I0764521

The Literary Adventures of Sherlock Holmes:

A Collection of Short Sketches

[Containing additional manuscripts found in the dispatch box of
Dr John H. Watson
In the vault of Cox & Co., Charing Cross, London]

Edited

By

Daniel D. Victor, Ph.D.

First edition published in 2019

Hardcover ISBN 978-1-78705-469-1

MX Publishing
335 Princess Park Manor, Royal Drive,
London, N11 3GX
www.mxpublishing.com

Cover design by Brian Belanger

Also by Daniel D. Victor

The Seventh Bullet:
The Further Adventures of Sherlock Holmes

A Study in Synchronicity

The Final Page of Baker Street
(Book One in the series,
Sherlock Holmes and the American Literati)

Sherlock Holmes and the Baron of Brede Place
(Book Two in the series,
Sherlock Holmes and the American Literati)

Seventeen Minutes to Baker Street
(Book Three in the series,
Sherlock Holmes and the American Literati)

The Outrage at the Diogenes Club
(Book Four in the series,
Sherlock Holmes and the American Literati)

Sherlock Holmes and the Shadows of St Petersburg

Sherlock Holmes and the London Particular
(Book Five in the series,
Sherlock Holmes and the American Literati)

For David Marcum,
without whose encouragement
these stories would never have seen the light of day

Introduction

*A*s compiled by Arthur Conan Doyle, the original cases of Sherlock Holmes may be categorized in any number of ways. There are, for example, those that feature animals such as *The Hound of the Baskervilles*, "The Veiled Lodger," and "The Lion's Mane." Others, like "A Case of Identity" and "The Noble Bachelor," may be labeled as stories of love gone awry. Some, like "The Three Garridebs" and "The Dancing Men," feature American villains. And still others, like "The Second Stain" and "The Bruce Partington Plans," depict political subterfuge.

The eleven stories gathered together in this anthology share their own common feature. All have connections to the world of *belles lettres*, the world of literature—some to authors in particular, others to themes or to stories associated with various writers.

By way of introduction, allow me to establish the literary associations (in the chronological order of the cases presented):

- "The Missing Necklace" tells of Holmes's friendship with French author, Guy de Maupassant, which led to the writing of one of the French author's most famous stories.

- "The Amateur Emigrant" pairs Holmes with Robert Louis Stevenson on the single night the writer spent in New York City.

- "The Second William Wilson" serves as a sequel to a frightening psychological tale by Edgar Allan Poe.

- "The Aspen Papers" offers Watson's account of a situation that Henry James fictionalized in his acclaimed short story, "The Aspern Papers."

- "For Want of a Sword" and "Capitol Murder" identify the role of Sherlock Holmes in two historical events—one involving the British Navy in the Mediterranean; the other, the assassination of an American governor—both occurrences originally reported by American journalist and novelist, David Graham Phillips.

- "The Smith-Mortimer Succession" illustrates a case referenced by Holmes's Boswell-like biographer, Dr John Watson, in "The Golden Pince-Nez."

- "An Adventure in Darkness" completes the story about the country of the blind first made public by author H.G. Wells.

- "An Adventure in the Mid-Day Sun" presents a case in the voice of the young American mystery writer Raymond Chandler, who in his youth served as a page-boy at 221B Baker Street.

- "The Star-Crossed Lovers," like the title, echoes the primary theme of Shakespeare's *Romeo and Juliet*.

- Finally, "A Case of Mistaken Identity" documents the meeting between Sherlock Holmes and the American novelist F. Scott Fitzgerald that took place late in the detective's life.

Let others plumb this collection for more subtle themes. From Maupassant to Fitzgerald, the authorial giants who populate these pages are explanation enough for its title. As interesting as such literary associations may be, of course, one cannot never forget that these sketches depict a series of heartless criminal acts—some more gruesome than others—in the finest tradition of all the other adventures of Sherlock Holmes.

Daniel D. Victor, Ph.D.
Los Angeles, California
May 2019

Sources

"The Adventure of the Missing Necklace" originally appeared in *The MX Book of New Sherlock Holmes Stories, Part IV,* ed. David Marcum, (London: MX Publishing, 2016).

"The Adventure of the Amateur Emigrant" originally appeared in *Sherlock Holmes: Before Baker Street*, ed. Derrick Belanger (Manchester, NH: Belanger Books LLC, 2017).

"The Adventure of the Second William Wilson" originally appeared in *The MX Book of New Sherlock Holmes Stories, Part VII*, ed. David Marcum (London: MX Publishing, 2017).

"The Adventure of the Aspen Papers" originally appeared in *The MX Book of New Sherlock Holmes Stories, Part I*, ed. David Marcum (London: MX Publishing, 2015).

"For Want of a Sword" originally appeared in Holmes *Away from Home: Adventures from the Great Hiatus, Volume Two*, ed. David Marcum (Manchester, NH: Belanger Books, LLC , 2016).

"The Adventure of the Smith-Mortimer Succession" originally appeared in *The MX Book of New Sherlock Holmes Stories, Part XII* ed. David Marcum (London: MX Publishing, 2018).

"Capitol Murder" originally appeared in *The MX Book of New Sherlock Holmes Stories, Part X*, ed. David Marcum (London: MX Publishing, 2018).

"An Adventure in Darkness" originally appeared in *Sherlock Holmes: Adventures in the Realms of H.G. Wells, Volume 1*, ed. Derrick Belanger and C. Edward Davis (Manchester, NH: Belanger Books, LLC , 2017).

"An Adventure in the Mid-Day Sun" originally appeared in *Beyond Watson: A Sherlock Holmes Anthology of Stories NOT Told by Dr John H. Watson,* ed. Derrick Belanger (Manchester, NH: Belanger Books LLC, 2016).

"The Adventure of the Star-Crossed Lovers" originally appeared in *Sherlock Holmes: Adventures Beyond the Canon, Vol. 3*, ed. Derrick Belanger (Manchester, NH: Belanger Books LLC, 2018).

"A Case of Mistaken Identity" originally appeared in *The MX Book of New Sherlock Holmes Stories, Part VI,* ed. David Marcum (London: MX Publishing, 2017).

A Note on the Text

Footnotes followed by (JHW) were supplied by Dr. John H. Watson.
Footnotes followed by (DDV) were supplied by the editor.

Table of Contents

The Adventure of the Missing Necklace

How would it have been if she had not lost that necklace? Who knows? Who knows? How singular is life and how full of changes! How small a thing will ruin or save one!
--Guy de Maupassant
"The Diamond Necklace"

I

Throughout the decades that I chronicled the cases of my friend and colleague, Mr Sherlock Holmes, his criticism never wavered. Indeed, upon looking back over the years, I can see how much his complaints had become a continual sticking point between us.

Take as an example the cold February evening in '98. Holmes and I were sitting before a blazing fire whilst a steady rain pelted our windows.

"In your hands, Watson," he observed yet again, "a story that should be edifying turns out to be merely diverting."

I am afraid I rolled my eyes. I knew we had no intention of leaving our rooms as long as the downpour persisted. Yet my vision of a warm wool blanket and one of Mrs Hudson's hot toddies was dashed when I realised that to Holmes our evening together translated into another opportunity to resurrect the same tired criticism of my writing that he had presented on so many previous occasions.

To be clear, I am not alluding to the annoying little side-comments he would make from time to time as in his complaint during our investigation of Wisteria Lodge that I told stories "wrong end foremost". I am, in fact, referring to the much broader kind of dissatisfaction he regurgitated with undue regularity towards my entire literary approach.

In a nutshell, Sherlock Holmes thought my emotional nature undermined his intellectual accomplishments. For instance, at the start of the case in which I met my late wife Mary, he argued that tingeing accounts of his investigations with romanticism made about as much sense as working a love story into the fifth proposition of Euclid. And on our way to the Abbey Grange just a month before our current dust-up, he had complained about my love of the histrionic.

"You slur over work of the utmost finesse and delicacy," he said to me as the Kentish train pitched and swayed, "in order to dwell upon sensational details, which may excite, but cannot possibly instruct, the reader."

On a cold winter's night like that which we were now experiencing, one might not expect terms like "edifying" and "diverting" to draw attention away from the comforts of a crackling fire. But no sooner did I hear their juxtaposition than I sensed I had to prepare anew for a fresh argument over a familiar subject. Here we go again, *I thought to myself,* another discussion of how the few literary embellishments I occasionally employ serve to diminish the significance of Holmes's intellectual triumphs.

None of these charges surprised me. I had always known that Holmes craved some sort of textbook to be derived from his criminal investigations. But as his promoter as well as the chronicler of his cases, I consistently sought means to engage my readers in the thrill of the hunt rather than putting them to sleep with descriptions of what were generally routine procedures.

It was not that I disagreed with Holmes's goal. Given the number of times he bested the traditional constabulary, the need for the kind of volume he desired seemed obvious. But I aimed for a grander audience than the local police force! It should surprise no one, therefore, when I confess that the more success my writing achieved in England, the more I dreamed of presenting the adventures of Sherlock Holmes to a worldwide reading public.

To this day, I maintain that in some part of Holmes's mind, he shared my point of view. Otherwise, how can one explain the contradictory stance from a man so universally identified with rationality? At the same time he criticised my accounts of his exploits, he also appeared to savour them. In his investigation of Irene Adler, did he not refer to me as his "Boswell"? At the start of our enquiry into the Baskervilles, did he not describe me as "a conductor of light"? In our search for the Bruce-Partington Plans, did he not call me his "trusted biographer"? And when the demon known as "the lion's mane" prompted him to try his own hand at composition, did he not acknowledge how much more of the tale I *could have made of it?*

Such obvious encouragement did little to prod me to change my style. Let someone else write the textbook Holmes desired. For that matter, let Holmes complete the task himself. In point of fact, during the train ride in Kent, he had speculated that when it came time for him to retire, he just might compile such a volume on his own.

During that cold night in Baker Street, however, Holmes could not let the matter rest. A flash of lightning punctuated my frustration, and suddenly I vowed to get to the bottom of our on-going contretemps. *I would take advantage of our enforced time together to discover the source of his lingering dissatisfaction.*

"Why is it," I asked him between rolls of thunder, "that you harbour so basic an objection to what the public find so engaging?"

"Hah, Watson," said he, filling his pipe. "You pose such a question because you've *never seen your own accomplishments twisted into something completely different—a true story made unrecognizable in a way that not even* your *romanticised writings have done. It happened early in my career, old fellow, and I've been fearful of similar distortions ever since."*

Early in his career? *Here was a history I had never heard before.*

"Who was the architect of this distortion?" I asked, eager to learn more of my friend's past.

Sherlock Holmes flashed a quick smile. "I trust I won't be the first Englishman to blame our rivals across the Channel for something I find distressing. It was the late French scrivener, Guy de Maupassant, who demonstrated to me how, in the hands of a fantasist, fundamental truth can be completely altered. The experience has served as a warning to me ever since."

"Maupassant," said I, charging my pipe with Arcadia mixture. "Do tell. I had no idea you'd ever met the fellow. Not your usual type, was he? As I recall, he'd been incarcerated as a madman before he died."

My friend shrugged. Thunder rocked the room again, and both of us took the opportunity to light our pipes. Once the silence returned, Sherlock Holmes proceeded to relate the following narrative. (Readers sympathetic to his point of view will appreciate the fact that I offer the account uninterrupted by any of the appeals to emotion and drama that I have been accused of employing.)

II

In the summer of '79 [Holmes began], not long after I had taken rooms in Montague Street, I got word from my brother Mycroft that our grandmother had died. She had moved back to France following the death of her English husband, my grandfather, and the funeral was to take place in Paris. I never pretended to be close to the French wing of our family, but Mycroft—much more mobile in those days than the sedentary figure into which he has devolved—was planning to attend the interment and asked me to join him. With the chance to please my brother—not to mention the opportunity for a summer's trip to the Continent—I readily agreed.

The list of mourners was quite distinguished. My late grandmother, the sister of the artist Vernet, had frequented the highest of artistic circles—and not just those of the painters she had met through her brother. Foremost among such artists who arrived at the cemetery that day was the celebrated novelist Gustave Flaubert, whom I recognised from his balding pate and drooping moustache. By his side stood a striking young man with a thick head of wavy dark hair, a full handlebar moustache, and a subtle *mouche* just below his lower lip. As I was to learn later, the young man's mother—said to be quite close to Flaubert—had encouraged a literary relationship between the great man and her son. In fact, the young man became Flaubert's *protégé*. His name was Guy de Maupassant.

By 1879, M. Maupassant had already gained some fame as a spinner of fictional tales; but unlike so many of our modern novelists with their unbounded flights of fancy, Maupassant displayed a practical nature and cynical point of view not unlike my own—or so I thought at the time. With similar philosophies and ages—he was but four years older than I—we quickly found much to talk about once the funeral had ended.

In fact, at Maupassant's invitation, I agreed to remain in France for an extra week; and after seeing Mycroft off for England at Calais, I travelled by railway to the young man's home in Étretat, a beautiful town on the Normandy coast. Its massive chalk cliffs and magnificent blue waters put one in mind of the Seven Sisters in the South Downs. Even at so young an age—I was but twenty-five—I remember thinking that such a coastal setting would make a wonderful place to spend one's retirement.

It took very little time indeed for M. Maupassant to discover my passion for detection and to regard me as a treasure trove of possible story-lines for his writing. Now I was new at my profession in 1879 and, sensing that neither the singular facts regarding the case of the *Gloria Scott* nor the arcane details related to the Musgrave Ritual need be made known to strangers, I had few selections to offer him. Nonetheless, young Maupassant picked my brain, and I confess to enjoying his responses to my feats of deduction.

"C'est magnifique!" he was always quick to remark followed by the clap of his hands.

Fortunately, I hit upon a case, one that had taken place not long before my departure for France, that I thought would interest the writer. Not only did my investigation present a number of odd clues and a most convoluted solution; but also, as the events had occurred so recently and thus remained fresh in my mind, I was confident that I could report the facts to my new acquaintance in great detail.

"*Eh, bien,*" said M. Maupassant. " Please begin."

*****

Towards the end of last November [I told him], a series of chill nights served to keep me indoors. On the evening that I discovered the initial clues in this case, however, a thaw had occurred that allowed me to resume my accustomed postprandial walks through Bloomsbury.

Cloaked in a long, warm coat, I swung open the outer door of my lodgings, passed between the pilasters framing the portal, and strode down the steps. Upon negotiating the metal gate, I immediately found myself staring up the dark and deserted pavement of Montague Street. To be fair, a few gas lamps did offer some light, and the lack of traffic was none too surprising. During daylight hours, countless visitors to the nearby British Museum filled the walkways; but in the evenings, with far fewer attractions, there was a significant drop in the number of pedestrians ambling about.

My usual route took me through Russell Square, up to the Euston Road, and sometimes as far as Regent's Park. To that end, I set out in a north-easterly direction past the familiar line of late-Georgian, four-storey row houses. With their similar *façades*—black doors positioned towards the right-hand side of two-toned brick walls (white below, dark-red above)—most of the structures looked just like the one I had exited. Black railings fronted each house; and shallow, black-railed balconies, some sporting empty flower boxes waiting for spring, looked down from above. Owing to the broad fanlights over the doors, half-circles of brightness pooled on the sidewalk in front of many an entrance.

It required but a few minutes for me to reach the confines of Russell Square. Once inside, to the accompaniment of babbling distant fountains and the snaps of breaking twigs, I crunched my way along the gravel walkways. Even in the dark, I knew there were curiosities to observe; and as was my wont, I kept a keen lookout among the holm oaks, yews and hollies for any strange flora, fauna, or bits of detritus that might stimulate my interest.

On this particular excursion, what caught my eye was a shabby grey bowler lying on the grass a few feet away. I reckoned the thing was probably just someone's lost old hat; but my enquiring mind prompted me to investigate.

The hat appeared to be a typical old-fashioned, dark-grey derby with rounded crown and abbreviated brim. Upon closer examination, however, three curiosities presented themselves. First, located on the leather band inside the crown was the distinctive imprimatur of "Lock & Co. Hatters, St. James's Street, London." Clearly, despite its scruffiness, this hat was no inexpensive head-covering. Second, there appeared on the side of the brim opposite the outer band's bow the bite marks of a small animal. Now all kinds of creatures roam the parks of London: hedgehogs, rats, badgers—as well as the more traditional dogs and cats. But due to the size, sharpness, and structure of the indentations, these marks seemed obviously feline. Fact number three created a circumstantial case as to the animal's identity: as it turned out, the bowler was resting neatly atop a small pile of what I recognised as cat droppings, waste not easily confused by the initiated with that of any of the other creatures in question.

At first glance, I had thought the singular location of the bowler to be random. Upon further reflection, however, it seemed quite evident that the hat had been intentionally dropped on exactly the spot the cat had fouled. What is more, the deep impression of the teeth-marks in the brim gave the suggestion of strong resolve. As absurd as it appeared, logic indicated that the animal had used its jaws to pick up the bowler and carry it for deposit upon its own excreta.

Much can be learned from the actions of cats, and one need not be an alienist to recognise a similarity between the behaviour of those small creatures and that of man. I myself have indicated how the cat that purrs before attacking a mouse appears no different from the human predator who hopes to distract his victim before setting upon him. With no other cases pending and a constant desire to challenge my mental skills, I concluded that there might be worthwhile insights to be derived from discovering the relationship between bowler and cat.

Though I had no idea what sort of evidence I was seeking, I attempted to scour the immediate area for clues. In truth, the nearby gas lamps did not project their light very far, and my vision was all but useless. Luckily for me, however, I literally stumbled upon an old potting shed.

Even in the darkness I could see that the small structure was decidedly run-down. Wooden sideboards hung askew; a triangle of broken glass partially filled the solitary window; shingles were missing from the roof; and the door, attached to its frame by a single remaining hinge, stood ajar. Yet in spite of this dilapidation, I realised that it was not the shed itself but rather the freshly turned earth of the surrounding flowerbed that had tripped me up. Striking a match for a better look among the shadows, I bent down on one knee to examine the soil.

Anyone familiar with cats knows that loose earth offers them the perfect toilet. Perhaps, it was the very soil before me that had originally attracted the bowler-stealing cat to the shed. Yet almost immediately I could sense that this dirt was not all that it seemed—or rather it was more than it seemed. For mixed in with the damp soil and decaying leaves was a jumble of refuse that looked and smelled strangely out of place in the gardens of Russell Square.

I scooped up a handful of the stuff in one hand and, bringing it to my nose, was instantly struck by the stench of old garbage. Next I ran my forefinger through the muck and studied the foul mixture through my glass. No wonder it stank: it was full of bits of orange peel, black pepper, coffee grounds, and pipe tobacco—a peculiar *mélange* to some, perhaps, but not to those familiar with tried-and-true methods for turning away cats.

No doubt, someone had sprinkled this mess into the soil to discourage any feral cats from nosing around the potting shed. In the process, one animal in particular had obviously taken great exception to such rudeness. Not only had the slighted cat stolen the offender's bowler from whatever perch the hat had been placed upon, but the creature had also deposited it in such a spot as to deliver a universally-understood insult—apparently, even understood by inhabitants of the animal kingdom.

I snorted loudly at the irony. Here I was, new in my career of detecting; and my first case dealing with revenge featured that of the feline variety. Yet thanks to the potting shed, one could not forget the human element; and I immediately refocused my attention on identifying a connection between the run-down structure and the owner of the hat. I pushed at the half-open door—though in spite of striking another match, I could see nothing of interest inside. Shovels and spades had long since been removed; and whilst shards and larger fragments of clay pots littered the ground, unbroken cobwebs indicated that nothing within had been recently disturbed.

I next turned my attention to the area immediately outside the shed. The darkness did not prevent me from carefully running my fingers over the boards on each wall, and eventually I came across a slat near the ground whose corner lacked connection to the joist behind it. Needing no further invitation, I slid the wood upward and discovered a moderate-sized hollow between the boards.

It took but a moment to insert my hand, encounter the knobby folds of a burlap sack, and extract it from its nesting place. Inside the bag, I found a small collection of gold jewellery—bracelets, tiepins, rings, and such. But the *pièce de résistance* appeared to be a fine-looking necklace whose fourteen identical gems mirrored the flame of my match.

And yet the reflections failed to sparkle as they should have in the facets of true diamonds. When I found that the gems would not make a scratch in the fragment of glass in the shed's window, I was convinced. In truth, the necklace held little value.

No matter the worth of the jewellery, a cloud of suspicion darkened my mind. It certainly looked like a thief's secret horde. Else, why would it be hidden in such a manner? I had no compunction about carrying away the forgotten bowler; but though I seriously doubted it, this cache of jewels might turn out to be some poor soul's legitimate collection of wealth—a poor soul, I assumed, who had no intention of letting stray cats draw people's attention to the hiding place.

Determined to learn more, I replaced the sack and its contents where I had found them; returned to the nearest footpath; and having made the decision to defer the rest of my evening walk, exited Russell Square. On my way out of the grounds, however, I cast one final look back and could not help noticing in the darkness a pair of green, almond-shaped eyes that were faithfully tracking my departure from the garden.

*****

As soon as I reached my rooms, I picked up the copy of the *Daily Telegraph* I had left lying on my desk and searched the Agony columns for advertisements regarding Lost Property. It took less than a minute to find what I was seeking. "Lost last week near Park Lane," the announcement read, "a diamond necklace consisting of fourteen similar stones on a thin, gold chain." Mentioning a reward but offering no specific amount, the listing gave one James Laws as the person to contact at a street number in nearby Bedford Place.

The description in the *Telegraph* was close enough to the piece I had found to warrant further investigation. Pleased by Mr Laws's proximity, I immediately sent a message via my landlady's son to the address printed in the column.

Although the night was growing late, James Laws sent word via the same messenger that he could come meet with me post-haste. The loss of the necklace, he wrote, had been weighing heavily on both him and his wife. Of course, I agreed to the visit.

I was at my worktable fiddling with some malodorous chemicals when I heard the hesitant knock at the door. Upon opening it, I discovered a young man in his twenties pulling at the tip of his manicured moustache. Over his left arm hung a folded long coat. Here was someone, I surmised, that hoped his sombre, store-bought suit and matching waistcoat gave him a grander appearance than that of the clerk he admitted to being.

"Mr Holmes," said he, brushing back a shock of brown hair, "My name is James Laws. When my wife Matilda and I received your message concerning the missing necklace, we felt hope reborn."

"Pray, come in and sit down," said I, waving him into my sitting room and indicating the soft chair I reserved for clients. I apologised for the chemical smell and, occupying the desk's turning chair that I'd placed opposite him, announced the bad news.

"I must tell you, Mr Laws, that I no longer have the necklace in my possession."

A wave of disappointment washed over his face, and I marvelled that an inexpensive piece of jewellery should be the cause of so much concern.

"But," I went on, "depending on your answers to my questions, I do know how to get it."

The look of hope returned. "Ask me whatever you want, Mr Holmes. Recovering the necklace is all that matters."

"I trust you won't mind, then, if I ask you to describe the piece."

In response, he reached into his jacket and produced a pencil sketch.

"Matilda drew this," said he. "She has a much better recollection of such things than I."

Before me lay a perfect likeness of the necklace with its fourteen jewels that I'd discovered in the potting shed.

"It looks to be the same article I've seen, Mr Laws."

At these words, he allowed himself a smile.

"Yet I must tell you," I went on, "that to my untrained eye, the stones do not appear to be diamonds. Have you had the necklace appraised?"

"No," said he, looking downward. "We never had the chance." Suddenly, he glanced up, his dark eyes flashing. "You mean that it doesn't have much value then?"

"I shouldn't think so. But since a theft may still have been committed, I trust that you can describe how the necklace came to be lost."

"Of course," said he, strangely energised by my low evaluation of the piece. "Last night, Matilda and I were honoured to attend a social gathering in Park Lane—a ball, actually—at the home of Mr George Rimpon, the Minister for the Committee of the Privy Council of Education. I'm employed by the Committee as a clerk, you see—though I have much loftier goals, I do admit—and my poor wife has been longing to go to any kind of social event. Mr Rimpon took it upon himself to celebrate all of his employees in appreciation of the good work we do. A number of cabinet ministers were also to be there, you see, so such a party was a god-send for both Matilda and me."

"For the *both* of you?"

James Laws cast his eyes downward again. "I'm rather afraid," he confessed, "that my wife equates the importance of my position with the number of social engagements it offers her. And this ball has been the only one."

"Quite so," said I, pressing my fingers together. "And the necklace?"

"After the *soirée* had ended and we returned home—it was about four in the morning, actually—Matilda was horrified to discover that the necklace had gone missing."

"'Horrified' is a strong word for the loss of a trinket."

"*You* may call it a trinket, Mr Holmes; but don't you see? *We* believed it to be worth a fortune. I know you must be wondering how unassuming people like ourselves could afford what we thought to be such a lavish piece of jewellery; but the truth is that Matilda borrowed it."

"'Borrowed', you say?"

"Yes. When I first told her about the invitation, she advised me that she couldn't attend because she had no appropriate frock. To make her happy, I reluctantly gave her the money I'd been saving for a hunting rifle. She bought a charming dress, but no sooner did she show it to me than she realised she had no jewellery to go with it. I suggested she wear flowers.

"'Flowers are always fashionable,' I suggested, but in response she simply cried."

I sympathised with the poor fellow, for I understood the temperament he was describing. I'd seen similar reactions during my short-lived career in the theatre. Like a neglected actress, his wife felt as if she was pining away; and here at last arrived the opportunity to appear on the stage, and she wanted to make the most of it. However high both of them wanted to climb, only Mr Laws had the opportunity. His wife, facing a life of drudgery at home, had none.

"Matilda rejected the invitation a second time, Mr Holmes; and I was beginning to grow frantic. I couldn't afford to give my employer a negative response. To my great relief, however, it was then that Matilda remembered Mrs Forrest, a friend with whom she'd gone to school. Mrs Forrest had married a wealthy man and now possessed a grand selection of jewellery. On some previous occasion, she'd offered Matilda the chance to wear a pair of earrings, and Matilda felt certain that her friend would loan her an appropriate piece for the upcoming ball. In fact, Mrs Forrest allowed Matilda to select a piece herself. It was my wife who chose the necklace. Little did I realise the trouble this transaction would create."

Laws rubbed his hands over his face, and shook his head once more.

"As soon as we discovered the necklace was gone, we immediately retraced our steps to Park Lane."

"Had you taken a cab from the ball?"

"Yes—after walking a bit in the cold, we found a hansom. We did contact the company—"

"But without knowing the cab's number," I interrupted, "you got nowhere."

"That's right, Mr Holmes. Believe me when I say that we searched high and low. Matilda remembered that the necklace had a secure clasp; it couldn't have simply fallen away. No, in the end, we were forced to conclude that the thing had been stolen."

"I take it that you went to the police with your suspicions."

"Indeed. But since no other guests had offered similar complaints, Inspector Goforth preferred to blame the entire matter on my careless wife."

I knew the policeman. "Goforth," said I, "a good man, but lacking imagination. Of course, he'd blame it on an innocent. What about your wife's friend, Mrs Forrest? How did she react upon hearing the news of her missing necklace?"

James Laws smiled. “My wife hasn’t told her yet. Matilda wrote to her that the clasp had broken and that we were going to have it repaired before returning it.”

“And what was her response to this presumptuous offer?” I wondered if Mrs Forrest sensed that too much was being made over a string of glass baubles.

“Matilda told me that her friend seemed more vexed about the clasp than the delay.”

“Quite so,” I said again.

I informed James Laws that I might have information that could shed new light on the matter. If he and his wife could wait but a day or so, this matter might reach a happy conclusion.

“I hope to hear from you as soon as possible, Mr Holmes. We must be certain about the value of the necklace. This afternoon Matilda went to the jeweller whose name appeared on the inside cover of the black satin box in which Mrs Forrest had kept the necklace. Matilda could only show him the drawing, of course; but assuming the stones to be real diamonds, the salesman put the price at one thousand pounds. *One thousand pounds,* Mr Holmes! The news was devastating. Matilda is a proud woman, sir; and we both are honest people who will undertake to do whatever is required to repay such a vast sum to Mrs Forrest. I need not add, of course, that raising so much money will probably take ten years; for certain, it will ruin our lives.

“I understand completely, Mr Laws.” Without the necklace in hand, I dared not offer confirmation of my suspicions that the gems were false, but at the same time I hoped to convey my sympathy. “I’ll do whatever I can for you and Mrs Laws to get to the bottom of this.”

Following these words, we both rose to our feet and shook hands. Mr Laws, uncertain whether he should be exuberant or apprehensive, gave me a final nod, and walked out into Montague Street. It would take him just a few minutes to return to his wife with my report.

III

The next morning, I visited Inspector Goforth at Scotland Yard. A professorial figure behind round spectacles, Goforth stood tall with a baldhead and red side-whiskers. Whenever the light reflected off the lenses of his glasses, his eyes seemed to disappear; and it was difficult to imagine what he might be thinking. None the less, in previous dealings, he had showed that he was willing to pay attention to a young investigator like me for whom his colleagues usually had little time. This occasion was no different. Accompanied by his curious habit of waggling the fingers of each hand in the small pockets of his waistcoat, he listened to my description of the potting shed in Russell Square. The story of the vengeful cat and the curious bowler, however, did not interest him at all.

"We'll put a man near that shed," said he when I had concluded my story. "We'll watch the cache night and day; and when that rogue returns for his loot, we shall have him."

"With all due respect," said I, "such a plan could take days—even weeks, or longer."

"Do you have an alternative solution?"

I did, actually, but I thought better of announcing it. "Not as yet, inspector. I was merely lamenting the amount of time to be spent in Russell Square by your men. Personally, I will try another approach."

*****

With a storefront of small, square windows and dark brick, Lock's Hatters is an unassuming establishment at 6 St. James's Street. Outside, its most noticeable attraction is the round sign hanging above the door. The name and address of the shop appear in the same block-lettering as the imprint within the crowns of Lock's hats. Inside, the walls are piled high with white, oval-shaped boxes, pasteboard containers filled with the top hats and bowlers that have maintained the company's reputation for more than two centuries The business itself is directed by smartly dressed salesmen in frock coats, starched collars, and silk cravats.

A look of dismay from one of these persons greeted the well-worn bowler I had extracted from my Gladstone. The salesman producing the aforesaid look, however, became more sympathetic when, after offering my name, I confessed that I was a consulting detective in search of answers. I have found it to be true more often than not that once people discover they themselves are neither the presumed targets of an investigation nor the possible victims of any danger, they become most eager to lend their expertise to solving a puzzle. Whatever the cause, Mr Robbins—for that was the gentleman's name—proved extremely cooperative.

"How can I be of service to you?" he asked.

I told him of my history with the bowler and wondered if Lock's, being so traditional an establishment, might have some way of tracing the hat's original owner.

Mr Robbins smiled and motioned me to follow. We proceeded to the end of a long mahogany counter where he exhibited a strange looking device made of metal—a piece of machinery, in fact.

"This, Mr Holmes, is our *conformateur.*"

The machine resembled a short-top hat with a brim fashioned of dark metal and a rounded crown composed of some fifty, six-inch-tall, flexible black arms. As Mr Robbins demonstrated on my own head, when the lid of the crown was gently pushed down upon, the arms—the bottoms of which now tightly encircled my skull—activated tiny pins at their upper ends that perforated the sheet of paper Mr Robbins had placed upon the top of the device. In such a manner, a precise impression of a person's head—bumps, ridges and all—was conveyed through pinpricks on the paper.

From these perforations, an accurate block of one's head could be fashioned. And after steam had been applied to the interior band of a hat, the hat could be set down upon the newly formed block and moulded to its shape. When the hat was transferred from block to head, the resultant outcome was a perfect fit.

It was quite a clever device and put me in mind of the French savant Bertillon. He was just then developing his system of body-measurements called anthropometry; and I could not help wondering how he might employ such a machine to further his hypotheses about the contours of criminal skulls. *I,* however, needed more practical information.

"What happens to the perforated paper once the hat is purchased?" I asked, fearing the pages might be discarded.

Mr Robbins's proud answer, however, was exactly what an investigator loves to hear: "We keep them in storage. That way, should a customer desire another hat, he can avoid undergoing the tiresome fitting process a second time."

He directed me to a wooden cabinet whose shelves were stuffed with boxes of those perforated pages. The files were organised by surname; but, of course, I did not posses that titbit related to the man I was seeking. In a quarter of an hour, however, Mr Robbins, working backwards from the old bowler I had brought in, was able to create a newly perforated sheet. All I needed to do was sort through the files to find the paper with the tiny holes that lined up with those of the head that fit the bowler.

With the hatter's permission, I proceeded to employ what the Americans call "legwork"—that is, good, old-fashioned labour—to match the pinpricks in my sheet with those in one from the boxes of files. To determine if the holes coincided, I held up to the light one perforated page after another, placing it over my unknown hat-wearer's pattern. It should not be a laborious task, I reasoned, just a tedious one. During the course of its long history, Lock's had accumulated a great many customers.

Fortunately, the matching holes belonged to a surname near the front of the alphabet—"Dimweather"—and the work took less time than I had feared. A man called Albert Dimweather, I discovered, was whom I was seeking.

I thanked Mr Robbins for his help and even promised to return some day when I could afford to purchase for myself the handsome tweed deerstalker I had seen there on display. Once outside the shop, I hailed a hansom and was soon rattling down St. James's Street on the way to Scotland Yard.

IV

"Dimweather" turned out to be a name familiar to Inspector Goforth. The man had previously been arrested on burglary charges, but recently seemed to be succeeding with temporary employment in service. The police knew where he lived—in a boarding house just off Tavistock Square near the British Museum. To no one's surprise, it was an address not far from Russell Square.

"Care to join us, Mr Holmes?" asked Goforth, his fingers dancing in the pockets of his waistcoat.

"Of course," said I and followed him out the door.

The police van drove down Montague Street on its way to gather up Dimweather; and once we arrived at the man's residence, I followed Goforth and two uniformed constables inside. The landlady gave us the directions to Dimweather's rooms.

Goforth pounded on the door. "Open up!" he commanded. "Police!"

The door was opened by a tall, thin man in formal black livery, the uniform of a footman dressed for an evening's work. His middle-parted black hair was neatly combed; his cheeks, clean-shaven. He was holding the brim of a black short-top hat, which was turned in such a way that I could discern the name of Lock's Hatters inside the crown. A number of other fashionable hats sat on little posts positioned on a cherry-wood side-table near the door. One could not help noticing that a solitary post remained empty. Confronted by the police, Dimweather stood at attention like the most disciplined of military men and allowed the cuffs to be fastened round his wrists.

Once the man was thus secured, Goforth placed a hand on his shoulder. "Albert Dimweather," the inspector proclaimed, "I am arresting you for the theft of various pieces of valuable jewellery too numerous to itemise at this time. Anything you say may be taken down in writing and used against you at your trial."

There was no slumping in Dimweather's stature as he listened to this announcement. In spite of being manacled, he managed to place his hat atop his head. Then, accompanied by the two constables, he marched stiffly out the front door and into the police van.

During his trial at the Old Bailey, Dimweather freely confessed to committing his thefts at various social gatherings including the ball in Park Lane for the Committee of the Privy Council of Education. Whilst masquerading as a footman, he was able to commandeer wallets and watches, cop a wayward necklace, and even lift a bracelet or two.

"I'd just walk in and pretend to go to work, sir," he told the bewigged barrister. "Nobody bothered me as long as I looked like I knew my way round. All I had to do was act like a footman, didn't I? I'd help ladies and gentlemen into their coats and wraps and then slip a hand into a pocket or unfasten a jewellery clasp. Nobody noticed, did they? The police never caught Albert Dimweather in the act."

Near the end of his testimony, he admitted to managing the cache, which I had uncovered.

"Better a hidey-hole in Russell Square," said he, "than some nook in my boarding house where any busybody might peek in."

Not to mention the odd cat in Russell Square, I mused.

To no one's surprise, Dimweather was pronounced guilty and sent off to prison. Once the trial had ended, the police returned to James Laws and his wife the necklace that Dimweather had taken, reporting in the process the relative worthlessness of the piece. Though Dimweather had illegally acquired some highly-priced gems, the false necklace he had stolen from Matilda Laws had obviously fooled him as much as it had originally fooled the couple. Mrs Laws did finally return the necklace to her friend, but I do not believe the lady ever learned it had served as evidence in court.

In fact, according to Matilda Laws, the only comment Mrs Forrest made about the necklace was, "You surely took your time returning it. What if I had wanted to wear it in the interim?" She never checked to see how well the alleged broken clasp had been mended—let alone if the necklace that was restored to her was the same necklace she had loaned out. In short, she treated the necklace like the cheap piece of jewellery she knew it to be.

The story of Albert Dimweather, the man who loved hats, was not the most dramatic of my cases; and yet in the manner of drawing conclusions, its unusual aspects rendered it most instructive.

V

"An intriguing tale indeed, Holmes," said I exhaling a cloud of smoke. The hearth fire danced lower though now the room was full of tobacco haze. "But you haven't told me how M. Maupassant liked it? You've neglected to wrap up the aspect of your story that seems to have bothered you the most."

Holmes flashed a quick smile.

"Oh, he listened to the story with great attentiveness. But the features that any logical mind would consider most compelling—the human-like nature of the cat, the strange elements in the garden soil,

the mechanical workings of the conformateur*—these seemed to interest him not at all. In fact, M. Maupassant ignored my feats of ratiocination and, leaning forward with a most maniacal gleam in his eye, asked me a singular question: 'What if it had taken years for the innocent couple to learn the diamonds were false—long enough, at any rate, to have ruined their lives paying off the loss?'"*

I raised my brows in horror at the thought. "But, Holmes," I reminded my friend, "you said that you had informed James Laws and his wife early on that the jewels were glass. And you said the police confirmed the fact."

"To be sure, Watson; and mighty happy were they both as a result. But surely you can understand that a truthful story in the hands of a fabulist like Guy de Maupassant provides a recipe for disaster. If you could only see it, the concerns I express about your *writings are my humble attempts to prevent* you *from making the kinds of distortions that writers of his ilk do."*

I resented being grouped with authors Holmes thought could not be trusted. But before I could say anything in my defence, he stood up, reached for a green-covered book from a nearby shelf, and handed it to me. "The Short Stories of Guy de Maupassant" was printed in gold on the spine.

"It took the Frenchman a few years to twist the plot into the form he desired," observed Sherlock Holmes, "but read the abomination called 'The Diamond Necklace'; and then talk to me about the wisdom of putting true crime stories into the hands of fiction *writers!"*

He left the room in a huff whilst I leaned back, pipe still in hand, and opened the pages to the narrative in question. The fire crackled in the background.

The Adventure of the Amateur Emigrant

Family and friends insisted that *The Amateur Emigrant* be pruned . . . even though that which was excised not only was every bit as finished as the parts deemed publishable but also was integral to an understanding of the situation as Stevenson saw it
and to the work as a whole.
--James D. Hart*

I

***R**are were the days that Sherlock Holmes dragged the large tin box into the sitting room and surveyed the contents therein. But no sooner had I returned to our rooms one mid-December morning in '94 than I saw him in the centre of the floor puttering through his collection of papers and artefacts from old cases.*

Poor fellow, *I thought,* he must be seeking distraction.

Following the sale of my medical practise to Verner a few months before, my position as locum at Barts had been keeping me away from Baker Street most mornings. Even Mrs Hudson was off preparing for the Christmas holidays. Holmes, having recently completed the investigation into that business at Yoxley Old Place involving Professor Coram and the Golden Pince-Nez, had nothing else to do but rummage among his things.

Of course, *I reflected*, he might also be researching the past to shed some kind of light on a new case I know nothing about.

Whatever Holmes's reason, I should confess that the sight of the box had always aroused in me a twinge of jealousy. Careful readers will recall that the contents of the receptacle in question represented a part of Holmes's detecting career in which my role was nowhere to be found. In point of fact, the items consisted of notes and

---

* Introduction to Robert Louis Stevenson's *From Scotland to Silverado*, an anthology that includes *The Amateur Emigrant*, Stevenson's storied account of his travels from Glasgow to California. (DDV)

memorabilia saved from Holmes's earliest cases, those investigations undertaken before he and I met in 1881. Here were his notes on the Gloria Scott, *the Musgrave Ritual, the Tarleton Murders, and that strangest of tales involving the aluminium crutch—all fascinating glimpses into the world of crime, to be sure, but all lacking any contribution or analysis from me, the scribe Holmes once had called his Boswell.*

The bulk of the material consisted of papers gathered into small stacks, each held together by red ribbon. There were numerous such bundles, yet I knew that beneath the papers lay additional treasures, specific objects Holmes had preserved from the investigations themselves—the peg of wood and attached ball of string from the Musgrave affair, for example, or the leather hand-grip from the aluminium crutch.

"A trip into the past?" I asked my colleague.

"Quite so, Watson" said Holmes. "I have always held that a periodic review of former cases helps stimulate the brain. Through such analysis, one may discover recurring patterns in the criminal mind. You may recall how my recollection of the Hindu snake charmer of Brixton helped me predict the behaviour of the villainous Dr Grimesby Roylott and his so-called 'Speckled Band'."

I did not recall the anecdote he cited—presumably because he had never bothered to report it to me. Yet all I said was, "Certainly, Holmes, but these things here"—I made a dismissive gesture in the direction of the tin box—"represent cases from your callow youth."

"However true, old fellow, such remembrances are still ripe for the picking—though today I must confess that I'm looking for a set of papers that are more nostalgic than instructive."

I had no idea to what he was referring, but none the less I watched him continue to riffle through the bundles. In the process an unbound collection of pages caught my eye. Unlike the other papers, which were held together by the ubiquitous red ribbon, these appeared torn from a notebook. What is more, though written in a tiny, cribbed style not unlike that of Holmes himself, the lettering on these pages appeared shaky; and the spaces between lines, much wider than in the writings of my friend.

"What are those?" I asked, pointing at the notebook pages. "They're different from the rest."

Holmes's long fingers reached for the papers I had identified and lifted them out of the box.

*"The very thing I was looking for," said he. "You have excellent eyes, old fellow. No doubt, it takes a writer to spot the work of a fellow scribbler. These pages were sent to me by an old acquaintance, Louis Stevenson—*Robert *Louis Stevenson to the world at large."*

"The Scotsman who died just the past fortnight? The writer?"

"The very same. In memory of his passing, I wanted to review an unpublished chapter from an early volume of his. Do you know, Watson, though I don't trumpet it about, I was instrumental in inspiring one of his most famous novels."

"Surely not that scandalous thriller, Dr Jekyll and Mr Hyde? *You do know that there are more than a few naïfs who believe that the monstrous Mr Hyde was real and that Sherlock Holmes played some role in ending his reign of terror."*

Holmes dismissed the notion with a wave of his hand. "No," said he, shaking his head, "my contribution was to a more swashbuckling kind of tale."

Clearly, I was about to hear a new bit of Holmesian history. In preparation, I poured us both a glass of sherry and settled into an armchair. "Do tell," I encouraged him.

Holmes sampled his drink and then began the following account: "As you are aware, Watson, a month or so after I had come up from Cambridge, I joined a troupe of actors called the Sasanoff Company. Not long thereafter, in the summer of '79, I found myself performing on the stage in New York—that is, before I ran out of money and had to return to England. Fortunately, within a matter of months I was able to re-join the Sasanoff group."

I knew of Holmes's brief acting career as well as his appearance on the New York stage. Indeed, but a few years earlier I had written that the stage had lost a fine actor when when my friend turned his mind to criminal detection.

"As it happened," Holmes continued, "Stevenson arrived in New York in the middle of August. He was on his way to San Francisco to join the American divorcée *with whom he had fallen in love during a trip to France. In point of fact, he planned to begin his railway journey west the day following his arrival."*

"After just one *night in New York City, Holmes?"*

"He had Cupid to propel him, old fellow. I should have thought that a romantic like yourself would admire his haste."

"But a single night, Holmes, in so vibrant a metropolis!"

"True," Sherlock Holmes nodded, "but let us not forget that the specific night in question was the occasion of our meeting. In fact, I remember the evening quite well. We were staging a pantomime of Robinson Crusoe. *It had been raining heavily, and the members of the cast were wondering how many people in search of an evening's entertainment would be willing to brave the elements. A small hole in the red-velvet curtain allowed us to scrutinise the audience as they arrived.*

"'Maybe half full,' I remember Nelly Ross observing as she backed away from the velvet to give me a look. 'But better than I expected for so wet a night.'"

"Nelly Ross?"

"The ingénue *playing Robinson Crusoe."*

"Ah."

"With her encouragement, I too peered through the aperture. The number of empty seats was indeed sufficient to catch the eye, and yet my gaze was attracted to a slight young man just then entering the rear of the hall. It was his burgundy-coloured velveteen jacket that first caught my attention—I noted it once he had removed his wet Mackintosh. But it was his cadaverous mien that sustained my curiosity.

"His pale, oval-shaped face seemed all the whiter in contrast to the frame of dark damp hair falling almost to his shoulders. The scraggly moustache and hollow eyes set widely apart added to his frail appearance. Why, even before he reached his seat, he was covering his mouth with a free hand, and I could tell from the shaking of his body that he was fighting a paroxysm of coughing. Only when it subsided did he settle into his chair next to the nondescript man with whom he had entered.

"The longer I stared, the greater my realisation that there was something familiar to me about the young man's bohemian aspect. Yet it was only after he had replaced a common flat hat with a gilt-embroidered Indian skullcap that I identified him. For, you see, I had observed the same man thus distinctively apparelled at Hatchards a few months before I had left England. He had coughed

then as well. It was all quite remarkable. Before me in a New York theatre sat the little-known Scottish writer, Robert Louis Stevenson.

"Though I had yet to begin my detecting career, it was the man's insightful depictions of murder that originally attracted me to his work. I need not remind you, Watson, that criminal pursuits have intrigued me from the beginning; and the passages Stevenson read at Hatchards that day were taken from a tale of death he had written two years before—one of his first, actually—called 'A Lodging for the Night'. It dealt with the reactions of the infamous French poet, François Villon, to a vicious murder. Even then, Stevenson seemed fascinated with how the soul of a poet and the soul of a criminal might be embodied in a single being."

"Jekyll and Hyde," I murmured.

Holmes nodded and continued his story. "Stevenson's appearance at the theatre that evening triggered a jumble of memories—of Hatchards, of the story he had read there, and of his haunting eyes. At the same time, however, I also knew that we had a show to put on; and with the curtain about to rise, I needed to assume my role. I was portraying a villainous pirate—a one-legged sea cook, no less—and I had to take my spot before the curtain rose.

"Happily, in spite of the incessant rain and an only partially-filled house, we put on a rousing performance that night; and to show his appreciation, Stevenson requested permission to come back-stage to congratulate the entire company. He greeted us all with equanimity, certainly having no cause to single me out in any way. No, Watson, as you might well imagine, it required a singular crime to bring the two of us together."

I am afraid I knit my brows at this last proclamation. "I can understand not hearing of such an occurrence from you, *Holmes," said I, "but Stevenson was a prolific chronicler of his journeys. As I recall, he produced at least two works,* Travels with a Donkey in the Cévennes *and* An Inland Voyage, *that report his adventures on the continent before he ever wrote about his trip to America. He loved the dramatic anecdote, and yet I have never seen in print any account by the man of some crime that had been committed against him in New York."*

"Quite so," said Holmes with a quick smile. He then finished his sherry and, setting down the glass, picked up the papers he had withdrawn from the tin box.

"News of our meeting," said he, '"never appeared in the published reports of Stevenson's travels in America. In the letter he wrote me that accompanied these pages, he explained that he had sent the account home for publication. In order to maintain a positive image of the writer, however, his friends and publishers chose to omit any stories they found objectionable or controversial. Apparently, Stevenson's depiction of himself as a target of a criminal in New York City stood no chance of being published."

At this point, Holmes handed me the unbound pages.

"Enough of my blather," said he. "Why not read it for yourself."

It was with great excitement that I took up the bundle. Scrawled across the top sheet in Holmes's penmanship were the words, "Excised from the chapter 'New York' in The Amateur Emigrant *by Robert Louis Stevenson (translations from the Latin rendered by S. Holmes)". My friend filled his pipe in preparation for an uninterrupted smoke; I leaned back in my armchair in anticipation of learning about the night in question from Stevenson himself.*

II

I have already mentioned my debarkation from the *Devonia,* a steam-ship of considerable tonnage. Maintaining the admittedly weak alias of Robert Stephenson, I clambered down the gangway at Castle Garden in the company of Mr Jones, the Welsh blacksmith and fellow traveller I had befriended during the course of the voyage. You would be hard-pressed to find a more uncomfortable crossing than we had experienced—the unsavoury food, the constant vomiting, the constipation, the incessant scratching, not to mention the haughty looks that the so-called "lords of the saloon" cast down upon those of us inhabiting the second cabins and steerage.

And yet our misery continued when, upon arriving in New York City that Sunday, the 17th of August in '79, we were greeted by a deluge that must have rivalled the downpour witnessed by Noah himself. Indeed, my entire stay, however brief, in the city nicknamed "Gotham" was accompanied by the steady drumbeat of falling water. No matter the discomfort or my desire to reach California as quickly as possible, I had to spend the night in the watery metropolis. There were no westward-bound railroads available to me that evening because the economical "emigrant trains" did not run on Sundays.

It had been raining when we docked, and the showers showed no sign of abating as we sought transportation to our digs. Though we had been warned aboard the *Devonia* about the New York City hucksters seeking to separate us from our money, we none the less paid dearly for spots on the soggy straw bottom of an open baggage wagon for the short ride from the docks to our lodgings.

It was still light at just past 6.00 that evening when our conveyance deposited us at Reunion House, the small establishment at No. 10 West Street advertised as presenting private rooms at low rates. To be sure, its location—just a few minutes' walk to the steamboat landing—was especially convenient. The following evening I would be sailing from that very dock the short distance across the Hudson River to Jersey City where I would board the train heading west. And yet owing to my financial duress, the low rates of Reunion House presented an even greater allure.

You should understand that problems with money plagued both Jones and me. Jones had been married and prosperous earlier in his life; but his wife had died, and his money had run out. As for me, my father—either disappointed in my failure to pursue a career in the law or disapproving of my current quest for love—had cut off my finances. Thus afflicted, Jones and I agreed to share a single room at twenty-five cents a night. With individual meals costing the same "two bits" (as the Americans call the quarter of a dollar), we exchanged nods and signed the register.

What a bargain we had struck! The bed was small enough to send me to the floor for sleeping. The other amenities—a solitary wooden chair and well-worn, wooden clothes-pegs for our wet coats—were not much better. In short, except for the not insignificant roof above our heads, we found no relief within our tiny cell from the dampness and gloom permeating the city that night. My skin itched, my lungs rattled, my teeth ached, my stomach growled (I still couldn't *sh*—) and now the walls appeared to be closing in.

Yet in spite of all this misery, I sensed that conditions had to improve. I took the time to remind myself that I had indeed reached the "promised land". I was in America, after all. My luck would have to turn. "O brave new world!" I reassured myself, "*post nubila*

Phoebus." [After dark clouds, the sun.] Tomorrow would be a better day.

In the meantime, our melancholia persisted, a condition that did not go unrecognised by Michael Mitchell, the proprietor and publican of the Reunion. How often must he have encountered travellers like Jones and me, pilgrims who had suffered a ten-days' tumultuous voyage at sea and now faced the vagaries of life in New York City sodden with rain.

"Boys," said he, wiping clean some glasses at the bar, "I have just the remedy for your downcast spirits."

Expecting an offer of gin or rum or some other variety of alcohol on his shelf, I was duly surprised by his suggestion.

"What do you say to a night at the theatre? A British pantomime's going on this evening at Booth's. *Robinson Crusoe.* It's just the thing for wandering Brits. The theatre's at 23rd and 6th Avenue. It's a couple of miles from here; but even with all the rain, if you hurry, you should arrive just before the curtain goes up."

"Booth's?" I queried. It was the only word I had retained.

"*Edwin* Booth," Mitchell said with a nod, "the actor who built the theatre, *not* his goddam traitor of a brother you're probably thinking of—John Wilkes Booth who murdered Lincoln. Edwin's one of our greatest players."

The sensational has always interested me, and I confess to having cultivated a ghoulish curiosity in the Booth family since I had first learned of the President's assassination some fourteen years previous. Jones too expressed interest in seeing the place, yet our interests were quieted when Mitchell informed us that the theatre no longer belonged to brother Edwin.

"He couldn't make it work and lost the place to bankruptcy five years ago. As you can expect, the new owners wanted larger audiences. Oh, they continued to put on classical plays the way Booth did—you know, Shakespeare and the like—but to attract new people, they staged more crowd-friendly shows like these British pantomimes."

I was impressed with Mitchell. For an American, he displayed a keen sense of British Theatre. Within the world of *belles letters,* it was common knowledge that a great many Americans confused the word "pantomime" with the silent affair called "mime". But as I am certain Mitchell could attest, anyone who has ever attended a pantomime can tell you that, thanks to all the singing, joking, and—dare I say—participation from a spirited audience, the British "panto" is anything but silent.

In fact, most pantomimes—often inspired by popular children's tales like *Robin Hood* and *Aladdin*—take the original stories down a few pegs. You might expect the democratic audiences in America to demand more appearances of these irreverent productions; and yet the British pantomime remains a *rara avis* [rare bird] in the States. If you believe *hôtelier* Mitchell, it is the desire to witness so uncommon a phenomenon that causes crowds to fill the local theatres when pantomimes are put on.

Thanks to current literary fashion, however, I was prodded by a more personal motivation. With narratives like *Robinson Crusoe,* Daniel Defoe's fictional account of the castaway sailor called Alexander Selkirk,* serving as inspiration, I myself had for some time been contemplating the composition of a sea adventure. That the panto version of *Robinson Crusoe* was being performed that very night was reason enough to see the show. No matter the cost of a ticket, visiting Booth's had just become my major objective for the evening.

All this I explained to my fellow-traveller Jones. With the promise that we would dine after the performance, I had every expectation that he would join me. After all, did each of us not consider himself the other's right-hand man? Such was the camaraderie we had cultivated aboard the *Devonia.* He moaned a bit about the cost of tickets; but when I suggested we could save money by walking to Booth's Theatre in the rain instead of hiring some sort of transport to take us there, he acquiesced. We stored our belongings in the room we had agreed to share—I, my knapsack, small valise, and railway-rug; Jones, his solitary travelling bag—pulled on our mackintoshes (mine over my favourite velveteen jacket), patted down on our flat caps, and gritted our teeth. Only then, armed with Mitchell's directions, did Jones and I emerge from Reunion House prepared to confront the elements.

---

* More recent scholarship has suggested Robert Knox, who lived as a captive on the island of Ceylon for nineteen years (1659-1678), as DeFoe's model. See Katherine Frank's *Crusoe: Daniel Defoe, Robert Knox and the Creation of a Myth.* (DDV)

How relentless the rain! It pelted us as we plodded along the flooded roadways. Massive buildings towered above, the odd awning or overhanging roof offering the most minimum of shelters. Gas lamps flickered in the rapidly falling darkness, the reflections of their light dancing in the wet and deserted sidewalks. No pushcarts, no vendors, no police interrupted the scene. The occasional hansom or carriage might roll past, but you did not have to be a native New Yorker to know that this evening was a time to remain indoors.

Lest it sound otherwise, let me reassure you that we did reach our destination just in time for the curtain's rise. Booth's Theatre itself was modern in its *accoutrements* and beautifully done up. Neither the darkness nor the rain could obscure the three towers rising above the mansard roof. Eager to escape the downpour, we quickly made our way into the foyer through one of the high-arched portals facing the street. Though the lobby smelled of sodden coats, the shiny marble floor remained continuously mopped. An imposing statue of Junius Brutus Booth, a distinguished Shakespearian performer as well as father to Edwin and John Wilkes, lorded over the scene.

On days less fouled by the weather, countless theatre-goers would have been mulling about the spacious lobby. As it was, we had no difficulty in locating the ticket window and purchasing inexpensive seats. Dashing to their location at the rear of the cavernous hall, Jones and I removed our coats. He sat down, but my hands began to itch again, and I scratched at them. Before I could take my seat, a cough racked through me, and I employed my right arm to cover my mouth.

Still, I did my best to settle into my chair. Even then, a chill coursed through my weakened body—I had already lost some fourteen pounds during the voyage—but, fortunately, I had my old skullcap to confound the cold, and I placed it atop my head moments before the overture began. Immediately, I felt improved. As if in sympathy, the sprightly music featured a gay tune or two, and I vowed to attempt them on my flageolet some day.

It was at the overture's end, with my maladies now in abeyance, that the curtain rose, and I caught my first glimpse of the actor William Escott. You should not believe that I focused my attention on that singular man during the entire performance. Yet in spite of all the pretty girls, menacing pirates, and diverting melodies, the way the one-legged Escott thumped about with a single crutch made him quite hard to miss.

It was in light of how the evening progressed, however, that I have chosen to concentrate my attention upon him at this point in my narrative. Although Jones and I came to learn the man's history only later that night, I believe that at the risk of upsetting the night's chronology, I should provide Escott's background before describing his performance. Such a detour should serve to help you navigate the troubling events that occurred following the play's conclusion.

*****

William Escott had begun his acting career in 1879 by joining the Shakespearian Company of Michael Sasanoff. And yet, though boasting of having performed with such theatrical giants as Sir Henry Irving and Sir Max Beerbohm Tree, Escott confessed to never having truly considered the stage as his calling. In point of fact, at age twenty-five, he had begun to envision his future not as an actor, but rather (in his own words) as a "consulting detective"—"the world's first," he hastened to add.

For Escott, acting served as necessary preparation. "There is no better way of penetrating a disguise," he announced, "than by being able to assume one." Without envisioning a theatrical career as his goal, he remained generally content—especially in the beginning—with small parts like the first or second "walking gentleman" or even "low comedian". For Escott, impersonation was the thing—learning the tricks of make-up and costume to appear convincingly in the persona of someone other that oneself.

In the early spring of '79, "Old Sasanoff" (as he was affectionately called by the actors) announced that he had arranged a lengthy tour of America for the troupe. Beginning in November, they were to spend a short time in New York City, proceed to Chicago, and then travel west. To Escott, such a trip posed more than the simple opportunity to further his acting skills. To him, the trip provided the perfect opportunity for familiarising himself with American life.

"I'd heard New York City described as 'The Modern Gomorrah', he told me, "and I wanted to know why. I needed more time there than Sasanoff was offering."

Although he never explained how he intended to go about it, Escott envisioned the metropolis as the perfect spot to examine the full range of criminal behaviours. As a consequence, having no central roles to perform in London, he asked Sasanoff if he might leave for America well before the others in the troupe and re-join them once they arrived in the fall. Apparently, Sasanoff liked Escott's work well enough to consent to the plan. Save for muttering about the need to find a replacement, Sasanoff agreed to rehire him upon reaching New York. In August, therefore, William Escott sailed off on his own for the United States.

Despite his inexpensive lodgings near Broadway, it did not take Escott long to consume most of the money he had set aside for his adventure; and he realised the need to find employment if he was to fend off starvation before November when the Sasanoff company was scheduled to arrive. As luck would have it, during a sightseeing venture to Booth's Theatre, he discovered that not only was a *Robinson Crusoe* panto about to be mounted there by the Watley players, a visiting group from England under the direction of Malcolm Watley, but also that the company stood in need of actors.

"*Robinson Crusoe* contains a number of stock characters," Escott explained, "the ship's crew, villagers, pirates, immortals, and the like—and the company required additional players to round out the large cast."

Upon seeing the advertisement, Escott applied to Watley himself and, thanks in equal parts to the actor's British upbringing and his theatrical experience, was immediately hired. In keeping with the tradition of the pantomime, his was a character that contained many parts—that of sea cook and pirate and one-legged man all rolled into one.

Silly though the panto may have been, it was thanks to that production of *Robinson Crusoe* that Escott learned how to contort not only his face, but also his body. To appear to be missing a limb, he was fitted with a leather, belt-like harness that kept his right-leg pulled up behind him. A long coat concealed this subterfuge, and Escott offered that it didn't take long to get used to hobbling about with the aid of the weathered crutch he was given to facilitate his movements. Although Escott said that he had actually come to like the illusion, he none the less admitted that once a performance ended, he had no hesitation in removing the harness and stretching out his liberated leg.

*****

Booth's Theatre provided us a brief respite from the weather, but not completely. At the performance Jones and I attended that Sunday evening, not only could you hear the rain pummelling the roof of the theatre, but you could also count the empty seats. And yet, as Lucretius tells us, *Ut quod ali cibus est aliis fuat acre venemum.* [One's man's meat is another man's poison.] Safely ensconced within the walls of a dry auditorium, Jones and I were not complaining. On the contrary, once the gaslights were turned down in the half-empty hall, we took the opportunity to improve our seating.

Replete with action, song, and dance, the performance offered much diversion. But through it all, the audience kept a collective eye on Escott. With a ridiculous wooden parrot of emerald green attached to his shoulder, the actor convincingly hobbled his way across the stage as pirate- ship's cook, eagerly flipping cloth pancakes into the air or uttering fierce growls while brandishing an ominous blade.

So fearsome an aspect did Escott project (in spite of the silly parrot) that members of the audience would shout out to warn the innocent Robinson Crusoe, "Hist! There he is!" "Be careful!" Such calls were particularly easy to distinguish in the half-filled auditorium; and Robinson Crusoe—played, in fact, by a young lady—would flit away in the nick of time. As a consequence, the sea-cook and the rest of the pirates, supposedly motivated by drink, broke into some sort of garbled song-and-laboured-dance about the evils they planned to perform the next time they caught up to Crusoe—something about fifteen sailors on a "dead man's chest" and a refrain of "yo ho ho and barrels of rum". Of course, the audience (what there was of it, at any rate) loved such antics.

As did Jones and I—so much so, in fact, that when the performance ended, I sent my card backstage—it contained my true name—to enquire if I might personally offer my appreciation to the actors. After all, it was not as if I was unknown in artistic circles. It was then that Jones learned my real name. Upon discovering that I was a recognised author, however, he offered no inclination to share the limelight and said he would await me in the lobby.

I learned later that it was William Escott who, upon hearing my name, had told the stage manager to allow me to join the actors. Apparently, Escott was able to identify me by dint of having attended a reading of mine at Hatchards; and after removing the harness and giving his previously hidden leg a few swings, he took the lead in introducing me to the rest of the company.

"Your panto was just the antidote I craved," said I to the assemblage of pirates, cannibals, and villagers. "I've been at sea for ten depressing days. I only just arrived this afternoon."

Scattered applause greeted my explanation.

"In fact, I'm leaving for California tomorrow."

"So soon?" someone said.

"What's in California?" asked another.

"Fanny Osbourne," I answered without thinking. "The woman I love."

Their collective warm-hearted sigh embraced me, and not a few female performers did the same. Some of the men patted me on the shoulder or even put an arm round my waist in congratulations. Yet people had their jobs to perform, and the stage-hands began moving props about in preparation for shutting down the set.

It took about a quarter-hour for the farewells to dissipate; but with the auditorium empty and the actors ready to leave, I offered my final compliments and began to move towards the exit and my meeting with Jones.

It was then that the trouble began.

*****

Reaching the wings to my left, I patted my pockets, as men are wont to do to check their contents. Suddenly, I stopped and began searching in earnest within all the pockets of my trousers, jacket and rain-coat.

"My wallet's missing!" I shouted. "My railway ticket is inside."

The players on the stage froze instantly. First there was chatter, and then there were people looking at the floor to see if the wallet had simply fallen out of my clothes. Following my directions, a uniformed usher still in the hall dashed to the rear of the theatre to the seats Jones and I had initially occupied and then to the seats we had later appropriated. In neither case did he find any sign of the missing billfold.

Watley muttered something about sending for the police; but Escott, harbouring a gleam in his grey eyes, immediately spoke up.

"Let's try solving this problem on our own," said he. "We don't need the authorities to settle the matter."

Watley furrowed his brow, but he said nothing. Escott took the expression as one of approval and immediately directed the stage-hands to commandeer the exits so no one could leave the stage. He then asked all the actors to assemble before the scrim. How strange to see the *dramatis personae* [characters in a play] posed in front of a background depicting the shingle of a deserted island. Some had already donned their street clothes; and even I, untutored sleuth that I was, could understand that a trip to the changing rooms provided an opportunity for hiding the pilfered billfold, a supposition that provoked Escott to request that a pair of stage-hands search the dressing areas. Yet it was apparent from his lack of interest in their investigations that the actor believed anyone trying to make off with the wallet would more than likely still have it on his person in order to facilitate a quick escape.

At the same time Escott began manoeuvring people about, my friend Jones reappeared from the lobby through a rear door. My outburst had obviously summoned him back. You must know that while I never considered him capable of theft, I was pleased that his absence from the stage ruled him out as a suspect. Even now he displayed the common sense to occupy a seat at the rear of the auditorium and not become involved in the confusion at the front. On the contrary, I do believe he understood that yet another stage performance—a more serious production—was about to begin, and he wanted to watch the new scene develop.

"I suggest, Mr Watley," Escott said, "that we begin by searching the group. We might ask Miss Ross to conduct the service for the women. Her Crusoe costume is so form-fitting that it precludes any opportunity for hiding away a billfold."

The young woman blushed, but proceeded to assemble the other females in the cast. Escott himself motioned for the men to group together. In retrospect, such actions must have been a diversion. For after Escott had looked one particular man over from head to toe, Escott placed his arm about the man's shoulders and ushered him to centre stage. It seemed obvious that the amateur detective had reached a preliminary conclusion.

James Flint had exchanged his pirate's costume for tweed coat and trousers and was carrying a rain-coat in preparation for departing. With high, chiselled cheekbones, a strong chin, flashing eyes, and luxuriant black hair, he possessed many of the features required for major roles. But standing barely five feet high, he remained too short.

"Mr Flint," said Escott, "might we check your pockets? You—"

Before Escott could say anymore, the actor laid his mac on a chair and pulled a brown-leather billfold from inside his coat. With a mocking grin, he announced, "Just my own wallet," and he held it high in the air for all to see.

Escott looked at me questioningly.

"Mine's black," said I, shaking my head.

"Let's see what your other pockets hold."

Flint made a show of turning out all his pockets, including those in the cast-aside rain-coat, maintaining his grin all the while.

But Escott was not to be denied. With the silly wooden parrot flopping on his shoulder, he turned and began to stride uphill to the back of the stage on a floor raked about five degrees. The rest of the company followed; and after some ten steps, he halted before a six-foot-square trap door, the onstage egress to the storage or trap room below the boards, an area called the "cellarage". It was through just such an opening that "bodies" were seen to be buried and ghosts to magically rise.

"Here!" Escott announced, pointing downward with his long forefinger. His eyes were shining, and his cheeks were tinged pink. But only for a moment.

Just as Escott had bent forward, Flint leapt upon him from behind, knocking the parrot to the stage in the process. The villain was grasping a fearsome knife and, holding his hand low, brought the six inches of flashing steel up into Escott's chest. I myself witnessed the knife pushed in all the way to the hilt, a thrust that could not have failed to penetrate poor Escott's heart.

*****

With screams and shouts filling the auditorium, a burly stage-hand grabbed Flint and pulled him away from Escott. The knife clattered to the floor, and I expected to see gouts of blood gush from Escott's chest. Instead, he rose to his feet and with the calmest of demeanours faced a circle of wide eyes and raised brows.

"You—you're all right then, William?" Nelly asked. "How can that be? I saw the knife enter your body."

Hushed voices and bobbing heads reflected the concerns of the entire troupe.

"Sleight of hand," Escott explained with a dry chuckle. "I suspected Flint from the start. He was already dressed and too eager to leave. I was able to check his pockets for the missing wallet when I escorted him to centre-stage. Though I felt no wallet but the one he displayed, I did detect an unseen dagger tucked into his belt. It was mere child's play to replace the real item with the retractable-bladed knife that still resided in my own pocket. Flint acted so quickly against me that he had no chance to note the switch."

Flint struggled all the more mightily to free himself—fortunately, to no avail.

"I can only assume," Escott went on, "that such reckless behavior confirms his guilt. Shall we see?"

Escott now stood about a foot downstage from the trap door amidst the sawdust employed to represent sand. So positioned, he fell to his knees and, raising the trap door, crawled round its frame, running his fingers along the wooden moulding just inside the cavity. He obviously believed that the recess served as a cache for the stolen wallet.

"Bah!" Escott shouted in frustration. Having discovered nothing secreted within the woodwork, he searched again—still to no avail. "It *has* to be here," I heard him mutter just before he jumped down into the trap room itself. Moments later, the under-stage room took on a yellow glow; he had obviously found a lantern.

I moved close enough to the opening to see a few of the treasures below—a small oaken table, a discarded tree of *papier-mâché*, a furled red flag leaning against the back wall. I caught a glimpse of Escott as well. Ignoring the slight stoop, there was just enough room for him to stand. Then suddenly the light extinguished.

"No need for a thorough search here," he announced in a voice muffled by the below-stage enclosure. "Flint didn't have enough time to be too clever."

Curiously enough, though Escott climbed out empty-handed, a look of genuine surprise appeared on Flint's face. Almost immediately, however, it transformed into a self-satisfied smirk.

"No wallet, eh, Escott?" he declaimed, squirming in the arms of the man who was holding him. Flint might have been orating in the midst of a play. "May I ask why you thought it was *I* who took it? Why you felt you could besmirch my good name in front of my colleagues?"

Escott looked momentarily puzzled. "I thought it was obvious, Mr Flint," said he at last. "In the world of detection there is much to be learned from trouser knees. Yours, sir, are flecked with bits of sawdust, sawdust precisely the same as that scattered on the floor near the trap door. Anyone can see that you were on your knees by the opening."

The stage-hand released his grip, and immediately Flint brushed the legs of his trousers clean. "Proves nothing, does it?" said he.

Escott's eyes now turned back to the assembled actors. Slowly, he scrutinised the appearances of them all. He seemed to be seeking out another thief. *Incidis in Scyllam cupiens vitare Charybdim.* [From the frying pan into the fire.] If he could not produce an alternative culprit, I assumed that he and the young actress would have to search the entire group.

Suddenly, Escott turned to face a white-bearded fellow identified by Watley as Bennie Gunn, the actor who had played a shipwrecked old sailor. He was still dressed in his costume of heavy blue cotton trousers and billowing white shirt.

"Do you mind, Mr Gunn?" Escott asked.

Gunn looked quizzical as Escott examined the man's shirtsleeves. Even I could detect the dark stains at the right cuff, which Escott was just then sniffing.

"Darjeeling, I should judge," Escott observed.

Immediately, Gunn pulled his arm back and sprang for the small stairway downstage that led into the auditorium and the exit. At that same moment, I saw my friend Jones rise in the back of the hall though I could not fathom what he might do if Gunn were actually to confront him. But the actor never even reached the stairs. Another of the stage-hands blocked his escape, grabbing him round his upper arms.

*****

Escott made his way to the wings where a dull brass samovar stood on a table. "This container," said he, resting his palm on the metal lid, "is filled with tea before every performance and is generally tapped out by the end." So saying, he carefully raised the lid, peered inside, and nodded. "Dry," he announced, "but not completely empty." He proceeded to thrust his hand inside and to pluck out a black leather wallet, which he held up for all to see.

"That's it!" I cried, dashing towards him. "That's mine. You can see my tickets inside—though not much else."

Indeed, there were but a couple of dollars within—little enough to attract a thief. But then a thief cannot detect a wallet's contents in advance. Escott also produced my ticket for the next day's evening-ferry to Jersey City as well as my railway ticket for travel from thence to San Francisco and even my cancelled ticket from the ship *Devonia*. There could be no doubt that the billfold was mine.

"Well done, Escott," said I as he handed it over. To the actor's great embarrassment, the entire theatre company broke into applause.

"You may have found the wallet," snarled Gunn, "but you can't prove it was I who stole it."

"I mentioned trouser-knees before, did I not?" Escott replied. "In my eagerness to confront Flint, I neglected to mention the equally important cuffs of shirtsleeves. There is much to be learned from them as well. It was Flint who initially pickpocketed the wallet and placed it beneath the trap door. But it was Gunn who, having watched all this transpire, removed the wallet from Flint's hiding place and hid it in the now-empty samovar—though not carefully enough to prevent some errant tea from staining his right-sleeve cuff. I have no doubt that after removing his costume, he would have gone straight to the samovar to retrieve his booty."

Watley now took command of his company, issuing orders to the stage-hands regarding Gunn and Flint: "Throw them out! The both of them. Take them to the alley in the back."

Grabbing the thieves by the shoulders, the big men shoved the two through the wings and to the rear of the theatre. Moments later, we heard a door open and the rush of falling rain. Cold air accompanied by a wet smell wafted onto the stage. Then there were the thuds of bodies being struck and the slam of the door.

"Well done, sir!" Watley crowed, slapping Escott on the back. "Well done, indeed! No need for the police when William Escott is present, eh?"

Amidst a final cascade of compliments, the members of the cast began to disperse. The moment offered me the opportunity to express my own appreciation.

"I'd like to thank you, Mr Escott," I said. "Perhaps you would honour me as a my guest for a late-night dinner. If you can recommend a place within my meagre means, I would be happy to host you."

Escott clasped my hand. "I would be more than happy to spend the time with you, sir," said he, "but there's no need for you to go to any such expense. I shall pay my own way."

I am rather afraid that a blush crossed my face, and I nervously scratched at my hands. This clever fellow had clearly noted the economical status of my travel tickets—the second-class cabin arrangements aboard the *Devonia* and the seat aboard one of the infamous "emigrant trains". Everyone knew that such a railway was devised to convey the newly arrived—and therefore the most frugal of travellers—westward in the least expensive manner. Yet if Escott recognised that my claim to literary recognition had so far produced no outward signs of monetary success, he kept silent on the matter.

"My father," I said and explained to him my financial predicament."

"We each must follow our own paths, Mr Stephenson," Escott observed.

The actor requested a few minutes to exchange his sea-cook's costume for more traditional garb. He soon reappeared, and after once again being congratulated by the remaining members of the troupe, he donned his mackintosh and soft cloth cap, a unique affair with bills in front and back and earflaps that tied together at the top. Jones and I put on our own rain-coats and flat caps and, thus prepared to face the drenched streets of New York City, set out to find a restaurant that fit my requirements.

*****

Escott guided us to a French establishment not far from the theatre. Happily, it took but a glance at the bill of fare to assure me that the restaurant would fulfil not only my culinary desires but my financial requirements as well. With my skullcap safely secured atop my head again, I eagerly joined Escott and Jones in a most satisfactory repast. It was during this meal that Escott reported to us the facts concerning his life that I presented to you earlier—the details of his acting career, his visit to Hatchards, his trip to New York City, and his interest in becoming a consulting detective.

Even if the wine and chicken did not pass for authentic *coq au vin,* I must say that in light of all the challenging events of the day, it was quite the feast. Yet to be honest, I was most appreciative of the coffee. The wretched brew on the ship had tasted of snuff; indeed, you could scarcely tell it apart from the tea.

Following dinner, we shared cigarettes—I rolled my favourite Three Castles—and after a few puffs began to cough.

Both Escott and Jones showed signs of concern as my hacking went on. But I waved them off with a few flicks of my hand.

"Not to worry," I told my companions and immediately changed the subject. "You know of my scribbling," I said to Escott. "I'm hoping to produce a narrative of this trip worthy of publication."

My new friends both raised their glasses.

"To your next work," said the actor.

I smiled, appreciative of Escott's support. In point of fact, I had been elaborating the plans for my sea story that very evening as I watched Escott hopping about on stage. The affair with the wallet had simply put it out of mind.

Now, however, I felt ready to announce my intention. "Escott," I said, "for some time now, I've been mulling over the idea for a sea-faring adventure tale; and I owe it to you that—no matter what happens during my journey west—I'm actually going to begin the thing."

The actor cocked an eyebrow.

"No, really, Escott, your portrayal of the one-legged sea cook inspired me. The crutch. The parrot. And later, when you uncovered that empty hidey-hole below the stage. It's all helped me move the plot along—as, indeed, have some of the colourful names I heard tonight."

Escott shrugged. "Glad to be of service," said he, clinking his glass with mine.

A chuckle escaped my lips. "I expect that people are going to say that my hobbled pirate was modelled after my one-legged friend, the poet William Henley. I must admit that, thanks to him, writing a story about someone so afflicted had crossed my mind. But *your* performance—not to mention that wobbly parrot—seems to have been just the inspiration I needed to touch off the action. And for that I am truly grateful."

Escott sat silently staring at me for a few moments. There are those who say that my widely-set eyes cause people to become meditative. Whatever his motivation, he seemed to be contemplating his next words carefully. Finally, he gave a brief nod, as if indicating to himself that he had decided in the affirmative. "Speaking of role-playing, " said he, "you should know that William Escott is not my real name; it is my acting pseudonym. In reality, I am called Sherlock Holmes."

In the Bohemian world of theatre, such news caused no great excitement. "Well then," said I, "here's to Sherlock Holmes," and I raised my glass. "Call me 'Louis'," I added with a smile.

"I'm still Jones," chuckled the third member of our group.

Jones had always known me as "Robert" and must have wondered if all of us artistic types—indeed, all of humanity—harboured dual identities. I know I contemplated the question. I should imagine, for instance, that few members of the Watley Company realised that the calm exteriors of James Flint and Bennie Gunn concealed the hearts of thieves. Actors were trained to hide their true natures. We were in America at the time, so I offer you Wilkes Booth as the pre-eminent example.

We finished our smokes, and Escott walked Jones and me back through the rain to Reunion House. The showers were not as heavy as earlier in the day, but the rain was still coming down in watery curtains. The next evening I would begin my long railway excursion to the west. I had no reason to think that I would ever again hear the name Sherlock Holmes. But at least I could complete this part of my journey in the belief that, however inadvertently, I might have played some small role in helping forge the career of the world's first consulting detective.

III

The day after I had read Stevenson's narrative, I made my way to the London Library in St. James's Square. It was there that the sub-librarian Lomax procured for me a copy of the very novel whose creation had been triggered by Stevenson's visit to the panto at Booth's Theatre. Book in hand, I proceeded to the Northumberland Arms near Trafalgar Square. My literary agent, Arthur Conan Doyle, and I had scheduled a holiday meeting at one of his favourite public houses to discuss my idea for a story about Holmes's recent return to life. (It had been just a few months since Holmes had shocked me with his dramatic re-appearance following his encounter with Professor Moriarty at the Reichenbach Falls—"shocking" since Holmes had been thought dead for close to three years.) As Conan Doyle and I exchanged literary strategies, we also enjoyed a tankard or two. Conan Doyle paused, however, when he noted the book at my side.

"The late Robert Louis Stevenson, I see," he observed grimly. "What a loss. Another Scotsman with genius—a wonderful teller of tales. If I do say so myself, Louis was one of the great storytellers of the race. He glorified the 'masculine type', if you take my meaning. Do you know that there are those who call that book next to you the finest narrative in the English language? He wrote it in the two years following his meeting with Holmes—no doubt the reason for originally titling it 'The Sea Cook". Louis himself employed the pseudonym of Captain George North and first published the thing in serialised sections in the children's magazine called Young Folks. *The rest, as they say, is history."*

Conan Doyle paused to sample the ale. Then, almost as an afterthought, he added, "Do you know, John, that way back in April of '83, not long after The Sea Cook *had appeared, Louis wrote to me just how much he enjoyed Sherlock Holmes? To tell the truth, I didn't know if he meant the man himself or the hero of your accounts—though he did say that reading one of your stories had given him momentary relief from a bout of pleurisy."*

My agent broke into a round of hearty laughter. "As a doctor myself," he said, "I regard that as quite a compliment. Don't you agree?"

I nodded sadly, thinking of Stevenson's early death.

Later that evening, following a meal of lamb and potatoes excellently prepared by Mrs Hudson, I settled into my armchair in the sitting room with the book in my hands. Holmes's tin box and the Stevenson manuscript were no longer in sight. A fire crackled in the hearth, and I prepared myself for a relaxing read. With Christmas but a week away, 221B seemed the most ideal spot in the world.

With a satisfied smile, I opened the book called Treasure Island. *In no less than three pages, I encountered young Jim Hawkins and the Admiral Benbow Inn and Billy Bones, the fierce-looking sailor with the sabre cut on his cheek. It was Bones who warned the lad to keep his "weather-eye open for a sea-faring man with one leg . . . ."*

The Adventure of the Second William Wilson

The mask and mantle of the unknown drop off, and Alfonso discovers his own image, —the spectre of himself.

--Washington Irving
"An Unwritten Drama of Lord Byron"

Straightway the door opened, and a shrivelled, shabby dwarf entered . . . . This vile bit of human rubbish seemed to bear a sort of remote and ill-defined resemblance to me.

--Mark Twain
"The Facts Concerning the Recent Carnival of Crime in Connecticut"

One cannot play a role in the detecting business—let alone *write* of the profession—without harbouring an opinion on the subject of Edgar Allan Poe. The American author so often referred to as "The Father of the Detective Story" evokes strong reactions in all kinds of readers, but especially in those directly connected to criminal investigations. Sherlock Holmes himself was not immune to Poe's sway. And yet for so clear a thinker as Holmes, his views on Poe's crime-solving skills were known to waver.

As much as he might deny it, my logical-thinking friend had always been of two minds regarding the writer. At the start of his career, Holmes appeared to look down upon the man. In our first investigation together, the account of which I titled *A Study in Scarlet*, he labelled Poe's fictional detective "a very inferior fellow".

"You should note, Watson," Holmes said, "C. Auguste Dupin is by no means the phenomenon Poe imagined him to be."

But Holmes also harboured another opinion. In a later case, an investigation I called "The Cardboard Box", he praised Dupin as a "close reasoner"—not unlike himself. Never comfortable with reversals of opinion, however, Holmes duly suggested that it was I, not he, who had initially doubted Dupin's credibility.

Though it is an easy matter for me to plead not guilty to such unfair charges, my faithful readers need not accept my pledge of innocence on its own. Events themselves offer corroborating evidence. In late 1882, the details of a strange new case forced Holmes to confront both sides of his conflicted attitude towards Poe. It required no less than a gruesome crime to cause Sherlock Holmes to question the dichotomy between Poe's celebrated psychological insight and the writer's equally renowned literary flights of fancy.

*****

Poe himself would have appreciated the beginnings of the matter. It was a dark Monday evening in a suitably bleak and dreary December, when Billy the Page came suddenly rapping at our chamber door.

"Enter!" Holmes called, and Billy stepped inside.

Holmes and I rose as the lad adjusted his livery and announced, "Mr William Wilson."

Directly behind Billy came a distinguished-looking gentleman. Dressed in a bespoke dark suit that contrasted nicely with his grey side-whiskers, he maintained a fine head of black hair combed straight back. Yet in spite of his august appearance, he had the unusual habit of constantly glancing round our sitting room. His blue eyes darted everywhere—peering beyond the chairs and tables, examining the windows, looking backward at the door, which Billy had closed upon exiting.

I judged him an obvious paranoiac, demonstrably worried that he had been followed. Indeed, he went so far as to check that the door latch had been secured. After assuring himself that all was in order, he began bouncing his gaze back and forth between my friend and me.

"Mr Holmes?" he asked.

"I am Sherlock Holmes," said my companion. Gesturing in my direction, he added, "This is my friend and colleague, Dr Watson. Whatever you have to say to me, you may say to him as well."

"I am called William Wilson," came the reply. "It is a name with which you might be familiar."

Holmes cocked an eyebrow.

"From the story with that title by Edgar Allan Poe," the man added.

It took me a moment to recall the piece. Once I did, I wondered how the man dared to identify himself so definitively. It is always dangerous to trust one of Poe's narrators; but if I remembered correctly, the storyteller states that so abhorrent is the tale he is about to relate that he fears sullying the "fair page" with his "real appellation". In light of our visitor's claim, one had to question whether the storyteller's denial was a ruse, or whether our guest was guilty of a ridiculous charade.

"I know the story," said I coldly. "I'm sure Mr Holmes does as well."

"Indeed I do," said my friend with a nod. "It is a difficult story to forget. The aforementioned William Wilson encounters someone he believes looks and sounds just like himself—an intriguing mirror-image the Germans term a *Doppelgänger*. This alter ego, who even bears the same name as William Wilson, follows Wilson to the Carnival in Rome. Driven mad by the constant pursuit, Wilson employs the rapier that is part of his costume to stab his double to death. Or so it appears."

Leave it to Holmes to hit exactly the right mark with his ambiguity. For as I then remembered, it is in a conclusion left open to interpretation that renders the entire story so perplexing. Through literary sleight of hand, Poe forces the reader to question whether Wilson, rather than having killed some evil tormentor, has in reality viewed himself in a mirror—a mirror that might or might not exist—and inflicted the bloody wounds upon his own person.

"What relationship does the story have to *you*?" Holmes asked our visitor.

The man stood tall. "The original William Wilson was my father."

"Preposterous!" I cried. "The story is mere fiction."

The visitor shook his head. "Gentlemen," said he with a dry chuckle, "I can assure you that you are mistaken. Neither is the story untrue—nor am I mad.'"

"You present a singular situation, sir," said Holmes, reaching for his favourite briar. "I'm certain I speak for Dr Watson when I say we wish to hear you out."

Stifling my scepticism, I muttered some words of agreement. At the same time, Holmes indicated that our visitor take a seat. The man calling himself William Wilson did just that, and Holmes and I occupied armchairs opposite his. "Now," said my friend as he filled his pipe, "pray, explain yourself."

Wilson took a deep breath. "As you are doubtlessly aware," he began, "Edgar Allan Poe was born in America. John and Frances Allan, the people who took him in following his father's abandonment and his mother's early death, brought him to England at a young age."

"To Stoke Newington, was it not?" Holmes asked as he lit his pipe.

"Quite right. They settled in the picturesque village just north of London. Poe's biographers will tell you that the hamlet described in his narrative about William Wilson was based on that very locale right down to the thick, cloying mist and the massive, twisted trees. For that matter, Bransby, the headmaster of young William's prison-like school in the story, bears the same name as the headmaster of the school attended by Poe himself."

Tenuous proof, I remember thinking at the time. *Poe may simply have liked the name.*

"I provide this information, gentlemen, to enable you to make the leap that literary critics seem so unwilling to perform—that is, to accept as fact a supposedly fictional story, however bizarre. Poe was describing the actual location where, as a youth, he had befriended a real lad he called William Wilson. As a consequence, I implore you to recognise the narrative in question not as a mere fabrication but rather as a true chronicle of past events."

Holmes's response to this singular request was to exhale a cloud of blue smoke towards the ceiling. I, on the other hand, confess to experiencing a degree of sympathy. After all, to this very day, my own accounts of the true exploits of Sherlock Holmes continue to be misidentified as fiction.

"To their delight," Wilson resumed, undaunted by Holmes's indifferent reaction, "the boys discovered they shared the same birthday; and soon thereafter they became fast friends. Once Poe returned to America a few years later, the youths began a correspondence that continued into manhood.

"Poe's letters are gone now; but being the wordsmith that he was, he recognised not only the attraction of the details Wilson recounted in his letters, but also the reckless abandon with which he described them. There seems little doubt that Wilson too appreciated what he himself had written. We'll never know the precise reason, of course, but presumably some dubious promise of anonymity from Poe prompted William to grant his friend permission to convert the many letters into a single, factual narrative."

Holmes allowed another cloud of smoke to escape his lips.

"You have read," our visitor continued, "of Wilson's attendance at Oxford and his intemperate behaviour there."

"In particular," I felt compelled to add, "his involvement with licentious women."

"'Profligacy'," stated Holmes, the pipe clenched in his teeth. "'Miserable profligacy' is the phrase employed by Poe."

"Quite right," said the man. "'Miserable profligacy' is exactly the term. So is 'debaucheries'. He used others as well—'soulless dissipation' and 'dangerous seductions' to name two more. I can assure you that such demeaning language most accurately describes his foul actions."

"You seem to speak from experience," I observed drily.

Our visitor smiled. "No, Dr Watson, I wish the answer was that simple. You see, gentlemen, much as it grieves me to report the fact, my own mother, whom I loved very much, was one of those young whores who serviced Wilson and his chums."

"Good heavens!" I cried. "One doesn't usually hear a gentleman speak so rudely of his own mother."

"I note," said Holmes coldly, "that you refer to the woman in the past tense. May we assume that she has died?"

"Yes, Mr Holmes. She died a few weeks ago at age seventy-two."

"A ripe old age," I observed.

"To be sure, Doctor; and yet the longer she lived, the more she feared going to her grave without providing me with the truth about my birth. I am no student of literature, you see, and had no cause to be familiar with the writings of Mr Poe. I can assure you that his works occupied no place on the shelves in our home. This last fact was the primary reason for my surprise when after her death. I discovered that my mother had left me an anthology of Poe's stories. Needless to say, it included Poe's account of William Wilson—along with a letter from my mother that explained the story's significance.'

"A letter, you say? Do you have it with you?"

"Yes, Mr Holmes. I thought that you would want to see it."

Sherlock Holmes extended his long fingers in anticipation whilst Wilson withdrew a set of folded papers from an inner pocket and placed them in Holmes's open palm. My friend proceeded to read the missive and then passed the pages to me. Here is the letter that we read:

10 October 1882

My Dearest William,

By the time you read this, I shall be gone, happy to face a better world, but happier still to know I have left you comfortable in this one. I cannot move on in peace, however, without providing you with specific knowledge of your own peculiar background. For all your lifetime I have been fearful of telling you your history, but during every one of those years my silence has gnawed at me. I cannot deprive you any longer of the knowledge of your past. No parent likes to advertise the misdeeds of their youth or to describe for their children the crumbling foundation upon which a false family history has been constructed. Yet I find myself in precisely that situation. Just as I confront my own fate, I cannot turn away from showing you yours.

You know of my early youth. Although my mother died in childbirth, I was brought up in a proper home in Gloucestershire. My father—your grandfather—was a vicar and provided me with an education. But I found such a simple life unappealing; and thanks in great part to my comely appearance, I came to believe at a youthful age that I might travel to Oxford and find some rising young man who could provide me not only with a family, but also with a material improvement in my fortune.

Sadly, difficult though it is to admit, I was taken advantage of. As a result, my dreams faded. I lost hope in securing a suitable man to be my husband—and yet I could never ignore the appeal of lucre. On the contrary, my lust for riches continued to grow. In short, though I hesitate to write the words, I spent most of my evenings in the arms of young men who sought nothing more than paying for all manner of delights of the flesh. Needless to say, amidst words of righteous indignation, my father, your grandfather, abandoned me.

My reputation as a bewitching temptress brought me gold and infamy, and it was not long before I met one William Wilson, a debauched young man with lots of money. Inflicting pain and humiliation were his chief desires, and he seemed intent on fulfilling his wants. In a word, he appeared a ruthless master. It was only later that I discovered the inner torment he suffered. He claimed to fear the vengeance of some sort of evil twin, a double that he said had haunted him from their first encounter years before. On occasion, he would whisper that I should run away. But no sooner did he dismiss me than he would cry out for protection from the devilish creature that was driving him mad. The longer I knew your father, the more I heard him rant and rave, and yet I assure you that no such phantom ever showed itself to me.

But why dwell upon the macabre?

You can read of his horrific escapades and nightmares yourself in the story by Mr Poe that bears your father's name. As for the two of us, William and I remained together until I discovered I was with child. When I told him I would not rid myself of it—of you*—he wanted nothing more to do with me. Not even Mr Poe, famous for his tales of the depraved, could bring himself to include my tragic chapter in his own history of William Wilson.*

And yet I must give the devil his due. Thanks to the largess of his parents, William was awash with money, and—quite the cheat at Écarté*—raised his own small pile at the gaming tables. As a result, he was willing enough to supply me with enough funds to live quite comfortably during my confinement. He required but two conditions. I was to give my child* his *name (if I was lucky enough to have a son), and I was never to reveal the source of my income. I am pleased to say that the fund was generous enough to allow me and you (for you were, indeed, the son I was blessed to have) to live comfortably. Happily, the money was sufficient for me to send you to school even after William's death. To spare you the pain, I invented all that business about a military father who had served his country nobly and died in battle. Although secrecy no longer matters, not even* *when you came of age did I have the courage to inflict upon you the ugly truth of your conception. That you have become a solicitor with a successful practice could make no mother more proud.*

Though I have said that your father, despite his latent cruelty, could never bring himself to completely forsake his former mistress and his son, neither did he ever wish to see us again. So utterly damning did I find his rejection that I began to fear that you, my only child, might have inherited some aspect of his deeply distorted nature. That is why I never encouraged you to marry or to start a family of your own, but rather to stay by me and care for your aging mother. Read the words of Mr Poe to understand your awful beginnings. Even as my time on earth draws to a close, you must become aware of the hidden dangers lurking within your soul; they threaten every fibre of your being.

Take heed and avoid the fate of your father.

It was signed, "Your adoring mother."

After I had finished reading the letter, Holmes addressed Mr Wilson: "With all due respect to the deceased, one cannot treat the account of an illusory *Doppelgänger* as Truth. Even your mother, the authoress of this fable, admits that she never saw the alleged simulacrum, that she had only read Poe's account of it. Not to speak ill of the dead, sir, but perhaps your mother had become delusional towards the end of a very long life."

Our visitor nodded. "So I thought too, Mr Holmes; and following her death, I read Poe's story just as she had instructed. Though the plot substantiated many of the events described in her letter—and, by the same token, made me question the basic touchstones of my life—what else could I do but consider her fears the ravings of a demented mind? I continued to doubt her warnings—continued doubting until a week ago. That was when I saw him."

"Saw *whom*?" I asked.

Wilson ran a hand through his thick black hair. "I know you will find this hard to believe, gentlemen," said he. "In fact, I fully expect you to resort to all the predictable explanations—delusion, dream, hallucination. But as I sit here now in Baker Street, so last week did I see a man who looked very much like me—very much indeed. He's followed me to and from work for most of the last few days. Sometimes he waits across the road from my club to dog my heels. When I attended the opera last week, I saw him lurking in the shadows of Covent Garden. And always, he follows me home. On one occasion, he got close enough to whisper my name."

Sherlock Holmes showed his teeth in what can only be described as a condescending smile. "I must confess, Mr Wilson, that your situation prompts my curiosity; yet I must also caution that in no way should my interest cause you to assume my belief in your imaginings."

Our visitor's face flushed. "See here, Mr Holmes, I'm willing to pay you to look into this affair. The police are not interested."

"I should think not. I doubt the name Poe means anything to the Yarders—let alone the name William Wilson. But though your case warrants attention and you have come to the right place to register your fears, I make no promises about how any such investigation may be resolved."

"But you *will* look into the matter, Mr Holmes? You *will* uncover whoever or whatever it is that tracks me? I shall go mad if you turn me down."

Holmes placed his pipe in a nearby ashtray. "The addresses of your chambers and rooms, if you please," said he, offering Wilson a sheet of paper and pencil. "Give it to Dr Watson."

Wilson scribbled the information about his rooms near Long Acre Street and his law office at the Inns of Court. He handed the paper to me, and in exchange Holmes gave him one of his visiting cards upon which he had written his fee. Wilson nodded his approval and thanked us both.

"One final question, Mr Wilson," said Holmes as he opened the door.

Wilson turned to face him.

"I must ask if you have recently committed some 'folly of vice'?"

"I beg your pardon," said Wilson.

"A folly of vice—the expression employed by Poe to describe an immoral act. Such behaviour on your part might have summonsed your father's double. A less-discerning critic might call that double a conscience."

"I-I should say not," replied Wilson with a bit of hesitation. Seemingly uncertain about the merits of his response, he walked hesitantly out of our sitting room and down the stairs.

Once Holmes heard the outer door close, he moved to the window and drew back the white curtain.

"From this vantage," said he, still facing the glass, "it would appear that no one is following our Mr Wilson. Tomorrow, however, we shall investigate more thoroughly." Holmes settled back into the armchair. Steepling his fingers and narrowing his eyes, he observed, "If Wilson's tale is accurate, we are in deep waters, old fellow. Tomorrow, we shall put to the test the question that underlies Wilson's story: was Edgar Poe merely inventing diversions or was he, in fact—as our client seems to believe—relating a frightening historical truth."

I nodded. Holmes's own conflicting views of the American writer could not have been expressed more clearly.

*****

I came down to breakfast the next morning expecting to find Holmes at table. Instead, I encountered an officious, grey-haired fellow with a clipped painter's-brush moustache. He was dressed in dark-blue kepi and uniform and seemed to be inspecting the gas lines leading to our light fixtures.

"May I help you, sir?" I asked rather sharply, wondering why Mrs Hudson would let so offensive a personage into our rooms without first gaining our permission—unless, of course, it was Holmes himself who had admitted him. But there was no sign of my friend, and the Inspector had moved from examining the pipelines to rearranging some of Holmes's laboratory equipment.

"I say, take your hands off that test tube," I commanded.

"I'm simply trying—" the intruder attempted to explain in a high-pitched voice.

"Nevermore!" I interrupted, surprised at how easily a refrain from Poe had crept into my vocabulary.

"Why, Dr Watson," the man squeaked, "cannot a fellow"—and suddenly his voice became more familiar—"move about his own paraphernalia?"

The inspector, of course, was Sherlock Holmes, and I had been taken in. I looked to the heavens for solace.

"A test, Watson. If I can fool you, I should easily be able to fool someone who does not know me at all, eh?"

"And what sort of costume are you in today?"

"I am whatever kind of inspector I need to be. I shall follow Mr Wilson from a distance, stopping when necessary to examine whatever is close by—metal pipes, street lamps, broken window glass—whatever causes no commotion by having a uniformed person like myself scrutinizing it. In such a manner, I should be able to blend into the scenery."

"And I? What am I to do?"

"As you are not an early riser and also have your patients to attend in the morning, I thought that you might follow Wilson home from work."

I nodded in agreement. "And do you have a disguise for me to wear?"

"No need," Holmes chuckled. "Just wear your usual dark suit and bowler, and you will look like all the barristers and solicitors running about the Inns of Court. No one will notice you."

With a wave, he was off; and I, before setting off for my surgery, was free to sit down with a breakfast of Mrs Hudson's eggs and ham.

*****

Wilson's law chambers were located just beyond Lincoln's Inn Fields, the large square laid about by Inigo Jones in the seventeenth century. In spite of the dark clouds that afternoon, it seemed safe enough to eschew a hansom; and as I walked the two miles from our rooms to the very centre of the British legal system, I found no need to open my umbrella.

Sherlock Holmes correctly predicted that, dressed in a dark suit and bowler, I would blend in with the similarly attired barristers, solicitors, benchers, and clerks parading through the Inns of Court. On grey days like the one in question, even my furled brolly appeared *de rigueur*.

Fortunately, I had no difficulty locating the redbrick Georgian building whose address Wilson had provided; and beneath a plane tree near the green, I found a wooden bench to sit upon whilst waiting for the man himself to appear.

The December night fell quickly, yet I had no problem discerning Wilson's distinctive black mane beneath his bowler as he exited his chambers. Indistinguishable from the legal types surrounding me, I trailed after him at a safe distance along the narrow, gas-lit confines of Bell Yard on the way to the Strand. As Wilson had done during his visit to Baker Street, he would frequently turn his head in all manner of directions, presumably in search of someone seeking him harm. I had no desire in his detecting me, however; and I dodged his glances by turning away to ogle the contents of shop windows, slipping into shadowy alcoves, or hiding behind any nearby walls.

At the same time, I had to keep my eyes open for any suspicious characters among the similarly attired that were heading in the same direction. Even when Wilson reached Fleet Street and began to mix with the general populous, he remained in the proximity of personages from the Inns of Court. Might his pursuer be mingling unseen among them? I did identify a man of equal height and weight who was matching Wilson's pace; yet hidden as he was by bowler and scarf, I could not distinguish the stranger's features. When Wilson reached his home, however, the other man was nowhere to be seen; and to be honest, I could not swear that anyone had been trailing Wilson in the first place.

The next few days passed just as uneventfully. In spite of leaden skies and intermittent showers, Holmes and I continued our routine of watchfulness—Holmes taking the morning shifts; I, the afternoons—but no suspicious characters made themselves known.

It was late in the evening of our third day of surveillance that an irate William Wilson burst into our sitting room. I had been reading *The Times*, and Holmes had been tuning his violin.

"I hired you to watch out for my double!" Wilson shouted.

"And so we have," answered Holmes, calmly twisting a peg.

"Bah! I've seen no one."

"The way it should be," observed Holmes with a smile.

"As yet, Mr Wilson," said I, "we have been unable to corroborate your suspicions. When we have proof, you shall have it."

"Indeed," said he with an imperious look, "I *do* have it. I was visited by the man late this afternoon."

"But I saw no one following you," I protested.

"That's because he was already within my flat when I got there. No sooner did I enter than I encountered this—this—frankly—this image of myself."

"Really, Mr Wilson," said Holmes plucking at some strings. "Are we to hear of a chimera yet again?"

"I tell you, Holmes, he is *real*. He warned me to stay away from you—not to let you meddle in his relationship with me."

"And yet here you are."

"I will not be cowed, sir—not even by the threats of a phantom."

"Threats?" I questioned, raising my eyebrows. If the man had actually warned our client of harm, then the case had become more ominous.

"Yes, gentlemen, this bogey said he would kill me if I continued with my attempts to find him out. When I came here tonight, I did my best to be sure I wasn't being followed. But as you have already discovered, the creature is hard to detect."

"Did you recognise his voice?" Holmes asked.

"No. It was a hoarse whisper."

"Pity," said Holmes, picking up his bow and pointing it at Wilson. "You must be careful, Mr Wilson. Tomorrow, friend Watson and I will work in concert and lengthen our observations."

On that reassuring note, Holmes and I slipped on our coats and escorted Wilson out to the sidewalk. With a cold rain adding to the night's gloom, I secured a hansom for our caller. Only after Holmes noted no other carriages trailing the cab did he breathe a sigh of relief. There was no way to know it at the moment, of course, but that carriage ride was the last time we would see William Wilson alive.

*****

Late that same night a sharp knock rattled our door. I started at the noise, but Sherlock Holmes simply rose and went to see who it was that had come calling so late. At the threshold stood a drenched Inspector Lestrade, a look of grim determination pinching his face in spite of the rain. Holmes gestured him in; and as the policeman marched towards our fire, he held his wet bowler in one hand and passed Holmes a small white card with the other.

From what I could see, it appeared to be Holmes's visiting card containing his name, our Baker Street address, and a handwritten number. Though it could have been any one of the numerous cards Holmes distributed to his clients in identifying himself, this one was unique: tiny drops of red dappled both sides.

"Sorry to call on you so late, gentlemen," said Lestrade, "but we found your card in the pocket of a dead man, Mr Holmes. In rooms near Long Acre Street in Covent Garden."

"Good heavens, Holmes!" I exclaimed. Do you suppose—?"

"What's this?" the policeman interrupted. "Are you connected to this case? I left a corpse and a murder scene to come here. I need to find out straightaway how you are involved in this nasty business."

"To whom did I last give a card, Watson?" Holmes asked calmly. I knew he could answer the question himself, but I reckoned he was trying to slow Lestrade's pace.

"William Wilson," said I. "It was just a few days ago. You don't think—"

"*Wilson*, you say?" asked Lestrade, taking out pencil and note pad to record his findings.

"Not that I'm surprised," Sherlock Holmes muttered with a furrowed brow. "Stabbed, was he, Lestrade?"

The policeman's mouth dropped open. He often reacted in such a fashion when Holmes revealed some bit of evidence beyond the Inspector's detecting skills. "Out with it," he commanded. "Tell me what you know, or I'll be forced to think you had something to do with it yourself."

Holmes shrugged. "The man came round Monday claiming to be one William Wilson. He appeared quite the successful barrister. Chambers in Lincoln's Inn Fields."

"He also seemed quite upset," I put in.

"About what?"

Holmes sighed. "All this requires some explanation."

"I don't have time for lengthy explanations, Mr Holmes. I've just told you that I've left a corpse lying on the floor in the front room of a flat. In fact, when I found your card, I was hoping I could convince you to return with me—you and Dr Watson—to make sense of this affair. I need to get back there as quickly as I can. I have a four-wheeler outside."

Holmes shrugged again. "Care for a ride, Watson? The weather's not the best, but when Scotland Yard's finest comes a-calling, we really should not decline the invitation."

I quickly agreed, and Holmes and I donned our rain-coats and hats. We followed Lestrade out to the kerb where a growler stood waiting in the darkness. Soon we were clattering down a wet Baker Street in the direction of William Wilson's rooms.

"Watson," said Holmes, "you're the literary man. Explain to the inspector what it was that upset our caller. I find these matters regarding Poe too tedious."

"Poe?" Lestrade blinked his eyes. "You don't mean Edgar Allan Poe, the writer? The same Poe who wrote that brilliant poem, 'The Raven'?"

"The same," said I in surprise. I had never taken Lestrade for a fancier of poetry. The fact that he had heard of Poe's celebrated poem, let alone liked it, showed the vast appeal of the American's work. "There's a story by Poe called—"

Lestrade waved me off. "I'm not interested in literary theory, Doctor. Let me tell you the facts before we get there. The poor bloke arrived home and entered his rooms. At some time past eight, a grand disturbance was heard by the landlady. She ran to the victim's door, which she found ajar, and entered. After taking one look at the bloody mess, she immediately sent her boy for the local constable, who summoned help from the Yard. I arrived, surveyed the horrible scene myself, and found your card in the dead man's pocket. Which brings us up to date."

We rolled to a stop in front of Wilson's residence, an apartment block of three storeys, just as Lestrade finished his description. The two constables at the door straightened up when they saw the Inspector emerge from the carriage.

How to describe the horror we encountered inside? Chairs and end-tables were overturned; blood smears stained the walls and carpet and streaked down the window glass. Upon the floor at the centre of this gory scene lay the body of the man we knew as William Wilson. He was sprawled on his back, his right leg dangling over the edge of a small table that had been knocked on its side. Near his hand lay a large carving knife. Discarded in a corner was an open copy of a book, its pages damp with blood spots. I could see the letter from Wilson's mother spread out on the desk. It too contained spots of blood. Near us by the door, the fractured remains of a large mirror framed within a wooden hall tree stood against the wall, shards of glass shimmering on the carpet before it.

Lestrade and I remained at the door as Holmes began to scrutinise the scene. Though initially he did not approach the body, one needed no close examination of the deceased to conclude that Wilson had been attacked and that the encounter had produced this blood-soaked *abattoir*.

Holmes was generally quiet in scrutinising such scenes, but on this occasion he spoke out when he looked at the blood-spattered book. "A collection of Poe stories," he observed, "open to the last pages of 'William Wilson'." He studied the door lock, the windows, and the carpeting. He took out his glass to examine the bloodstains.

Finally, he reached the body itself, noting the cuts, the blood, the knife. Following such work, Holmes usually kept his conclusions to himself. On this night, however, he announced definitively to Lestrade, "Aside from your familiar boot marks and the man's turned-out pocket from which you obviously extracted my card, I see no evidence of another person's presence in this room."

"Surely not suicide, Holmes," said I. "Wilson didn't seem the type. Besides, no one could attack one's own person so viciously."

"We found the door ajar," the Inspector added. "The killer could have made an escape."

"Never forget, Lestrade, that every murderer leaves some trace of his presence at the scene. It is the prime tenet of detecting. As investigators, our job is to find those traces. In this room, there are none. Thus, I conclude that no one else was here besides the dead man."

Lestrade shook his head. "A murder with no murderer? This is more of that Poe business, I should judge. As much as I hate to say it, Mr Holmes, I think you must be consumed by Poe's lunatic fantasies. 'The Raven' is one thing. But it's just a poem. From what I hear, his stories are not to be believed—a murderous ape let loose in a city? A vengeful dwarf? Body parts hidden under a floor?"

"On the contrary, Lestrade," said Holmes. "It was not I, but William Wilson himself who had been consumed by Poe's stories—so much so that in his own mind, like one of Poe's characters, he invented someone he believed was following him and whom he actually envisioned committing murder. Only it was he himself that he was really seeing, which is probably why he broke the mirror."

"Like the end of Poe's William Wilson," I said, "seeing himself in the glass."

"Exactly, Watson. That poor wretch on the floor killed himself with a long-bladed knife in the same manner as his namesake in Poe's story."

Lestrade leaned back on his heels and allowed a broad grin to work its way across his face. "It's not often I can get the best of Mr Sherlock Holmes. Yet you persist in mentioning this William Wilson. But, you see, that was *not* the dead man's name. Regardless of what he might have told you gentlemen, he was called Gordon Bleechford. His landlady gave us his lease agreement. Not only did he sign it that way, but that was how she addressed him. What's more, we knew of him at the Yard. He seems to have recently taken up cheating at cards. *Écarté* was his game. Played at the Tankerville."

Holmes allowed himself the briefest of smiles.

"William Wilson, you say?" repeated the policeman with a self-satisfied grin. "No, Mr Holmes, this time round I judge that you backed the wrong horse."

"Confound it, Lestrade!" Holmes fairly shouted. "The man's name is irrelevant. Read the letter on his desk. Learn his background. He can call himself whatever he likes. The important fact here is that no one performed this atrocious act but the victim himself."

"Unless," I felt obligated to put in, "there really *was* some sort of *Doppelgänger* that no one but Wilson could see, some spiritual double that followed him about, some villainous twin that performed this heinous act."

"Listen to yourself, Watson," said Holmes. "You're beginning to sound like Poe!"

"Some do say," Lestrade observed as he rubbed his chin, "that Edgar Allan Poe could see things in this world that others could not."

Holmes stared at the policeman in disbelief, then merely shook his head. Striding into the carpeted hallway, Holmes opened the outer door and walked down the few steps to the sidewalk and into the rain. Hailing a cab, he called to me, "Come, Watson! Back to Baker Street where reason reigns."

We left Lestrade standing in the hallway holding his bowler in one hand and scratching his head with the other.

With the horse's hooves clattering in the background, Holmes leaned over to me and said, "Let Lestrade comb the earth for a suspect. Wilson or Bleechford, whatever his name, we know what the poor man did to himself."

Of course, thought I. *What other answer can there be?*

A peal of thunder punctuated my certainty. Or mocked it.

The Adventure of the Aspen Papers

Nine-tenths of the artist's interest in [bare facts]
is that of what he shall add to them
or how he shall turn them.
--Henry James
The Art of the Novel

I

Mrs Hudson recognised a man of noble bearing when she saw one. Those were the visitors she most often reserved for herself to introduce, leaving to the boy in livery the task of announcing the guests she deemed less important. As a consequence, when she appeared at the door of our sitting room one morning in late October of 1887, both Sherlock Holmes and I looked up with great expectation. Sensing the drama her presence created, she smoothed down her skirt, cleared her throat, and proclaimed, "Mr Henry James."

It was not that I thought she had actually recognised the cerebral American author of *Roderick Hudson* and *The Portrait of a Lady*. Rather, it was the man himself who presented quite the authoritative figure. He appeared to be in his forties, with piercing light-grey eyes, a high forehead, and thin dark hair at his ears that accented a balding pate. Combined with his short, grizzled beard and sensitive mouth, his features conveyed a sense of dignity, perspicacity, and intelligence. What is more, having recently moved to London from the States, he was attired in a smart, three-piece English suit, a gold chain stretched taut across his waistcoat. Taken as a whole, his was an image destined to command respect from anyone, even those like Mrs Hudson, who had never heard of him—let alone his reputation. Quietly, she closed the door and exited.

"Mr Sherlock Holmes?" said our visitor to my friend, somehow aware of which of us to address.

Holmes bowed slightly, introduced me, and indicated that James take a seat.

No sooner had we settled ourselves than he addressed us. "Gentlemen, I come to you—I come to you—with a problem."

Let me say from the start that for so accomplished a writer, Henry James had the startling tendency to hesitate and repeat—almost to stutter—when he spoke. And yet his manner of speech seemed less a bumbling with words, than the rehearsing of finely-tuned sentences. To spare the reader superfluous repetition, however, I have taken the liberty to minimise this characteristic throughout the narrative that follows.

In point of fact, James's voice was rich and melodious, almost mesmerizing; and I was pleased to observe that Sherlock Holmes was immediately engaged. As I have reported elsewhere, the previous spring had been a difficult time for my friend. He had been worn down by the months he had devoted to resolving the matter of the Netherland-Sumatra Company, not to mention the unpleasant business near Reigate in Surrey where ironically he had gone to regain his strength. To see him devote his complete attention to Henry James was most reassuring indeed.

I hoped it would be equally reassuring to James; for as he sat drumming his fingers on the velvet arm of the chair, he certainly looked in need of some sort of aid.

"You don't mind if I smoke," said Holmes. It was more of a statement than a question, and it left to me the obligation of offering James a cigar.

"Not today, Doctor," said he, waving off the suggestion. "I'm—I'm in need of quick answers. This is not a social call."

Holmes ignored the implied criticism with a quick smile. Filling his briar with dark shag, he asked, "How can I be of service?"

"It's a moral issue, Mr Holmes," said James and immediately got to the point. "An acquaintance of mine has gone missing. Since I'm the one responsible for having gotten him into a sticky situation, I feel responsible for finding out what's become of him." He placed one hand on top of the other, interlocking his fingers in the process. It was as if he was signalling the complexity of the story he was about to tell.

"Pray, start at the beginning," said Holmes, blowing a blue cloud upward.

"The acquaintance in question, gentlemen, one Thomas Warren, arrived in London from New York at the end of the summer. He's an aspiring young academic, though a bit headstrong and compulsive. He's a professor—an instructor—at the University of Virginia, and the two of us have exchanged some correspondence. He hopes to advance his career through a biography of the American poet, Jeremy Aspen—Jeremy Bishop Aspen."

"Jeremy Aspen," I repeated. It was a name unfamiliar to me. Holmes, who took little interest in poetry, showed no recognition at all.

Henry James pulled at his beard. He resembled a frustrated instructor, annoyed that his students had not remembered his previous lecture. "Aspen was famous for the romantic poetry he composed at the turn of the century. His devotees call him 'The Orpheus of the New World'. A few months ago, I learned through my arcane literary connections that a former paramour of Aspen, an English woman named Olivia Borden, is rumoured still to be living here in London. I forwarded this information to Professor Warren in Virginia, and so great—so intense—was his interest that he dropped everything he'd been doing and immediately sailed to England."

"Quite the dedicated scholar," I chuckled.

A frosty glare from James quieted me. "I thought so too, Doctor; but he's gone beyond so benign a description. He considers Aspen a veritable god. More to the point, he's obsessed with the idea that Miss Borden—if located—will be able to further his career. He believes that not only could she be a fountain of knowledge regarding Aspen, but that she might actually possess letters of an intimate nature from the poet himself. Such a find—such a discovery—would elevate Warren's career in an instant."

"The paramour of a poet who wrote so long ago?" said I. "She must be well advanced in years."

"Close to ninety, I should imagine," said James, waving away Holmes's smoke that had begun to envelop us all. "Her age explains Warren's haste. He rightly fears that she could die at any moment, in which case *his* opportunity would dissipate as well. Little is known of the years Aspen spent away from his home in New York, you see. Oh, we're well aware that he lived for some time in

England—but nobody knows the details. The scholar—the researcher—who publishes such information would certainly receive grand honours, and now Warren—thanks in great part to my encouragement—believes he can get the answer from this old woman, a lady with whom Aspen supposedly fell in love over seventy years ago. Warren thinks this Olivia Borden must be the reclusive muse that scholars have been seeking for years."

"If these letters exist," I observed, "I imagine that in literary circles they'd be worth a fortune."

"To be sure, Dr Watson," said James. "Thomas Warren's quite right. The discovery of the letters—not to mention the woman herself—would go far to establish not only his career but also his bank account. He can't afford to miss out."

"And how well has he succeeded?" Holmes asked.

"That's just it. I don't know. Not long after he got here, he wrote me a lengthy letter. He said he'd established that the old woman really does exist and that he'd been able to track her to a run-down manor house in Southwark called The Hollows. She lives in rented rooms there with her niece."

Holmes exhaled another blue cloud. "You're a literary man, Mr James. Hasn't this singular information from Warren sparked curiosity in *you*? Why haven't you endeavoured to meet the woman yourself?"

"A fair question, Mr Holmes, but Aspen is Warren's province. He staked out the scholarly territory for himself, and I respect his boundaries. Oh, it's true that I did go there once—to The Hollows, I mean—but only after Warren had gone missing. That's when I met the niece—Rita Borden. Miss Rita, she's called, a middle-aged spinster-type, quite plain and matronly. I learned very little from her. Indeed, most all that I'm telling you I gleaned from Warren himself."

"Pah!" Holmes cried out. "Little comes from second-hand tales."

Henry James arched his eyebrows. Accomplished writer though he might be, I was certain he was unused to people discounting his narratives.

Nonetheless, he ran his hand across his balding head and continued. "Warren wrote me about an overgrown garden within the grounds. Apparently, he managed to convince the niece of his love for flora. More important, he convinced her of his need for seclusion. He told her he was a writer seeking a place to live, you see, and that he required peace and quiet in order to compose. It was the grotesqueness of just such a garden, he told her, that soothed his soul. And I should imagine that she believed him."

"Quite so," murmured Holmes, the pipe clenched firmly between his teeth.

"The niece told him that her aunt craved money; and in the end, he offered the old woman much of his life savings to rent two rooms. For a three-months' stay at The Hollows, he paid the amount he might be charged for an exclusive flat for a year—that's how important the Aspen papers are to him. Not surprisingly, the old woman agreed; and he delivered the money to her in gold in a bag of *chamois*-leather. Or so Warren told the story to me. Accompanied by his manservant, he moved in soon after and seemed to be getting along. I myself had just returned from a lengthy stay in Italy—Venice and Florence, in particular—and have been quite busy with my own writing. Quite frankly, I didn't think much about not having heard from him."

"How long has it been?" Holmes wanted to know.

Henry James looked to the ceiling the way some people do when they calculate sums. "It's three months since he moved into the house. And another few weeks since I received no answer to a letter I sent him. It was last week that I went down there—to Southwark—and encountered the niece. At first, she sounded worried. She said that she didn't know what had become of Mr Warren—that he seemed to have disappeared. And that was all. She said she didn't want to talk to me. It was quite strange, really. She seemed both reticent and direct at the same time. All around, I must tell you, The Hollows was not too inviting a place."

"And the old woman—she still lives?"

James flashed a quick smile. "Yes—as far as I know. Though I for one never got to see her."

"And the Aspen papers?" Holmes asked, taking the pipe from his mouth. "I assume that while Warren was living at The Hollows, he never stumbled across them. If he had, I suspect he would have shared that knowledge with you."

"I don't know, Mr Holmes. At the beginning of all this, I would have expected him to tell me of his discoveries. Now I'm not so sure. When I asked Miss Rita about his work, she shut the door in my face. That's when I thought of turning to you."

Sherlock Holmes put down the briar and smiled at the writer.

Good fortune was smiling upon Henry James as well. Appealing to my friend's investigative talents was a sure-fire method of engaging his services.

"I would like it very much, Mr Holmes, if you could go to Southwark—to the house—and find out what's become of Thomas Warren. It was I, after all, who set him off on this course; and it will be I who'll feel culpable should something tragic have happened to the poor fellow."

James reached into his inside coat pocket and produced a wallet.

Sherlock Holmes put up his hand to stop the writer. "Let us see what I can uncover before we talk about finances, Mr James. Perhaps there will be very little mystery at all. What say you, Watson? Are you set for an afternoon drive to Southwark in search of a missing scholar?"

I readily agreed. The page-boy could take a message to my wife, who was more than understanding when it came to matters involving Holmes. As for my surgery, I had no patients scheduled for the next day and could easily be available then if more time should be needed.

"Then it is settled. Dr Watson and I will look into this matter, Mr James. It seems quite the curious puzzle."

Shaking hands with Holmes and me, Henry James offered a formal nod. Then he turned and marched down the seventeen stairs to the outer door, his footfalls ringing steady and certain.

II

A hansom carried us to London Bridge where we crossed the river and entered the Borough of Southwark. As per James's instructions, we took the specified turnings below Long Lane and soon found ourselves in a low, wooded area where the abundance of foliage all but obliterated the afternoon sun. A final bend in the roadway brought us to the aging manor house known as The Hollows.

Owing to the massive oaks that surrounded it, the place stood draped in shadow. Two tall chimneys rose like bookends at each side of what appeared to be a single square building, its once honey-coloured walls turned black by a century of soot, grime, and neglect. The curtained windows looked dark; many on the ground floor were barred. The rusting rails of a black metal fence framed the primordial landscape, presenting to the unlucky visitor a tangle of gnarled and overgrown hedgerows.

Our driver pulled his sorrel horse up before the access road. The black metal gates, mired by the damp soil in the open-position, might gape wide for eternity.

"Do you know this place?" Holmes asked.

"Aye," said the driver, pulling down the front of his flat cap as he surveyed the gloomy scene, "but just to pass by. Nobody in there but a pair of daft old ladies. There's some what calls 'em witches, but that's just a tale. I hear they live in a couple of rooms downstairs; the rest of the place stays empty."

Holmes nodded and instructed him to wait: paying for the added time would be far easier than trying to hail another cab on this deserted road.

Amidst a dank, cloying smell that attacked our nostrils as soon as we set foot on the broken flagstones, Holmes and I carefully negotiated the irregular pathway through the unruly grounds. It came as no surprise to encounter neither bell nor knocker when we reached the entrance, and Holmes pounded on the massive oak door with his fist.

After a few moments, it was opened only a few inches by a short young woman dressed in a blouse and skirt of white linen. Through the small gap between door and wall she stared out at us suspiciously. A single eyebrow extended above both eyes, and thick black hair appeared to hang in a long plait down her back.

"*Si?*" said she in Spanish.

"Is your mistress in?" Holmes asked, but already we could sense someone approaching behind her.

"Yes?" this latter asked, stepping in front of the maid and opening the door a few inches wider. She was a heavily-built, middle-aged woman draped in a formless dress of navy blue. "Rosa doesn't speak much English. What do you want?" She wore her dark hair tightly wound in a bun, its severity accenting her prominent nose;

and she stared at us with wide-set eyes. This was obviously the matronly niece, Rita Borden, about whom Henry James had spoken.

"Yes?" she asked again.

"You are Miss Borden? Miss Rita Borden?"

"I am Miss Rita. And who are you, I should like to know?"

"My name is Sherlock Homes, and we're looking for a gentleman who lodges here, Mr Thomas Warren."

"Oh," said she with a gasp "He's gone. Left suddenly. Didn't even take his man with him. It's been more than a week now—though it seems much longer . . . . "

One could hear sadness in her voice as it trailed off. But, suddenly, just as Henry James had forewarned, she countered, "And what's it to you?"

"I'm a colleague of Mr Warren," Holmes declared.

"You're another book critic then?" said she with a touch of venom.

"Not exactly. But we haven't heard from him in months, and we are concerned about his welfare."

She smirked. "He said he was interested in our garden—that's what he told my aunt. He said he wanted to rent a room, but she told him no."

"And yet," Holmes countered, "I understand that he did secure lodgings here. What changed your aunt's mind?"

"What else?" she said with a snort. "Money, of course. Lots of it. Say, you do ask a lot of questions. I don't know why I should be telling you all this."

"To help find Mr Warren, of course."

Holmes seemed to be offering hope, and she softened a bit at his response. "My aunt gets a trifling amount each year from someone in America—hardly enough for us to live on. That's why she accepted a lodger. She wants the money for *me*."

During the course of this discussion, Miss Rita had allowed the door to open wider, and it was through this larger gap that I was able to gaze upon the ancient woman herself. The maidservant had pushed a three-wheeled Bath-chair towards the door. Staring up at us from the brown, wickerwork seat was a decrepit little figure cloaked in black—or in what must have at one time been black; her dress was now a faded dark-grey, worn shiny by many years of wear. Sitting hunched over like that, she could have been a hundred years old.

Henry James's estimate, however, was probably nearer to the mark. She had to be close to ninety—infirm, frail, desiccated. Breathing seemed to be a chore as well. But it was not her cadaverous form that caused the most alarm. That distinction fell to a black veil of tightly drawn lace that covered the upper half of her visage, leaving visible only her withered lips and skeletal jaw. It was as if she were wearing a ghastly mask. Worse, in the darkness of the room, though her eyes were barely discernible, one still had the sense that they possessed the power to bore directly into one's soul.

"Who's there, Rita?" she called in a grating voice. "Who's come to disturb our afternoon?"

"Two men looking after Mr Warren." Her tone was matter-of-fact.

"Show them in, dear. *They* might have money as well."

Miss Rita led us into a large sitting room, the thick green-velvet curtains pulled shut before a row of French windows. Heavy beams ran across the ceiling, and oak panelling lined the walls. Although white sheets concealed most of the furniture, a few wooden chairs and a low mahogany table stood uncovered and ready for use in a far corner illuminated by a pair of yellow candles. One got the feeling the room had been like this for ages.

The old woman leaned forward and gestured for us to sit down in the uncovered chairs.

"We're looking for Thomas Warren, Miss Borden," Holmes said as soon as we were seated. "We know that he roomed here for months and has now disappeared. We were hoping you might shed some light on the matter."

Below the unyielding vizard, the old lady worked a small smile—more of a smirk, actually.

"He came here under false pretences," she rasped. "He said he valued our garden. He said it was exactly the sort of quiet place he was looking for in which to do his writing. He said he'd seen the garden through the fence and wanted to revive it. All it needed was some work, he said. He promised to find some geraniums or 'Jack Frost' that would flourish in the shade. He festooned the house with flowers. For weeks on end he played his game, and only lately did he show his hand."

"He talked to *me* of plants and nature as well," added Miss Rita. "At first. Then he moved on to art and books. It took him months to get round to talking about the research he did on writers. And when I asked if he knew about Jeremy Aspen, he said he didn't know the name—didn't even know Aspen was a poet, he said. The rogue was lying, of course. In point of fact, he knew lots about Aspen. But it was only early last week that he finally got round to asking about him. He said that since he did research on other writers, he might as well enquire about Aspen. He wanted to know if my aunt might have some papers or letters concerning the man."

"As if I would leave Mr Aspen's papers lying about," the old lady said. In a confidential whisper she added, "Once I realised those papers were all he was interested in, I told him he would *never* get them from me." In a sudden burst of energy, she actually raised herself and hissed, "*If* I had any such papers to give, that is." This last utterance seemed to have tapped all of her strength; for after saying the words, she dropped back down in her wickered chair and appeared to fall asleep.

Miss Rita gestured sympathetically at her aunt. "It's late," said the niece, rising and moving towards the entrance hall.

When she opened the door, we could see a finger of late-afternoon sunlight poking its way through the leaves. "I fancy you won't be nosing round here again," she said, her wide eyes registering a degree of triumph as she closed the door.

"That was no great help," said I to Holmes as we walked along the broken flags. "Not only did we learn nothing about Warren, but we haven't even determined that the Aspen papers are real."

"Did you not notice, Watson, how Miss Borden spoke of the poet as '*Mr* Aspen'? When one refers to public figures that one *doesn't* know, one tends to identify them by their surnames only."

"I've never thought of the matter."

"Well, please do. We say, 'Shakespeare wrote' or 'Shakespeare said'—not *Mister* Shakespeare."

"Of course, now that you mention it."

"But when one speaks of an acquaintance, one might well employ a title like 'Mister'."

"And the old woman," I now remembered, "did indeed call the poet '*Mister* Aspen'."

"Precisely, old fellow. I'd be willing to wager that a relationship between Miss Borden and Jeremy Aspen is, as Henry James suggested, more fact that fiction."

"Then how do you explain Warren's disappearance? If she's the right lady, why would he have left?"

"Since I expect him to return, the reason doesn't concern me. No doubt, he was frustrated. He'd spent months cultivating his relationships with the two women and saw nothing come of it. As long as the papers are here, however—not to mention his manservant—he'll be back. The Aspen papers remain too important for him to abandon."

The hansom stood where we'd left it, the sorrel horse impatiently pawing the dirt.

"Back to Baker Street, if you please," Holmes instructed the driver as we climbed into the cab. To me he said, "I shall speak to the Irregulars." He was talking of the young street Arabs whom he frequently hired to provide information from the byways of London. "They can keep an eye on The Hollows for us. That way, when Thomas Warren does return, we shall know."

The carriage took off with a jolt, and Holmes leaned over to me. "After I instruct the boys, Watson, I think a dinner in the Strand might be in order."

I smiled in agreement, but Sherlock Holmes was already staring out the window submerged in thought. I do not imagine he noticed the pink and purple swirls of sunset painting the sky.

III

"Dead!" came the cry as the street urchin burst into our sitting room the next morning. We were just finishing breakfast when he gave us the news. "There's somebody in that house what's died! Popped their clog. Hopped the twig!"

Sherlock Holmes put down his coffee and rose to meet the lad. "Who?" he demanded.

"Dunno, do I?" said the boy, brushing a lock of dirty brown hair from his eyes. "But I seen the wagon arrive. Only there was no black feathers on the horses. And no coffin inside it. Just a bloke in a tall hat and black togs. He went into the house."

Sherlock Holmes was already donning his coat.

"Come, Watson! There's not a moment to lose! We must get to the body before it's taken away. That was the undertaker the boy saw—come to make final arrangements with Rita Borden."

*****

Thomas Warren must have been keeping his own watch on The Hollows. For no sooner had Olivia Borden died than Warren returned. In all probability, it was his manservant who had informed him of the old woman's death. In any event Warren was already there when we arrived.

Rosa admitted us, and Holmes and I introduced ourselves in the sitting room. In black suit and sombre mien, the American certainly dressed the part of a concerned mourner. Attired for a funeral, he had obviously packed his luggage for England contemplating the possibility of bereavement. Yet with those dark, penetrating eyes and black hair combed straight back, he appeared more dashing young suitor than heavy-hearted scholar.

"We're here at the behest of Henry James," Holmes told the professor. "Mr James is concerned about you and the progress of your business here."

"I'll contact him when it's appropriate," Warren said without much concern. "'*Comme il faut*', as James himself likes to say."

Holmes and I exchanged glances, but fell in line behind Warren as he crossed the sitting room and, passing through the doorway to the ground-floor sleeping quarters, led us to Olivia Borden's inner sanctum. It was there that Miss Rita stood beside the bed, the diminutive body of her aunt lying before her.

The late Olivia Borden commanded the centre of an anachronistic tableau. With her veil no longer in place, one could see the prominence of her aquiline nose and the roundness of her skull. Wrinkled hands folded on her chest, she was clothed in luminescent white, a dress no doubt kept hidden away in anticipation of this particular occasion. The threadbare quilt upon which she rested had yellowed over the years, and the bed itself might have come from another century. With small winged suns carved into a rectangular headboard the colour of dark chocolate, the entire rosewood piece suggested a Regency design. Redundant hairbrushes and depleted unguents adorned the dressing table, and a mirror replete with spidery cracks presided over the futile *homage* to vanity. Atop the nearby chest of drawers, a japanned wooden box that could have contained any number of rings or necklaces or letters stood conveniently open—open and empty. Owing to the dusty white drapes that covered the windows, the whole scene, illuminated as it was by floor-candelabras on either side of the bed, seemed a setting from some antique mystery play.

Warren had positioned himself next to Miss Rita and bowed his head. Despite his show of sympathy, I felt certain that his concern dealt less with the dead woman than with the papers he had suspected her of possessing, the same papers—if they existed at all—presumably now in the custody of her niece.

We took our cue from Miss Rita and, following a decent period of respect, prepared to exit. I made one last visual sweep of the chamber, hoping to detect the evidence of someone's final frantic search for the missing papers. But aside from the open wooden box, there appeared no signs of any such disruption.

As I turned to leave, however, Holmes caught my arm. "Watson," he whispered. "Engage the others in conversation elsewhere. I need time to examine this room more fully."

"I wonder," he now said to Miss Rita, "if you'd mind giving me a moment alone with your aunt. Many people will tell you that I am a private person who prefers to keep his personal thoughts strictly between the deceased and himself."

"You hardly knew the woman," she scoffed, but Holmes seemed sincere; and fortunately Miss Rita, no great master of recognizing deceit, did not require further convincing. For his part, Warren seemed eager to talk. Indeed, no sooner did we find our places in the sitting room than he began discussing what he knew of the elder Miss Borden and Jeremy Aspen.

"Looking at that old woman," said he, "you wouldn't think her to have been a beautiful, vivacious, even rebellious young lady. But she must have been *all* those things. It would explain why Aspen was so attracted to her. For that matter, I often wonder how they met."

Miss Rita shrugged. "He came calling on her."

"I know *that*," replied the professor, "but why? Aspen was an aristocrat; Miss Borden's background was more modest. What prompted him? My own guess is that she must have been connected to someone with whom the poet had dealings here in England. She could have been a governess to a child of one of Aspen's friends. Or the daughter of someone he'd employed—a secretary, perhaps, or a portrait painter. Americans love to have their images immortalised by English artists. Whatever the circumstances, she held the man's attention—so much so that she became the object of his love. She was, after all, the precious *'l'ange'* in his cycle of love sonnets."

I shrugged my shoulders, hoping that the conversation would prevent the others from wondering what Holmes was up to.

Suddenly, Warren's eyes flashed, and he changed the subject. "I think she hid his letters somewhere." He pointed at a tall mahogany secretary's desk with brass fittings. "That was my first choice. I'd always suspected it was locked, but I couldn't be sure. Yet I was afraid to look. Not that I would ever steal the papers, mind you; but a few weeks before her death, I finally worked up the courage to see if the desk would open. I was just about to test the lock when the old lady interrupted me."

"Why," Rita cried, "that must have been just before you left."

"In truth," Warren said, "with that black veil of hers, she gave me quite the fright. 'Stop that!' she'd cried out while teetering on her cane in the doorway—all those months and I didn't even know she could walk. In such a fury was she that she tore off that infernal mask and threw it to the floor. That was when I saw her magnificent eyes."

"My word," I barely whispered.

"Oh, yes—her eyes. They were wide and deep and full of hatred. And yet, strange to say, they also filled me with a kind of comfort. For looking into those extraordinary orbs, I somehow felt closer to Aspen. Her rage at me was a short-lived imitation of the torrid flames that must have burned so brightly when she was in his arms, a fiery passion that I thought had been all but extinguished."

Warren's own eyes were wide open now, a man staring full-on into a vibrant past as he described the confrontation.

"'I know what you're looking for,' the old woman screeched at me, '—why you've come here.' She nodded at the secretary desk. "Go ahead and look inside, if you must.' Reluctantly, I tried the lid and, discovering that it was unlocked after all, lifted it open. I expected to discover nothing, and nothing is precisely what I found. The old woman stared triumphantly at me.

"It was when she turned and hobbled resolutely back to her room that I realised she would never be giving me the letters. Mortified—and not a little angry at Olivia Borden—I left the house the next day."

Miss Rita sat open-mouthed. There was obviously a lot about her aunt she had apparently never got to know.

Just then Rosa entered the room with two large vases of Calla lilies.

"I ordered them," Warren said.

A look of admiration appeared in Miss Rita's wide-set eyes. I couldn't say whether she had ever experienced a social engagement with a man, but she was certainly appreciative of Warren's gesture.

I, on the other hand, was more cynical. With the papers as Warren's goal, I could not help regarding all of his acts as empty motions designed to get Miss Rita to share her aunt's literary trove with him. In fact, I was beginning to suspect that the letters had motivated the behaviours of everyone in that house. Why, perhaps the old woman had been dangling them in front of the professor to unite him with her niece. Or perhaps the middle-aged spinster herself was hoping to inherit them and use them to entice the man.

Holmes's return interrupted my thoughts. He arrived in the sitting room just as Miss Rita was rising to help Rosa set up the flowers.

"It's a bit stuffy in here," he observed, striding to the green-velvet drapes. Drawing one of them aside, he opened the French window an inch or two. As he moved the curtain back in position, he turned back to Miss Rita. "One last question, if I may. Did your aunt write a will?"

Miss Rita looked down. "No. She had nothing to leave me."

"Except for the papers," Thomas Warren muttered.

Holmes glared at the professor, but all he said to him was, "Don't fail to let Henry James know that you're safe." Then he motioned to me that it was time to leave, and once more we expressed our condolences to Miss Rita.

"If you don't mind my asking," Holmes said to her, as we were about to exit, "should I want to pay my respects yet again, when will the undertaker come for your aunt."

"At nine o'clock tomorrow morning."

With Holmes nodding at the information, we left that frightful house and hurried back to our waiting hansom. I climbed in as under darkening skies my friend exchanged a few words with the driver. Then Holmes joined me, and we began our journey back to Baker Street. Or so I thought.

IV

After making the first turn that hid us from The Hollows, the cab came to an abrupt halt. The horse whinnied in protest, but Holmes stepped out and bade me follow. As I would learn later, he had arranged earlier for the driver to stop once the house was out of sight, and Holmes dropped a healthy number of compensatory coins into the man's hand. As the hansom disappeared in the darkness, the two of us stood out in the road listening to the diminishing clink of the horse's hooves.

"Should anyone be watching," he explained, "I wanted it to appear that we'd actually left. The old woman was murdered, Watson; and I fear there may be more violence yet to come."

"Murdered?" I cried. "But she looked so peaceful, Holmes. What makes you say such a thing?

"You know my methods, old fellow. As soon as I was alone with the body, I drew my lens and examined the corpse. It was absurdly simple to discover the bits of down in Miss Borden's nostrils, the tiny feathers she must have inhaled gasping for her final breaths with a pillow held down over her face."

"Who could have committed so heinous an act?"

"That is what I hope to confirm tonight."

"But, Holmes, surely we must inform the police."

"We don't have the time," said he, shaking his head. He then motioned me to follow, continuing his explanation as we edged back down the dark road towards The Hollows. "We know that Olivia Borden's body will be collected by the undertaker tomorrow morning at nine. I fear that the immediacy of that appointment may precipitate some harmful action."

"You think that Miss Rita is in danger then?"

Holmes smiled. "On one level, I think not. The death of the old woman leaves the niece as the sole link to the papers. Anyone seeking the papers would be foolish to silence her."

“Unless,” I added, “the miscreant has already acquired them.”

“If he had acquired them, Watson, he would no longer be here.” We were approaching the house now, and Holmes lowered his voice. “When I searched the old woman’s room, I spied a blanket and sheet that appeared dishevelled on the far side of the bed. I immediately ran my hand beneath the upper mattress.”

“Did you find anything?”

“A single scrap of very old foolscap containing a few strokes of faded ink. But even so small a morsel was enough to suggest that somehow the withered old woman had mustered the strength to hide the papers between her mattresses.”

“Surely such a hiding place could not be secure. When Rosa changed the bedding, she’d discover the cache.”

“You’re right, of course,” replied Holmes. “Perhaps Olivia Borden had originally kept them in the secretary desk just as Warren suspected or even in the japanned box so conveniently left open for us. But move them she did, and somehow—maybe with Rosa’s help—hid them beneath her mattress. In any case, I suspect that Rita has found her aunt’s hiding place—or may even have been given the papers. At the very least, Rita is probably the only one who knows their current location.”

I was about to respond; but we had reached the railing of the metal fence, and Holmes put his finger to his lips. In the darkness, we slipped through the open gates and tiptoed to the garden at the side of the building. It was here that we encountered the French window that Holmes had earlier so presciently left open. Although we could see nothing of the sitting room through the curtained glass, we could hear quite clearly the conversation that was going on inside.

“I thought that you *liked* spending time with me,” Miss Rita was saying to Warren.

“Of course, I do,” said the professor. “I enjoy your company. Remember those summer evenings out in the garden?”

“Yes,” she sighed. “They were grand.” One could hear the longing in her voice. “For years I’ve been imprisoned here with my aunt. And then *you* came round, someone who took an interest in me.”

There was a moment of awkward silence. I imagined Warren dwelling on her final few words. “Now listen,” he said at last. “I don't believe I've ever acted in an ungentlemanly manner towards you."

"I thought that the flowers—"

"They were intended for your aunt as well as for you."

"So *you* might get the papers. Perhaps that's what my aunt was thinking all along. In the end, bringing you and me together must have meant more to her than spending her final hours with her niece."

But Warren would not continue Miss Rita's narrative. "I should imagine that all along her plan had been to give me the papers."

"No!" said Miss Rita firmly. "She never wanted outsiders to get their hands on them." There was a pause of a few moments during which Miss Rita must have been fashioning her most convincing smile and most flirtatious voice. "Now if you were a *relation* . . ."

The word could have but one meaning.

"Me—and *you*?" Warren spat out.

"I've enjoyed our time together."

"But for the rest of our lives?" One could not ignore the disdain in his voice. "Not even the receipt of *all* your aunt's papers would be worth such misery!"

We heard her gasp and then the rustle of clothing and the stomp of heavy feet. Warren had obviously stood and was about to make a grand exit up the stairs to his room. "I'll be leaving in the morning!" he shouted. "Early!"

Muted sobs filled the silence.

*****

Sitting cross-legged on the damp ground by the open window, Holmes and I managed to stay awake through an uneventful night. With only the routine activities of nocturnal creatures to distract us—mice scrabbling among the tree roots, crickets drumming their songs, an owl hooting his displeasure at our presence—we had to wait until the next morning for human passions to become enflamed.

Sometime before dawn, Holmes reached inside the window, which no one had bothered to close, and adjusting the green-velvet curtains that had blocked our view, created a gap of about half-an-inch through which we could peer. The morning activities in the house played out before us as if we were attending the theatre. Off-stage, the clatter of dishes and clanging of pans announced that Rosa was preparing breakfast in the kitchen. At half-seven, Miss Rita made her entrance from the sleeping quarters on the ground floor. Dressed in austere black, she was prepared for her meeting with the undertaker. At almost the same moment, as if he had been waiting for Miss Rita to appear, Thomas Warren emerged from his chamber and hurried down the stairs. Despite his threat to leave before the removal of the body, he wore the same black suit we'd seen the previous day. Miss Rita turned at his approach, a melancholy look colouring her downcast face.

"I'm sorry," Warren said, reaching for her right hand. "I've been cruel. I should have taken your proposal more seriously last night."

She raised her head.

"In fact," he said, sounding full of contrition, "I've given myself the chance to examine your offer once more, and I believe I now see much wisdom in its implementation. I owe my career to the securing of those papers; and while I did all I could in the most proper way to obtain them from your aunt, I believe she never seriously appreciated my efforts. I think that for as long as she lived, she intended to use those papers as bait to bring me closer to you."

Miss Rita's wide eyes looked even wider. And more melancholy. Perhaps she sensed what Warren was about to suggest.

"In fact, I now believe that we should honour your aunt's wishes and agree to such a union. I believe she intended for you to do with the papers exactly as you had proposed to me last night. I am, you see, quite prepared to accept your aunt's papers—the Aspen papers, if you will—as a dowry."

At some point during Warren's last few words, Miss Rita's left hand had begun a slow journey upward until it was covering her now open mouth.

"Why, what's the matter?" asked Warren. "I know it's what you want. Everyone will be pleased. You will get a husband; I will get the letters; and your aunt's memory will be honoured."

Miss Rita lowered her head.

"What's the matter?" Warren asked again. His eyes signalled fear; his tone had grown desperate.

"Oh, Thomas," she said slowly, "I burned the papers last night. In the fireplace in my bedroom. Once you refused me, I saw no point in keeping them."

"You—you *burned* them? The key to my life's work?"

"I was going to have them buried with my aunt," she explained, realizing that she'd also destroyed any future she might have envisioned with this man. "But you made me so angry last night that I burned them one by one. It took a long time."

Warren's eyes began to bulge. "After what I've already done?" he muttered, his face turning dangerously red.

"What?"

"And to think," he snarled, "I almost found you charming."

"We can still marry," Miss Rita urged. "You'll see. I can make you a good wife."

Thomas Warren glared at her. The silence seemed interminable. In the end, he threw back his head and laughed. It began as a loud, raucous laugh, but it slowly transformed itself into a maniacal shriek. Suddenly, he was upon her, his white fingers tightly gripping her throat.

Without a word, Holmes sprang up, jerked open the French window and raced towards the struggling pair. Wrapping an arm around Warren's neck, he yanked him off the poor woman, who fell heavily to her knees on the hardwood floor.

In an instant, I had joined Holmes; and between us we managed to wrestle Thomas Warren onto one of the sheet-covered chairs. Rosa ran out from the kitchen to see what the trouble was. She helped her mistress to stand, and Holmes ordered her to go out in the street to find the nearest constable.

"La policía!" he instructed.

Soon we heard the blast of a police whistle, and within the hour Inspector Gregson arrived at The Hollows.

Not long thereafter, we had the satisfaction of seeing Thomas Warren charged with the murder of Miss Olivia Borden—whom he confessed to smothering after he had secretly returned to the house—and the attempted murder of Miss Rita Borden. Between two uniformed officers, he was marched to the police van, which immediately drove off in the direction of Scotland Yard.

As it clattered down the road, it passed the undertaker's hearse, which was just then approaching the house from the opposite direction.

V

The next afternoon, Henry James joined us for tea at Baker Street. Following Warren's arrest, Holmes had sent a request to the writer at his rooms in De Vere Gardens, and James eagerly accepted. In addition to the tea, Mrs Hudson set out small chocolate biscuits and a few of the sugary doughnuts that, according to Holmes, James was known to enjoy.

Sherlock Holmes reported the details of the case to our guest as we sampled our tea.

"Good Lord," said James, when Holmes had finished. "I had no idea my letter regarding Jeremy Aspen would create—would weave—such a tangled skein."

"More tangled than you can imagine, Mr James," Holmes observed. "For it is my conjecture that the Aspen papers contained more value of a personal nature than even your world of *belles-lettres* could estimate. I have no valid proof, you understand; but judging from my own observations—the similar facial structures, the widespread eyes, the curved nose—not to mention the concern that Olivia Borden expressed regarding her niece's welfare—I can only conclude that a major topic of the correspondence between Jeremy Aspen and his mistress was the welfare of their child—a daughter I believe to be Miss Rita Borden."

At this revelation, the doughnut Henry James was poised to devour fell onto his plate.

I found myself equally astonished. After catching my breath, I asked Holmes, "And does Miss Rita know of your conjecture?"

"Only if she read the letters before she burned them—and, of course, only if my supposition is accurate. Based on so little evidence, it is certainly nothing I would share with her."

James retrieved his doughnut and took a small bite and then another. "So," he said after finishing the morsel, "in addition to the tale—the mystery—surrounding the Aspen papers, we also have a story dealing with the secret love-child of a writer and his mistress. Not to mention the cunning machinations of a so-called scholar."

"Just so, Mr James," said Holmes.

The author did not respond for a moment. Staring off as they were, his grey eyes suggested his mind was somewhere else. If my own writing experiences might serve as a guide, I imagined him already at work, composing in his head some sort of novel dealing with the bizarre triangle of old woman, forlorn niece, and obsessed academic.

"One writer to another, Mr James," I dared to say, "quite a story, is it not?"

"Indeed, Dr Watson. Perhaps one we might both attempt to record—each in his own fashion, of course."

"An excellent suggestion," said I, already devaluing my factual narrative when compared with the intimate psychological embellishments so typical of James's fiction. His ornate and methodical style could perfectly reflect the labyrinthine twists and turns of a mind diseased.

"I would, of course, purge the story of obvious references," said he. "I could fudge or doctor my notebooks—change Jeremy Aspen to Byron. Or Shelley. And shift the scene of the adventure to somewhere outside of London. Maybe even outside of England." Suddenly, he clapped his hands together, the notion of subterfuge obviously gaining in appeal. "This very afternoon I shall walk—no, I shall drive—to the National Gallery and look at landscapes for inspiration. Turner's watercolours of Venice might be just the thing!"

Sherlock Holmes poured himself more tea. "I envy you, Mr James. The world of detection offers no such escape. *My* boundaries are limited by the rules of logic and the confines of reality. The detective cannot go willy-nilly where inspiration calls him."

"Ah, yes, Mr Holmes," said Henry James. "But it is the claustrophobia created by such rules that leads the literary artist to the world of fiction. Imagination trumps reality every time."

Such abstract arguments usually make my head spin. But on this occasion, I was ready to do battle. "I—I take your remark about writing a story as a challenge, sir," said I to Henry James. "Let us each report the sordid tale of the Aspen papers in our own manner and leave it to posterity to judge who has rendered the stronger case."

With a smile, Holmes pointed first at the gasogene and then at the spirit case. I understood his gestures and, producing three glasses, mixed the sparkling water with brandy. Once everyone was served, we hoisted our drinks.

"To the judgment of posterity," proclaimed Sherlock Holmes.

"Hear, hear," Henry James chimed in, and then the three of us emptied our glasses.

For Want of a Sword

I

Although the gathering marked a ten-year-anniversary, it was not a celebration in the usual sense, but more of a memorial. I had no prior knowledge of the occasion save for the small white card I had received earlier in the day from Mr Sherlock Holmes. Billy the page hand-delivered the message, which was dated 22nd June 1903 and read:

My dear Watson,
Join Mycroft and me at the Diogenes Club this evening at 8.00. New material to add to your histories. Wear mourning black.

More of a command than an invitation, it was signed with the single letter "S".

I have written elsewhere that no matter how demanding, it has always been difficult for me to refuse any requests from Sherlock Holmes. They always present so many intriguing possibilities, and tonight's appeared no different.

"Of course, you should go, John," said my wife, a most understanding woman when it came to my friendship with Holmes. "And please offer my condolences for whoever it is who has died."

"I wish I knew," I answered.

Whoever indeed? *I found myself pondering that question throughout our dinner of lamb and potatoes. Curiosity prompting, I hurried through the orange sorbet, more than ready to don black suit and cravat*

"How do I look?" I asked my wife once I had dressed.

"Suitably funereal," she replied with a half-smile, still struck, no doubt, by the selfsame mix of interest and sympathy that were continuing to plague me. Assuring her I would provide a complete

report upon my return, I secured a black band on my trilby and hailed a hansom.

It was a beautiful evening for a drive. In what had been a very wet June, temperatures were finally on the rise; and the seemingly constant blanket of clouds had all but dissipated. As we clattered along beneath the darkening sky, a few stars were beginning to twinkle and the lights of the city to take hold. On so splendid an evening, not even the thought of being cooped up in Mycroft's stodgy club could dampen my spirit—especially when charged with the question of who it might be that the brothers Holmes were remembering.

I alighted directly in front of the Diogenes in the western end of Pall Mall, the home of so many of London's distinctive and celebrated clubs. Maypoole, the ancient doorman, took my hat and bade me enter. Though it felt as if my arrival had been expected, the man offered no hint concerning the nature of the event I was there to attend.

Certainly, *I thought as I tiptoed up the stairs to the Strangers' Room,* there are no clues to be gained from Holmes's recent activities. *Earlier in the month he had solved the riddle of the Mazarin Stone; but as far as I knew, he had no new cases with which to occupy himself. Oh, there had been a time when Sherlock Holmes would have raged against such inactivity; but by the summer of '02 it was common knowledge to those with whom he was acquainted that he was planning to retire soon and that, as a consequence, he remained uninterested in acquiring additional clients.*

"Ah, Watson," said Holmes as I silently entered the Strangers' Room, "so good of you to join us."

Behind me, a serving man in a white tunic glided silently out the door. He had just finished placing a cut-glass bowl filled with almonds and Brazil nuts on the low mahogany table. A decanter of similar cut-glass design had already supplied two small copitas with a ruby-red port. A third glass, presumably mine, remained empty.

Dressed in traditional mourning attire, the two Holmes brothers rose to greet me—my friend easily enough, Mycroft with a great deal of difficulty punctuated with an elongated grunt. On account of the lingering twilight that dimly illuminated the large bow window, they appeared before me in silhouette, their figures accounting for the difference in their efforts. Sherlock Holmes stood tall and thin. His brother, though of similar height, carried much greater weight. Despite the celebrated acuity of Mycroft's mind, the least physical movement seemed to him an anathema.

We shook hands all round and exchanged warm greetings, not a common experience in the Diogenes Club. As faithful readers will remember, the establishment, founded by a group of men that included Mycroft himself, was desirous of strict quietude and thus maintained a list of rules that forbade all nature of speech within the walls. Only here in the Strangers' Room, a venue set aside for just such occasions as tonight's, would speech be tolerated.

"Gentlemen," said I, taking the leather armchair indicated by Mycroft, "I am pleased to be here though I must confess that ever since I received the invitation, I've been wondering for just whom this memorial has been planned."

The brothers exchanged well-practiced glances; and once they too had seated themselves, Mycroft nodded at his younger brother.

Sherlock Holmes filled the empty glass before me with port and then refilled Mycroft's as well as his own. Handing one glass to his brother and another to me, he stood again and indicated that we should join him. Once more, Mycroft struggled to his feet; and when we were all three facing one another, Holmes raised his glass.

"To Admiral George Tryon and the three–hundred-fifty-eight brave lives lost," he proclaimed with due solemnity, "in the sinking of H.M.S. Victoria *on this same date ten years ago—22 June 1893."*

Of course.

We drank and remembered.

Though I had not that day recalled the anniversary to which Holmes had alluded, no true Englishman could ever forget the catastrophe. During military manoeuvres in the Mediterranean a decade before, two British warships, the Victoria *and the* Camperdown, *had tragically collided. By all accounts, the results were devastating. The* Victoria, *pierced below the waterline some nine feet by the steel battering ram of the* Camperdown, *required less than fifteen minutes to sink. As evidenced in Holmes's toast, the resultant loss of life was immense. There were those within the Admiralty who labelled it the most disastrous accident in the history of the Royal Navy.*

The sheer horror of the tragedy was quite sufficient to make it memorable, but the event maintained a personal connection to Sherlock Holmes and me as well. The collision had occurred off the coast of Syria at the same time that Holmes—presumed dead following his encounter with Professor Moriarty at the Reichenbach Falls—happened to be travelling incognito through the Levant. Upon that day in particular, he found himself in Tripoli, a part of Syria before the Great War, where he actually witnessed the horrible accident first-hand.

As it turned out, the British press was either too reluctant or simply forbidden to print anything critical about the much-loved Royal Navy. But through a series of complicated events, some of which I would later chronicle in the account I titled The Seventh Bullet, *Holmes managed to convey the story by telegraph to the American pressman, David Graham Phillips, the newly appointed London correspondent for Joseph Pulitzer's newspaper,* The World. *As a result, despite Pulitzer's reluctance to publicise his pressmen's by-lines, Phillips gained international fame for reporting the story. To thank Holmes for his help in sending out the details, the dapper Phillips had actually come to visit us at Baker Street in 1896. Sad to say, it was this same friendship that would ultimately lead us to New York years later to investigate the writer's untimely murder. That enquiry, of course, was still years off and another matter entirely.*

I assumed it was the Graham-Phillips aspect of the disaster that had sparked Holmes's desire to remember the lost seamen. As for Mycroft, I could not account for his lingering sentimentality unless it was due to his relationship, however opaque, with the Foreign Office and the Ministry of Defence.

No matter the reason, paying our respect to the naval dead was an honourable gesture. Yet once having done so, I felt it equally appropriate to honour our friend Phillips. It was he, after all, who had brought the matter to the public's attention. Raising my glass a second time, I offered, "To Graham Phillips and the printed word."

"Graham Phillips," Holmes echoed with a smile and proceeded to drink.

Mycroft, however, furrowed his massive brow and resumed his seat. "I salute the dead of the Victoria,*" said he tartly, "not the conniving Yank who almost single-handedly set back the forces of peace in Europe."*

"Now, now, Mycroft," said my friend as he and I also settled back in our chairs. "I believe you're overstating the case."

"Am I?" replied Mycroft, leaning forward with some effort to grab a handful of nuts. "Of course, I'd expect you *to say that, Sherlock. To admit otherwise is to confess your own sorry role in the delicate affair—not to mention your Bohemian* naiveté. *There was much going on behind the scenes, brother-mine, of which you had not an inkling." He placed an almond in his mouth and emphasised his accusation with a definitive chomp.*

I looked from one Holmes to the other, each with clenched jaw and fixed gaze. It was clear that though ten years might have passed, the tension over the matter had not.

Sherlock Holmes suddenly focused his gaze on me. *"I say," he suggested to Mycroft, "why not let Watson here be the judge? As much as it will pain me to recount the horrors of that day, I shall detail for him my recollection of the events, and you may offer him yours. I'm sure that with the passage of an entire decade, your secrets can safely be exposed."*

Mycroft knitted his brows again as he considered the offer. Finally, he nodded. "As long as you understand that some constraints still bind me," he cautioned, "I'll drink to that proposal." Without rising this time, he drained the rest of the ruby liquid from his copita and popped another almond into his mouth.

Sherlock Holmes moved to refill our drinks, and I offered him my glass. At the same time, I could not help noting that no one had asked for my own opinion about participating in such a debate. I should laugh. With the steel-grey eyes of both Holmes brothers trained upon me, I knew it would be virtually impossible to deny their collective will. Besides, though I already possessed some familiarity with the grim outline of Holmes's narrative, I confess to anticipating with great interest any new secrets of state that Mycroft Holmes might volunteer to divulge.

What follow are the respective statements of both brothers.

II

Sherlock Holmes's Account

How I came to be in Syria following my flight from the falls of Reichenbach remains a tale for another time. Suffice it to say that the ancient mysteries of the Arab world have always beckoned; and following some two years spent in Tibet, I made my way to the Middle East. By the early summer of '93, bearing a rucksack and draped in white *kafeyah* and loosely-woven *haik*, I had traversed a good part of Persia and, civil unrest notwithstanding, gone on to investigate the treasures of Mecca. Then—who knows, Watson, perhaps inspired by your old portrait of the murdered General Gordon—I put aside my knowledge of all the blood spilt in Khartoum and decided to travel to that historic city as well.

I knew that ports in the Levant offered a wide array of ships bound for northern Africa, and so I set out from Mecca for the west coast of Syria. In spite of some harrowing adventures along the way, I eventually found myself in a wagon laden with wool prayer rugs lumbering through the Syrian highlands northeast of Tripoli.

The driver, a grizzled old man with deep-set eyes, took me along the twisting paths through the mountains, but it wasn't until mid-day of 22nd June that I actually observed the seaport. In point of fact, the old man had purposely pulled up his horse when we reached a broad turning in the road. He had wanted to give me the proper vantage for my first look at the glorious panorama below—the small white houses sprinkled about the descending foothills, the ebony cluster of ships' masts bobbing by the wooden docks, and the vast, deep-blue Mediterranean whose gentle waves shimmered brightly beneath the overhead sun. I tell you, gentlemen, it was a sight to behold; but like its more celebrated Edenic counterpart, this paradise too contained its dangers—in particular, a tell-tale blot of dark smoke off in the distance serving to mar the scene.

The old man followed my gaze. He spoke little English, but none the less pronounced the familiar word, "Bri-tish."

Extracting the field glasses from my rucksack for a better look, I immediately saw that he was correct. Far to the south—splayed out for two miles, single-line abreast—sailed eleven warships, each flying the Union Jack.

"British," I repeated with a nod.

Indeed, there could be no doubt that this was Her Majesty's grand Mediterranean Fleet. Through the glasses, I could clearly see the large flagship and her pair of massive guns mounted low in a single turret at the prow. She was accompanied by a line of other low-slung, ironclad steamers—by my reckoning, eight battleships and three large cruisers in all.

It was quite a display. Oh, they may have lacked the billowing white sails of the splendid vessels from yesteryear, but I knew that those ships before me featured the strongest and most modern weapons in the world. The Mediterranean provides England a gateway to the East—to the Ottoman Empire, the Suez Canal, and ultimately India. The Royal Navy is not about to let so important a shipping lane be interrupted by any foreign nation dim enough to have forgot that Britannia rules the waves.

I lowered the glasses so I could watch the entire Fleet approach the wide waters of the bay in which they would ultimately be anchoring. The vessels themselves may have appeared small in the vastness of the scene, but one couldn't miss the cloud of black smoke that had originally caught my attention. Rudely belched from the steamers' funnels, it was now spreading throughout the calm sea air. Beneath this ominous veil, the ships seemed to travel in a kind of darkness, the cloud itself dissipating into purposeless wisps only after drifting far astern.

It was a warm summer's day—nearly eighty degrees, I should judge—and the humidity was already causing the air to feel close. In short, conditions augured just the sort of afternoon any sensible Englishman would choose to remain indoors. And yet with the prospects of a grand naval spectacle about to unfold before me, I nodded to my driver to proceed down the dusty road to the sea so I could have a closer look. Hours later, he deposited me near the wharves where, after offering thanks for his services, I paid him what he asked and then some. The piping of sea birds announced my arrival.

Before approaching the water, however, I realised I had business to conduct. Ever since the wagon had rattled past the central telegraph office in the heart of Tripoli, I had been thinking of sending a cable to Mycroft. He and I had been out of communication for the last few weeks; and now that I had reached a seaport on my journey to Khartoum, I thought it time not only to inform him of my whereabouts, but also to ask him for additional funds.

(What, Watson, still the long face after all these years? You know I couldn't contact *you*. Recall that during my travels, I needed to keep my existence unknown from the remnants of Moriarty's gang. I couldn't risk your open and honest nature revealing my secret, old fellow. Mycroft remained my only confidant; and even when communicating with him, I identified myself as the Norwegian explorer, "Sigerson".)

Upon nearing the docks, I spied an old woman selling *hummus* and flat bread. Hungry as I was and in need of information, I purchased her wares and, using my hands to imitate the action of writing, made her understand that I was seeking a telegraph office. She pointed down the road and with the wave of her fingers indicated a pair of turns. I thanked the woman, followed her rudimentary instructions, and soon found myself standing before a small, whitewashed building not more than a mile distant from the sea.

A few steps took me inside where I saw a squat, bearded man perched behind a barren desk. It took but a moment to ascertain that he knew no English, only French and Arabic. But after I printed out a brief note and offered him some money, he dispatched my cable with little problem. Munching on a piece of the flat bread I'd stored in my rucksack, I exited the telegraph office; and along alleyways crowded with weathered sailors, wide-eyed travellers, and shrewd buyers and sellers of anything one could imagine, I made my way to the docks.

The salty smell of the sea embraced me as I edged past busy fish stalls, piles of sails, and rows of wooden boats. I removed my boots upon reaching the strand and ambled through the pebbles at the water's edge. By 3.30 I found a deserted stretch of sand along the bay's eastern shore—not far, as it so happened, from the stone ruins of the Tower of Lions, an ancient, square-sided fortress adorned with worn-down carvings of the king of beasts. Unknown to me at the time, it was to serve as a landmark for the British Fleet.

The sun was now baking hot. The warships, still a few miles out, were pointed in my direction—that is, towards the eastern edge of the bay. From where I was positioned, I could easily discern their white upper works, long black hulls, and polished brass fittings. With the thrumming of the steam engines as background, I squatted on the beach to watch the show.

Whatever my notable talents, gentlemen, knowledge of naval manoeuvres is not among them. At first, I was content to gawp at the military splendour of the vessels—the colourful flags, the disciplined formation, the mighty guns. I confess to you that it was truly quite sufficient for stirring one's national passions, especially those of the traveller so many miles from home. Yet within a few short minutes even I could see cause for concern.

In order to enter the bay, the broad line of ships had magically rearranged itself into a pair of close, parallel files. The two divisions were just now heading into port, and anyone with a cursory knowledge of measurements could intuit that, as they neared the shore, they would by necessity very soon—that is to say, almost immediately—have to turn about or risk running into the boats already at anchor—if not into the very docks themselves. The closer they sailed, the more distressed I became, unable to comprehend their failure to reverse direction.

Within seconds, however, all seemed to be righted. The flagship began her turn, and I breathed a sigh of relief. Obviously, or so I assumed, *all* the ships in both columns would turn-about in the same manner at the same time and continue sailing in reverse order in the direction from which they had come. Such a course seemed the reasonable manoeuvre. Yet moments later the lead ship of the second file also began to turn—but to turn *inward, towards* the flagship! There could not have been more than a thousand yards between them—surely not enough space for the two lines to turn safely *towards* each other, one after another. And yet that was precisely what they seemed bent on doing!

Alas, there was no time to ponder the options. The two lead ships—the *Victoria* and the *Camperdown,* I was soon to learn—were turning directly into each other. Within seconds and at an almost perfect right angle, the *Camperdown* ploughed straight into the *Victoria*.

Gentlemen, I tell you, it was an event that I shall never forget! Everyone watching—on the hills, on the strand, on the docks—heard the impact, an explosive roar that ripped through the clouds of dust and dirt filling the air, a cacophony of noise trailing in its wake: the screams of frightened bluejackets, the trill of a bugler's call to action, and finally the mournful lament of the *Camperdown's* foghorn.

I sprang to my feet at the initial contact, grabbing my binoculars and shielding the sun from my eyes. There was nothing I could do, of course, save stand and observe—though I did check my watch. It was 3.34.

A shudder surged through me as with an ear-splitting, half-human shriek, the *Camperdown* now slowly backed away, its engine thrown into reverse and the underwater ram—about which I would only hear later—surgically extracting itself from its victim. By 3.36 the ships had separated, but the *Victoria's* low-slung prow was already dipping dangerously low. It had taken only two minutes to complete the act; and yet the damage was not unlike Hamlet's prick of Laertes: "a hit—a very palpable hit."

The scene came alive with confusion. Lifeboats dropped from the nearby ships even as those large vessels were manoeuvring out of the way of the two damaged craft. And all the while, the *Victoria* continued to take on water. In only five minutes, her bows had sunk some fifteen feet, and the sea was beginning to lap at the muzzles of her huge guns. A few minutes later, with a sickening rip, the gun-turret broke free; and as the pair of long barrels slid forward over the deck, their weight lowered the prow ever farther until the stern of the ship began to rise out of the water. Through my field glasses, I could actually see her turning screws break the white surface of the now-roiling sea.

At the same time, displaying unimaginable discipline, some six hundred of the *Victoria's* bluejackets lined up four-deep on the deck to await instructions. In point of fact, they were anticipating the command to leap into the ocean. Suddenly, the ship lurched to her starboard side, and even I could hear the cry of "Jump! Jump!" from an officer on the deck.

The *Victoria* was capsizing! And hundreds of bluejackets—swimmers and non-swimmers alike—dived into the water to escape being dragged down. At 3.43—a mere nine minutes after the collision—the ship rolled over and, keel up, began to spin full-circle like the needle of a compass—slowly at first, but quickly gaining speed.

Now, with water pouring into the furnaces, an explosion blasted from below. The boilers had burst, and horrific shrieks from scalded sailors marked the brutality of the escaping steam. Then the air that had been trapped within the ship erupted, vomiting up to the surface a knot of bodies, furniture, spars and yardarms that had all got entangled somewhere within the inverted wreckage.

The *Victoria* continued to spin as she sank, and it was to the creamy pool at the centre of this wheeling circle that a *mélange* of living and dead was inexorably sucked. Many who had not drowned within the vortex were slammed into by the spiralling snarl of metal and wood that had shot up from below; still others were torn to pieces by the screws that continued to run even as the hull, which by this time had turned vertical, plummeted straight down. In less than a quarter of an hour, she was gone.

Caught up in the frenzy of sinking, the *Victoria* had failed to release her lifeboats. Later I would discover that the hydraulics needed to free them no longer operated. Fortunately, the teams of men in the small boats sent out by the other ships were able to retrieve both the living and the dead who floated past in the blood-red sea.

*****

It was just then that I saw some movement among the flotsam floating in my direction—a white-shirted sailor clinging to a spar was washing towards the shore. Once he saw me, he struggled to raise an arm.

Needless to say, I dashed into the small waves and, half-running, half-swimming, grabbed the wood to which he clung and guided it and him to safety. He sputtered his thanks as I helped him stagger from the water. Then I gently lowered him to the sand, where bloodied, worn out, and drenched, he lay panting before me.

"My God," he said at last. And then he repeated it over and over again. "My God. My God."

It took a few minutes for him to catch his breath; but once he settled down, he looked seaward at the limping *Camperdown*, the ship that had crashed into his own. By this time, she had backed well enough away from the point of impact that she seemed ready to drop anchor.

"Are you all right?" I asked. "You've suffered quite a shock."

He looked surprised at my words. I imagine that my Arab garb, along with my sun-baked complexion and bearded face, may have put him off. Hearing me use the Queen's English, however, seemed to assure him that I was a fellow countryman.

He took a few more breaths; and when he appeared to have collected himself, he said, "I'm a midshipman from the *Victoria*, sir. I saw it all."

Had the young man still been wearing his blue frock coat, I would have recognised his relative rank. Wisely, he had taken to the water without it. He'd discarded his shoes as well.

"How came this tragedy?" I asked, "I mean, besides the obvious. How came these two ships to collide?"

The midshipman shook his head. "Stupid," he muttered.

"Sorry?" I pressed him again.

"Admiral Tryon," he gasped.

"Sir George?" Even then I knew the name—Vice-Admiral Sir George Tryon, K.C.B, a big bear of a man with a personality to match—one of the most loved and feared officers in the Royal Navy. A disciple of Lord Nelson, he seldom made mistakes—some would have said, "never".

"Right," said the midshipman, "Sir George."

"What was he thinking?"

The sailor shook his head. "We'd been in Beirut for five days, and we weighed anchor this morning at 9.45. Beirut's forty miles to the south, and it was supposed to take us six-and-a-half hours to get here. We were sailing along quite well at about nine knots. Because of her long, low forecastle, the *Victoria* moves—moved—easily in the water. She was nicknamed "the slipper", you know, because her ride was so smooth. We arrived here right on schedule; and after dividing into two divisions, we headed for the eastern shore."

The midshipman raised a limp forefinger in the direction of the nearby stone ruins. "The Tower of Lions over there," said he. "That was our landmark. The Admiral intended to have the lead ships of both lines turn inward when they reached the head of their columns at a point parallel to the Tower of Lions. That was the plan at any rate. Then we could put in at our anchorage in the same order in which we'd entered the bay."

The young man rubbed a hand across his eyes. As his hair dried in the sun, I could see that it was dark-blond rather than the black it had appeared when I'd fished him out of the water. No doubt he would make quite the smart officer when he advanced.

"Once the Admiral gave the initial order," the midshipman went on, "I saw the other officers exchange looks. To a man, I don't believe any of them thought there was enough distance between the two columns to complete the manoeuvre. The *Victoria* needed at least four cables length to turn."

"Cables?"

"Sorry," he muttered. "About two hundred yards. The *Camperdown* would have required the same. And yet we appeared to be but six cables apart. We probably needed twice that space."

"Did no one question the order?"

The sailor managed a faint smile. "One doesn't question the Commander-in-Chief of the Fleet. Certainly not a midshipman like me. One *should*, of course, if the safety of the ship is threatened. A couple of officers mumbled some concern, but not with any purpose. Still, the danger seemed obvious. I'm convinced that's why Admiral Markham, the commander of the *Camperdown*, was reluctant to begin his own turn."

"'Reluctant', you say?"

"Aye, sir. He failed to respond to Admiral Tryon's initial signal to turn. He hoisted his flag in agreement only after repeated demands were flashed to him from the *Victoria*, and by then we were too close to the shore. There was no time left for either ship; that's when we turned into one another.

"The collision was bad enough—though even then we might have weathered it except for the *Camperdown's* bloody ram—begging your pardon. It holed us below the waterline. When the *Camperdown* backed away, you see, the water rushed into the breach. If the two ships had remained locked together, maybe the *Victoria* wouldn't have sunk. Who's to say? There might have been just enough time to seal the watertight doors and save the ship.

"As it was, we slammed a few doors closed—and, God forgive us, locked in some poor souls by accident. We tried to shut all the doors; but, my God, there was just too much water. The Admiral was trying to reach land; but the distance was more than four miles, and we couldn't move any faster than four knots. Then there were the heavy guns near the prow. They weighed her down. Once she tipped forward—well, in seventy fathoms of water the result was inevitable."

"Did Admiral Tryon say nothing?"

"As we were going down, I heard him talking to another officer. 'My fault,' the Admiral said. 'It is entirely my doing, entirely my fault.' And then he was gone. I myself was thrown free. Thank God, I grabbed onto something that floated by. I managed to tear off my coat and shoes and hold on till you came to my aid."

Clearly exhausted, the poor fellow leaned back. Talking to me had worn him out. Meanwhile, the rescue missions continued. Small boat after small boat returned to land filled with the quick and the dead.

Suddenly, we were engulfed in a shadow. A figure from out of nowhere loomed over us and eclipsed the sun. It was a naval officer, who had seen the two of us conversing. With his black-billed white hat and dark-blue frock coat in perfect order, he commanded the midshipman to stand and report to the docks where inventories of the survivors were being completed.

"Under no circumstances," the officer commanded as the bedraggled sailor shakily got to his feet, "are you to speak with anyone about what occurred here this afternoon. Do you understand?"

"Aye, sir," said the midshipman.

The young man and I exchanged glances. I trust he realised that the Royal Navy would hear nothing from me about what he had said. With a trembling hand, he saluted his superior, completed a ragged about turn, and marched off as best he could. I had not even learned his name.

The officer now looked *me* over from head to toe. Thanks to my local dress, I suspect he saw no cause for worry. Whom was *I* going to tell? Besides, the collision—a deadly accident of the greatest magnitude—had been a naval flummox of the grandest order; and though I knew the Royal Navy to be reluctant to announce its failings, I could not imagine that the Admiralty would consider attempting to conceal so horrific a mistake.

I was wrong, of course; but it took a night in a small hotel and plenty of thought to make me reconsider my silence. Upon Friday, having decided to report the disaster I had witnessed, I returned to the same telegraph office from where I had cabled you, Mycroft. Although I hoped my look of assurance the day before had conveyed to the midshipman that I would not report to the Navy what he had told me, I had not intended such an understanding to prohibit my communicating with Fleet Street. The public deserved to know what had occurred that fateful summer's day.

*****

The same diminutive clerk was sitting at the same barren desk he had been facing the day before. It was as if he had not moved. Perhaps if I spoke distinctly enough, he would understand me. "I need to cable London," said I slowly. "About the collision at sea."

"You're wasting your time," said a gentleman with an American accent. "The news is already abroad."

In so great a hurry when I had entered the office, I failed to notice the man standing to the right of the door. He had been leaning both elbows on the counter, and now he removed his straw hat to mop his bald head with a well-used handkerchief. Perspiring freely, he wore neither collar nor necktie; and dressed in wilted white shirt and trousers, he looked overwhelmed by the heat. He seemed to perk up, however, when he heard me informing the telegraph operator that I intended to send a wire about the naval tragedy.

"I appreciate that you want to tell the world what happened here yesterday, but that fellow"— he gestured with his straw hat towards the clerk, "doesn't speak any English. Besides, like I said, the world already knows."

"I can well imagine," said I.

Though I felt thwarted in my personal plans, news that the story had got out made perfect sense to me. At the time, I did not know of Rear-Admiral Markham's cable to the Sea Lords describing the collision, but I none the less assumed that some official would be duty-bound to send the Admiralty a report.

"And yet they want more," said the man, raising a forefinger portentously.

"Who?"

"The press, who else? Pierre, the cable operator over there, showed me a request that's just come in from London. Since he doesn't read the language, he asked me for help. I'm Ira Harris, by the way," said he, extending his hand, "Dr Ira Harris from Fayetteville, New York."

I clasped his hand, responding with my Sigerson alias.

“Glad to meet you,” said he. “For a Norwegian, you’re pretty far from base. I’m with the Presbyterian Board of Foreign Missions—been running the Tripoli Hospital here for the past ten years. The locals trust me.”

“What did you mean,” I asked, “when you said ‘they want more’?”

The American slid a wrinkled, yellow cablegram along the counter-top to me. It had been lying in front of him, but was actually addressed “To the Telegraph Agent, Tripoli, Syria”. The printed message had come from an American pressman in London called David Graham Phillips of the *World.* To my astonishment, he was offering $500 for two thousand words about the naval disaster, which he had somehow got wind of.

“Any such offers from the *British* press?” I asked. *“The Times? The Evening Standard? The Daily News?”*

“No,” Dr Harris answered, shaking his head, “not one. But I can vouch for the *World*. I’ve been a subscriber for years.”

“Well then,” said I, clapping my hands together, “I see no good reason to deprive this Mr Graham Phillips of the story—if we can figure out a way to send it, that is. At least, he’s in London.”

“Tell me what you know,” Harris offered, reaching for a pencil and blank sheet of paper on a nearby table. “I’ll write it down in big block letters so that Pierre here can read it. Without knowing any English, he can still copy the words and send them off.”

Having got Pierre to dispatch my own cable to Mycroft the day before, I understood the procedure and agreed to the doctor’s proposition. Careful not to identify my source, I combined the first-hand experience that the midshipman had described to me with what I myself had observed. Taken together, the two accounts produced a comprehensive narrative of the terrible collision.

Dr Harris took it all down slowly whilst I kept an eye out the window. I remained on the lookout for suspicious naval authorities seeking to quash any news that might be heading for England. Since I had already been scrutinised once by such a figure, I decided to exit the office as soon as I had finished my report, trusting the American to see that the message would be safely sent.

It was years later that I came to learn how much responsibility I had placed on the poor man. It took Dr Harris and Pierre until 10.00 that night to compose the piece; and only then did the doctor discover that in order to send so lengthy a story to London, it first had to be relayed from Tripoli's central office to Beirut. Not only did it require another hour for Dr Harris to reach the central office by tram and foot; but upon reaching the place, he had to wait an additional thirty minutes for the operator, who also knew no English, to finish his cigar. Once again, Dr Harris was required to spell out each word of the story. What's more—much to his credit in light of what he had already experienced—he borrowed $500 from an acquaintance to facilitate the money exchange that Graham Phillips had originally promised to Pierre.

I suppose one could say that the rest is history. In spite of the pressures that the Admiralty put on Fleet Street to hush up an account of the British Navy's incompetence, Pulitzer's *New York World* could publish the news with impunity. As Watson can attest, after my own role in securing the details was made public a couple of years later, Graham Phillips himself came round Baker Street to thank me.

Actually, I have always believed that Phillips did quite a nice job with the story. Who can forget his terrifying description of the screws? "Frightful, swift, revolving knives," he called them. It was indeed a horror, but a horror that cried out for reporting—and not only for the sheer drama of the event. One could but hope that the news of so catastrophic an accident would provide the impetus for strengthening our military. It was a decade ago that this horrific accident occurred, gentlemen; but even then the winds of war were blowing. Preparation is all, and the collision at sea needed to be exposed as a warning. How else to know of our ironclads' vulnerability? How else to encourage officers to question perilous orders? Indeed, how else, gentlemen, to hold the Royal Navy accountable?

III

Sherlock Holmes refilled his copita and drank more port.

Throughout his brother's narrative, Mycroft had sat fidgeting with his watch chain, constantly checking the time, as if he could scarcely wait for the misguided tale to conclude. Save for the light cast by the electric street lamps outside, the world beyond the bow window had turned black.

"Quite important for you, was it, Sherlock," asked Mycroft at last, "to tell an American pressman all about our mishap—all about one of the greatest peacetime naval disasters in the history of the world? Content to wash our soiled linen in public, were you?"

My friend offered a slight smile. "I believe I told Watson during that business with the busts of Napoleon that the press is a most valuable institution if one only knows how to use it."

I did not recall the quotation, but made a note to employ it if I ever recorded that singular case. Or perhaps I would insert it in another.

"Well, brother-mine," grunted Mycroft Holmes as with no little effort he leaned forward refill his glass, "I should imagine that now it falls upon me *to set the record straight—as much as one can, anyhow." He sighed and fortified himself with another pull.*

For his part, Sherlock Holmes drew a Havana from an inner pocket, struck a Vespa, and lit the cigar. In anticipation of his brother's speech, Holmes leaned back into his chair and stretched out his long legs. Almost immediately, the cloying smell of his tobacco filled the room.

IV

Mycroft Holmes's Account

We came here tonight, gentlemen, to mourn the dead. And yet as I might have predicted, our memorial has unfortunately devolved into yet another recapitulation of the tragic events that occurred this day ten years ago. How many times must one hear the agonizing details? No doubt, the fault is mine for suggesting this remembrance in the first place—unless, of course, this new vexation is simply the price one pays for having failed to reveal all the facts ten years ago. There is, you see, more to the story of the collision than both of you are aware—much of which, I'm pleased to say, the Foreign Office has now permitted me to share with you.

To begin with, the true subject of this discussion should not be some broad question regarding the military readiness of our forces at sea. Not that such issues are not relevant, mind, but in discussing the tragedy of *H.M.S. Victoria*, the focus must really centre upon a single plot—the attempt by the Germans to steal an object that *was*—and in all probability still *is*—the greatest artefact in the possession of the Royal Navy—certainly, in the possession of the Mediterranean Fleet. I am referring to no less than the grand battle sword of Vice-Admiral Horatio Lord Nelson, the same sword that Nelson brandished in his epic victory over Napoleon—in a word, gentlemen, the very quintessence of British naval supremacy. I need not overstate how the loss of such a treasure would convulse the nation.

Yet in addition to so keen a symbol of British military might, there was in the early nineties an even greater matter concerning the country. Oh, I freely acknowledge that you didn't know it at the time, Sherlock; but when the dispatch that you composed concerning the naval accident in Tripoli was sent off to David Graham Phillips, you were in effect tinkering with the political equilibrium of all Europe. Truth to tell, gentlemen, we meet here this very night during a grave period of contemporary history. Current diplomatic efforts bear significant implications for the fate of the entire world, a fate that the ten-year-old collision of the *Camperdown* and the *Victoria* may actually have played some role in shaping.

You will recall that it was just a few weeks ago that His Majesty King Edward travelled to Paris, and it is now but a few weeks prior to the reciprocal trip to these islands of French President Loubet. As I'm sure you are both aware, the purpose of these meetings is highly political—to finalise the agreement called the *Entente Cordiale*, an understanding between France and England that will solidify the bonds between our two nations in the face of growing German strength—growing German strength at *sea* in particular.

As you know, under the guise of an intricate balance of power, the late German Chancellor, Otto Von Bismarck, worked hard at masking his goal of German hegemony. As a consequence, for more than a decade now, England and France have been striving to confound the Kaiser's ambitious wiles and weaken the strength of the German Empire. Not with much success, I am afraid. With French and British concerns on the one hand and the Kaiser's subversive schemes on the other, I fear this competition can have but one result.

Personally, I cannot envision another decade slipping past without a monstrous confrontation among the nations of Europe.

But enough about the future, gentlemen. Let us not forget that we are here tonight to memorialise the past. Which brings us back to that terrible day in June of 1893. Allow me to set the stage. Recall that in the early nineties the Royal Navy was *nonpareil.* The Germans hoped to match us, but simply could not. And yet, ironically, it was the very *lack* of opposition, which was based on our strengths, that engendered complacency in our ranks.

Sir George Tryon rightly believed that, short of having an enemy at whom to fire, confronting our navy with challenging manoeuvres remained our next-best chance of staying alert. As Commander-in-Chief of the Mediterranean Fleet, Sir George put his ships through their paces, as it were, inspiring them to conduct all sorts of innovative drills and in the process display the Union Jack to all the sheiks and sultans of the area—not to mention any potentates of Europe—who might be observing the manoeuvres.

As for his vessel, as you rightly noted, Sherlock, *H.M.S. Victoria* was the flagship of the Fleet. The Admiralty was most proud of her. Her 100,000 tons of steel made her among the largest, fastest, most powerful ironclads in the world. With two 16.25-inch, 111-ton guns, the largest in the Royal Navy, she was also the best protected. Why, within the Mediterranean Fleet alone, we possessed six of the most feared battleships afloat.

All of which made the sinking of the *Victoria* so distressing. The Sea Lords received word of the tragedy at 12.30 the morning after—twenty-two officers killed; over three hundred men lost. That a first-class warship costing close to one-million pounds could capsize in ten minutes and completely sink in thirteen called into question the fundamental designs of our most important ships.

Take the *Victoria's* side-armour, for example. It stopped short of encasing the entire hull. Would extending it further have protected her from the *Camperdown's* ram? And what of her heavy guns? Would not lesser weapons have increased the time it took her to sink? For that matter, what about the chain of command throughout the Navy? As you suggested earlier, Sherlock, should we have been doing more to encourage officers to countermand orders that seemed to threaten the safety of the ship? The Admiralty wanted answers. After all, if such a catastrophe was the result of a mere collision, what damage could enemy guns produce?

We can surely agree that resolving such difficulties is vital to military success, and yet in point of fact these questions bear little relation to what was actually going on that day ten years ago. What you did not know then, Sherlock—and what the Foreign Office is allowing me to tell you tonight—concerns a German plot set into motion during the early summer ten years ago when a small band of English-speaking German spies arrived somewhere on the coast of Syria and, disguised as British bluejackets, eventually managed to insert themselves among the *Victoria's* crew.

You already mentioned, Sherlock, that it was no secret how much Vice-Admiral Tryon admired Lord Nelson. Indeed, an avid collector of all matters related to his beloved hero, Sir George had made large purchases at an auction featuring many of Nelson's valuables. The prize of the collection was the famous battle sword that we have previously discussed—the same sword, incidentally, which served as model for the blade held by Nelson's statue atop the Corinthian column in Trafalgar Square. (Do you know that in the daylight one can almost see it from this very window?) And, of course, it was public knowledge that the artefact in question was hanging on display in Sir George's cabin aboard the *Victoria.*

Because of the sword's great symbolic value, the German high command—perhaps, von Tirpitz himself, their *Kapitän zur See*—were bent on stealing the thing. In fact, once the Kaiser heard about it, he himself became obsessed with obtaining the blade. You can understand their nefarious thinking. What better way for the German Imperial Navy to demonstrate its dominance over the greatest naval force in the world than by securing so valuable a possession?

It was the job of those German spies who had been set down in Syria to masquerade as English sailors and grab the sword. They planned to steal it as the *Victoria* was sailing into port at Tripoli and then commandeer the ship away from the fleet and escape via a commercial vessel waiting for them at the docks. Even though it was staring you in the face, Sherlock, I doubt that you noticed the merchant ship flying the German flag that day. She had been anchored in the harbour to be used in their getaway.

No? I thought not.

How many Germans there were and how and where they masterfully infiltrated themselves among the hundreds of sailors aboard the *Victoria*—not to mention how the Admiralty got wind of the plan—all this I am not at liberty to reveal. Actually, no one with whom I have ever discussed the matter understands just how much of the scheme the Sea Lords knew. I was told that the Admiralty had hoped to send a secret group of marines to overtake the Germans in Beirut, but that our men could not be deployed quickly enough.

The remainder of this story, I'm afraid, is all rather hearsay. There were rumours to the effect that Vice-Admiral Tryon knew about the secret contingent of marines aboard the *Camperdown* and that he formulated a scheme to enable the marines to board the *Victoria* when the two ships met. Bringing the ships close enough for such a transfer may be the reason that, even with such insufficient space between the two, he so ill advisedly attempted the evolution. Sir George, dynamic officer that he was, apparently had no fear of executing the manoeuvre. The German merchant ship left port just moments after the disastrous collision. As for the spies stranded on the *Victoria,* one supposes that those who were not killed in the accident somehow managed to escape. Whatever their fate, they were officially listed as "presumed dead".

Unfortunately, Sherlock, you were present to witness the results of a plan gone awry. As you have already described, within minutes of having been penetrated by the *Camperdown's* ram, the *Victoria* plummeted prow first straight down to the bottom of the Mediterranean. Our mathematical experts conjecture that it must have stuck upright like an arrow shot into the ground. They surmise that it hit with such force that some three-quarters of the hull buried itself into the ocean's floor. It goes without saying, of course, that even now, a decade later, the sword of Lord Nelson remains somewhere within the wreckage.

*****

Enter the American, Mr David Graham Phillips.

Following the receipt of Rear-Admiral Markham's dispatch that arrived after midnight in London, the Admiralty assumed that some news of the affair was bound to leak out to the public. According to the Foreign Office, however, Phillips had access to more official sources than do most pressmen. It seems that he maintained contact with a Portuguese minister who in turn had informants in the Turkish Embassy. It was through these channels that news of a major disaster in the Mediterranean was first reported.

Much to the dismay of the Ministry of Defence, the British press did manage to print a few lines about the affair but nothing of any significance. And yet this mere whiff of trouble was sufficient to inspire the publicity-seeking Phillips to gamble two shillings per word for any additional news regarding the accident. As you know, Sherlock, it was upon Friday, the day after the collision, that Phillips sent the cablegram to Tripoli offering money for the story to the telegraph agent, the man you identified as Pierre.

Though Phillips received Pierre's answer on Saturday evening—"Will send account," it read—by early Monday morning Phillips had yet to receive any details. Nor, for that matter, had any British newspapers. But then, at 11.00, half a dozen sentences about the collision began trickling into the *World's* London office; minutes later, some more came in, and every ten minutes thereafter another batch arrived until the report was completed. These cables, of course, comprised the account that you gave to Dr Harris, Sherlock, which he, thanks to the Herculean effort you have already described, managed to have telegraphed to London.

For his part, Phillips made these facts known throughout the world. I'll give the man his due. He pulled no punches when it came to laying blame. He called Vice-Admiral Tryon an "insane commander" and the decision to turn the ship inward an "insane order". He compared the sinking of the *Victoria* to the "sounding" of a whale.

And yet, in retrospect, I suppose it was fortunate for the American that Mr Pulitzer denied him a by-line. That way, you see, Phillips himself was able to dodge much of the anger the Admiralty aimed at those papers deemed to have revealed too much about what had occurred in the Mediterranean that fateful day.

On the other hand, to deflect any criticism regarding Fleet Street's inability to acquire the relevant facts, British publishers labelled the *World's* story a "fake". Presumptuous, to be sure—and ironical as well. For not only did the attack by the British papers fail, but in the end most of them felt duty-bond to reprint in full the *World's* initial report.

As I am sure you have already inferred, gentlemen, it was political motivation that caused the Admiralty to quash any news of the collision. First and foremost, they worried that if Germany's secret role in the ugly affair had become known, the war hawks in Whitehall would have demanded a military response—a response, which, thanks to the Kaiser's newly built navy, we could not be confident of winning. It also did not help to advertise how easily the Germans had infiltrated our forces. Fortunately, at least that part of the story has never reached the public.

But there was still more about the accident that needed to be contained. With German sea power growing, the Sea Lords wanted to suppress any news concerning the vulnerability of our sturdiest warships. Iron clad, heavily armed, strongly powered—it all mattered not a whit if the things could sink to the bottom of the sea within thirteen minutes!

And that was not the worst of the affair. One cannot forget the humiliation—the loss of more than three-hundred able-bodied seamen due to the miscalculation of an overly aggressive commander! At so delicate a time, we could not afford trumpeting to the world the news of what was perhaps the greatest blunder in the history of the Royal Navy. And all for the desire of an antique sword!

So at long last, brother, we come to the crux of our disagreement. *You* believe people have the right to know what happened; *I* believe that in light of the welfare of the country, the government has the right to control such information. I willingly acknowledge that your position is the more noble. Mine, however, is the more practical; for my position ultimately allows philosophers like you to breathe the air that enables them to speak of freedom.

I have talked quite enough now. It is time for more liquid refreshment.

V

Mycroft drank rapidly his glass of port and then turned to stare at his brother.

Staring right back, Sherlock Holmes exhaled a cloud of smoke. He seemed to be searching for an appropriate response as he slowly laid his cigar in a nearby ashtray. It was none too soon; for by now, a tenebrous haze had filled most of the room.

"Are you aware, Mycroft," he drawled at last, "that in his Areopagitica, *the great Englishman John Milton wrote the following: 'Give me the liberty to know, to utter, and to argue freely according to conscience, above all liberties'?"*

Waving away the smoke, Mycroft Holmes offered the same slight smile that I had seen on many an occasion in the muted reactions of his brother.

"And are you *aware, Sherlock," said Mycroft drily, "that in his great monument to British freedom called 'On Liberty', John Stuart Mill wrote: 'Despotism is a legitimate mode of government in dealing with barbarians'?"*

Nostrils flaring, Sherlock Holmes sat up straight as he prepared his riposte. "Speaking of your new friends, the French," he hissed, steel-grey eyes flashing with menace, "no less a figure than Voltaire has said: 'Je déteste ce que vous écrivez, mais je donnerai ma vie pour que vous puissiez continuer à écrire.' "

"Hah!" Mycroft exclaimed. "'Niemand ist mehr Sklave, als der sich für frei hält, ohne es zu sein'. " As if a punctuation mark were needed, he spat out the single name "Goethe".

I understood the French. In point of fact, while the sentiment *about writing free from censorship was most assuredly Voltaire's, there was some lingering controversy about whether the words themselves—"I detest what you write, but I will give my life so that you may continue to write"—were actually those of the Frenchman.*

As for the German, I looked to Mycroft for a translation; but Sherlock Holmes answered me first: "'None are more hopelessly enslaved than those who falsely believe they are free'."

Mycroft seethed at having been outdone by his gloating brother. Grotesque mirror images, both men sat warily eyeing the other, each breathing heavily, as if he had just completed a mile-long foot race. For my part, I might as well have not even been there.

It was Mycroft who finally broke the uncomfortable silence. "We must do nothing to endanger the fragile Franco-British alliance that is being constructed as we speak. Mark my words, brother-mine—war is in the offing. We can ill afford to fight among ourselves when we should be working together to build solid resolve."

Sherlock Holmes raised his glass of port. "Agreed," said he. "But don't forget that we also agreed to let friend Watson here decide which one of us has proffered the more compelling argument."

To be honest, I was hoping that they had indeed forgotten the proposition. But Mycroft touched his glass to his brother's, and they sipped their port. Holmes picked up his Havana, and then both combatants turned to me.

"Well, Watson," said my friend, "what do you make of it all?"

Now I have been in tight fixes before, and I have never lost my nerve—not whilst facing Jezail bullets in Afghanistan nor stalking that supernatural hound in the Grimpen Mire nor even being shot just a year before by "Killer" Evans. And yet all those dire predicaments paled when compared to fending off the imperial gaze of the brothers Holmes for a second time in a single evening. Like gimlets, their sharp eyes bore into m; and I feared alienating either one.

I needed to gain additional time for consideration of my answer. Opening a window would serve the purpose.

"Fresh air," I explained as I rose from my chair.

"Do you not find," asked Mycroft, "that a concentrated atmosphere enables one to maintain more concentrated thoughts?"

"There is a limit," said I definitively—though Mycroft's remark had a familiar ring. I seemed to recall hearing something similar from his brother early in our investigation of the Baskerville business. Perhaps the observation was a family tenet. I let it go, however, and raised the sash, content to inhale the cool night air.

At the same time, I considered my alternatives. In point of fact, the arguments of both brothers warranted defending. As a writer, I could easily support what America's Bill of Rights calls "the freedom of the press". No author on earth wants to be censored. And yet, whilst the sanctity of the written word demands preservation, the siren song of military preparedness also clamours to be heard. In my heart, I could feel the correctness of the writer's calling; in my brain, I could not ignore the voice of reason. I needed to establish a middle ground.

It was whilst returning to my chair that I experienced the epiphany. Suddenly, I recognised the goal of both of the brothers. Ignore their lofty language, *I thought. It was with the* author *of a theory—not with the theory itself—that each brother really wanted me to side.* Of course. *Once I determined that this standoff was more personal than philosophical, my role became clear. More important than deciding which principle to support was encouraging each brother to make peace with the other.*

Thus it was that I settled on the word "compromise" as a solution to my dilemma. It would be the tool that would guide me between this modern Scylla and Charybdis. "Compromise" may seem a simple remedy, for it is a course of action tolerated and even respected by most people in a civilised society. But then the two men sitting before me did not represent "most people"; and to judge by my own experiences, I expected neither one to appreciate my conclusion. And yet, in truth, I regarded my attempts to reconcile the pair to be among the most challenging situations I had ever faced.

"Gentlemen," said I, waving my hand to clear the air, "this is nothing but a silly feud between two siblings. Forget the fate of the Victoria *and Nelson's sword. That business took place ten years ago. As of now, one can only assume that each of you has solidified the righteousness of your own position in order to trivialise that of your brother. Simply put, Mr Sherlock Holmes, you must recognise that, like many a criminal investigation, matters of state require caution when one makes them public. Mr Mycroft Holmes, for your part, you must accept that, like many a political moment, the public require the Truth and will somehow—and sometimes at great cost—work hard to discover it."*

During the silence that ensued, it was obvious to me that both men recognised the fundamental principles I was exhorting. Yet I must point out that whenever brothers are involved, not even the skills of a master arbitrator can be counted upon to settle disputes. Cain's treatment of Abel aptly dramatizes the situation.

To my great relief, however, simultaneous sighs finally broke the stillness. The penetrating gazes that had fallen upon me *now turned to focus more softly on each other. The two men spoke at the same time.*

"Quite right," said my friend.

"Just so," said Mycroft.

And the two brothers leaned toward each other and clasped hands.

"You know, you're quite correct, Watson," said Sherlock Holmes, "and yet even as you artfully unite the two of us, I fear that all of Europe will soon be in need of statesmen like yourself. For who else will be capable of resolving the hostility that Mycroft so rightly describes as permeating the atmosphere?

"No matter our resolutions here tonight, the world remains divided; and ultimately all of us will have to take a stand. For battle-lines will be drawn, old fellow, and I fear that even the greatest of nations will be unable to field ministers with your admirable negotiating skills. Soon we shall all be forced to choose. What then? *Must we muzzle the voices of liberty in the name of our security?"*

"Whatever we do, Sherlock," Mycroft answered, "friend Watson here is quite right. We must do it together."

It was not often that I intervened in the life of my friend and colleague Mr Sherlock Holmes. Seldom was I given the opportunity. But as we all shared a final drink together that evening, I knew that I for one should always regard my reconciliation of the two Holmes brothers as one of the bravest and most noble deeds I have ever done. *

* More information about the naval disaster may be found in Richard Hough's *Admirals in Collision* and in "A Famous Newspaper Beat," the chapter in Isaac F. Marcosson's *David Graham Phillips and His Times* that deals exclusively with Phillips's reporting of the story. (DDV)

One final point: *HMS Victoria* still remains buried where she sank in 1893, some 500 feet below the surface of the Mediterranean Sea off the coast of what is now Lebanon. In early 2012, however, news media reported that eight years earlier an explorer and salvage-diver named Mark Ellyatt had actually discovered Lord Nelson's treasured sword within the wreckage. To avoid issues over ownership, the Ministry of Defence requested that the coveted artefact be left on board the *Victoria*, and Ellyatt complied, admitting that he had hidden the sword somewhere within the ruins of the submerged ship. *The Daily Mail* has suggested that for the sword alone collectors would pay up to one million pounds.

The Adventure of the Smith-Mortimer Succession

The famous Smith-Mortimer succession case
comes also within this period [1894].
--Dr John H. Watson
"The Adventure of the
Golden Pince-Nez"

No detective, not even an amateur, wants to admit that he has been the victim of thieves. And yet that was precisely the situation in which I found myself after moving back to Baker Street in May of 1894, some two weeks after the dramatic return from the dead of my friend and colleague, Mr Sherlock Holmes.

By now the whole world knows the astounding story of how Holmes had appeared to plunge to his death at the Reichenbach Falls in Switzerland on 4 May 1891, how he had spent the next three years travelling incognito, and how he had finally reappeared in London in the spring of '94 to solve the murder of one Ronald Adair. Though today such facts are readily available, it must be remembered that for reasons never made entirely clear to me, Holmes prohibited my publishing an account of the case for some ten years following his resurrection.

Adhering to Holmes's request, I waited patiently until the autumn of '03—actually, a year prior to the end of his self-proclaimed moratorium—when he finally allowed me to produce the sketch I entitled "The Empty House", the narrative that detailed Holmes's so-called "hiatus".

Though he had made it quite clear that my account was not to be published for a decade, I stood firm about recording the facts as soon as Holmes reported them to me—that is, in April of '94. Only by noting the details while they were still fresh in my mind, I told him, would I be able to fulfil the role of faithful Boswell that he had attributed to me.

To that end, I maintained a notebook in which I set down the salient features of the Reichenbach affair as soon as Holmes provided them to me. I kept the thin volume in a drawer of the writing desk in our sitting room, and it was the purloining of the notebook in question that placed me in the predicament to which I referred at the start of this narrative.

I discovered the theft one balmy afternoon in late May. It happened this way. Upon returning from my surgery, I encountered the perfect opportunity to write. There was no Sherlock Holmes to be found, and an hour yet remained before Mrs Hudson would bring up our tea. No sooner had I seated myself, however, than I opened the desk-drawer and discovered that my notebook had gone missing.

I immediately summoned Billy the page. "Has anyone entered our rooms recently when Mr Holmes and I have been out?" I asked him.

"Why, um, yeh, Doctor," said the boy, tugging self-consciously at his burgundy tunic. "Funny you should ask."

"And why is that?"

Billy shifted uneasily from foot to foot. "Some bloke, a young fellow 'e was and very short, come in yesterday with a bucket and sponge—said 'e was 'ere to wash the windows."

"And you," I charged in disbelief, "let him in without so much as a 'by your leave'?"

Billy blushed, unable to conceal his miscalculation. "Mrs H was out, Doctor, so I couldn't ask no one about the fella's story. Both you and Mr 'olmes was gone; and, strange enough, the chap sounded like an educated fellow. I reckoned no 'arm could be done, so I opened your door for 'im. You know 'ow Mrs H allows the police inspectors free run of the place."

"Window cleaners are not Scotland Yard detectives, Billy," said I, shaking my head in annoyance. "You should be aware, young man, that this window cleaner took an important notebook that belonged to me."

Rather than apologizing for his blunder, Billy raised a forefinger and said, "Do you know, Doctor, I thought something seemed a bit dodgy about 'im—besides 'is posh speech."

"And why is that?" I said, my voice tinged with irritation.

"Because 'e 'aint been in 'ere but five minutes, and then out 'e rushed, bucket in 'and, saying 'ow 'e forgot 'is soap, and just like that 'e runs out the front door."

Now that Billy mentioned it, the begrimed windows looked no different from the day before. The strange behaviour of the window cleaner certainly seemed to confirm the intruder's guilt.

Whilst I could not let Billy leave without admonishing him for his poor judgement, I also found myself thanking him for offering so straightforward an admission. Only after the lad had gone did I stop to consider the peculiarity of the theft. Nothing else seemed missing, and I had no clue concerning what vital interest there could be in my simple notes of Holmes's return to London. They contained no secrets.

If the details of Holmes's escape from Moriarty's clutches were not already public knowledge, Holmes's reappearance in the fight against London's criminal class most certainly was. How could it not be? Elsewhere I have noted the many cases he tackled in 1894, and his presence was obviously known to all the participants in each of those investigations. One need not be a Yarder to understand that word travels quickly among the denizens of London's underworld when it comes to matters of survival.

Holmes himself returned in time for tea, and I related to him the mystery involving my notes.

"Curious, Watson," said he, cocking an eyebrow. "But 'tis no great matter. Disturbing as it is to be the victim of a minor crime, no major harm can come from missing the notes of my reappearance. I shall merely repeat the details for you, and you may take them down again. Fear not. I have no doubt that with the passage of time your little puzzle will be solved."

Although we did not know it that afternoon as we sat sampling Mrs Hudson's tea and biscuits, the solution to that so-called "little puzzle" was destined to appear much sooner and with greater implications than we ever could have imagined.

*****

It was a week to the day since I had discovered the thievery in our sitting room, and I had almost succeeded in pushing the matter out of mind. Having questioned Holmes about his escape from

Moriarty once more and recorded for a second time the facts required to complete a satisfactory account of his actions in Switzerland, I no longer had the need to dwell upon what I had come to call "The Singular Case of the Missing Notebook". That morning, in fact, along with the breakfast dishes and the coffee, Billy presented a letter that had been left for Holmes. Such communications usually suggested new cases, and thus I felt doubly certain that more weighty issues would replace my concern over a loss that no longer mattered.

"Brought in early this morning by a footman in livery, sir," said Billy on his way out the door.

My friend examined the envelope with its thick-stock paper, overly large monogram, and red-wax seal.

"Someone important," said he with a wry chuckle, "or at least someone who thinks he is." Holmes broke the seal and quickly scanned the letter. "Note the shaky hand in contrast to the firmest of tones," he said as he pushed the paper in my direction. It was dated that morning at Windstone Hall, Gloucestershire.

Dear Mr Holmes [it read],

I shall meet with you this morning at 11.00 in your rooms. It is of the utmost urgency, and I must insist that you cancel any other plans you might have.

It was signed, *"Sir Lionel Smith-Mortimer, Bart".*

"Watson," Holmes said over the rim of his coffee cup, "The *Who's Who?* if you please."

I gulped down a piece of toast and rose to fetch A.C. Black's familiar listing of influential people. It took but a moment to locate the book with its dark-blue boards and gold-lettered spine. I thumbed the pages, found the appropriate entry, and handed the open volume to Holmes.

Sipping his coffee, he read the passage quickly and summarised the salient features for me: "Lionel Smith-Mortimer, Baronet. Born 1822. One son named Leigh. Wife died in childbirth. In addition to an inherited title and fortune, he is the owner of Windstone Hall, a manor house in Oxfordshire. He—"

"Wait a moment, Holmes!" I cried. "I remember reading something about the son called Leigh just yesterday in the *Times*—a rather tragic piece about a suicide, as I recall." I retrieved the newspaper from the small pile of spent dailies residing on a nearby table. It took me but a moment to locate the report. "Here!" said I, pointing to the story. It was indeed a melancholy announcement—"Death of Baronet's Son"—so sad an account that I had not gone on to read the details. Had I done so, I would certainly have called them to my friend's attention.

"Holmes," said I after quickly reviewing the piece, "it says that the young man died in the Falls of Reichenbach."

Sherlock Holmes put down his cup and stared at me with his steel-grey eyes.

"'The coat of the deceased,'" I read aloud, "'was discovered neatly folded on the path above the falls. His footprints along the path led to the edge of the precipice above the water—a drop of more than eight hundred feet. His body has yet to be recovered.'"

I laid down the paper and looked at my friend. If I did not know better, I could have sworn that the slightly upturned corners of Holmes's mouth displayed a hint of amusement.

"I returned from death but a month ago," said Holmes, "and already I seem to have created imitators." He looked at our mantel clock. "Come. It is almost eleven; and unless my ears are very much mistaken, a pair of disciplined horses are pulling a four-wheeler to the kerb. We should prepare to meet our distinguished guest."

Sherlock Holmes exchanged his mouse-coloured dressing gown for a dark jacket, and I proceeded to don my coat. It was a matter of minutes before Mrs Hudson herself climbed the stairs to introduce our guest. No page-boys for the likes of a Baronet.

"Enter!" Sherlock Holmes commanded at her knock.

Mrs Hudson opened the door and stood at the portal. "Sir Lionel Smith-Mortimer," she announced. Then bowing her head, she straightened her skirt, backed out into the hallway, and closed the door.

I must say that whilst I knew this Baronet to be a septuagenarian, I nonetheless expected to behold someone of erect and noble bearing. Instead, I saw before us a scowling old man with a stoop to his back and a hand curled like a great claw over the round, silver head of his walking stick. With a nod to fashion, he wore an expertly tailored suit, its dark frock coat contrasting with his yellowing white hair. Patent leather boots complemented his attire.

"Sir Lionel," said my friend, "I am Sherlock Holmes." He introduced me as well and gestured towards the armchair Holmes reserved for his clients.

The Baronet gave a quick frown in my direction and then with some effort shuffled to the proffered seat, and sat down. Holmes and I took chairs opposite him.

"Let me first say, sir," announced the elderly client with a thump of his stick, "that I don't fancy being here one bit." He rapped his stick on the floor a second time to punctuate his point. "Only because of Leigh's faith in you have I come at all."

Holmes stared at the man, offering no discernible response.

"Without doubt you have seen the reports of my son's accident."

We both nodded respectfully.

"Simply put, I don't believe them. I want to know what really happened. All I do know is that he was wandering about in Switzerland with a friend."

"A friend?" Holmes asked.

"Yes. One Reginald Bentley. A barrister by profession. Known each other for about a year. Bentley and my son travel together when the opportunity presents itself. London not good enough for them. They want to see the world."

"And where was this Bentley at the time of your son's death?" Holmes asked.

"*Alleged* death, may I remind you. He remained at the hotel near the Reichenbach Falls, don't you know."

"At the *Englischer Hof*?" I asked. Noting the similarity to our own ill-fated trip three years before, I guessed the two men might have stayed in the same hotel Holmes and I had occupied.

As if he believed I possessed too much arcane information, Sir Lionel knit his brow. But all he said was, "By Jove, when I hear of a mysterious death and no corpse is produced, I have my doubts. You may think I sound like some suspicious figure in one of your adventures, Holmes, but that may be in part because of the interest that Leigh expressed in reading about them."

"I appreciate the kind words, Sir Lionel," said Holmes, ignoring the fact that the compliment might better have been directed at the author of those adventures. "But under the circumstances," Holmes went on, "one cannot escape an uncomfortable conclusion.

The apparent death of your son mirrors—however imprecisely—my own rumoured demise. Given the fact that I myself have only just returned from that narrow escape, one has to marvel at the coincidence."

"Quite," muttered Sir Lionel.

It was at that moment that the thought of my missing notes popped back into my head. The young man posing as a window cleaner whom Billy had observed, the one with an educated manner of speech—might he be none other than Leigh Smith-Mortimer whose father now sat before us? Recreating the death of Sherlock Holmes, someone he admired, could have been his morbid motivation. Perhaps Leigh Smith-Mortimer had sought to end his brief life in dramatic fashion not unlike the storied suicide of the Romantic poet Thomas Chatterton who succumbed to arsenic at the age of seventeen.

"I must confess," said Holmes, "that the role of my personal history in this situation adds impetus to my curiosity. I too would like to know what happened to your son, Sir Lionel. I shall take your case."

The Baronet withdrew a wallet of light-coloured leather from inside his jacket. "Name your fee, Holmes," said he.

"Later," my friend replied. "All my clients pay at the same rate, Sir Lionel. But concerning this case in particular, its proper resolution will furnish me with additional reward."

The Baronet gazed at his wallet. "I almost forgot," said he, extracting a photograph and a small card from the billfold. "My son and Bentley," he explained in reference to the photograph, "inseparable friends. The card contains information about Bentley's chambers in Gray's Inn."

Holmes took the items, examined them briefly, and handed them to me. In the photograph, two serious-looking young men in straw boaters—the taller one with a moustache, the shorter, clean-shaven—stared back."

"Leigh is the one without the whiskers," said Sir Lionel as, using his stick as a brace, he struggled to rise. "As for Bentley, he works at Mapplethorpe and Ruggles, and I have already prepared him for your visit at 2.00 this afternoon. He awaits you in Gray's Inn Gardens."

"That gives us a half hour," said Holmes in spite of the old man's presumptuousness. "We must leave poste haste," he added, ushering Sir Lionel to the door.

But the Baronet had more to say and stopped to address my friend. "This matter is of great importance to me, Holmes. In addition to the welfare of my son, I feel compelled to point out that he is my only issue. He arrived late in my life, and his mother died tragically during his birth. It was quite horrible really. The babe chose to appear when Lady Smith-Mortimer and I were vacationing in the mountains near Lake Windermere. It was all so sudden. We were alone in the woods, and I had to deliver the child myself as my wife lay dying."

"Horrible," I said.

Sir Lionel ignored my response. "What's more," he added, standing up as straight as seemed possible for him, "neither can I neglect the deposition of my estate."

"It is entailed?" Holmes asked.

"Indeed. All I possess will be inherited by my closest male heir. If Leigh is truly no longer living, then Windstone Hall will be dealt off to some distant cousin in Canada. That is why it is imperative that I find out what happened to my son."

"Understood," said Holmes. "I will report to you as soon as I learn anything."

We listened as Sir Lionel made his way down the seventeen steps, his walking stick producing a distinctive thump on each one.

I heard the latch of the carriage door and then the clatter of the wheels as Sir Lionel's four-wheeler drove off down Baker Street.

"Come, Watson," said Holmes, already moving towards the door. "We shall begin this investigation with our pre-arranged interview of Mr Reginald Bentley, Esquire, the travelling companion of Leigh Smith-Mortimer."

*****

We flagged a hansom at our front door and were soon rattling along Oxford Street. Southampton Row brought us to High Holborn and the Inns of Court, the legal centre of London. We alighted at the wood-panelled frontage of the Cittie of Yorke public house that stands at the narrow alleyway leading to Gray's Inn. Entering the grounds through the main gate, we passed the South Square to our right and made our way under the archway leading to the green swards of the Walks, as the spacious Gray's Inn Gardens are more commonly called.

It had just gone 2.00, and under the afternoon sun we walked quickly along the gravel path enveloped by the iridescent colours and sweet aromas of the season. Spring seems so wrong a time to hold discussions of death—especially among the yellow daffodils and blue hyacinths and roses of pink and white and red attempting to distract us. After a few additional paces, however, we recognised the moustachioed chap from the photograph seated on a nearby bench.

Reginald Bentley was sitting in the shade of the London-planes and elms that populated the Walks, and he rose upon our arrival. "Gentlemen," said he, "Thank you for agreeing to see me outside of chambers. This tragedy is no one's business but our own." He pointed to a low-slung block of yellow-brick offices across the lawn. "Besides, Mapplethorpe and Ruggles have suffered the confinement of the Raymond Buildings over there since the early years of the century. I appreciate the moments I can spend away from my desk. As you must already know, Leigh and I always enjoyed our walks through the countryside."

"Which leads us to the Falls of Reichenbach," said Holmes. "As I understand it, your friend seemed intrigued by my personal history—so much so that he literally walked in my very footsteps. How does one account for this obsessive interest?"

"Let us sit," said Bentley, gesturing towards the bench. "Justice was paramount for Leigh," he explained once we were settled. "I should imagine his concern was based upon his own sense of victimhood."

"Victimhood?" I echoed, imagining the rich surroundings of Windstone Hall in which the boy had grown up. "In what way?"

"I know what you're thinking, Dr Watson—the money that must have smothered Leigh when he was a child. But, you see, it was that very legacy that constantly weighed him down. His father had made it clear to Leigh that he had to marry and have sons to carry on the line—you know, gentlemen, the usual upper-class prattle."

"You don't approve of the British aristocracy?" I could not refrain from asking.

"Look," he said, "my own father is a banker and fortunately for me was able to send me to university. I have benefitted greatly from my education. After all, here I sit, installed in the legal profession and quite able to pay my own bills."

"Rather proves my point, eh?" I said.

"Within reason, Doctor. I don't believe one should be forced to live the life one's father confers upon him however much money that involves if that is not the life one chooses for himself."

The young man may have had a valid point for the common fellow, but one cannot allow the upper classes to make such choices. Where would we be if the heirs to the throne could choose willy-nilly whether they wanted to be king? One could scarcely imagine a royal monarch giving up the crown to marry a commoner! Of course, such dilemmas did not concern a mere medical man like myself—not that sort of money in my family, I am afraid.

Holmes brought the conversation back to practicalities. "Tell me about this trip the two of you took to Switzerland."

Bentley patted down his moustache. "When Sir Lionel notified me that you'd be coming to talk about Leigh, I assumed you would ask about that final journey." He withdrew a map from an inner pocket and, unfolding it, proceeded to lay the sheet flat on the bench between Holmes and himself. "Leigh invited me to join him with the understanding that I would follow his instructions without questioning them. He told me he had a plan, and I agreed to go along."

Sherlock Holmes studied the chart, his eyes flashing as he noted the familiar route now coloured in red.

"I took the liberty to mark our course," said Bentley. "It was a singular excursion." As the young man spoke, he traced the progress of their trip with his forefinger. "We boarded the *Continental Express* here at Victoria. I had originally thought we would cross the Channel at Dover and sail the twenty-two miles to Calais, but Leigh had other plans. He insisted we change trains at Canterbury for the run to Newhaven, a decision that caused us to switch twice more at Ashford and Lewes. When I asked him why, he answered with your name, Mr Holmes."

"Quite so," Holmes nodded. "Pray, continue."

"I'm sure you yourself can supply the details. At Newhaven, we sailed to Dieppe,"—here Bentley's finger on the map slid across the blue of the Channel—"a crossing, I might add, three times the duration of the crossing at Dover. From Dieppe we travelled by train to Brussels and then on to Strasbourg and Geneva. Following a week's walk through the Rhone Valley, we made our way to Leuk, climbed the Gemmi Pass in the Central Alps, and finally arrived just a short distance from the Reichenbach Falls in a town called Meiringen. We stayed in the *Englischer Hof* run by—"

"Let me guess," I interrupted, "Peter Steiler the elder."

"Correct, Dr Watson. But from what I understand, you and Mr Holmes stayed in the same hotel."

"Quite so," said Holmes again. Then he added vaguely, "It was all done for professional reasons."

Leigh Smith-Mortimer may have stolen my notes concerning the geographical route Holmes and I had taken to Meiringen, but obviously Holmes still wanted to conceal the details connected with the criminal activities of Professor Moriarty and his associate Colonel Moran.

"To be sure, gentlemen, we had travelled a great distance in a roundabout fashion; and yet we finally did reach our destination, and so I could fathom no reason to suddenly start doubting my friend's sanity. Thus, when early the next morning Leigh told me he wished to go alone to view the Reichenbach Falls, I acquiesced. It was the last time I would ever see him." Here Reginald Bentley hung his head. Had I been less sympathetic, I might have regarded it as an altogether too theatrical a pose.

"And then?" Holmes asked. "No doubt you alerted the police."

"When Leigh failed to return, I myself walked up to the Falls—ran, really."

I nodded with appreciation. Had I not made the same fateful run under the most similar of conditions?

"That," Bentley resumed, "was when I found Leigh's folded jacket and tweed cap lying at the end of the small path leading to the rushing waters. Once I saw those personal items, I suspected that something was truly wrong, and I summoned the police. We all returned to the scene, and they examined the footmarks leading to the edge and not returning. Alas, there was but one sad conclusion to draw—that Leigh had thrown himself from the precipice, his body disappearing in the churning waters below."

Holmes arched his eyebrows. "It would certainly seem so," said he. "Did you detect anything in Leigh's nature that would lead you to imagine he could perform such an act?"

Sighing heavily, Bentley stared up into the cloudless blue sky. Perhaps he was hoping to find an answer somewhere in the heavens. "I can only tell you that he hated the role his father had placed him in. But I assure you, gentlemen, that I never suspected that Leigh was unhappy enough to do himself in. There's really not much else I have to say on the subject—except that I miss my friend greatly."

Holmes stood up. "Thank you, Mr Bentley. You've been a great help to us."

The barrister collected his map and gently folded it along the creases. Replacing it in his coat pocket, he shook hands with the two of us and wished us well. We accompanied him as far as his chambers and then bade him good day.

"Do you realise, Watson," said Holmes once we reached High Holborn, "that thanks to Mr Bentley—not to mention the dead Mr Smith-Mortimer—we are going to have to return to the scene of some of our most unpleasant memories?" When he raised his hand to flag a hansom, he bore the gravest of expressions.

*****

Unlike our first trip to the Reichenbach Falls, we required no subterfuge on this occasion. We faced no adversary like Moriarty in his special train to fool into thinking we were going to Paris. The *Express* from Victoria took us directly to Dover. From there, a ship conveyed us to Calais. With no need to pose as carefree pedestrians touring the Valley of the Rhone or exploring the Alps of central Switzerland, we utilised the various railroads traversing the French and Swiss countrysides to deposit us at the chalet-like train station in Meiringen.

Holmes and I may not have looked like the tourists we had hoped to resemble three years before, but even on that earlier occasion we had no cause to conceal our true identities. When we reached the *Englischer Hof*, therefore, old Peter Steiler greeted Holmes in particular like an old friend.

"*Ach*, Herr Holmes," said Steiler, his English helped by an earlier stay in London, "it is as though you come from the dead. I heard of your return and am pleased to know that you did not die in the Reichenbach waters."

"And yet someone else just did, *nicht wahr*?" Holmes asked.

"*Ja,*" answered Steiler. "A young Englishman. Like you, from here he went walking on his own."

"It is his death, Herr Steiler, that we are here to investigate. How was he dressed?"

The old man thought for a moment, then smiled broadly as he remembered the details. "Heavy trousers. Heavy coat. Good boots. Flat cap."

Holmes nodded. "Nothing else?"

"But of course," said Steiler, "*schon vergessen.* A large rucksack he carried on his back."

"Ha!" cried Holmes, slapping his hand on the counter. "Precisely as I expected. Come, Watson. We shall soon get to the bottom of this mystery."

Snow-covered mountain peaks served as backdrop when for the second time in our adventures Holmes and I marched up the incline towards the series of falls. From the bottom of the road one cannot see the water itself, only the winding trail leading up and past the three mighty torrents that ultimately rain down as one. It took us some ten minutes to reach the lowest of the falls, an additional fifteen to reach the central, and another thirty to get to the uppermost.

Veiled in the shadows of the numerous fir trees, we plodded upward. Holmes kept his eyes on the ground searching for any tell-tale clues. For me, however, the path served only to conjure terrible memories. During that first ascent three years before, I had been called back to the hotel on a ruse; and I shall never forget the horrible fear I experienced when I rushed back up this same mountain trail hoping against hope that my friend still lived.

Now as then, the fearsome roar of the waterfall attracted us like a magnet. Skirting the ominous rock walls that towered above, I followed after Holmes in the direction of the thunderous din. To witness the waters cascade in waves of white foam down the glistening black walls of stone and plunge into the cavernous abyss is to see unmasked the overwhelming power and beauty of Nature.

Yet once we reached the narrow path leading to the edge of the final precipice, my morbid recollections eclipsed the grandeur. A wave of nausea overcame me as soon as I encountered the very boulder against which Holmes had leaned his Alpine stock and upon which he had left his farewell note. Enveloped by the clouds of mist and spray that hovered above the roiling waters, I forced myself to halt at a safe distance from the brink. The world around me was beginning to spin. With the mountain wall on one side and the straight drop a short distance before me, I placed my palm against the wet stone and took a series of deep breaths.

Holmes, who was stooping over a handful of black soil a few steps ahead, looked back over his shoulder and saw my condition. Whether my unsettled appearance affected his judgement, I shall never know, but with a quick shake of his head, he shouted at me over the water's roar, "No need to go any farther!" Then he gave the dirt in his hand a final peremptory look and tossed the stuff to the ground. "The path is of no use to us," said he loudly, slapping his hands together to rid them of any residual muck. "It's too moist, and too many footprints have already marred the trail. I should imagine that the authorities themselves have stomped across it and obliterated whatever clues we might have hoped to find."

"Are we done here, then?" I shouted back hopefully.

In answer, Holmes looked up at the sheer mountain wall by our side. "Do you see it, Watson?" he asked, pointing to a projection some twenty feet above our heads. "The ledge that shielded me when you brought the police here to examine the scene."

So long ago, and yet the memory of my exclusion from his plan still stings. I imagine that I will always harbour some resentment towards Holmes for letting me continue to think him dead. It was only the ultimate jubilation I experienced upon his return that alleviated the pain.

"We need another point of vantage," said he; and keeping his eye on the wall to our left, he proceeded to march back in the direction from which we had come. Though each step away from the edge helped restore my strength, I suddenly feared Holmes was searching for the invisible footholds he had employed in his earlier escape in order to scale the wall once again. At the point where the wall fell away, however, he stopped and, turning to his left once more, stared at a network of overgrown brambles and ferns.

"Aha!" he cried out at last and roughly pushed aside the overgrowth.

In an instant I perceived a hidden pathway ascending round the back of the mountain, and together Holmes and I scrambled up the steep terrain. Only when we reached a small plateau did I realise that we must be at the same spot where Colonel Moran had watched the struggle between Moriarty and Holmes unfold. It would have been here that Moran, intent on completing the job that Moriarty had thankfully been unable to consummate, rained down upon Holmes a shower of large rocks and stones.

Today, of course, there were no such dangers. In spite of the tumble of tree branches that blocked a part of the view, we could now readily discern some twenty yards beneath us the rectangular outcropping that had served as Holmes's hiding place. The ledge was several feet deep; and verdant moss, like a green wool rug, blanketed the small nooks and crannies of its stone floor.

From an inner pocket, Sherlock Holmes drew a pair of binoculars, which he trained on the area below. "Owing to the proximity of the Falls," he observed as he peered through the lenses, "the moss-bed remains continuously moist. I can assure you from experience that not only does it provide a comfortable nest, but it also retains footmarks exceedingly well."

For a few moments more he proceeded to scan the ledge. "*Eureka!*" he suddenly shouted and, handing me the glasses, commanded, "Look for yourself."

I adjusted the lenses and observed the patterns in the moss more closely. Where before I had seen only gentle folds, I now made out among the rear shadows a long indentation where a body had recently lain. I could also begin to distinguish a few scattered footprints. At one edge of the projection, I detected what appeared to be the broad marks of a man's boots. At the other edge—

"Hold on," I said to Holmes. "Are those not the footprints of a woman's shoe?"

"Precisely what I expected," said Holmes, clapping his hands together.

"But what can such footprints mean? For that matter, Holmes, what does any of it mean?"

"To London, Watson," said he by way of answer. Motioning me to follow, he hurried along the downhill trail, his eyes focused on the path before him. Thanks to the information furnished by the binoculars, we now knew for what to look. And truth be told, clearly discernable along the way were the occasional woman's footprints mingling with all the other marks that had churned up much of the earth.

"We have learned all that we could hope for here in Switzerland," proclaimed Sherlock Holmes. "It is now time to reacquaint ourselves with Mr Reginald Bentley."

*****

Amberwell House, a modest building of soot-darkened stone, can be found in Southampton Row between Russell Square and Theobalds Road. Thanks to its proximity to the Inns of Court, the establishment provides lodgings for many of the solicitors and barristers who work nearby. Two days after our return from the Continent, Reginald Bentley suggested the Amberwell in response to our request to speak with him.

"Amberwell House at the end of my workday," he had wired back.

As he led us to a group of grey-leather-backed chairs in the corner of the small lobby, the moustached barrister seemed ill at ease. He continually looked round although, except for the clerk at the front desk and a man across the way hidden behind a newspaper, the lobby was deserted.

"We have just returned from the Reichenbach Falls, " Holmes began. "Let us get straight to the point, shall we?"

Avoiding Holmes's gaze, Bentley fidgeted with the cuffs of his jacket. "I don't know what you mean," he mumbled.

"We believe that your friend, Mr Leigh Smith-Mortimer, stole Dr Watson's notes that dealt with my near-death experience three years ago in Switzerland. As you previously confirmed with the map you showed us, just a few days later, you accompanied him in the re-creation of our previous trip. You alleged that he left you in your room at the *Englischer Hof* in order to go walking on his own. Further, you maintain that he never returned—that he fell, or hurled himself, to the bottom of the Falls."

"As I have already said."

"Then, sir," came Holmes's blunt reply, "not to put too fine a point on it, I do not believe you."

Bentley's eyes grew wide. He was about to sputter out some retort, but Holmes kept speaking.

"Oh, I do not doubt that Smith-Mortimer went off to the Falls on his own, but I must conclude that you knew of his plans from the start—that, in fact, the two of you conspired to make it appear that Leigh Smith-Mortimer had leaped to his death never to be heard from again."

"Now, see here, Mr Holmes," Bentley countered, "I won't have you disparage Leigh that way, not to mention myself. Do you not remember that it was I who notified the police?"

"And yet, Mr Bentley, it was also you who failed to inform them that the presumed-dead Smith-Mortimer was in reality hiding on the ledge not twenty feet above them when they investigated the scene. You must admit, sir, that—" But Holmes never finished the sentence.

"Enough!" came the forceful, high-pitched voice of the man whom I supposed to have been reading the newspaper. He slammed the pages to the floor and stalked over to us. "Leave Reginald alone, Mr Holmes. *I* am the one you seek. I am Leigh Smith-Mortimer."

Holmes and I both stared up at the man—though, in truth, not very far up. From his photograph, we knew him to be shorter than his friend. But in the flesh, his entire stature appeared much slighter in spite of the Saville Row cut of his dark suit. His face bore delicate features, and his dark hair was trimmed short.

Reginald Bentley offered him his own seat while Bentley himself collected the chair that Smith-Mortimer had just been occupying.

"Well, well," Holmes said with a quick smile. "The very man we speak of. He who has dogged my footsteps to death's door at the Reichenbach Falls appears very much alive. What do you have to say for yourself, *sir*?" This last word was heavily emphasised, and at the same time there appeared in my friend's eye the same inexplicable twinkle that I had seen when he had first heard the details of the young man's disappearance.

"Reginald has told me," Leigh Smith-Mortimer replied, "that you already know how much I detest my father and his domination—all in the name of his legacy. A plague on that legacy! I tell you, Mr Holmes, that I could take it no longer. I wanted a means of escape.

I've read of your investigations; and when I heard of your so-called death and resurrection, it gave me the idea to do the same.

"Your return being so recent, I assumed that Dr Watson would have his notes concerning the affair lying about. As you have surmised, I entered your rooms in disguise and stole his notebook. Reginald and I then followed all of your steps to be certain we didn't miss any of the planning that led to your success."

"Stealing my notes," I muttered. "Not very sporting."

"I'm sorry, Doctor, but your notebook furnished me with the kind of details I needed—like the footholds leading to the ledge above the path. As you did, Mr Holmes, I hid there from the police during their investigation; and when they had gone, I made my way back to London. Under a pseudonym, I took a room here at the Amberwell down the hall from Reginald. Now, I suppose, you will notify my father, and he will attempt to have me return to Windstone Hall."

"Your father is my client," said Holmes. "He has contracted me to find you. And yet, should I so choose, a rejection of his money would rid me of the responsibility."

The young man's eyes suddenly blazed with hope. "You'd do that, Mr Holmes?"

"I assure you, Mr Smith-Mortimer, that in the name of fair play, I have committed a number of unconventional actions. I am no official police force, you understand. But I must give your situation some thought. I don't overturn my clients' requests lightly. And whilst there is no law that will force you to go back to your father, the law of decency makes it imperative for me to let him know that you are alive and well. I suggest that we meet at Baker Street tomorrow afternoon. I shall send you a telegram once I have arranged the matter with Sir Lionel."

With that Holmes rose, and I followed. As we exited the Amberwell, I could not fail to notice that behind us an animated discussion was going on between the two young men.

*****

"Well, Watson, what do you make of the situation?" Holmes asked once we had found ourselves in Southampton Row again and walking towards the Strand.

"I believe that you were quite right in reserving additional time to consider your responsibilities. Still, I must say that there seems no let up in young Smith-Mortimer's grudge against his father. Unreasonable, I should think—in light of the rules that dictate the responsibilities of a titled son."

Sherlock Holmes stopped in his tracks. "Good old Watson—forever faithful to the traditions of our culture. And yet you miss the salient feature."

I could not see where Holmes was leading me. The antagonisms between father and son seemed quite clear.

"My dear fellow," said Holmes. "You have failed to recognise the fact that Mr Leigh Smith-Mortimer—'the titled son', as you call him—is in reality no son at all. He is, in fact, a woman."

Even I, the so-called man of words, was speechless. At last I spat out, "You—you can't be serious, Holmes."

"But I am, old fellow. Of course, you noted the delicate features, the smooth chin, the short but luxuriant hair, the small frame, the lilting voice."

"Yes, all of which proves nothing."

"But when you couple those decidedly feminine characteristics with a masculine life dictated by the unforgiving laws of primogeniture, you discover a wretched soul forced to play a part counter to her nature."

"But, Holmes. Surely birth certificates, doctors' statements—all would discount your inflammatory charges."

"Remember the birth, Watson. The couple were alone wandering the woods. Who knows? Perhaps Sir Lionel had purposely arranged their isolated perambulations to coincide with the time the birth was expected. Fortunately, he himself managed to deliver the child; but unhappily, he could do nothing regarding the complications that killed Lady Smith-Mortimer. Clearly, there would be no more children. I imagine that in the confusion that followed, the doctors devoted their attention to saving the poor mother and simply taken Sir Reginald's word for the sex of the baby. Money paid out to wet-nurses and nannies would have purchased the silence of any others who knew the truth."

Such a wild plan certainly explained Holmes's fantastic accusation.

"I suspected some sort of ruse," said he, "as soon as Sir Lionel began complaining so bitterly about his son. I thought the old man protested too much. Upon observing the young person, I am now convinced."

"But the pretend suicide, Holmes, the climb up the mountain to the ledge. Surely, no *woman* could be expected to perform such feats!"

"Ah, Watson," Holmes smiled, "how did Hamlet put it to Horatio? 'There are more things in heaven and earth than are dreamt of in your philosophy.' I find women quite as capable as men in accomplishing whatever they put their mind to." He turned silent, and I knew he must have been thinking of the machinations set up by Irene Adler a few years before that had succeeded in thwarting Holmes himself.

"But what's the point?" I asked breaking into his thoughts. "Even if Sir Reginald had succeeded in passing the girl off as a boy, there could be no children in her future, no male heir to claim the estate."

"A crazed old man trying to hold on to what is his for as long as possible," Holmes offered. He grew silent again. In fact, the only words he uttered after we had reached Aldwych, were, "Let us continue on to Simpson's. Afterwards, I shall make arrangements with Sir Lionel for tomorrow's meeting."

With the late-afternoon sun in our faces, we negotiated the Aldwych crescent, the walls of the buildings we passed casting shadows along the curve. I remember thinking at the time how well those shadows epitomised the case. Whatever had been going on in the mind of Sir Lionel Smith-Mortimer for the past twenty years must have been very murky indeed.

*****

Mrs Hudson had prepared tea for five people as we had requested. The stooped form of Sir Lionel arrived first, his trek up our stairs again punctuated by the beat of his cane. He looked at the tea service and chocolate biscuits set out on the dining table, shook his head, and selected an armchair to sit upon that was far removed from the table.

"Tell me your news, Holmes," he demanded.

"In due time, sir. We await the others."

"What others?"

As if in answer, a sharp knock rattled our door. Holmes opened it to Reginald Bentley. The barrister entered the room, but not by himself. He was accompanied by a magnificent young woman in a dress of yellow cotton, accented in white at the neck and cuffs. Adorned with a white feather, a small yellow hat was perched coquettishly upon her short black curls. It nearly took my breath away to realise that only the day before I had been conversing with this very person under the impression that I was speaking to one Leigh Smith-Mortimer, the only son of a Baronet.

"Watson," said Holmes with a gesture towards the lady, "may I re-introduce you to Leigh Smith-Mortimer. That is, *Miss* Leigh Smith-Mortimer.

"Now see here!" interrupted Sir Lionel. "I won't stand for this *charade*."

Miss Smith-Mortimer had been about to take my hand when she wheeled upon her father. "*You* won't stand for this *charade*?" she charged, cheeks reddening, nostrils flaring. "I've been play-acting in your little game for as long as I can remember. Always the boy—to preserve the line! Even though you've always known that the line would end with me. You knew I could never marry as a man. And now I have found someone who has seen through this masquerade and wants to love me as a woman should be loved. I am through with your game, Father. May Windstone Hall crumble to the earth for all I care!"

"Leigh," Sir Lionel said, holding out both hands. "After your mother died and there was no possibility for a male heir—"

"Stop, Father!" she cried. "I have heard all this nonsense before. Let the succession fall to cousins twice-removed—or *three*-times removed. I don't care! It doesn't matter any more. You robbed me of my proper childhood, and I won't allow you to rob me of my marriage." She turned to Bentley. "That is," she said, her voice now lowered, "if you'll have me."

Reginald Bentley took her in his arms. "I love you, Leigh. Your beautiful nature has always shone through your disguise. We did our best to kill off the male version of yourself; and now, thanks to Mr Holmes, you've been able to speak the truth."

The young woman stood as tall as she could. "I am leaving you now, Father," she said simply. "As you've just heard, Reginald and I will soon be married. Good man that he is, he has convinced me to invite you to the wedding. It is your choice whether you want to gain a daughter and, God willing, grandchildren or live on in isolation. The choice will be yours."

Before leaving, the couple turned to Holmes and me. "Thank you, gentlemen," said Bentley. "At first I feared you might bring ruination upon us, but now I see that shining a light on this bizarre story has instead brought us salvation." The two of them smiled and hand in hand slowly made their way down the stairs.

With a dissatisfied grunt, Sir Lionel leaned on his cane in order to stand. He took a deep breath and, without looking at either Holmes or me, placed a one-hundred-pound note on the table as he shuffled to the door.

No one uttered a word. Once the door closed, I walked to the table set for tea and sampled one of Mrs Hudson's chocolate biscuits.

*****

Reginald Bentley had relatives who lived in the hamlet of Icomb in Gloucestershire It was there in the tiny church of St. Mary the Virgin a few short weeks after the events described that he and Leigh Smith-Mortimer chose to marry. Holmes and I were invited to the ceremony, but we decided not to attend. It was to be a small affair, and our presence would only serve to raise uncomfortable questions. Happily, there were no pressmen in attendance, and Miss Smith-Mortimer sent us an account in her own hand of all that had transpired.

True to her word, she did request her father's presence. And I am pleased to report that, difficult as it was for the old man both physically and emotionally, Sir Lionel travelled to Gloucestershire to give his daughter away. Villagers must have wondered about the splendid carriage and liveried footman at so simple a ceremony, but their wonder never reached the spiteful arena of London gossip—at least not then.

It would take three years and the death of Sir Lionel for the facts regarding his mistreatment of his daughter to become the fodder of scandal throughout the land. Just as the Baronet had predicted, with no son to inherit the estate, the grand manor house along with the rest of the riches was passed on by virtue of entailment to a distant Canadian cousin called Randolph Carlton Smith.

It had been my desire to maintain the privacy of the newly-married couple. To that end, I included the Smith-Mortimer affair in the collection of cases from 1894 that I chose not to make public. Yet however noble in intent, the gesture turned out to be laughably feeble.

Periodicals could not print enough about the story to satisfy the public. Newspapers constantly rehashed the details; magazines furnished long-winded biographies of the principals. So widespread were the accounts of the ugly business that one can understand why I had originally referred to the entailment case as "famous". In retrospect, I believe that "infamous" would have been the more appropriate adjective.

Capitol Murder

For an educated human being to arrange an assassination,
he must have a streak of the monster in him—
even if the man he purposes to be slain
is regarded by him and by multitudes
as an enemy of God and man.

--David Graham Phillips
"The Assassination
of a Governor"
The Cosmopolitan, April 1905

I

I suppose that the appearance of yet another American should not have been surprising. After all, a great many of them have played significant roles in some of the most celebrated adventures of my friend and colleague Mr Sherlock Holmes. Why, our very first investigation together, the case I titled *A Study in Scarlet*, involved the American Jefferson Hope and the Mormons of Utah. And Holmes himself will never forget Miss Irene Adler of New Jersey, the female adversary whose successes earned from him the distinctive accolade of "*the* woman". For that matter, I myself was shot in the leg by one James Winter, the notorious "Killer" Evans from Chicago.

I might also add that my literary agent, Arthur Conan Doyle, who knows a thing or two about successful publishing, has always encouraged me to promote the American angle. "It's good for business, Watson," he constantly reminds me. "Sprinkling your adventures with Americans broadens the market." How else to interpret Sir Arthur's delight upon meeting William Gillette, the American actor famous for depicting Holmes on stage, and who at the time of the encounter was fully dressed in ear-flapped travelling cap and long grey coat?

According to the reports, Gillette approached Sir Arthur with magnifying glass in hand and, after examining him closely, proclaimed, "Unquestionably an author!"

Though it would be a few years before I personally witnessed Gillette's impersonation of Holmes, I was never convinced by it. Not only did I not see the resemblance, but I could also not forget that it was Gillette who popularised for the entire world the inaccurate notion that Holmes smoked a calabash pipe and always donned a deerstalker.

There was simply no need for false *accoutrements*. With so many English trappings already associated with the man—the Baker Street address, the London backdrop, *Bradshaw's Railway Guide* (not to mention his generally stoic nature)—Sherlock Holmes fully epitomised the British character. He required no help from the Americans.

Yet in spite of such misinformation that appeared in the United States, I continue to marvel at the large number of Holmes's investigations that truly did have connections to America. One need only glance at some of our most celebrated adventures to discover just how much of Holmes's career depended upon cases linked to the States.

These cases include (to name but a few): "The Noble Bachelor" featuring the ill-fated marriage of Hattie Doran from San Francisco; "The Problem of Thor Bridge" dealing with a former American Senator; and "The Dancing Men" involving the peculiar stick-figure code employed by American gangsters. Two cases, "The Five Orange Pips" and "The Yellow Face", suggested the pernicious effects of Southern prejudice; and in "His Last Bow", Holmes himself assumed the role of an England-hating Irish-American before the onset of the Great War. One must also not forget two other cases, "The Red Circle" and *The Valley of Fear*, that brought within Holmes's professional circle Agents Leverton and Edwards, a pair of investigators from Pinkerton, the renowned American detective agency.

There is, however, a hitherto unknown investigation linked to this same Birdy Edwards that involves yet a third Pinkerton operator. Though much less dramatic than Edwards's clandestine work in Pennsylvania's Vermissa Valley, equally significant was the simple act he performed in referring a colleague to our Baker Street rooms.

In point of fact, it was this innocent recommendation that led to the conclusion of a political drama containing one of the most cold-blooded operations Holmes ever undertook. The less charitable among us might even say that the adventure I publish here for the first time lays at the feet of the world's first consulting detective the indisputable charge of premeditated murder.

*****

The origins of the ugly business occurred in the middle of a wintry morning in late February of 1900. Holmes and I sat warming ourselves by the fire when Billy the page brought to our rooms a tall, thin, clean-shaven gentleman with a strong, square jawline. He wore a long black coat over a dark suit, white shirt, bowstring tie, and stovepipe trousers. Square-toed Western boots peeked out at the cuff, and his left hand was holding what appeared to be a dark-brown, wide-brimmed Stetson hat with a flattened crown. One did not need to hear him speak to conclude that yet another American was about to make his presence known.

"Wyatt Steele, Mr Holmes," said our visitor, extending his hand. "I'm a Pinkerton agent." His flat intonations confirmed his provenance.

Holmes offered his own hand and then introduced me.

"Glad to meet you, Dr Watson," said Steele, gripping my hand with an air of confidence. He appeared to be in his mid-thirties, and I must admit that he cut quite a figure, every bit the straight-backed American that the Pinkertons had the reputation for hiring.

"I know it was a few years ago, Mr Holmes," he went on, "but if you recall my old pal Birdy Edwards, he was the one who said to look you up if I ever needed help in London. He wrote a quick note to me before he vacated Birlstone Manor. It was right after you investigated a murder there. He didn't sign the letter, but I knew it was from Birdy all the same."

Sherlock Holmes smiled. "I do indeed remember Mr Edwards, a fearless Irishman with a singular mind. Lost at sea a few years back—or so the story runs—presumably, another victim of the late and unlamented Professor Moriarty." The smile waned as he contemplated the destructive power of his former enemy.

"Hold on," said Steele, raising his hat as a kind of stop-sign, "I had no intention of setting off so dark a mood. To tell you the truth," he announced, "I'm actually here on Pinkerton business."

Holmes took the man's hat and coat and hung them on a peg near the still-open door. Then, indicating to our guest a cushioned chair near the fire, he proceeded to shout down the stairwell at the page-boy. "Billy!" he cried. "Ask Mrs Hudson to send up tea—on second thought, make it coffee in honour of our American friend."

I heard a murmur of what sounded like assent from below before Holmes closed the door and joined me in his own armchair opposite our guest.

"Now, Mr Steele," said Holmes, "pray, tell us what sort of Pinkerton business has caused you to seek me out on so miserable a day. Other than the assassination of Kentucky's governor a few weeks ago, I recall no other recent crimes in America that might have caused you to come all this way."

Steele's mouth gaped wide. For a moment, the calm and cool Pinkerton agent seemed to have lost his composure. "Wh—how? How did you know?" he stammered.

I shared his amazement. Holmes's words were the first I had heard of any such affair.

"The newspapers provide all sorts of information," he said with the wave of his hand. "And when it comes to more vital issues of state, my brother Mycroft also keeps me informed."

"However you've come by the news, Mr Holmes, you're quite correct. I am indeed on the trail of the killer of William Goebel, the short-lived governor of Kentucky. He was shot in Frankfort, the state's capital; and I have good reason to believe his assassin has come to London. But then you seem to know much of this already."

"I make it my business to keep abreast of a variety of crimes, Mr Steele, though I must confess that political assassinations generally fail to interest me. They're too prosaic. One politician doesn't like another and—bang!" Holmes pointed his long index finger like a gun at Steele and pretended to fire. "Motives are obvious, and means are generally unimaginative. Not much to hold my attention, I'm afraid. This case, however, features some curious echoes."

I had participated in most of Holmes's investigations, yet I remained at a loss regarding the so-called "echoes" to which he alluded.

"Allow me to tell you what I know about the case," offered Steele. "Perhaps we might then combine our knowledge and reach some sort of conclusion. It's the sort of thing Birdy said you were so good at."

Just then Mrs Hudson arrived with Billy in tow. He was holding a tray with her silver service and a few biscuits neatly arranged on a large plate. Mrs Hudson herself placed the fixings on the low table near our guest, filled our cups with coffee, observed that all was in order, and only then—with a brief dip of her head—fairly pushed Billy out the door ahead of her.

Whilst we listened to the two of them thumping down the stairs, Holmes leaned forward to sample the coffee. Finding it to his satisfaction, he placed his cup back on its saucer and turned to our guest. "Now, Mr Steele, pray tell us about this unfortunate William Goebel. What had he done to bring about his death; and, for that matter, what is there about his murder that is mysterious enough to have engaged the likes of the Pinkertons?"

As if to fortify himself, the American drank some of his coffee. Thus prepared, he began his tale. "First, one must understand William Goebel the man. Ironically for a politician, he wasn't a particularly likeable fellow—at least, according to those who knew him. Not many people were close to him. Besides his brothers and sister, he seemed to have few friends. There were no women in his life besides his sister; and while he advocated reforms for working people, most folks believed that it was their votes he sought rather than their true well-being."

I grunted in agreement. I could name many a duplicitous politician in England who fit the same bill.

"Nor was Goebel much of a speaker," said Steele. "I'd been to one of his political rallies when I was travelling through Frankfort. Oh, he'd go through the motions, but his words didn't soar. You'd have to turn elsewhere—to someone like William Jennings Bryan, who had, in fact, campaigned for him—if you wanted to get your blood flowing. Goebel's looks weren't much to speak of either. He had pale skin, narrow eyes, and plastered-down, black hair. To tell the truth, there was something reptilian about him."

Holmes and I exchanged glances. I knew that we were harbouring the same suspicions. Holmes had once compared the ruthless blackmailer, Charles Augustus Milverton, to a serpent, but the only person I had ever heard Holmes specifically describe as "reptilian" was the cold-blooded Moriarty himself.

"And yet despite such obstacles," continued the American, "Goebel successfully climbed the political ladder. In the name of the common people, he stood up to the L & N—that's the Louisville and Nashville railroad—the major line in Kentucky. He called them 'blood-suckers', said their labour practices were unfair, their ticket prices too high, their interests only concerned with financial gain. It was a good sales pitch all right, and he rode it straight to the leadership of Kentucky's Democratic Party. He became quite the power broker. People called him czar, King Goebel, even William the Conqueror."

"One presumes," observed Holmes quietly, "that in the process he also collected some formidable enemies—the so-called L & N in particular."

"Precisely, Mr Holmes. It was, in fact, the leadership of the L & N—Basil Duke and Milton Smith, to be precise—that hired Pinkerton to find out who killed Goebel. They want L & N's name cleared. You see, as Goebel's principal adversaries, they fear being held responsible for the assassination themselves—as by some, I can assure you, they already are. There are plenty of Kentucky Democrats who'd think nothing of shooting a likely suspect—especially if he runs a railroad."

"So I have read," said Holmes. "No, offense, Mr Steele, but even before this latest outrage, a number of pressmen have already referred to Kentucky as the most violent state in your country."

"No offense taken, Mr Holmes." With a chuckle, he added, "I'm from Montana," and proceeded to revisit his coffee.

"Kentucky's a dangerous place all right," he went on. "They have their own methods for working things out. It's funny. Though Goebel wasn't born there either, he seemed to fit right in. A while back, he had a dispute with a banker named Sanford. Planned or not, they happened to meet out on the street. Within seconds, guns were drawn, shots were fired, and Goebel's bullet struck Sanford in the head. The man died not long thereafter. That's how they take care of things in Kentucky."

Frontier justice, I could not help thinking. To the average Englishman, myself included, Kentucky seemed no different from the rest of that lawless country.

"Which," continued Steele, "brings us back to that fateful day last month when Goebel was shot. The election for governor took place in early November."

"The election presumably won by Goebel," I noted. "You already told us he was the governor."

"If it only were that simple, Doctor. A Republican named William Taylor—'Hogjaw' Taylor, they call him—came out ahead and was actually inaugurated in December; but, you see, Goebel had previously set up his own legislative committee to rule on the integrity of the election, and he appealed to them in hopes of having the results reversed.

"Yet much to everyone's surprise—especially Goebel's—his handpicked committee confirmed Taylor's victory. Goebel still had another card to play, however; and he appealed the committee's decision to his allies in the heavily Democratic state legislature. In fact, it was when Goebel was on his way to hear the final deliberations that he was cut down. It was only *after* he was shot that the Democratic legislature overturned the election results and declared Goebel the new governor. Mortally wounded—some say he was already dead—he was sworn in the next day, the 31st of January 1900. He died three days later."

"My word," said I. "Quite a dramatic tale."

Holmes leaned back in his chair, steepled his fingers, and closed his eyes. "Describe the scene of the shooting, if you please, Mr Steele."

"With your permission," said the American, withdrawing a small pocketbook from inside his coat. He flipped through a few pages to consult his notes and then reported the following: "On the morning of Tuesday, January 30—a cold, crisp day it was—Goebel set off with two friends for the state house from the Capital Hotel where he was staying. It was just a short walk—one block down Main Street and up St. Clair to Broadway.

"You must understand that due to the contested election, feelings were running high. This was Kentucky, after all; and most of Frankfort seemed an armed camp. Mountaineers from the south-eastern counties that supported Taylor—some called them '*desperadoes*'—roamed the streets with pistols, rifles, and shotguns—presumably with the intent of intimidating the legislature into supporting Taylor. For their part, the Democrats responded with newly-sworn-in police to help maintain the peace. With all the talk of violence, of course, it was feared that somebody might eventually try to shoot Goebel himself.

"Which is why those two friends who accompanied Goebel to the Capitol that morning also served as bodyguards. At first, it seemed they weren't needed; for when the three arrived at Capitol Square, they found the area—it's a full city block—almost completely deserted."

"The scene, Mr Steele," Holmes repeated, eyes still closed. "Describe the scene."

Steele nodded. "The grounds themselves are pretty flat, interrupted here and there this time of year by barren hackberry trees. The square is surrounded by an iron-rail fence. That morning, a thin layer of snow covered the ground. The water in the four-tiered fountain near the Capitol's steps had frozen. The Capitol building itself, a two-storey, brick and white-stone structure, stands at the centre of the square. It's one of those places in the Greek revival style and has a portico with six large columns that hold up the gabled pediment."

Sherlock Holmes opened his eyes at the preciseness of the description. "Six columns you say?"

"I know what you're thinking, Mr Holmes," said Steele. "An assassin hidden behind one of those columns could do some damage. But, you see, a shooter in the portico would be easily detected; there isn't enough cover. The front of the building contains no windows and only a single entrance."

Holmes nodded, and the fire crackled in accompaniment.

"At 11.16," Steele continued, "Goebel and his two bodyguards made a turn into the square through one of the two open gates and proceeded up the wide stone walkway. No doubt you could have heard their shoes crunching the leftover snow on the pavement. It's about a hundred feet from the street to the portico, and the walkway itself inclines slightly as you approach the building. One of the bodyguards went ahead to check that the interior was safe; the other dropped back a step or two.

"It was just then—right before Goebel reached the fountain—that shots rang out. Some say Goebel tried to draw his own pistol; but the wound was too great, and he fell to the ground. 'Get me away,' he's said to have uttered, 'I'm afraid it's all over for me.'"

"How many shots?" Holmes asked.

"Not certain. Maybe five. Maybe fewer. There were too many conflicting accounts. Needless to say, the assassin escaped, identity unknown."

"Of course," said Holmes. "A situation you plan to rectify."

"One may hope," Steele replied. "But what I *can* tell you with certainty is that a single bullet traveling downward pierced Goebel's right side; splintered a rib; passed through a lung; and exited his back. He was carried to his hotel room; and doctors were summoned. But ultimately, the damage was too great.

"A few days later, after having been sworn in as governor and visited by his sister and one of his brothers—the other couldn't get there in time—Goebel died. I suppose it's fitting that controversy dogs his last words. Democrats say that he told his friends to 'be brave, fearless, and loyal to the great common people.'"

"Quite noble in the end," I observed. "A confirmation of the man's social concerns."

"To be sure," said Steele, "if true. One of his doctors reported that his final words were in fact a complaint about his last meal. 'Damned bad oyster,' he's supposed to have said."

I shook my head in disbelief and changed the subject. "What did the police make of all this? Surely their investigation must have turned up some valuable information."

Steele allowed himself another short laugh. "Well, Doctor," he drawled, "at least I can't say they didn't try. They did determine that a rifle had been fired from a window in the next-door Executive Building. It's a three-storey brick structure some forty feet to the east of the Capitol."

"You said 'from *a* window', Mr Steele," Holmes pointed out. "Not from *the* window?"

"Good point, Mr Holmes. Exactly *which* window wasn't so easy to identify. Remember that there were just a handful of people walking around at the time. A few of them pointed at the nearest open window. It was in the southwest corner of the Executive Building—which, incidentally, just happened to be the private office of the newly-elected Secretary of State, a Republican named Caleb Powers. The shade was down most of the way, and the window was raised about six inches."

"There you have it," said I.

"Not quite, Doctor. You see, a number of other people maintained that the shot had actually come from higher up. A few said they'd actually seen a rifle barrel in a third-floor window."

"Certainly," said Holmes, "an immediate investigation would turn up the appropriate evidence to establish the facts."

Now anyone familiar with the investigative methods of Sherlock Holmes could predict that, had Holmes been there himself, he would have invaded the offices on both floors, fallen to his hands and knees in each, and begun peering through his glass in search of vital clues.

"So one would assume, Mr Holmes. So one would assume." Here Steele paused—almost as if to draw keener attention to his next few words.

Holmes did, in fact, lean forward. "I sense that you're suggesting some impediment to the investigation."

Steele laughed again. "Indeed I am," said he. "You see, Bill Taylor, the soon-to-be *deposed* Kentucky governor, had been paralyzed by fear even before Goebel' shooting. And with good reason. Upon the arrival of Taylor's mountain men, Goebel's people had begun marching around with guns.

"The assault on their Democratic leader brought matters to a boil; and seething with anger they screamed about killing the Republican Taylor. Fearing for his own safety, not to mention that of his family, Taylor had no hesitation in ordering in the state militia. Within minutes of the shooting, five-hundred strong of the Louisville Legion and the 2d Regiment filled the square. Their bayonets at the ready, the fully uniformed militiamen stood positioned to prevent anyone from entering the area—which obviously included the scene of the crime. '*Anyone*', of course, meant the police as well."

"Preposterous!" I exploded. The thought of soldiers hindering a criminal investigation—let alone blocking the state's elected representatives from convening in the Capitol building—seemed unworthy of a democratic nation.

Steele merely shrugged. "As you could have predicted, the local authorities got no help at all from the Republicans. In fact, to the best of my knowledge, Taylor and his crew are still holed up in the Executive Building. By my count, it's been some three weeks now. Taylor told the Republican legislators to meet in the town of London—London, Kentucky, that is; and the Democrats are gathering in the Capital Hotel in Frankfort. It's like the state has two governments."

Holmes offered a single, sarcastic clap of his hands. "Wonderful!" he cried, "a regular comedy of errors."

"Don't get me wrong, Mr Holmes," countered Steele. "Plenty of arrests were made. In fact, some twenty-seven people were rounded up at the start—clerks, politicians, even a state-police officer. But from what I've been hearing lately, suspicion has focused on three: Caleb Powers, the Republican Secretary of State—"

"From whose office the bullet was fired," I interrupted.

"*Might* have been fired, Doctor," Steele corrected. "Powers was thought to be the mastermind. A stenographer and notary public named Henry Youtsey, was charged with being the go-between. He worked in the state auditor's office just down the hall from Powers. Youtsey's the one they think hid a pair of rifles—a Marlin .38-55 and a Winchester .38-56—behind a loose wooden plank in Powers's office. The last of the three, a Republican county assessor named Jim Howard, had previously been charged with some other murder. Apparently, *he* is now considered the gunman. I should add that Powers himself had conveniently arranged to be out of town at the time of the shooting."

Holmes nodded. "It sounds like the authorities have constructed a logical case, Mr Steele. But you still seem to harbour doubts?"

"I do, Mr Holmes—to a point. All these charges against Powers and the others may, in fact, be true; but I have to believe there's more. A full ten days after the shooting, the police discovered a .38 calibre bullet in the trunk of a hackberry tree not far behind where Goebel had been hit. The bullet matched one of the rifles found in Powers's office. As a consequence, the police employed an engineer to show that one end of a taut string held at the bullet hole in the tree and the other end at Powers's corner-window would have passed directly through the point where Goebel had been standing, thus proving the origin of the shot."

"One moment," said Holmes. "How high was the bullet hole in the tree?"

"About four-and-a-half feet from the ground."

"And the distance between the ground and the bottom of Powers's window?"

"About the same."

"Hah!" Holmes cried. "Earlier you said that the bullet which struck Goebel had travelled *downward*."

"Exactly." Steele grinned. "You're an excellent listener, Mr Holmes. What's more, you're also giving voice to the same thoughts I have."

Sherlock Holmes cocked an eyebrow.

"You see, I couldn't forget the witnesses—more than a dozen, actually—who'd mentioned a third-floor window. They all agreed the shots had come from somewhere between the Capitol and the office building, which I took to mean from the office building's west side, not from a front-corner window like Powers's. For that matter, I'm told that Howard, the alleged shooter, didn't seem a calm enough type to have lain in wait and done the deed. Oh, some people did swear they'd seen him on the Capitol grounds near the time of the shooting, but he produced his own witnesses to say he was elsewhere.

"Assuming you're the sort of investigator I perceive you to be," said Holmes, "I imagine that you tried to confirm your doubts."

Steele smiled again. "On the second day of the occupation by the militia, I was able to check that third-floor office myself. I bribed one of the men—$20 of L & N money was quite a sum to convince him to lend me his uniform for an hour or two."

"Excellent!" cried Holmes.

"Disguised as a soldier, I entered the Executive Building, climbed the stairs, and visited the room in question."

"What did you find?" Holmes asked, his grey eyes blazing.

"The room itself had been swept clean. And yet in front of the window stood two boxes, one on top of the other, reaching to the level of the windowsill. Need I say, a perfect place to rest a rifle? But there's more. The wooden floor revealed scuffmarks in front of the boxes that suggested a person had been moving around at that spot. And that's not all. You see, there was something strange about the markings."

"Strange?" Holmes repeated. "In what manner were they 'strange'?"

Steele consulted his notes again. "Most were long, sweeps—as if a foot had been dragged along the floor rather than simply having stepped upon it—as if whoever made the marks had a bad leg."

"Well done, Mr Steele!" cried Holmes. "At long last. Anything else?"

"One more thing, Mr Holmes. I found *this!* It must have been brushed into a corner." As he spoke, he drew from inside his coat a long, white envelope, which he handed to my friend.

Like a starving man reaching for food, Holmes shot out his hand to receive it. Carefully opening the flap, he slowly drew from the envelope what looked to be a short, metal rod. It had a small wooden handle at one end and a tiny, round, bolt-like device at the other. Only after scrutinizing the entire piece, did he roll the thing between his thumb and forefinger.

"*Ein Hebel,*" he murmured.

"What's that, Holmes?" I asked.

"*Hebel* is German for lever."

"You recognise it then?" asked Steele. "I figured it must be important, but I didn't know what it was."

"It is the lever," Holmes said, holding the rod vertically so Steele and I could examine it as he spoke, "used for priming the bellows within an air rifle. You'll remember, Watson, that back in '94 Sebastian Moran employed such a weapon (what the Germans call a *Bolzenbüchse*) for shooting at me—though in Moran's case, it had been modified by that tinker von Herder. I told you that this case offered familiar echoes."

Who could forget the horrible night when the dummy-likeness of Holmes that he had placed in our Baker Street window had taken the bullet meant for the man himself? It seemed like yesterday though almost six years had passed.

"If I understand you correctly," Wyatt Steele addressed my friend, "you're suggesting that the assassin was, in fact, at the third-floor window of the Executive Building with an air-rifle."

"Quite so. I shouldn't doubt that, as you yourself have described, there were also shooters in the office of the Secretary of State. Let's not forget that there were gunmen running rampant throughout the city. Still, I'm willing to wager that the shooters in Powers's office were meant to be diversions. Oh, I have no doubt that they fired upon Goebel—one even hit a tree!—but whoever wanted him dead had put his true faith in the shooter with the silent weapon on the third floor. He's the gunman we're really after."

"A gunman with a gamy leg," I said.

"Exactly, Watson. And unless I am very much mistaken, I believe it is the same conclusion that has compelled Mr Steele to continue his investigation.

"Indeed, Mr Holmes. But not with the assuredness that your confirmation provides. While I was still in uniform, I asked some of the soldiers nearby if they'd seen anyone limping about."

"And?"

"'Now that you mention it,' said one, 'I do remember a beggar hanging around. A cripple he was. He had a bad back and twisted leg. He was wearing a pea coat and bell-bottomed trousers—you know, the kind that sailors wear. I remember his sea-faring clothes because I thought they looked pretty strange out here in the middle of Kentuck.'

"'And another thing,' a second soldier chimed in, 'even though he looked young, he walked with a cane. I guess 'cause he was all hunched over.''

"A walking stick, Watson," said Holmes. "Do you mark that?"

I did though I failed to make anything of it. That a deformed man required a walking stick did not seem unusual to me.

"Where was he seen?" Holmes asked.

"On Broadway in front of the Capitol grounds. Apparently, he was holding out a tin cup for money; but in all the commotion, he started hobbling east towards Ann Street. You should know, Mr Holmes, that just past the corner of the square is the L & N railroad depot. It's quite close by actually—only a couple of blocks away. Once I got back into my regular clothes, I checked there myself. A ticket agent told me he'd seen a cripple begging out in Elk Alley next to the station. As far as I could tell, no one actually saw him get on a train, but you know how it is—once word gets around about a shooting, people start running every which way. I don't imagine they'd pay any mind to a beggar, not even a deformed one."

"You're suggesting," I said to Steele, "that this cripple boarded a train at the railway station and got out of town."

"I am," said the Pinkerton agent. "And depending on time and destination, he could have made connections to most anywhere. Say he got to Cincinnati. Then he could travel north. "

"Or west," I suggested, images of frontier gunslingers springing to mind.

"I wagered on New York," offered Steele. "The pea coat and flared trousers made me think of a seaport—a place where he could fit in—and New York is the major point of departure—"

"—For ships sailing to almost anywhere," said Holmes, completing the sentence.

"I figured it was worth looking into. I notified the agency to get some people out to the New York docks and keep an eye peeled for the twisted man."

"Excellent work, Mr Steele," said Holmes. "I can only assume that someone saw him board a ship for London, which is why you are here."

"That's right. The Pinkerton Agency has had many dealings with the Metropolitan Police, and I cabled Scotland Yard to be on the lookout at the London docks for the suspect. An Inspector Lestrade was put in charge, but I guess that the crippled man somehow managed to elude him."

"Fancy that," said Holmes drily, "a crippled man eluding Lestrade." He allowed himself a brief chuckle and then said to the two of us, "Well, gentlemen, I suppose it will be up to us to track down the fugitive."

Steele's eyes widened. "Do you actually have someone in mind, Mr Holmes?"

"By itself, I grant you that the naval attire doesn't tell us much. But when I match it to a deformed young man with the intent to kill, a certain profile most certainly comes to mind. What say *you*, friend Watson?"

There was indeed a ring of familiarity in the description, yet I could not place the figure in question.

"And if I tell you," Holmes said to me, "that a trip to Sussex might be in order—to Cheeseman's in Lamberley just south of Horsham?"

"Bob Ferguson!" I cried.

"More properly, Bob Ferguson's son, Master Jacky."

Steele knotted his eyebrows. His confusion could well be understood since I had not yet made public the case I intended to title "The Sussex Vampire". The narrative would dramatise for the reading public the young man to whom Holmes was referring.

"Jacky Ferguson is the son of an old friend of mine," I explained. "In our rugby days, the boy's father was known as 'Big Bob'."

Holmes cleared his throat to remind me to stick to the salient facts.

"By 1896," I continued, "Bob's wife—that is to say, Jacky's mother—had died, Fergusson remarried, and soon they had a new son."

"Not long thereafter," said Holmes, "the trouble started."

"In November of that year," I told Steele, "Ferguson came to Holmes seeking an explanation for the apparently murderous intentions of his second wife towards the baby. As it turned out, however, it was not Bob's wife but the pampered older boy Jacky—I called him *boy*, he must be close to twenty by now—who had attempted to poison his tiny half-brother. His was a decidedly murderous plan intended to prevent the baby from coming between himself and his father. After revealing the crime, Holmes suggested to Ferguson that his son spend a year at sea."

The Pinkerton agent furrowed his brow. "I don't understand how—"

"Sorry," I said. "I failed to mention that the boy Jacky had suffered a terrible fall during his childhood. The result was—"

"Let me guess," Steele interrupted. "A twisted spine."

"Quite so," said Holmes. "Now, Watson, wire Ferguson with the news that we're coming to visit. We can catch an afternoon train at Victoria. No need to mention Master Jacky until we actually get there. Mr Steele, I'm afraid we'll have to leave you to your own devices until we return. Three people descending on poor Robert Ferguson would be too many."

"Whatever you say, Mr Holmes. I'm in your hands. I never expected to have identified a suspect so quickly. Birdy Edwards certainly had you pegged correctly."

A brief smile flashed across Holmes's face. He was never one to ignore a compliment.

II

As Sherlock Holmes had proposed, he and I took the afternoon train from Victoria to Horsham. Though ashen clouds and a lingering February chill attempted to bedevil the Sussex landscape, hosts of golden daffodils, wild red clover, white snowdrops, and pink camellias maintained the beauty of the picturesque countryside.

Yet I had no desire to gaze out the carriage window. On the contrary, I preferred to fasten my eyes on Holmes as he revealed to me the various actions that had been going on directly under my nose but about which I clearly knew nothing.

"Surely, Watson, once we discovered Master Jacky's vile role in that vampire business, you didn't imagine I'd let him go off in the world unobserved? One doesn't expect a sour temper to sweeten overnight. That is why I requested your friend Ferguson to notify me as soon as he secured a ship's berth for the boy. It took a few weeks; but the shipping agents at Ferguson's firm, tea brokers Ferguson and Muirhead of Mincing Lane, were finally able to complete the assignment. A position 'before the mast', as it were, was established for young Jack on the *S.S Heraldic*, a tea-carrying steamer in the Merchant Navy. What's more, from all reports, the boy appeared ready, if a bit reluctant, to perform his shipboard tasks to the extent that his physical abilities allowed.

"Most admirable," I said, pleased that my friend's son seemed to be falling into line.

"And yet, Watson, I needed to be certain. No sooner did I learn that Jacky would be setting out to sea from Gravesend than I put Sammy Trout and the other Baker Street Irregulars on his scent. With comrades all along the river, I knew that the Irregulars would have little difficulty keeping track of a flaxen-haired youth that exhibited a decided limp. I instructed Sam to inform me when they actually saw him boarding.

"Once Jacky had set sail, it was a simple matter to chart the *Heraldic*'s comings and goings in the newspapers' recordings of commercial ship movements. My various contacts in European and American ports served to confirm what I had already learned, and such has been the case for the past three years."

Three years! —During which time *I* had suspected nothing. The railway carriage swayed back and forth, and under ordinary circumstances the movement might have lulled me to sleep. But on this occasion, so annoyed was I at having not been told about what was going on with the son of my old friend that drowsiness never threatened.

"How did young Jack fare as a sailor then?" I asked.

"As one might expect, Watson," said Holmes, unsurprisingly oblivious to my annoyance. "The boy viewed anything required of him as punishment. Let us not forget that Master Jacky regarded his attempts to kill the baby as perfectly logical. As a result, his exile to shipboard labour must have seemed very unjust punishment indeed."

"And yet a moment ago you described him as resigned to facing his sea adventure."

"Ah, Watson," Holmes sighed, "I'm afraid it only gets worse. As a not-too surprising consequence, the boy began to cultivate undesirable associates among his shipmates. One imagines that it took little effort on their part to interest the bitter young man in firearms, and Jack soon extended his so-called 'tour of duty' aboard the *Heraldic*. Guns, you see, made no demands on his deformity—indeed, here were weapons that allowed him to gain the strength that he'd always felt he was lacking."

"Surely, Holmes, you didn't learn all this from the Baker Street Irregulars? Good watchdogs, so to speak, but mere children lacking the psychological insights you are reporting."

"Hah, Watson! Sharp as ever. No, the Irregulars merely presented the facts; I supplied the inferences. As it turned out, Jack had returned to Gravesend with an unsavoury group of friends. One of our lads followed them to the marshlands outside of town and watched them shoot at bottles and the like. Jack, it seems, had become quite proficient.

"Once I heard that he'd begun taking aim at stray dogs and cats, however, my concerns grew. In fact, I arranged for my associates with the German police to follow him on the occasion the *Heraldic* berthed in Hamburg. Sad to say, my intuition paid off. He went to the *Reeperbahn* to see an elderly German with a knowledge of firearms—blind as it so happens—who, curiously enough, arrived at the rendezvous with two canes—and left with only one."

"Von Herder!" I exclaimed.

At that moment, like a warning cry, the train sounded its horn. We must have been getting close to Horsham.

"Quite so, old fellow," replied Holmes, ignoring the blast from the horn, "Von Herder, the gun mechanic. It was he, I have come to believe, who furnished Jack Ferguson with an air rifle. Though not the most talented of gunsmiths, Von Herder is competent enough. Not only could he obtain from gun-makers like Townsend and Reilly the basics of the hollow walking stick, but he could also combine the structural framework with the mechanism of his own air gun. Jack would certainly not be the first shooter to employ a rifle that resembled a walking stick. But I hazard a guess that he may be the first to render the employment of *both* of its features a necessity."

"Of course!" I exclaimed. "A malformed assassin concealing his weapon in the guise of a dependable cane."

"Quite so, old fellow. It may have been no more than coincidence that the *Heraldic* was delivering a shipment of tea to New York in early January of this year, but I'm willing to wager that Jack was no longer part of the crew when it left a week later. He had honed his skills with the rifle and somehow presented himself as an accomplished shooter to the lawless elements bent on exploiting America's East Coast.

"Word travels fast within the criminal underworld, and Jack must have learned that his services could be put to use in Kentucky. It mattered little that the *Heraldic* had sailed before the deed was done. No doubt he earned plenty for his work and could easily book passage back to England. My hope in meeting with your friend Ferguson, Watson, is simply to confirm my reasoning."

*****

Though a closed carriage conveyed us the few miles from Horsham to Lamberley, we had to hire an open dogcart for the final leg of the journey. A thin rain began as soon as we reached the road to Cheeseman's, forcing us to wrap ourselves more tightly in our long coats and pull our hats even lower over our brows. Only when we recognised the familiar winding lane of Sussex clay did we know our ever-dampening excursion was about to end.

No doubt, it was the unkind weather that made the seventeenth-century farmhouse appear more ominous than I had remembered. To be sure, the leaden skies and shadowy trees had darkened its redbrick walls, but I was certain that some element beyond the weather was rendering the atmosphere so oppressive.

"I have to admit to you, Mr Holmes," said a sombre Bob Ferguson, who met us personally at the dark-oak outer door, "that I'm of mixed minds talking with you. There's no two ways about it." Without so much as the briefest of smiles, he continued to speak as he slowly ushered us inside. "I will never forget the joy you restored to my life by revealing the causes of my wife's strange behaviour. And yet, though I know it was for the best, I cannot forgive you for compelling me to remove my Jacky from our family."

The reluctant host led us into a dimly-lit sitting room where bright flames danced in a cavernous fireplace, casting eerie patterns on the half-oak, half-plastered walls. Ferguson offered us each a brandy and motioned to seats on the leather couch, but his tone was anything but warm.

Recounting the recent history of his son Jack was obviously not to Ferguson's liking. After Holmes had asked what Ferguson knew of Jack's latest activities, the father required a pull of the brandy and began his report with a frown. "When Jacky returned home following his first voyage—it's been about two years now—I was hoping to see a positive change in the lad's attitude. Unfortunately, there was anything but. Oh, he did ask if we might go out shooting, not a sport in which he had showed a whit of interest prior to his putting out to sea. But he shot some grouse, don't you know, and seemed quite pleased with himself. At the very least, I thought the outing might help us strengthen our friendship, but he remained here just a day or two. In point of fact, gentlemen, he collected his belongings and told us he would be taking a flat in London, thank you very much. Then he left, making off with my German dictionary for good measure. I haven't seen him since."

"Do you know his current location, Mr Ferguson?" Holmes asked. "We have every suspicion that he has returned to London, and it is necessary for me to speak with him."

Ferguson scowled. "Is he in trouble again?"

"One can't be certain," Holmes replied. "That is why I need to see him."

I assumed that the boy's actual address was unimportant to Holmes. Certainly, the Baker Street Irregulars had dogged Jack

Ferguson closely enough to identify his residence. Still, had his father known the boy's whereabouts, it would have made finding Jack that much more simple.

"No," said Ferguson, his voice laced with bitterness, "he's never shared that detail with me. If he had, I'm not certain I would want to share it with you. The boy has been through enough."

Holmes nodded. Later he would explain to me, "I wanted to learn just how estranged father and son had become. That the father doesn't know where his son is living indicates the severity of their break."

During our visit, we saw no sign of either Mrs Ferguson or the young boy who had been the target of Jacky's wrath those few years before. But having exhausted our topic, we finished our brandies, thanked a sceptical Ferguson for his help, and promised to keep him up-to-date concerning any developments that involved his son. Then, with the much-appreciated aid of Ferguson's carriage, Holmes and I made our way back through the rain and wind to the small railway station in Horsham and ultimately home to Victoria and Baker Street.

Ringing in our ears throughout the journey, however, was Ferguson's final and unwarranted valediction: "None of this would have ever happened, Mr Holmes, had we not initially followed your cruel advice."

*****

I leave to my fair-minded readers the question of premeditation. For my part, I have never been totally clear concerning the exact role Holmes played in the shooting that concludes this account. At the very least, however, we have arrived at the point in the narrative that, as I have already indicated, presents Sherlock Holmes at his most cold-blooded.

Unfriendly winds had been blowing throughout the night of our return to Baker Street; and yet even as I was shuffling down the stairs for breakfast the following morning, I encountered my friend enveloped in cape and deerstalker entering our sitting room from the outer hall.

"Out so early in this foul weather?" I asked.

"Indeed," he answered, hanging his cold-weather garments on the pegs by the door. "Windy or not, it seemed the right time for the

Trout boy to show me Jack's lodgings. Sooner than later, I wanted to ascertain the lie of the land. As it turns out, Jack maintains a flat in the Hanover Buildings in Tooley Street."

"Just south of the river—not far from the London Bridge Station?"

"Quite so," Holmes nodded.

"I know the place—five identical six-storey blocks of yellow brick." I had ministered to a few of its residents when I had worked as a houseman at Bart's. Originally constructed to house the men who laboured at the nearby docks and warehouses, the buildings had been renamed the Devon Mansions during the Great War. As far as I was concerned, Jack Ferguson could not have found a residence of lesser distinction.

"And yet," I was forced to concede, "the location makes sense. It's near London Bridge Station, and from there it's a simple train ride to Gravesend where Jack's ship put out." Though not overly familiar with the South Eastern and Chatham railway lines that ran parallel to the Thames, I still would not soon forget the foul-weather excursion through which Holmes and I had suffered on the line the previous year when we travelled to Gravesend to meet the so-called "Baron of Brede Place". I refer, of course, to the American writer Stephen Crane who was returning to England following his adventures in Cuba during the Spanish-American War.*

Equally memorable was a trip we had taken along that same course a few years before. To gain an early start at resolving the business with Professor Coram and the golden pince-nez at Yoxley Old Place, we had boarded a train at six in the morning at Charing Cross, the first station west of London Bridge. The plan had been to get off just beyond Chatham at the Higham halt, which is within a few miles of Yoxley.

As luck would have it, however, we found ourselves on the "slow" train, the one that stopped at every last station along the way. Inspector Hopkins had required only ninety minutes to cover the identical distance the day before, and yet it took us twice as long to

---

* Interested readers may find Watson's account of his and Holmes' encounter with Stephen and Cora Crane in Watson's narrative titled *Sherlock Holmes and the Baron of Brede Place*. (DDV)

make the same journey. That infernal train ride seemed to last forever! The thought still rankles.

Interrupting my memories, Holmes held up a small piece of paper. "I've taken the liberty to write Jack Ferguson a note in your name."

"In *my* name?" I replied. "Why not in *yours*? It is with you he has a quarrel, not with *me*. *You're* the one who suggested he go to sea."

"Precisely, my dear fellow. No love lost there, I'm afraid, which is quite the point. I don't think he'd agree to see *me*. A request from *you*, on the other hand, might make him curious enough to want to hear you out."

"And just what did I say in this note?"

"You've asked permission to visit his flat."

"For what purpose?"

"Why, to request that he invite *me* in as well."

I thought my friend must be losing his senses. Had Holmes not just suggested that Jack would not welcome him? For that matter, Holmes suspected him of being a killer. Would it be safe for *me* in the lair of an assassin? Unable to mask my fears, I cast a concerned look at Holmes.

"Nothing to worry about, old fellow," said he. "I'll be standing just outside the building. Once he gives his approval, your job will be to open a window, and call me in."

I scratched my head in dismay. But knowing better than to question the rationality of my friend, I agreed to go along with his request. Still, as Holmes gave the page-boy the message for Jack Ferguson, I could not keep from wondering what trick my friend had up his sleeve.

Nothing to say to you, ran the note (including the underscoring) that Billy returned to me. *But I am curious about what you have to say to me. This afternoon. 2.00.* It was signed *JF.*

"Perfect," said Holmes, rubbing his hands together. "Now I have some last-minutes plans to put in motion. I'll be back at noon for lunch. Suggest beef sandwiches to Mrs Hudson. That joint I saw in the kitchen looked quite inviting."

And then he was gone.

*****

A hansom brought us to the Hanover Buildings just south of the Thames. The winds had died, but frantic traffic laden with tea and coffee and hops and leather bustled along Tooley Street as the nearby ships and warehouses and shops made their demands.

No sooner did we exit the hansom than Holmes pointed to the block nearest us. "That's his room," he said, indicating the second window in the first-floor line. "He'll be expecting you. Go." With that, Holmes turned his back and began to survey the other structures along both sides of the street.

A gate interrupted the short black railing round the building, and I made my way through it as well as through the unlatched outer door. Traversing a dark foyer, I climbed the equally dark stairs to the first storey and in the light of a meagre gas lamp managed to locate what I presumed to be the second flat facing the street. I knocked hesitantly and, receiving no response, knocked again more sharply. This time the door swung open, and I immediately found myself standing face to face with Jack Ferguson.

When we first had met, Jacky had been able to conceal the hatred he harboured towards his infant half-brother. Only when Holmes confronted him regarding the boy's foul plan did Jacky's murderous intent reveal itself. Now, however, with his thick, flaxen hair combed straight back, that same devilish look appeared permanently etched into his features. His knotted brow, curling lip, and narrow, brutish eyes conveyed a rage that he clearly no longer felt compelled to hide. Worse, as much as one might hope to deny it, his deformity added to his sense of menace. For though I would be the first to protest the casting of so general an aspersion, in this instance his twisted spine seemed to reflect his twisted nature.

"I welcome you to my home," said he, bidding me enter with an exaggerated sweep of his arm. He indicated an old armchair, which I took; and pulling out one of two wooden chairs nesting under a rickety table, he sat down with his bent-back to the window. I recognised the trick, one often employed by Holmes himself. With the window behind him, Jack's face became silhouetted by the brightness outside, the result rendering his facial reactions difficult to discern.

"I don't see my father much," he offered. "I should imagine that you came at his request—though I don't know how you discovered this place."

I thought of Sammy Trout and the Irregulars; but playing my cards close to the vest, I said rather cryptically, "As you know, I work with Sherlock Holmes; and when he wants to find someone, that person is found."

"Holmes!" Jack spat out, "the man who tore me from my family? The man who turned me into what I have become?" The more animated he grew, the more spasmodically his entire body jerked.

"Holmes wishes to speak with you," said I calmly, "but he fears that you wouldn't let him through the door."

"He's got that right. Quite the detective!"

"Holmes anticipated you would react in such a fashion. That is why he asked me to pave the way. He was hoping I might talk you into letting him come up here. You see, he's just outside the building, awaiting a sign from me at the window to summon him in."

With some effort, Jack turned his body and glanced suspiciously at the window behind him. White curtains of gauze-linen barely covered the glass.

"What does he want with me?" Jack questioned.

"I'm sure I don't know. Why not let me signal that he can come up?"

Jack glanced at his bureau, a sure giveaway that something he wanted lay concealed within. Except for drumming his fingers on the table next to him, however, he sat motionless for a moment or two. At last, with a sigh of resignation, he said "Why not? "and waved me towards the window.

All I had left to do was carry out my instructions from Holmes. I spread the two curtains apart and then pulled up the sash. Holmcs was pacing below, his eyes fixed on the window in search of any movement. I motioned for him to come up, at the same time being sure—as, for some strange reason, he had directed—to leave the window open and the curtains separated.

No sooner had I completed the task than I turned round and discovered myself face to face with the revolver Jack was now pointing at my head. As if playing a chord on a piano, he had arched the fingers of his free hand on the top of the bureau, their obvious strength helping him maintain his balance.

"No need for the gun," said I.

"Just a precaution." He pointed the barrel at the chair I had occupied. "Now sit."

I did, and with Jack still standing, we silently awaited the arrival of Sherlock Holmes.

Minutes later came a quick rap.

"Enter," commanded Jack, the barrel of the gun now turned toward the doorway.

Holmes walked in cautiously, eyed the pistol, displayed his empty hands, and opened wide his coat to show that he carried no weapons.

Motioning with the gun, Jack gestured for him to sit down.

Holmes pulled the second wooden chair away from the table, placed it to my right—opposite Jack—and turned it slightly so it wasn't in direct line with the window. He then seated himself and faced the gunman.

"Now, Mr Sherlock Holmes," said Jack, "be so kind as to inform me of the nature of your business."

Holmes flashed a brief smile and then, after stealing a glance at the window, got straight to the point. "I merely wish to ascertain, Jack Ferguson, that it was *not* the L & N Railroad that hired you to assassinate Governor Goebel in the American state of Kentucky last month."

For a man holding a gun, Jack displayed an alarming lack of control. His eyebrows shot up and he lurched backward upon hearing Holmes's charge. "Who claims that I assassinated anyone?" he demanded.

This time Holmes's smile lingered. "Please, Jack, don't take us for fools. We know of your recently acquired talent with guns. We know a man of your description was seen in the Capitol grounds in Frankfort. We know you met with the gun-maker von Herder in Hamburg when your ship put into port there last year, and thus we suspect that the walking stick you utilised in Frankfort was, in fact, an air rifle constructed by the German. Finally, we know that after shooting the governor, you boarded a railway in Kentucky, secured a ship in New York, and ended up here in Tooley Street."

Jack Ferguson's demeanour grew darker with each point ticked off by Holmes. "If you know so much, Mr Sherlock Holmes, how come you don't know who hired me?"

"That is why I am here, Jack, to find that out—before we hand you over to the authorities for shipment back to the United States."

"Ha!" he snorted. "That's funny with me holding the gun. Though I don't suppose it matters all that much since neither one of you is leaving here alive. When I explain to the police that I found two men burglarising my flat and shot them dead, you won't be in a position to tell them otherwise."

Shooting us dead? Consider me foolish; but though I had already experienced some concern for our safety, I had not anticipated so deadly a turn of events. Oh, I suspected that Holmes might enter the flat unarmed, and yet I also assumed that he would have some sort of plan for extricating us from this dilemma. Gazing at Jack's pistol caused me to see how naïve my thinking had been.

"I don't mind telling you," said Jack, "that L & N had nothing to do with the job in Frankfort. I was hired by a fellow called Rounceville—though I doubt that's his real name, and I don't really care because his money is good. He was a deputy to the Secretary of State in Kentucky, that fellow Powers; but I tell you honestly that I don't know if Powers even knew what was going on. This Rounceville told me the Republicans didn't want Goebel, a Democrat, stealing the election; and that to stop him once and for all, they wanted him dead. They told me when and where to lie in wait and promised diversionary gunfire when I performed the work. With my silent airgun, I knew I could shoot Goebel and escape undetected."

Holmes nodded. "As I thought," said he. Then he slowly stood and moved his chair to the right.

I suppose Jack could have shot him right then, but in point of fact he himself moved opposite Holmes placing his back squarely in front of the open window.

Holmes and I have been in some tight places together—but I cannot recall a moment that seemed more dire, a situation that seemed to offer no escape.

"Exit Sherlock Holmes," announced Jack, holding out his arm at full length as he pointed the pistol at my friend.

Suddenly—without a sound—a blossom of red erupted from Jack's white shirtfront. There was a momentary look of surprise that splashed across Jack's face, and then he fell forward. In a sense, it appeared that he had exploded from within; but the truth, of course, was much less fantastical. He had been struck by a bullet fired through the open window. That I had heard no report accompanying the shot made it all the more perplexing.

Needless to say, I sprang to my feet to administer to the stricken young man. I felt for a pulse, but there was none. Jack Ferguson lay dead; the man who had killed Governor Goebel had himself been assassinated.

Sherlock Holmes stood by the window staring silently across the street. Only then did it dawn on me that he had set up the entire deadly scheme.

"Holmes," I said, but he hushed me with a forefinger to his lips.

"Come," said he, and together we exited, leaving the body of Jack Ferguson sprawled on the floor of his flat in an ever-widening pool of blood. When we reached the pavement, Holmes hailed a hansom, and we made our return to Baker Street.

*****

"Not a word till dinner," said Sherlock Holmes in reference to our harrowing afternoon. "I have made plans with Mr Steele to meet us in Simpson's at 7.00. We shall discuss the matter then."

Leaving me to stand in wonder, Holmes retired to his bedroom; and soon I heard the strains of his violin as he attacked some concerto or other. For my part, I tried to pass the hours by reading the latest *Lancet* and keeping up-to-date on medical matters. But it did little good. I could not stop myself from wondering whether Holmes had possessed the notion of having Jack Ferguson shot from the start.

More practical queries coursed through my brain as well. The questions may appear obvious, but still I needed to learn who had actually done the shooting and why I had heard no shot fired? For that matter, I also wanted to know what had happened to the body Holmes and I had left on the floor of the flat and how my friend Robert Ferguson was to be told of the death of his son.

The answers to the first two questions came immediately upon my seeing Wyatt Steele at Simpson's. He entered the dining hall with the aid of a walking stick. Holmes and I were already sampling a pre-prandial sherry when the Pinkerton approached our table. As he settled into his seat, he carefully rested the stick against the chair's wooden arm. The significance of such a piece, especially in the hands of an accomplished agent like Steele, revealed all. The stick was a weapon fashioned by the gun-maker Von Herder.

"It is a little-known fact, Watson," said Holmes, "that the original air-rifle we'd taken from Sebastian Moran in '94 and bestowed upon Scotland Yard for safe-keeping had been misplaced and ultimately stolen. It seems that on his way to the Yard, Inspector Lestrade had alighted to quell some disturbance or other and left the thing in the hansom.*

"One of my Irregulars happened to be near the vehicle at the time. Happily, he managed to grab the rifle and bring it to me. As the one who had presented it to Lestrade, in the first place, I concluded that the thing would be far safer in my hands than in his. Since then, I've kept it—along with the ammunition I bought—secure in one of my London hidey-holes. Today, however, when the business with Jack Ferguson materialised, I decided it might be needed to help extricate us from a delicate situation. Fortunately, Mr Steele, who was positioned on a rooftop across the road, was up to the task. He is, just as I had surmised, an American sharpshooter."

Steele's face flushed. "This gun is a fine piece, Mr Holmes. Make no mistake. You did your part by manoeuvring Ferguson to the window, but I never would have fired if he hadn't pointed his pistol at you."

"I believe I also speak for Dr Watson when I say that we are both extremely glad that you did."

I raised my glass in appreciation, and the three of us drank to Steele's timely marksmanship.

"In anticipation of the other questions I assume you have concocted," Holmes said to me, "you will be pleased to know that I have anonymously notified the police of the presence of a body in the Hanover Buildings. I leave it to the Yarders to inform Robert Ferguson of the death of his son. I don't believe he wants to hear anything more from you or me."

---

* In his essay, "Colonel Moran's Infamous Air Rifle", (BSJ, Vol. 10, No 3, 1960), Ralph A. Ashton corroborates the theft of Moran's weapon. (DDV)

I felt a pang of guilt at not addressing Ferguson myself, but I have come to agree with Holmes's assessment of our intrusion into his life.

"I will also give to Mr Steele," Holmes continued, "a note in my own hand to pass along to his employers at the L & N Railroad. To protect Robert Ferguson's good name, I've written that, whilst not offering the identity of the prime actor in the plot, the assassin exonerated L & N in the planning of Goebel's murder. I believe my reputation in the States is strong enough to alleviate any anxieties at the railroad. It is, of course, near impossible to put an end to the common gossip and speculation that will no doubt go on indefinitely."

"I'm much obliged to you for putting the record straight," said Steele. Holding up his glass once more, he added, "To Birdy Edwards. It was he, after all, who set me on the track to Baker Street and ultimately to the revelation of Goebel's true killer."

"Birdy Edwards," Holmes and I chorused, both of us in agreement that the late Pinkerton would have been duly pleased at the outcome of our investigation. No sooner had Holmes put down his glass than he signalled for the waiter to have one of the domed silver trollies brought to our table.

"One final question, Holmes," I asked before the carver arrived. "Do you not feel responsible for leading Jack Ferguson to his death?"

My friend stared into my eyes. "The man had become a hired killer, Watson, a paid assassin. However much I am to blame for his departure from this world, the regret does not give me much pause."

With that, we all turned our attention towards the trolley that was just then arriving before us.

*****

Following Holmes's retirement in 1903 to a cottage in Sussex, he and I saw each other only sparingly. Yet long after our involvement in the death of Jack Ferguson, we continued to keep track of the latest legal developments regarding the assassination of William Goebel.

Thanks to the accounts of pressmen like Irvin Cobb and our friend David Graham Phillips (himself the victim of an assassin's bullet in 1911), we could follow the evolution of the legal entanglements related to primary figures in the case. It was on 21 May 1900, just a few months after Goebel's death, that the United States Supreme Court ruled on the legitimacy of Goebel's gubernatorial victory over Republican William Taylor. Citing the argument of states' rights, the Court refused to overturn Goebel's election that had earlier been upheld by the Democratically-inclined Supreme Court of Kentucky.

On the other hand, appeals courts dominated by Republicans nullified the convictions of Caleb Powers and James Howard. Although Powers himself would face three more trials and actually be convicted in two of them, sympathetic courts demanded new trials both times, the last concluding with what the Americans term a "hung jury"—that is, the members of the jury were not in agreement, and the case was dismissed.

Like Powers, Howard, the presumed gunman, also faced another trial; but though unlike his associate he was convicted, in 1908 both he and Powers were finally pardoned. For his part, Youtsey, the alleged go-between, was paroled in 1916 and pardoned three years later. In the end, Caleb Powers, who had been tried four times for murder without success, was elected to the United States Congress in 1911. He would go on to serve four successive terms.

One evening some years after the various aspects of the Goebel affair had been settled, Holmes came up to London. Whilst enjoying cigars together in my sitting room, we found ourselves discussing the contradictory resolution of the entire business.

"If I recall correctly, Watson," Holmes observed, "in the case you titled 'The Abbey Grange', you recorded an observation of mine regarding the law. At the time, I said that I would rather play tricks with the law of England than with my own conscience. Is that not right?"

"Yes, Holmes," I said with a nod, "I believe you quote yourself correctly."

"Well then, " said he stretching out his long legs and exhaling a plume of blue smoke, "allow me to also say that, judging from all we have learned in the Goebel case, it would appear that in America it is the law that plays the tricks and one's conscience that suffers."

I nodded; and both of us, yet again contemplating the protean relationship between England and the United States, proceeded to fill the room with ever-thickening clouds of smoke.

An Adventure in Darkness

"You don't understand," he cried in a voice
that was meant to be great and resolute, and which broke. "You are blind,
and I can see . . . ."
--H.G. Wells
"The Country of the Blind"

*D*uring the twenty years I had known Sherlock Holmes, I had come to accept his various eccentricities. The chemical experiments on the scarred wooden table, the bullet holes in our wall, the letters transfixed with a blade to the mantel—all these I had learned to tolerate. But seeing Holmes that November afternoon in '01—eyes hidden behind a black silk cloth, Alpine walking stick in hand, and posed at the centre of our dismantled sitting room motionless as a statue—I thought that perhaps the poor man had finally lost his senses.

It was late in the day, and I had just completed an invigorating round of billiards at the club with my old friend Thurston. The autumnal winds were blowing; and as I walked along the Strand, contemplating a sweet sherry and warm fire, the thought of Holmes's strange activities never crossed my mind. No sooner did I enter our Baker Street lodgings, however, than I realised my simple plans for the remainder of the afternoon had come off the rails.

The sitting room lay in shambles. In spite of the golden streaks of sun still lighting the sky, the green damask curtains were already closed. And yet even in the darkness, I could see that the place looked as if Lear's hurricanoes had passed through. The two armchairs had been shoved aside; a stool, knocked over. Under a scattering of newspapers, the bearskin rug lay in a heap. Shards of a broken yellow saucer decorated the floor, an overturned yellow cup leaving black coffee stains on the white tablecloth.

In the midst of all this mayhem, the blindfolded Holmes, clad in his mouse-coloured dressing gown, cocked an ear. "Watson," said he, "is that you?"

"Of course, it is I. Who else should it be? What on earth has possessed you?"

Holmes pulled up one side of the blindfold and, Cyclops-like, peered at me with a single grey eye. "I am soon to be visited by a blind young lady, and I was endeavouring to understand what having no sight must be like."

"But, Holmes," I protested, "you know every inch of this room. The placement of the chairs is part of your interviewing strategy, and you regularly count the number of steps from the outer door. If you pardon the redundancy, you could navigate this room blindfolded."

"Right you are, old fellow—which is why I asked Mrs Hudson to draw the curtains and to move things randomly about whilst my eyes remained covered. She was none too pleased with the task, I can assure you."

With a shake of my head, I turned up the gas to bring light to the room.

"*Fiat lux*," Holmes said, tossing the blindfold towards a chair. "I am afraid I did bump the table. Hence, the broken plate and the overturned cup."

I shook my head at Holmes's behaviour. "Who is the woman that has prompted all this?" I asked whilst righting the fallen stool. "A case, I presume?"

"Quite so," said he as he stooped to recover the newspapers from the rug. "She is called Anna Nuñez. You may have read in the *Times* of her husband, Juan Carlos Nuñez, the famed mountaineer from Colombia. He has just come back to England after having been lost for months whilst off trekking somewhere in the Andes. They have been married for only a short while."

"I cannot say that I remember the story; but if he is no longer missing, then what can his wife wish to speak to you about?"

"That, my friend," smiled Holmes, "I am afraid I cannot deduce." He was now employing his stick to flatten the lingering waves in the rug. "The request came via an oral message from her servant earlier today. Other than forewarning me that his mistress lacked sight, he had no knowledge of the matter in question." Holmes consulted the clock on the mantel. "She is due here at 5.00."

"Why, that is in less than a quarter hour!" I cried. "We must put the rest of these things back more quickly."

"Your enthusiasm suggests you wish to join the consultation."

"Of course I do," said I, "if I am invited."

"It goes without saying, old fellow," answered Holmes who, not without some amusement, was watching me attempt to set the armchairs at just their proper angles.

Holmes proceeded to prop his stick against the wall nearest the door; and I, taking care to wrap the coffee cup and pieces of broken plate within the stained tablecloth, moved the whole mess out of sight. Only after a final glance round the room assured me that we had corrected all of Mrs Hudson's handiwork did I feel comfortable in announcing, "All is in order."

"Well and good," said Holmes with single clap of his hands, "—though I am certain Mrs Nuñez will not notice the difference."

"Holmes," said I, ignoring the callousness of his remark, "we cannot have the poor woman tripping over the *débris* of your little experiment."

With another check of the clock, Holmes exchanged his dressing gown for a jacket. Fortunately, I had remained in my coat, for we did not have much longer to wait. Indeed, it was just a matter of minutes before we heard Mrs Hudson helping someone climb the stairs.

"Here we are, my dear," said our landlady just beyond the door, and then there was a sharp rap. "Mr Holmes," she called with motherly concern, "let's not keep this young lady waiting, shall we."

Holmes swung wide the door, and Mrs Hudson, casting an approving eye round the neatened sitting room, guided an attractive young woman into our presence.

"Mrs *Nunez*," our landlady announced, omitting the nasalisation called for by the tilde. Despite her polite attentiveness, Mrs Hudson's mispronunciation of the Spanish name exhibited the same acerbic tone she employed when referring to all manner of foreigners. Indeed, having delivered to Sherlock Holmes his client, our landlady seemed eager to depart the scene and quickly closed the door as she exited.

"Mr Sherlock Holmes?" the woman enquired in impeccable English.

I am bound to admit that with a surname of Nuñez, I had expected a dark-skinned, dark-haired lady. But now I realised that the appellation belonged to her husband and that the blonde young woman standing before us was properly English. With skin as white as porcelain and a dress of burgundy velvet, she looked like someone ready to step out for an evening's entertainment. Her hair was done up in a fashionable *chignon;* her small features were pleasing to observe. And yet, of course, she was blind.

No smoke-lensed spectacles concealed her affliction; and yet one could not detect whether the orbs appeared rheumy or glazed because in point of fact her eyes were simply closed. Detracting not a whit from her beauty, her eyelids, rimmed as they were with long, dark lashes, appeared capable of opening at any moment. It was as if she were Sleeping Beauty awaiting the kiss of a handsome prince.

"Mr Holmes?" she asked again, at the same time, pivoting her head slowly to the left and right.

"I am Sherlock Holmes, Madam," said he.

Upon hearing his voice, Mrs Nuñez turned to face him. "I am Anna Nuñez," she said, extending an ungloved hand. "Please forgive the informality, but because I rely so much on my sense of touch, I find gloves to be an encumbrance."

"Understood, Madam," said Holmes as his long fingers enveloped hers.

The lady turned her head in *my* direction. "Is there someone else present?"

"Indeed there is," Holmes said. "Standing next to me is my friend and associate, Dr John Watson. I assure you that you may speak as freely to him as you do to me."

"Charmed," said I. "Allow me to offer you a seat." And I took the liberty of placing a deferential hand on her arm as I guided her to a chair.

"It is unusual to have someone with your condition visit us, Mrs Nuñez," said Holmes as we seated ourselves opposite her. "Other than the fact that you have been blind from birth, that you do not like coffee, and that you are an accomplished pianist, I really cannot imagine what more I can tell you."

Mrs Nuñez's eyebrows shot up in amazement. "I—I have heard of your powers, Mr Holmes, but I must confess that you take my breath away. How do you know such details about me?"

"Elementary, Mrs Nuñez. You set your head so instinctually to listen for vital sounds and to catch stray aromas that one must assume you have cultivated the employment of compensatory senses since birth. You frowned when you detected the lingering aroma of our spilt coffee—hence, my inference that you do not like the brew. And then there are the calluses on the pads of your fingers—I felt them when we shook hands—thus, my reference to someone who frequents the piano keyboard."

"I might have been a typist," she shot back. "Memorisation of the placement of the machine's keys allows the blind to type, you know."

Holmes's quick smile indicated his appreciation of the woman's perceptiveness.

"I am afraid," said he, "that the rough spots at the outside edges of your thumbs are the quite distinctive results of striking keys in distant octaves. Such stretching is more common to the pianist than to anything a typist is required to perform."

"I fear," said she with a demure little chuckle, "that I shall have to wear gloves in the future."

"A trifle, Madam, I assure you. Yet I repeat that I am at a loss to suggest why you have come to see me."

Mrs Nuñez adjusted the small black reticule she held in her lap. "Let me first apologise for calling on you at so late an afternoon hour. But I must tell you that time is measured quite differently by those who cannot see."

"Is it not true," I offered, "that, when contemplating sleep, the blind relate more to heat and cold than to light and darkness?"

"Indeed, Doctor. I for one often find myself at odds with the schedules of sighted people. I am, you see, a very late riser and, as a result, tend to remain awake till the late hours of the night."

"The sleep patterns of the blind," murmured Holmes. "I confess it is a topic to which I have not given much thought. Perhaps I shall write a monograph on the subject. I would expect that your husband might be able to contribute some relevant observations regarding your own behaviour."

Holmes's mention of the woman's husband caused a reaction. She tightened her grip on her reticule and knit her brow. "It is about my husband that I wish to speak, Mr Holmes, though I imagine you came to the same conclusion, and that is why you so deftly brought the conversation back to Juan Carlos."

Holmes smiled again, another sign of respect for the woman's acumen though, of course, she herself could not see these responses. Holmes must have wondered, as did I, if Mrs Nuñez understood that in relation to a female client, trouble with a husband was always a safe guess for any detective to venture.

"For you gentlemen to understand our marriage," she continued, "I think that an explanation of my background would be helpful. I am sure you have realised that my trappings of success do not typify the conditions experienced by most sightless people. For them, life has not been so accommodating."

"By all means," I said, "tell us your story."

"My mother was an actress of no great repute," Mrs Nuñez explained. "And my father left her once he discovered that their baby could not see. But my mother was a fighter and would not allow her daughter to be pitied or condemned or even ridiculed—the way too many with my condition are treated in our society. She worked hard and saved enough money to enrol me in the Royal Normal College for the Blind here in London."

"That would be the school in Upper Norwood," I observed. I myself had directed a blind patient to that institution. It was renowned for its worthwhile programs.

"The very same. My mother heard that the school had been designed for children like me. That turned out to be true. In addition to my regular studies, I learned to read Braille and to play the piano. The college is well known for the piano tuners it has produced, but such work is generally reserved for men. None the less, I sharpened my craft; and when I was not mastering how to tune the instrument, I was perfecting my ability to play it. I grew quite skilled in the art; and whilst I would never think of performing at the Royal Albert Hall, I have been invited to play at various smaller venues here in London."

"Would that we had a piano," I said without thinking. Obviously, the woman was a client seeking help from a detective, not a pianist in need of an audience.

"It was at my performance of Chopin's *Études* in late March," she continued, "that I was approached by Juan Carlos Nuñez, he who was destined to become my husband. I could tell from touching his face—he has a straight nose and a square chin—that he was a handsome man. And I soon learned how, thanks to his mountaineering skills, he had made not only a name for himself among the rich but also the money to go along with it.

"Juan Carlos could have had his pick of many sighted women, and yet for some reason he seemed obsessed with me. Perhaps I should have recognised the danger signs then. But he followed me to my various concerts, took me to dinner, courted me, and in late May—within two months of our having met—asked to marry me."

"Only two months," I observed judgementally. "Not a lengthy courtship."

"No, indeed, Doctor. I was, in fact, a June bride." She added this last bit with the blush of a little girl. Within a moment, however, her mood grew sombre again. "You forget my condition, Doctor Watson. Any offer of marriage is far beyond what a blind woman can hope to expect—and I assure you that an offer from an attractive suitor like Juan Carlos Nuñez is not easily ignored. "

I knew that her charge was true. So compelling an image did this young woman present that one might almost be excused for forgetting her plight. Ignore the handkerchief she had removed from her reticule and begun to twist, and one might wrongly assume she had not a care in the world.

"In short, gentlemen, I accepted his proposal. We have been married for almost six months now, and it is only during the last few weeks that his behaviour has begun to disturb me."

Leaning back in his chair, Holmes steepled his fingers, as he was wont to do in anticipation of hearing the details of a case. "If you would, Madam," said he, "describe for us your concerns."

"Yes," said Mrs Nuñez with a sigh. "It is, after all, what I have come here for. My concerns go back about a month. It was then that Juan Carlos began muttering to himself."

"Muttering, you say?" asked Holmes. "Muttering what?"

"He repeats the same phrase over and over again—like a refrain. It is as if he is trying to reassure or convince himself of some strange matter. And he continues to this day."

Holmes bent forward, his grey eyes flashing. "And what is it that he says?"

"In the country of the blind," she said simply. "At least, that is all I can hear."

"'In the country of the blind'?" Holmes repeated.

"Nothing more?" I asked.

"Should there be more, Doctor? Needless to say, I am not well read. Does this phrase have some greater meaning?"

"It could be part of the old proverb," I responded, thinking of the common-enough utterance made by those with limited attributes who hoped to set themselves above those with even fewer. "In the country of the blind," I announced, "the one-eyed man is king."

Holmes did me one better; he stated it in Latin: "*In regione caecorum rex est luscus*—so stated the philosopher, Erasmus, in the early sixteenth century. Some trace the adage back to early Biblical interpretations."

A furrow marked the woman's brow. "I shall take your word for it, gentlemen, but what does it have to do with me? Juan Carlos and I live in Berkeley Square, not in some 'country of the blind'. And my husband certainly has the use of *both* of his eyes—not to mention his outstanding physical skill. He is most assuredly not someone of—what was your phrase, Doctor? —'limited attributes'."

"Sorry," I replied. "I had no intention—"

But Mrs Nuñez ignored my interruption. "I am at wit's end. When I ask him what he is saying, he just ignores me. Gentlemen, I do not understand why he should go about babbling some nonsense about a one-eyed man. Do you?"

Holmes did not answer immediately. Instead, he cast his gaze directly at our guest as he ruminated on her situation. It was a rude and intrusive posture, which he might have modified had she been able to observe him. At last, he said, "There is something else that troubles you, madam. I suspect that you have not told us all."

Mrs Nuñez lowered her head. With great difficulty, she admitted, "He—he has struck me, Mr Holmes."

"The blackguard!" I exploded. Hitting a woman is bad enough. But striking a blind person—woman or man—goes well beyond the pale.

"It was really more of a slap," she said. "But he had never done it before, and it goes without saying that I am easy prey. He apologised the first time he—"

"The *first* time!" I cried. "Do you mean to say there were more?"

She nodded. "That is why I came to see Mr Holmes, Doctor. I am afraid for my safety."

"Certainly the police—"

"Believe me, Doctor Watson," she said firmly, "I can assure you that the police take little interest in protecting wives from their husbands. There's many the judge who winks at wife-beating. And as for protecting the blind—let us just say that the odds against *us* are even worse."

I listened to her words, and I knew she spoke the truth.

Mrs Nuñez now turned back to my friend. "Mr Holmes, I was hoping that you could get to the bottom of what is causing Juan Carlos to behave as he does. For my own peace of mind, I have to believe his problem can be solved."

Sherlock Holmes does not easily display sympathy, but the knotting of his bushy brows told me that, like myself, he was greatly concerned for the welfare of this noble woman.

"I will help you, Madam," he said quickly.

She reached into her reticule once more and withdrew a small set of visitor's cards. They were held together with a red ribbon, and I would later learn that they contained her address in addition to her name. Slipping out the topmost, she offered it in Holmes's direction.

"Rest assured, Madam," said he as he snatched the card from her wavering hand, "we shall get to the bottom of this business." He moved his chair as he stood, a signal that we were finished, and Mrs Nuñez rose as well. "Watson will help you secure a cab," said Holmes and with a gesture of his head indicated my assignment.

It was a task I carried out with the utmost responsibility and concern. In fact, I carefully guided Mrs Nuñez to the stairwell, accompanied her down the stairs, and escorted her out to the kerb where I hailed a hansom. Only after she handed me another one of her cards to be given to the driver did I help her climb in.

*****

By the time I returned to our rooms, Sherlock Holmes had already begun reviewing the entries in his abstracts under the letter "N".

"Juan Carlos Nuñez, mountaineer," he announced as I sat down across the table from him. "Born in 1870 near Bogotá, Colombia. Mastered English at an early age, a diligent reader, sailed the seven seas, employed as a guide by numerous British hikers, including some of the most famous of the English aristocracy. Granted membership in the Alpine Club three years ago."

"Quite an accomplished fellow," I observed, "at least, in that line of work."

Even as I spoke, Holmes was reading ahead. "Listen to this, Watson," said he, raising a forefinger. "Apparently, Nuñez was thought to have died on his last excursion, this one near Quito, Ecuador. In May of last year, he replaced a Swiss guide, one of three leading a small group of Englishmen up Parascotopetl, the so-called "Matterhorn of the Andes". It was then that he disappeared. According to Pointer, a fellow-climber whose narrative is supposedly the best of the many written about Nuñez's disappearance,* they followed his tracks to the top of a long, steep slope. The disrupted snow revealed where he had lost his footing and tumbled to the bottom. Although there was no sign of the mountaineer himself, Pointer reported that they could just barely make out far below the edge of a sharp precipice over which, they presumed, Nuñez had fallen to his death. In light of the tragedy, the group discontinued the climb."

"But as we know from Mrs Nuñez," I pointed out, "that is not the end of the story."

"Correct," Holmes said without looking up from the text. "It says here that with little explanation, Nuñez reappeared in February of this year, about a month after the death of Queen Victoria."

"And it was just a month later," I added, "in March, that he met his soon-to-be wife."

"Quite so, Watson," said Holmes, closing the volume. "And yet in spite of Pointer's details, the stark truth remains that we have

---

* Pointer, Nigel. *"The Disappearance of Juan Carlos Nuñez." Alpine Journal.* 1900 [annual]. (JHW)

no information about what transpired between the time of Nuñez's disappearance and his return to civilization. It is a time-period for which we must account. To shield Mrs Nuñez from her husband's suspicions, we should begin our investigation at the Alpine Club. It is the London centre for all matters mountaineering, and you will recall that Nuñez is a member. We shall go there in the morning."

Having determined our plans for the following day, Holmes picked up his violin. A Bach partita was his choice on this particular evening. With all due respect to my friend, I would have preferred listening to Mrs Nuñez play Chopin on the piano.

*****

A breakfast of kippers, toast, and coffee preceded our departure for the Alpine Club the next morning. At 23, Savile Row, the club was situated not far from the Nuñez's house in Berkeley Square; and it was probably this very proximity that had caused Nuñez to establish his home there. Just as we were proceeding out the door, Holmes reached for his deerstalker and Inverness cape. The cold weather easily justified warm outerwear, but I believe that Holmes felt his *accoutrements* added credibility to his appearance as a hiker. I settled for my heavy coat.

The Alpine Club is located at the far end of Savile Row* next to the arched passageway to Conduit Street. The building includes a large meeting hall, a reading room, a map room and a library. In the lobby behind a desk of polished red-mahogany sat a bespectacled clerk, one Mr Horace Stringfellow according to the plaque in front of him, a slightly-built chap with middle-parted, black hair. Ironically, he appeared to offer no hint of a talent for mountain climbing.

Holmes presented himself to Stringfellow as a seasoned hiker looking for greater challenges. "I'm told," said Holmes, "that you have a guide here who's most adept at leading groups on foreign climbs. I've been up to the Reichenbach Falls and am currently thinking about an expedition to the Andes."

"The Andes?" Stringfellow queried.

---

* The building was demolished in 1936 to allow the construction of a throughway to Conduit Street. (DDV)

"Yes, and I've heard that you have a member named Nuñez who's quite familiar with the area."

"Ah, yes, Nuñez," said Stringfellow. He absent-mindedly began spinning the small globe to the right of his desk blotter. "Actually, Nuñez had some problems on his last climb and, as yet, has not seemed interested in going out again." Stringfellow smiled. "Funny thing, though. You are the second person today asking about the man."

Holmes smiled at the emergence of an unexpected development. "Interesting," said he. "Was it someone else asking about a venture to South America?"

"No," replied the secretary, stopping the globe. "A writer, actually. But you can speak to him yourself. He said he would be stopping in the reading room. I have not seen him leave, so I presume he must still be there. It is just down the hallway to your left."

Holmes thanked the clerk, and we were already in the hall by the time Stringfellow's last sentence reached our ears: "We do have other guides to recommend, you know."

The reading room looked quite inviting. Rather than the bookshelves one would expect to find in such a room, however, the walls below an upper border of pale rosettes were bedecked with paintings, majestic renderings of the world's great mountains. Oh, I could appreciate their beauty readily enough, but not their individuality. To me one snow-capped mountaintop set against a bright blue sky looked much like another. Fortunately, each frame contained a title. Here was the Matterhorn; there, Mont Blanc. Here a portrait of the American Mt. Whitney; there, a picture of the African Kilimanjaro. Featuring explosions of red and yellow, one singularly dramatic piece depicted the imagined eruption of ancient Mt. Vesuvius.

Actual flames danced in the fireplace on the side wall; in the centre of the room stood an oval oak table laden with books, most all of them dealing with various climbing expeditions. Half a dozen chairs filled the room including two plush armchairs on either side of the fireplace. In the armchair facing the open door sat a familiar-looking gentleman with a narrow face, thick moustache, dark hair, and piercing eyes. He was reading a newspaper though looking up at the doorway every now and again.

"There is our writer," I whispered to Holmes in the hallway.

"I am impressed, Watson," he replied softly. "Besides the ink smudges on his fingers and the frayed edges of his cuffs, how can you be so certain?"

"Because I know the man, Holmes," said I confidently (in spite of missing the details Holmes had pointed out). "He is the fantasy writer, H.G. Wells. Author of such books as *The Time Machine* and *The War of the Worlds*."

Holmes nodded in recognition. "Too superficial for my taste, I am afraid."

"Not my style either," said I, "but still a pleasure to read. You will recall that I met him at Brede Place when I was visiting Stephen and Cora Crane. We struck up quite the friendship."*

Holmes and I entered the room, and immediately H.G. Wells studied my face. "Could that actually be Dr John Watson?" he asked in his high-pitched voice.

"It is indeed, Mr Wells," said I.

"Bertie," he reminded me.

"It is so good to see you again, Bertie. And may I present to you my friend, Mr Sherlock Holmes."

"Sherlock Holmes, at last," said Wells rising to his feet. "I missed you at that year's-end *fête* at Brede Place, you know."

The two men shook hands, each one seemingly taking the measure of the other—on the one side, a master of unravelling crimes; on the other, a master of spinning fantasies.

Wells invited us to sit, and Holmes took the unoccupied armchair whilst I pulled over the straight-backed chair from the book table and placed it between them.

Holmes wasted no time with amenities. "Mr Wells, I must ask what brings you to the Alpine Club?"

"Just up from Spade House, our new home in Folkestone. I am always on the hunt for fresh story-material, you see; and I had heard some rumours from my hiking friends concerning a guide called Nuñez who had reportedly gone missing on an expedition to

---

* Interested readers may find Watson's account of his initial meeting with H.G. Wells in Watson's narrative titled *Sherlock Holmes and the Baron of Brede Place*. (DDV)

the Andes. Just my sort of thing. He was said to be connected to the Alpine Club here in London, so I came up to find out more about him."

"And did you?" Holmes wanted to know.

"That I did," chortled Wells. "In all due modesty, it was thanks to my literary reputation that the chap at the desk, Stringfellow, put me in touch with the man. Nuñez and I first met two days ago in this very room; and after I had agreed to give him an advance on half of any profits I might earn from writing about his travels, he agreed to bring me the notes he had made after having gone missing in the mountains. Believe me when I say that he hinted at having had quite an adventure in uncharted territory."

Holmes leaned forward. "And what, may I ask, did you learn, Mr Wells?"

The writer frowned. "With all due respect, Holmes, I am not one to give away the plots of my stories."

Sherlock Holmes narrowed his eyes. "I assure you, Mr Wells, that a person's life may hang in the balance."

"I should imagine no less," Wells said. "Else, why would Sherlock Holmes be involved? And yet even so . . . ."

My friend refused to be put off. "It is a young woman's life we are discussing here," said he. "But perhaps we can strike a bargain. Assuming that what we discover is not of a criminal nature and that, as a consequence, we do not have to involve the police, if you reveal to me what you have learned, I will do my utmost to see that you will be first to get any titbits we turn up in our investigation."

"I suppose that whether I agree or not depends on just what sort of investigation you are conducting."

Holmes took a deep breath. "Mr Wells," said he, "a moment ago you spoke of your own reputation. I ask you to consider the value of mine. I tell you again that a woman's life is at stake."

H.G. Wells stared at Sherlock Holmes for what seemed like a full minute. At last, with only the crackle of the fire breaking the silence, he nodded his assent; and I joined Holmes in leaning forward to hear Wells's account.

"This chap Nuñez told me of the horrific fall he suffered on his last climb in Ecuador. He tumbled from atop a towering precipice, and it was the soft snow upon which he landed that saved his life. Not only did he find himself in an unknown valley, but it was there that he also discovered a community of primitive villagers. They lived in stone huts totally isolated from the outside world. What is more, to his great frustration, surrounded as he was by towering mountains, massive glaciers, and dense forest, he could find no way out. After much futile searching, he concluded that he was going to have to live with these strange people."

"What made them so strange?" Holmes asked.

"Oh," said Wells, "did I not say? They were all blind. Been so for generations."

At the word "blind", Holmes and I exchanged glances. No doubt Holmes, like me, was recalling the proverb reported by Mrs Nuñez.

"Let me guess," I suggested to Wells. "When he discovered he could not find a way out, he quoted the old saying, 'In the country of the blind, the one-eyed man is king."

"Why, that is absolutely correct, Watson," cried Wells, clearly astonished by my prescience. "Nuñez figured that with all his knowledge, if he could not escape from these people, then at the very least he could become their leader. He would impress them with his grand knowledge of a world they knew nothing of—light, dark, colour, stars."

Sherlock Holmes shook his head. "To persons who have no frame of reference," he observed, "such concepts are most difficult to convey."

"Quite right, Holmes," Wells said. "The way Nuñez reported it, the people thought him mad. I should point out that all this did not occur overnight. Nuñez claims he has written an account that fills in the details, including his *affaire de cœur* with a young blind woman there. It seems his resolution to remain in the valley was enhanced by his infatuation with her."

"And yet," said I, "he attempted a dangerous and near-impossible escape in order to return to England."

Wells patted his moustache. "In the end, you see, he did find a way to climb out—a challenge he had considered hopeless till he finally worked up the courage to give it a go."

"But he could have been killed in the process," said I. "What made him take the risk?"

"Oh," said Wells again, "did I not say? To cure him of his so-called madness, the village leaders had decided to remove what they determined to be the cause of his derangement."

"And what was that?" the doctor in me wanted to know.

"Sorry. I seem to be omitting all the crucial bits. Perhaps I am just reluctant to reveal the best parts of the story I intend to write." Here Wells smiled and paused to stare into the fire. Like Sherlock Holmes, Wells too recognised the drama inherent in the facts behind a compelling narrative. Only after he reckoned enough time had passed to increase the suspense to its maximum did he resume. "It seems that the villagers had resolved to cure Nuñez of his madness by removing those two queer, distended growths that they felt just below his brow. After all, the villagers had no such appendages, and so they assumed those irritant bodies to be responsible for his problems. In short, gentlemen, they fully intended to put out his eyes."

The simple statement came like a thunderbolt. I no longer heard the outside din of voices, cries of hawkers, rattle of carriages. My own eyes would not focus. The conclusion of Wells's report seemed not unlike a death sentence for Juan Carlos Nuñez.

Now Holmes and I turned to stare into the fire. For his part, H.G. Wells, who apparently knew nothing of Nuñez's new wife, merely sat back in silence. We all remained that way for a few minutes.

It was Holmes who returned to the subject. "Mr Wells," said he, "you are a student of human psychology. What do you make of the fact that, upon his return, this Nuñez married a blind woman?"

"A blind woman, you say?" said Wells. "He never got round to telling me the most recent events in the story. But if one thinks about it, one should not be too surprised at such a marriage—at least, not if one remembers his Swift. Do you recall Gulliver's final voyage, his journey to the land of the Houyhnhnms?"

"The talking horses?" I recalled.

"The talking horses who were also philosophers," Wells reminded us. "Recall that when Gulliver returned to England, his distaste for human beings had grown so intense that he spent all his days in the barn with regular horses, the non-speaking kind. As I recollect, he said that 'the first Money' he laid out upon his return was to buy a pair of 'Stone-Horses',* and he admitted to conversing with them four hours each day."

Holmes flashed a smile. "You are suggesting that Nuñez was like Gulliver—that he may still have been so much in love with the blind lady he had left behind that he attempted to recreate the experience with a contemporary replacement. You are the literary man, sir; and yet I believe there are also readers who interpret Gulliver's admission as proof of his madness. I know that *I* do."

"Perhaps, you are right, Holmes. But why not see for yourself. Did I not say? The reason I have planted myself here is to meet with Mr Nuñez. In truth, he and I have an appointment at noon today."

Somewhere in the building a clock was striking that very hour. If the author of *The Time Machine* was correct, we should not have long to wait.

*****

After some five minutes had passed, H.G. Wells flicked his head at the open door. Holmes turned in that direction, and I looked to my right. Standing in the portal was a tall, dark-skinned man with a full, rich head of jet-black hair. Dressed in a snug brown suit, he was holding a bowler and gave a nod of recognition to Wells. Upon surveying Holmes and me, however, his expression changed. His brows knotted; and as he approached, the strong set of his jaw seemed to become all the more rigid.

"What's this then, Mr Wells?" the man asked with the faintest lilt of a Spanish accent. "You said nothing about bringing others to our meeting."

We all rose; and Wells attempted to introduce us, but Holmes was in no mood for delay.

"See here, Mr Nuñez," said he, "my name is Sherlock Holmes, and I believe you pose a threat to your wife. My associate Dr Watson and I have come to demand an explanation."

"I've heard of you, Mr Holmes," said Nuñez with a wry smile. "Many's the English mountaineer who carries your stories about in his rucksack. But that doesn't mean I'll tolerate your interference in

* Today we would call them stallions. (DDV)

my personal affairs." He turned to Wells and held out his palm. "You promised me money."

"You promised me your notes," Wells replied.

Nuñez patted his left breast as if to imply that his papers were stored in an inner pocket. "Now give me what's due," he insisted, still holding out his hand, "so I don't have to spend any more time with these pests."

Slowly, Wells withdrew a wallet from inside his coat and produced a number of notes.

Suddenly, Holmes grabbed Nuñez's extended wrist. "Tell me about your wife *now*!" he demanded, the abrupt action an obvious tribute to how much Holmes was worrying about his innocent client.

A beatific calmness suddenly seemed to engulf the mountaineer. *"¿Porqué no?"* he shrugged. "It matters little to me any longer."

Holmes let go his hold. "What do you mean?"

"Anna was a diversion," Nuñez said blandly, "a poor substitute for my true love, Medina-saroté. I am planning to return unencumbered to the country of the blind—and make her my bride."

"'Unencumbered', you say," repeated Holmes. "You plan to win some sort of divorce before you go." It was more a statement than a question.

"No, Mr Holmes, I intend to leave right now—from here in fact—as soon as I take my money."

Holmes nodded. "Then you will content yourself with becoming a bigamist?"

The word caused Nuñez to blanch. "No, I will *not*!" he proclaimed.

"What do you mean?" Holmes fairly shouted the question this time. "What have you *done*?"

Suddenly, Nuñez burst into maniacal laughter. It began as a high-pitched howl and devolved into a series of staccato barks. To this very day, the recollection of those animal sounds makes the hair on the back of my neck stand up.

Then just as suddenly, he turned complacent again. *"¿Quién sabe?"* he shrugged, gazing at Holmes.

My friend and the mountaineer locked eyes. In the moments that followed, it seemed that Holmes was picking the man's very brain.

Mere spectators, Wells and I watched as the two stared at each other. It was Nuñez who broke the tension with the wave of his hand. "Gentlemen," he exclaimed to all of us, "*adiós!*" And in an explosion of movement, he grabbed the banknotes, which still lay in Wells's hand, and raced out of the room. He paused only long enough to shout with a laugh, "She's a light sleeper, Holmes—be careful not to wake her!" and then he was gone.

Instinctively, I moved to follow; but Holmes clutched my arm. "No, we must attend to the woman."

With a quick nod to Wells, we rushed down the hall, past a confused Stringfellow in the lobby, and out into the cold air. As I noted earlier, the Nuñez home in Berkeley Square was not far from the Alpine Club. Our feet would convey us there more quickly than a hansom. And so with a blowing wind at our backs, we took off past the shops in Savile Row and zigzagged our way from Clifford Street to New Bond Street to Bruton Street and finally into the Square itself.

As we ran, Holmes pulled out the card Mrs Nuñez had given him containing her address.

"We have no precise idea what the man has planned," said he as we pulled up in front of a small terraced house of grey stone, "but I suspect we should not arouse the household when we enter."

No sooner had we reached the outer door than Holmes produced his lock-picking tools, and within seconds we were inside. No servants appeared, and I was about to leap forward, but again Holmes restrained me. Placing his forefinger at his lips, he signalled me to be silent.

Dark-blue velvet curtains had been closed to keep the house in darkness. None the less, we managed to tiptoe across the entry hall until we were facing a pale, hard-edged stone staircase. It was only then that I understood the nature of Nuñez's diabolical plot, a plot that Holmes himself had somehow already deduced. For that matter, it was only then that I understood the madman's final words to us: "Be careful not to wake her."

In spite of the gloom, I could just barely discern the lethal piano wire Nuñez had mounted at the top of the staircase some four inches above the penultimate step. The thin wire had been pulled taut between the two vertical rungs supporting the bannister rails on either side of the stairs.

At that moment, we heard a door swing open; and Mrs Nuñez, dressed in a white, silk dressing gown with her blonde hair askew, appeared at the head of the stairs. "Is someone there?" she called, moving forward at the same time.

"It is Sherlock Holmes, madam!" my friend shouted. "Do not move!"

She heard the name, but his command did not register.

"Mr Holmes?" she queried, walking forward all the while.

My friend bounded up the stairs just as the poor lady was reaching the wire. When her small, slippered foot encountered the obstacle, she let out a curiously mild "oh," and stumbled forward—directly into the arms of Sherlock Holmes.

*****

Would the fall have killed her? It is difficult to say. A week later, Holmes and I were still discussing the case. On this occasion, we were seated in our armchairs before the fire at Baker Street drinking the sherry that, thanks to Holmes's *charade* with the blindfold a few days earlier, I had never got to sample. As an ironic reminder of that madcap experiment, Holmes actually discovered the square of black silk with which he had covered his eyes. It was stuck between the cushion and the arm of his chair. He cocked an eyebrow and laid the blindfold in his lap.

"Recall, Watson, that Mrs Nuñez tuned pianos as well as played them. As a consequence, I assumed there would be any number of spools of the strong, thin wire lying about the place, a perfect tool for any number of different murderous acts—garrotting and hanging are but two examples. With such an idea in mind, I found Nuñez's remark about not waking his wife to be more predictive than cryptic. It suggested a plot still to be set in motion. If I was correct about the use of piano wire, perhaps the stuff had not yet accomplished its evil task."

Alas, Nuñez's motive was a hypothetical that would remain unresolved. All that we could conclude with any certainty was that, despite our alerting Scotland Yard to the villain's escape, Juan Carlos Nuñez was never found. No doubt, a man with his knowledge of travel possessed many a clandestine alternative for slipping aboard some ship bound for South America, the first leg of his return to the country of the blind. To this day, he remains unaccounted for.

On the other hand, we had little doubt that Mrs Nuñez, in spite of the obstacles she faced on a daily basis, would rebuild her life. In addition to the solace her music provided, she also retained the material properties Nuñez had left behind. As a blind woman who had learned to read Braille, master the piano, and move comfortably among the sighted, there was little reason to doubt she would continue to be successful in the future.

As for Bertie Wells, though neither Holmes nor I knew it at the time, it would take him another two years to write the adventure for which he had paid Nuñez so handsomely. Although Nuñez's notes never turned up—if they ever existed in the first place—Wells was able to construct a credible manuscript from what Nuñez had already told him as well as from—dare I say?—fabrications of his own making.

In 1904 H.G. Wells published the narrative he titled "The Country of the Blind" and in it depicted how life was lived in that hidden valley. The story related Nuñez's initial experiences among the sightless people and continued only until the time of his escape. "An adventure into the unknown—that is the part of Nuñez's tale that people want to hear"—or so Wells explained it. From a practical point of view, Wells left to me the task of writing the more pedestrian account of the mountaineer's escapades in London.

In contemplating my report of the matter, I realised that it was Nuñez's escape that galled me the most. Not only would the man responsible for all the grief escape an appearance in an English courtroom for attempted murder, but presumably he would also get to spend the rest of his days with the woman he loved. "Not fair at all," said I to Holmes.

"And yet, old fellow," Holmes assured me, "he quite literally faces a very dark future indeed."

"Reunited with his lover?" I countered. "Where is the darkness in that?"

"You forget, my dear Watson, the pre-condition of this second marriage—blindness is the price he is to pay." To emphasise the point, Holmes actually covered his eyes with the blindfold and tied it behind his head. "If Nuñez is to be believed, he is destined to lose his eyesight—a prospect once so terrifying that it had prompted him to risk his life in escaping from the valley."

Observing the blindfolded man before me made the judgement seem all the more real.

"It may actually be true," Holmes continued, "that in the country of the blind, the one-eyed man is king"—and here he raised half the cloth to expose a single steel-grey eye—"but let us not forget, old fellow, that unlike myself at this moment, Señor Nuñez will never be able to escape his newly inflicted world of total darkness."

I raised my glass to indicate my appreciation of Holmes's view of justice and then sampled my drink. At the same time, Holmes pulled down the silk so that it once more covered both his eyes. In spite of the blindfold, he had no trouble in bringing the glass of sherry to his lips, which at that very moment were curled into a self-satisfied smile.

An Adventure in the Mid-Day Sun

There was a desert wind blowing . . . . It was one of those hot dry Santa Anas that come down through the mountain passes and curl your hair and make your nerves jump and your skin itch. On nights like that . . . meek little wives feel the edge of the carving knife and study their husbands' necks. Anything can happen.

--Raymond Chandler
"Red Wind"

I

*C*old summers make the warm days feel all the hotter—the way the briefest of smiles from a frosty girl can set a man's heart aflame. That's why the blazing sun in the middle of the cool and wet July of '03 felt as if it were blistering the city. You don't easily forget such lingering heat, the kind that makes the roads shimmer and the horse-droppings and petrol fumes stink; the kind that turns drinking bouts into pub brawls; the kind that makes mild folks contemplate mayhem. On such a day you enter the street with an extra dose of caution; you regard all people with a wary eye.

And yet that very heat seemed to make no difference to Mrs Hudson. I may have been sweltering in my dark, wool tunic, the one with the buttons forming a V down the front; but even if the garbage did smell worse and the wool did stick to my skin, she still commanded: "Billy, remove the trash."

A bit of history: As far as I know, all the page-boys who've ever worked at the house numbered 221 in Baker Street have been called "Billy". In point of fact, I was born "Ray Chandler"—"Raymond", to be more precise—fifteen years ago in America; but when I was seven, my mum brought me to England.

We visited family in Ireland and ultimately settled in London, where I enrolled as a day-student at Dulwich College. Like any other healthy lad, my mind began to wander; and having recently got into some trouble at Dulwich, I was "encouraged" to take a job during the little free time I had, summer months included. According to Florence Thornton Chandler—that is, my mother—I would have much less chance of getting into mischief if I kept busy.*

With Uncle Ernest funding my education, I didn't need the meagre pay a page-boy's job provided. But to show contrition for my earlier transgressions, I agreed to work in Baker Street for Mrs Hudson, who conveniently had connections, however indirect, to my mother. Conveying the odoriferous garbage outside on the hottest day of the year is only one of the many chores I perform for Mrs H. Sweeping floors, running errands, announcing visitors also keep me busy.

Not that I'm complaining, mind. No fifteen-year-old ever wants to waste his time working, but relatively speaking I'm quite happy with my position. What teener wouldn't want to be employed at the residence of Mr Sherlock Holmes, the world's first consulting detective? Especially if that teener wanted to be a writer. For Dr Watson, Mr Holmes's friend and biographer, frequently gives me suggestions concerning my own writing, advice that I have much appreciated since I regard his own work so highly.

I may have read Aeschylus, Marlowe, and Twain at Dulwich, but I still find especially appealing Dr Watson's true-life crime sketches that appear in *The Strand*—not to mention the sensational fiction of his literary agent, Arthur Conan Doyle. Even though Dr Watson recently left Baker Street to be closer to his medical practice, he does come round frequently enough to peruse the new compositions I set aside for him.

Such perquisites, however, provided scant comfort in the heat of that day in July. On such a day, even a priest might loosen his collar. And outside with the garbage in tow, the sun seemed hotter; my uniform, thicker; the dustbin, heavier. If all that wasn't bad enough, I still had to heft the bin's contents—in this case, the detritus of Mrs Hudson's fish and chips from the previous night—into the large metal garbage bin in the narrow alleyway. To my great

* For details of Chandler's so-called misconduct, see Dr Watson's *The Final Page of Baker Street.* (DDV)

disappointment, there weren't even any distractions like servants or other pages dumping their own refuse at the same time. The dusty cobblestone seemed all but deserted.

And yet I did catch a glimpse of one figure out back—though technically he wasn't actually standing *in* the alley, but lurking behind the corner of a neighbouring house. From what I could discern before he ducked behind the wall, he appeared to be a young boy dressed in baggy, black trousers torn at the knee and a loose-fitting, collarless white shirt. The idea that he might be peeking at *me* flashed through my brain; but as I could conjure little reason for such behaviour, I picked up the now empty dustbin and, giving the lad no more thought, returned to my duties inside.

I was passing through the entry hall when the front bell clanged. Wondering who might be visiting on so hot a day, I opened the outer door and was greeted by an enchanting vision, a handsome young woman of fair complexion whose dark hair was swept up in in the latest style. With her trim figure clothed in a dress of white cotton buttoned to her neck and wrists, she was quite the looker. But then, like a moth to the flame, I've always been attracted to women some years older than myself.

"Is Mr Sherlock Holmes in?" she asked, her face flushed from walking in the sun.

I nodded. "I'll announce you," said I and asked for her name, which she provided. She then followed me up the seventeen steps, and I knocked on Mr Holmes's door.

"Enter."

The white muslin curtains of the sitting room had been pulled back to allow a greater flow of air; and as a result, the room was bathed in sunshine. The reflection from the yellow-brick building across the road added to the brightness. Attired in his purple dressing gown, Sherlock Holmes sat in his armchair reading a newspaper and, despite the oppressive heat, smoking his black clay pipe. As usual, his books and newspaper cuttings lay at odd angles round the room—collections that, as I valued my life, I'd been instructed never to touch.

"Mrs Frank Barclay of Hampstead to see you, sir," said I in what I hoped was my most imperious tone.

With a wave of his hand, he signalled that I should show her in. The woman brushed past me as Mr Holmes replaced his dressing gown with a jacket. The two exchanged quick introductions, and I started to exit and close the door.

"No, Billy," Mr Holmes surprised me by saying, "leave the door open. It might help cool the room."

I shrugged and nodded, then slowly left to resume my chores.

"Billy," roared Mrs Hudson from downstairs. "The hallways!"

Now I know that Dr Watson's readers think of Mrs H as some sort of mother hen. But let me assure everyone that, though she might keep after Mr Holmes and the doctor in a maternal fashion, she can call out orders like a cawing gull to those that work for her.

Fortunately, sweeping the hallways included the landing in front of Mr Holmes's rooms—out of Mrs H's line of vision from the ground floor. Had I not been so isolated, I would never have been able to prolong my dawdling and, at the same time, overhear the woman's story.

"—string of valuable pearls stolen from my home in Hampstead," she was in the midst of saying when I returned with the broom, "and I would like *you* to find them for me, Mr Holmes."

Although I'd been employed at Baker Street but a few months, I'd seen enough of the great detective in his listening mode to picture him sitting in his soft chair, his back to the sunlit window so his visitor would see him in silhouette unable to read his expression. His eyes would remain half-closed, his fingers steepled together—almost as if he wasn't paying attention. But, of course, he was—like a serpent about to strike.

"The pearls were given to me by my former *fiancé*—"

"'*Former*'?"

"Phillip Stanley," said Mrs Barclay softly. "Perhaps you've heard of him. He drove racing cars and was killed in a terrible crash during the Paris-Bordeaux Rally a couple of years ago. It was horrible. We were to be married, and—"

An abrupt silence followed except for a few hiccupping sounds which I took to be the woman's sobs.

After a moment to compose herself, she continued. "Phillip gave me the pearls as an engagement gift. The clasp was fashioned to look like a pair of racing wheels, spokes and all."

"Quite so," murmured Mr Holmes.

"I first met Frank Barclay at one of Phillip's races. Frank was charming, and I was vulnerable following Phillip's death, and Frank and I ended up marrying the following year—no doubt, a mistake for both of us. Frank worked on French racing cars, you see, and frequently journeyed off to the Continent to attend races—among the other pleasures he fancied there. To facilitate my own travels during his absence, I hired a driver, a young fellow named Waldo Mackintosh who'd been recommended to me. But Frank is a jealous husband, Mr Holmes; and upon his return, he sacked the man. I won't deny that I may have given him reason to distrust me, but I certainly can find better companionship than a mere *chauffeur*."

I didn't know what Mr Holmes might make of such a confession; but with a woman as pretty as she, I could readily understand her husband's suspicions.

"Here's where the strange part begins," she continued. "Just before his departure, in what appears to be some sort of misguided revenge, this Mackintosh, the driver, made off with the necklace Phillip had given me. I thought I'd never see the pearls again, but yesterday the villain contacted me. He wants to sell the necklace back to me for one hundred pounds. A *hundred* pounds! They're beautiful pearls, but I don't think they're worth *that* much.

"I take it that you never had them appraised."

"No, Mr Holmes. I'd always planned to, but I never did."

"More's the pity."

"Then I thought of *you*. I'd heard that you handle such transactions, and I've come to ask for your help. In fact, if you'll forgive my boldness, I assumed you would agree. That's why I told Mackintosh to meet me here today."

Dr Watson has already reported how Sherlock Holmes represented a woman of honour in a similar situation. Mr Holmes had hoped to offer mediation between her and the conniving blackmailer, Charles Augustus Milverton; but the man's murder intervened. Only with Milverton's death and the destruction of his incriminating files could much of aristocratic London sleep more easily. Still, like the poisonous weeds they are, such villains have a way of coming back for more. As a consequence, I reckoned Mrs Barclay had come to the right man. Mr Holmes was—

"You, boy!" Mrs Hudson cried, poking a finger in my back. "Don't be lollygagging round Mr Holmes's door. Sweep up this

hallway, and take the refuse outside. You know the way. We don't want to miss the dustman."

Leaning on the broom and listening to the woman tell her tale, I never heard Mrs H come creeping up on me. It didn't seem fair, her tiptoeing about like that. Nonetheless, within minutes I was traipsing back out into the hot sunlight, once again dumping refuse into one of the large, stinking bins.

Unlike my earlier venture into the alleyway, however, this time I discovered that I was definitely not alone.

II

Fists were flying some thirty feet down the alley. Despite the heat—or because of it—two combatants in black suits and black bowlers, one man pale, the other swarthy, were having at each other, shouting, shoving, punching. Suddenly, the darker of the two broke free and, extracting a small revolver from his jacket, fired off two quick shots. Both bullets found their marks, and the other man's hat flew off as he staggered backward, clawing at the air, then crumpling to the ground. The bowler, on the edge of its stiff brim, rolled a few yards away. It slowly spun to a stop and came to rest, right side up, near the corner of the neighbouring building.

The man with the gun used his foot to prod the inert form lying before him. There was no movement. Satisfied that his victim was dead, he snarled, "*Now* we're level," and stooped over to check the dead man's pockets. It was only after pulling out what looked like a packet of folded bank notes that he squinted up the alley and saw me gawping at him. My eyes must have been as round as a pair of Mrs H's fine-china tea saucers. Worse—baked by the sun, I couldn't move—not even when he raised the pistol in my direction and, pointing it at my heart, kept the barrel steady whilst marching toward me.

"Sorry, boy," said he breathing heavily. "No witnesses."

Fearing the worst, I shut my eyes, and I clearly heard the click of the cocking mechanism. I was sweating heavily now, and it had nothing to do with the heat.

I waited. And waited. But the gunshot never came; the pistol didn't fire. Instead, a new voice—a threatening whisper it was—greeted my ears. It was coming from behind my assailant.

"Hoy," it said with a cockney accent, "drop the rod, or your throat gets cut."

Unable to breathe, I opened one eye. To my great astonishment, I could see the boy with the baggy trousers positioned directly behind the shooter. He was pointing his blade into the gunman's neck. I'd originally reckoned him to be eight or nine, but from the way he was holding that long knife, I could tell that he was no young child. Though small in stature—undernourished perhaps—he had a large head, and he scowled fiercely as he pushed the blade harder against the man's soft flesh.

What the boy might actually have done had the shooter not conformed, I never asked. Thankfully, the man's icy demeanour turned to water, and a moment later I heard the clank of the revolver hitting the ground.

"Damn," the villain muttered to himself.

In an instant, I retrieved the pistol—a .44 calibre British Bull Dog, as Mr Holmes later identified it—and handed it to my rescuer, who now pointed the weapon at the man.

"I'll get help!" I cried. "Don't let him get away."

With that, I raced back into the house, past an open-mouthed Mrs H, and up the stairs. The door to 221B had remained open, and I burst into Sherlock Holmes's sitting room. He was still talking with Mrs Barclay, and he looked up in amazement at the interruption.

"Outside!" I gasped. "In the alley. A man's been shot! There's a boy out there aiming a gun at the shooter."

The detective jumped to his feet, excused himself to Mrs Barclay, and snatched up a small, shiny cylinder from the mantel. Then he rushed down the stairs and out into the blinding sun. I followed right behind.

"It's all right," I told the boy who was still pointing the pistol at the shooter. "You can give the gun to Sherlock Holmes."

A big grin crossed the lad's face, and he eagerly complied.

Holding the weapon in one hand, the detective raised a police whistle to his lips, for such was the object he'd grabbed from the mantel. A few short blasts followed. Then crouching low, he checked the pulse of the man on the ground. A moment later, he looked at me and shook his head. The poor wretch was dead. The scarlet pool spreading beneath the body underscored the fact.

With the gun still trained on the shooter, Mr Holmes proceeded to riffle through the pockets of the dead man. Finding nothing, he now turned towards the assailant and indicated with a flick of the gun that the man turn out his own pockets. Flashing an angry scowl, the villain produced a dirty white handkerchief and a cheap cigar broken at the centre. Reluctantly, he also revealed a handful of neatly-folded ten-pound notes—no doubt, the same notes I'd seen him steal from the dead man. Holmes took the money and secured it inside his coat.

At the same time, the heavy beat of running footsteps announced the arrival of a uniformed constable.

"Mr Holmes," the winded policeman managed to say, "What's the trouble?" The constable obviously knew the detective.

"Clamp the handcuffs on this man, Dalmas. Then notify your superiors. I'll take him inside and keep an eye on him until they arrive. I leave *you* to deal with the body here."

"Right you are, sir." He touched his forelock as if he'd been talking to Mr Balfour himself and proceeded to secure the metal bracelets round the prisoner's wrists. They fastened with a reassuring click, and the constable strode off to complete the rest of his assignment.

Sherlock Holmes marched the shooter past Mrs H, who by now was used to such goings on in her establishment, and back up the stairs to his sitting room. Mrs Barclay, who'd moved to a corner, started when she saw the villain.

"Excuse the disturbance," Mr Holmes said to his visitor, "but in my line of work, interruptions like this sometimes take precedence."

"Of—of course," she said with less conviction than her words conveyed.

"Stand by the door, Billy," he commanded, and I took up the position as instructed—though uncertain what I would do if the fellow tried to bolt.

As if he were hosting the villain for tea, Sherlock Holmes offered his shackled prisoner a chair not far from Mrs Barclay. Perhaps it was the lady's calming influence, but the bloke seated himself without incident. More likely, it was the pistol, whose butt end could be seen peeking out of the front pocket of the detective's coat. Mr Holmes paced up and down the sitting room as he addressed the man.

"Your name, sir?"

"I don't mind telling you my name or my business," the former gunman said proudly. "I'm Al Teasel, and in a different day I might have been called a highwayman. But that bloke had it coming. Worked a job with me, didn't he? We got caught, and he peached to the police, blaming it all on me. *He* walked free whilst I was four years in the nick. When I got out, I reckoned I'd settle the score. I spent months looking for him and almost gave it up. But then today—quite by accident, really—I spied him in Marylebone and followed him here to Baker Street. When he finally saw me, he ran into the alley. You know what tempers are like in this kind of heat. I guess you might say he made a fatal mistake."

"And what, pray, was the name of your unfortunate victim?"

"Waldo Mackintosh," spat out Teasel.

In the corner, Mrs Barclay gasped. "Mackintosh? Why, he's the man I told you about, Mr Holmes. My former driver—the one who stole my necklace. He must have been bringing it here to sell just as I'd asked." She stood and walked over to the detective. "Did you find any pearls on his person?" she asked him.

"The dead man was carrying nothing," said Mr Holmes, who now turned and fixed his grey eyes on Mackintosh's killer.

"Don't know nothing about no pearls," Teasel admitted, "but I grabbed the seventy pounds that was in his pocket—the same seventy *you* just took from me."

"Which I'll be giving to the police," Holmes advised.

Mrs Barclay shook her head. Word of the dead man's empty pockets had obviously crushed her hope of reclaiming the pearls that meant so much to her. She extracted a linen handkerchief from the end of her sleeve and dabbed at her eyes. But even so, she couldn't prevent the tears.

A heavy tread on the stairs interrupted the scene, footfalls announcing the arrival of the police. They turned out to belong to the moustachioed Inspector Youghal, the same policeman I'd first encountered when Mr Holmes settled the matter of "The Mazarin Stone".

"The body's on its way to the morgue," Youghal greeted us, pulling at his thick moustache. "Just as well. I wouldn't want to be spending any time with a corpse on a scorcher like today." Eying Mrs Barclay, he added, "Beggin' your pardon, Madam."

It took but a few moments for Mr Holmes to explain matters. The inspector copied into a small notebook the name of the victim and, placing in an envelope the seventy pounds Teasel had been holding, slipped the notebook and envelope inside his coat pocket. The inspector then placed a hand on the prisoner's shoulder, turned him toward the open door, and escorted him down the steps and out into Baker Street. Once Teasel exited the building, a uniformed constable carefully secured him inside the police van that had been standing by the kerb.

A lad doesn't get the chance to see a murderer herded into a Black Maria very often—especially not where I lived in quiet Dulwich—so I was quick to follow Mr Holmes and the others outside. At the same time, I also couldn't help noticing the boy that had saved my life. In all the excitement, I had forgotten about him, and yet there he was, peering over a garden wall at me from less than a hundred feet away. Despite the macabre nature of the day's events, he was smiling beneath the dead man's bowler. It fit his big head perfectly.

III

"That tall gent—that was really Sherlock 'olmes, the detective?"

The van had clattered off down the road, and the others had gone back inside. The boy and I were standing in the sun a few paces from the front door.

"Yes, indeed," said I, puffing out my chest. "I work for him. I'm the page-boy here at 221."

"I know that, mate," the boy surprised me by saying. "It's why I've been following you, hain't it?"

I stared at him in light of his curious comment. He took off the bowler, and I could see that he wore his dark hair neatly combed. Torn trousers or not, he was a handsome lad with sharp, piercing eyes and an engaging smile. What's more, as I suspected, he appeared not as young as I'd previously thought, but rather closer to my own age, perhaps a trifle younger. Now that he was no longer skulking in the background, he seemed friendly enough; and beneath his humorous exterior I sensed a kind of sensitivity as well.

"What do you mean, 'following me'?" I challenged.

This question produced a laugh. "I'm an actor, hain't I—a stage actor. I'm about to join a theatre company what's putting on a play titled "Sherlock 'olmes". We're going to tour the country—might even get up to Scotland."

"Go on," I scoffed, "you're just a kid. And Sherlock Holmes is a man."

The boy giggled infectiously. "Are *you* thick!" he cried. "I hain't the detective; I'm still the kid. I play the part of Billy the page."

"Billy the—" I began. "Wait a bit. That's *me*!"

"Right you are, mate. Which is why I've been following you. I'm studying up for my part, hain't I? If I'm good enough, maybe I'll end up on a stage 'ere in London."

"Wait a bit," I said again. "You know *I'm* Billy. What's *your* name?"

"I'm Billy too, hain't I?" said he with a grin. "Billy the page." And he repeated that winsome laugh.

"You're a regular comic, aren't you?" I shot back, my tone full of sarcasm. Practical joking wasn't designed for sweltering afternoons. "What are you really called?"

"Charles Spencer Chaplin," he smiled. "But m' friends call me Charlie."

"I don't know," said I, figuring it was my turn to prod. "You look a mite small for a role as important as Billy's. Maybe you're not big enough for the job."

I should have known better than to joke around on a day like that. Hot weather makes people do crazy things. The smile dropped from his face as, reaching down in his pocket, he produced the long knife he'd held at the throat of the gunman. Only this time he pointed it at *me*.

"This blade says I *am* tough enough. Been brought up in the streets, 'aven't I? See fights all the time. Though I must say, guns hain't usually part of the mix. What was that business with the shooting all about?"

I put up my hands in mock surrender. He'd saved my life. He deserved to hear the details, and so I filled him in on all that I knew, right up to and including the lamentations of Mrs Barclay, who'd lost her precious pearls.

"Why don't we fetch 'em for 'er then?" asked Charlie.

I snorted. "Where would we look? Where would we start? We don't even know where the dead bloke came from."

"*I* do, don't I? On my way over 'ere, I seen 'im walk out of a boarding 'ouse—Fremont 'ouse in Gloucester Place it was—just the other side of Marylebone." Charlie put his hand on my shoulder. "Let's go."

I glanced at the front door. "But Mrs Hudson—my job . . . ."

"Your job's to 'elp Sherlock 'olmes, hain't it? Let's give 'im a 'and by finding the pearls for the lady."

Maybe it was the heat, but I couldn't muster the energy to argue. Besides, he was right. It was very much my job to aid Mrs Hudson's boarders, Sherlock Holmes included. And so without a look back, I joined up with Charlie Chaplin, who'd replaced the bowler at a rakish angle atop his head. With the thrill of the hunt leading us on, we made our way to Gloucester Place and the rooms of the late Waldo Mackintosh. If I'd known what we were about to find, I might have been less eager.

IV

The original red brick of Fremont House was bleeding through the whitewash, and the black paint on its weather-beaten outer door was peeling in the heat. Worse, it was locked. As we stood at the entrance wondering how to proceed, the door was pushed open from the inside by a gent sporting a boater.

Charlie tried to slither in behind him, but the fellow used an arm to block his way.

"Here now," the man said. "You can't just go rushing in like that."

"Please sir, we're looking for Mr Mackintosh, m'uncle," said Charlie, hat now in hand, eyes wide, voice—minus the Cockney accent—tinged with innocence. Quite the actor was my new friend; there was no denying his persuasive manner. "M'dad's a carpenter, and he's cut his pinkie clean off. He needs m'uncle's help. D'you know what room he might be in?"

The man nodded. Whether or not he believed Charlie's story, the matter appeared not the sort to get him riled up about while baking in the sun. "Room four," said he, and he even held the door open for us. As soon as we were in, Charlie plopped the bowler back on his head.

"What if we get caught and somebody tells your dad?" I asked in the foyer. I could just imagine how angry my own mother would be down in Dulwich if she found out that her son had been sneaking into the digs of some poor bloke who'd been murdered—especially since I'd been sent to Baker Street to straighten out my evil ways.

"*My* dad?" repeated Charlie with a snort. "'E won't care. 'E's been dead for two years, hain't 'e? I never saw 'im much anyway—though 'e did start me clog-dancing on the stage. I do owe 'im that."

There was a boiling stuffiness to the ground floor where a single charwoman was listlessly dusting a white-pine sideboard in the sitting room. She showed little enough interest in us, so up the stairs we climbed. We found the room we were seeking on the first floor. The corridor itself was dark, but we managed to read the faded numbers painted on the doors.

Charlie placed his hand on the doorknob and turned.

"Locked," he whispered. "But not to worry." From inside a pocket he pulled out a set of small metal picks. "One of these should work." And sure enough, like a jeweller tinkering with a clock, he got the tumblers to fall and the door to open.

A ripe aroma instantly hit our nostrils, no doubt the stench of some food gone bad exacerbated by the heat. But we had a job to do, and so we covered our noses with our forearms and entered. A faded-red curtain covered the rear half of the room, the flimsy cloth setting off the sleeping area. A small window on the back wall let in enough light for us to see though, owing to the curtain, everything seemed bathed in a scarlet wash. Fortunately, the place was small, and we calculated that our search shouldn't take long. The area in front of the curtain contained only a wooden table, two cane-back chairs, wall-pegs for hats and coats, and a chest of drawers. The curtain itself concealed the bed.

"You look for the pearls back there," Charlie commanded, pointing in the direction of the curtain. "I'll check the bureau," and he yanked out one of the two top-drawers.

"Quiet," I cautioned.

Since there was so little furniture in the room, the worn curtain and what it might be hiding seemed to offer the greatest mystery. With the smell growing fouler as I approached and hesitant at what I might discover, I slowly drew back the thin red cloth. As it turned out, I had good reason to be concerned.

A large hook for a chandelier was fastened to the ceiling near the left-hand wall, no doubt a remnant of the building's more refined distant past. In this instance, however, it wasn't a lighting fixture that hung from the hook, but a black leather belt whose nether end was strapped tightly round the neck of the poor soul dangling below it. Clad in a worker's brown overalls, the hanging man clearly looked dead. With bloodshot eyes protruding and tongue coloured blue extending from between his teeth, such a conclusion seemed obvious. Beyond the noose-like belt, I could make out purple bruises at his throat. I'd learned enough from Sherlock Holmes to figure out that the man had been strangled before he'd been strung up.

"Ch-Ch-Charlie," I managed to say.

But he ignored me. Instead, he shouted, "Look 'ere!" and held up a string of white pearls in one hand and a stack of fat envelopes in the other.

He flashed a broad grin until he glanced over my shoulder and saw the grisly scene I'd just come across myself. Then his eyes grew wide.

"Let's get out of here!" he cried.

It was fine with me. Shoving the pearls and envelopes inside his shirt, Charlie checked that the hallway was clear, and then we both bolted down the steps, slowing up only long enough not to distract the char. She was still dusting half-heartedly in the afternoon heat.

V

When Charlie and I arrived back at Baker Street, Sherlock Holmes was sitting in his shirtsleeves by the open window and smoking a cigar. We were bursting to give him our report about the dead man in Fremont House, but he held up his hand to silence us. He closed his eyes and, reminiscent of the American Indian who sends puffs of smoke into the sky to signal his mates, blew a great white cloud towards the window. When he finally got round to focusing his grey eyes in our direction, it wasn't to question us concerning our discoveries but rather to ask me about my companion—that is, the boy who'd saved my life.

I was hoping to blurt out the story of the dead man! To scream the news of the pearls and letters we'd found! But I knew enough about Sherlock Holmes to understand that following *his* way of doing things ensured the greatest chance for success. And so in spite of the developments I longed to report, I ended up relating how Charlie had come to my rescue in the alley when Teasel had pointed the gun at me. My new friend and I had pressing information to impart, and yet Mr Holmes appeared more interested in learning that Charlie was a budding actor in a drama about the detective than in hearing what we had to tell him about the case he was working on.

"I am familiar with Gillette's play that bears my name," he said, his voice full of disdain. "It is a waste of dramatic effort." But then he added wistfully, "You know that I myself trod the boards a number of years ago. Even now I employ many of the techniques I learned in the theatre." He exhaled another cloud of smoke, this time into the room itself.

I understood full well the techniques Mr Holmes was referring to, for I'd read Dr Watson's descriptions of the various disguises the detective continues to utilise. And yet, sweltering as I was, I knew that those counterfeit dotty vicars and bent old ladies and grimy labourers would have to step aside. I could contain myself no longer.

"We found the pearls!" I exploded. "Mrs Barclay's pearls! Charlie knew where Mackintosh lived, and we went there, and we found the necklace and a pile of envelopes filled with letters. And there was a dead man in the room."

"A dead man? Letters?" Mr Holmes carefully placed his cigar in the ashtray next to his chair and leaned forward.

I told him about sneaking into Fremont House and the body hanging in the room and how Charlie had discovered the necklace and the envelopes in Mackintosh's bureau.

"We'll have to notify the police," Mr Holmes murmured; but even whilst uttering these words, he extended his open palm and motioned with his fingers that we hand over the necklace. Charlie pulled it out from somewhere inside his cavernous shirt and gave it to me to hand over. Mr Holmes frowned as soon as I laid the pearls in his palm. The closer he brought them to his eyes, the more quickly the frown turned into a scowl.

"The clasp is just like the racing tyres Mrs Barclay described," he observed, "and yet these pearls aren't real. A passable imitation, perhaps, but nowhere near as valuable as Mrs Barclay had suggested. I am amazed that it actually fooled her."

"Show him the letters," I told Charlie. Fishing inside his shirt again, Charlie produced the envelopes he'd taken from Mackintosh's room. Out shot the detective's palm once more, and this time Charlie himself filled it with the envelopes, through which Mr Holmes immediately began to thumb.

"Standard stationery. Postmarked in London. Addressed to Mr Barclay in a woman's hand. Written in cursive English, the dotless i's suggesting Russian training. Other than the sender's address on Sumner Place with no name given, there's nothing particularly noteworthy about the envelopes. Now let's look inside."

Mr Holmes proceeded to examine the letters themselves. He even sniffed the pages. A few minutes passed before he announced: "One doesn't need the aroma of perfume to infer that these letters to Mr Barclay are from a Russian lady. They suggest an intimate relationship about which neither the writer nor the recipient would want Mrs Barclay to know. I can only assume that just as Waldo Mackintosh had stolen the pearls from Mrs Barclay, so he must also have stolen these compromising letters from her husband. Quite a resourceful brigand, the late Mr Mackintosh! Unless I'm greatly mistaken, he had plans to extort money from wife and husband at the same time without either one of them knowing about the other."

The detective stood up and took his coat from the rack.

"Come, " said he, looking in my direction. "We shall pay a visit to the return-address on the envelope. It is time to meet Mr Barclay's lady-friend."

I pointed at Charlie. "*Both* of us?" I asked hopefully.

The hint of a smile crossed the detective's face, and he strode to the open door.

"Mrs Hudson!" he called down the stairs.

Within minutes Mrs H appeared, arching an eyebrow when she caught sight of me standing in the room.

"Here, Billy," said she, brushing away a strand of her grey hair that had come unglued in the heat. "Where have you been all afternoon? There's work needs to be done."

I exchanged glances with the detective. "I was engaged on personal business for Mr Holmes," I dared to say, hoping he'd support me.

In fact, he went a step further. "Actually, Mrs Hudson, Billy has been most helpful. As has his friend Charlie here. And I was wondering if you might do us a favour."

He proceeded to describe Charlie's upcoming role in the play about Sherlock Holmes. Though he told little about the details of the drama, he emphasised the importance of her Baker Street residence in the story and suggested how much more accurate the production might be if Charlie could be given an actual uniform and allowed to spend a short time performing as a page-boy in the real Baker Street rooms.

"Oh, I should be honoured," said Mrs H smoothing down her dress as if she too might be stage-bound. "I'll be right back."

She returned a few minutes later with a smaller version of the uniform I was wearing and handed it to Charlie.

"Ta," said he before going downstairs to change. Minutes later he re-appeared in the guise of a Baker Street page.

"You look swell," I greeted him. "Now 221 has two 'boys in buttons'."

Charlie looked down at himself and straightened his jacket. "This feels good," he said with a smile. "In m'old rags I felt like a tramp—even with that bowler I recently acquired."

In spite of his new uniform, however, I knew that Charlie wasn't satisfied. I understood that not being removed from an actual murder case meant more to him than learning the role of page-boy. But I needn't have worried; Mr Holmes had another job in mind for him. The detective had not yet notified the police regarding the hanged man Charlie and I had discovered at Fremont House. Appreciating Charlie's desire to be included, Mr Holmes now wrote a note detailing the matter and handed it to him.

"Give this to Inspector Youghal at Scotland Yard and to no one else," Mr Holmes instructed. "This information is very important. The police will know it's authentic when they see you in Mrs Hudson's livery."

It didn't matter to Charlie that he was already sweltering in the new wool tunic. He had an important service to perform. His eyes sparkled and his smile beamed; and like a soldier receiving an honour, he straightened out his uniform, clicked his heels together, and offered a small salute. Then he was off.

"Come, Billy," Mr Holmes said to me. "You and I shall travel to the address listed on these letters and see what we can learn about Mrs Barclay's husband."

VI

Though it was not surprising to discover that the Old Brompton Road in Kensington was just as hot as our own front steps in Baker Street, it was indeed a surprise to encounter Frank Barclay himself in the small flat in Sumner Place.

As it turned out, no servant answered our ring. A plain but heavily made-up young woman dressed in yellow cotton opened the door. Giving her name as Irina Glukhov, she turned out to be none other than Mr Barclay's lady-friend. As Mr Holmes had surmised, she was Russian.

A tall, portly man in shirtsleeves was standing behind her. When he heard who was calling, he donned a coat and joined the woman at the door.

"I am Frank Barclay, Mr Holmes," said he perspiring freely and offering no hand to shake. "I suppose my wife Emily hired you to snoop on me. Well, you found me out. Can't say I'm pleased to see you, but I suppose I will be rid of you more quickly if I speak to you now."

In spite of such seeming openness, neither he nor the woman made any effort to invite us to sit down. Rather, the four of us remained bunched together in the stuffy entry hall, as if Mr Barclay might usher us out at any moment.

Indicating his companion, he said, "I met Irina during a car race in Paris. I'm an automotive engineer and was working on a Mors."

"Ah, yes," Holmes nodded. "'The Mors Machine'. A V engine configuration, if I remember correctly."

"Quite impressive, Mr Holmes. Actually, it is a V4 side-valve. And though I could talk about such a racing car the entire afternoon, I assume that the Mors is not the point of your visit."

"Quite so."

"Well, mine is not a complicated story," Mr Barclay said, mopping his brow with a linen handkerchief. "Irina agreed to accompany me back to London. I got her this flat, and I spend a great deal of time with her—more time now than I do with my wife." He squeezed her shoulder as if to confirm his commitment.

Mr Holmes and I exchanged glances. My personal sympathies were obviously with the wronged Mrs Barclay.

"You are aware that Irina's letters to you are missing?" asked Mr Holmes.

"Alas, I am." Mr Barclay raised his eyebrows. "Do you know their whereabouts? I'd hidden them at the bottom of a desk drawer, but obviously not well enough. At first, I thought that Emily had found my hidey-hole. But when I heard nothing from her about them, I supposed they must have been stolen. In point of fact, I feared contact from a blackmailer."

"Any one blackmailer in particular?"

"Why, I don't know what you mean."

"I think you do, Mr Barclay. I think you suspected that the man you sacked not long ago, Waldo Mackintosh, your wife's chauffeur, had stolen your letters. So much did you believe it that you sent one of your employees—possibly a mechanic, judging from the description of his work clothes—round to Mackintosh's rooms in Gloucester Place to buy them back for you."

"The seventy pounds Teasel stole from Mackintosh!" I exclaimed.

"Yes, Billy. Mr Barclay here gave a man in his employ seventy pounds to buy back the stolen letters from Mackintosh."

"He's a French mechanic called Leon Grimaud," added Barclay. "And, actually, I paid him twenty pounds to complete the deal. The other fifty was Mackintosh's price for the letters themselves."

"Then this Grimaud," I remembered, "must have been the dead man in brown overalls."

"Dead man?" Barclay cried, eyebrows arched. He mopped his brow once more.

"Quite dead," answered Mr Holmes. "One can only assume, Mr Barclay, that the twenty pounds you paid the late Mr Grimaud wasn't enough for him. The man had obviously wanted more."

"Wait a moment," said Barclay, a wrinkle crossing his brow. "If Grimaud is dead and Mackintosh ended up with Grimaud's money as well as the money for the letters, how come I never got the letters back?"

"Really, Mr Barclay," the detective replied. "I believe it is no less a figure than Falstaff who complains that there is 'No honour among thieves'. Mackintosh stole the money out of the pocket of the man he'd just killed. Perhaps Grimaud paid out the fifty pounds, plotting to kill Mackintosh himself and steal it back. More probably, Mackintosh suspected Grimaud's murderous plan from the start and simply stole the money after strangling him."

"The bruises on the hanged-man's neck," I said. "Right, Mr Holmes?"

"Yes, Billy. A misguided attempt to make Grimaud's death look like suicide. Of course, we'll never learn exactly what happened since both men are dead."

"Mackintosh is dead too?" Barclay gasped, his face turning ashen.

"Oh, I neglected to inform you. Shot by an angry confederate late this morning, a fellow named Teasel."

Barclay took a deep breath, and his nostrils flared.

"The police are investigating both murders, Mr Barclay. They know about the money, but not about the letters. I am the one who has those."

Barclay now patted his lips with the linen. "May I have them back?" he asked. "Or do I now have to pay *you* for them. I don't want any trouble with Emily. While I'm sorry to hear of Grimaud's death—Mackintosh's too, for that matter—they have nothing to do with me. I never gave orders for anyone to be killed."

"It's strange," said Mr Holmes coldly, "but I believe you. And yet such a conclusion does not exonerate the contemptible treatment of your wife." The detective reached into his coat, produced the stack of envelopes and handed them to Mr Barclay. "I am returning to you all of your letters save one." And here he patted his breast pocket. "You will receive the remaining epistle once I am informed by Mrs Barclay herself of the satisfactory disposition of your marriage. She is my client, and I shall accept whatever resolution she prefers.

"Come, Billy," said Mr Holmes as he turned to the door. "We have yet another stop to make."

I thought we would be off to the Barclay home in Hampstead, but Holmes had the hansom drive to Golders Green where we stopped at a jeweller's shop. He told the driver to wait, and I followed the detective inside. A tiny bell above the door jingled when we entered.

Seated behind the counter and looking up at the sound of the bell was a bespectacled man with a greying beard. He wore a black skullcap and a white shirt open at the collar. I don't know much about gems and stones and such, but most of the gaudy pieces I saw within the glass cases looked like the kind you can win at some game or other on the Brighton Pier. A chessboard lay at the end of the counter. The game has always interested me, but these pieces stood in random fashion. A bishop lolled on its side as if too enervated by the heat to perform.

"Mr Lazarus," said Holmes, clearly having done business with the man before, "in very short order I need you to put together a necklace much like this one." From his coat pocket he produced the pearls we were soon to return to Mrs Barclay, the ones that had been stolen by Mackintosh. They shone in the sunlight that was pouring through the window and heating up the place.

The jeweller took out a lens and examined the necklace. After a few moments, he leaned back and removed his glasses. "Ah, Mr Holmes," he sighed, "Bohemian glass beads. A good reproduction, perhaps, but in the end, still a fake. I could easily create for you a necklace of false pearls, but mine would look significantly cheaper than this one."

"Precisely my wish."

The old man shrugged and replaced his glasses. Then he opened a drawer and scooped up a handful of tiny white balls. They could have been glass marbles.

"And, Lazarus," Holmes added before the jeweller got to work, "in the piece you are now making, be sure to include the clasp from the necklace I just gave you."

I looked at Mr Holmes questioningly whilst the old man nodded and disappeared into his workroom somewhere behind a wall at the rear of the shop.

"When we visit Mrs Barclay," said Mr Holmes, "I will offer her the cheaply-made necklace. She will easily identify it as a poor imitation and not the one that was stolen from her. I will then inform her that Mackintosh had sold what she thought was her 'valuable' original and was planning to give back to her a cheap imitation in its place."

"But the original was also a fake."

"Yes, Billy. *We* are privy to that information, but she is not. Recall that she said she'd never had the opportunity to appraise it. She still thinks it real. Why inform her now that the gift given to her by the late Mr Stanley, the man she loved so dearly, was just a handsome imitation? This way, she'll believe that Mackintosh sold away the cherished original and planned to fool her with a cheap replacement. Her romantic memory of Mr Stanley will remain intact."

I could see nothing wrong with the plan—nothing besides the fact that it undermined the common belief that Sherlock Holmes lacked sentiment. For what it was worth, I nodded my approval.

The jeweller reappeared and laid both necklaces in long, black rectangular cases. Mr Holmes gave the man some money and collected the boxes. I followed him out of the shop, the little bell ringing again as soon as the door was opened. We resumed our seats in the hansom as it rattled off down the Finchley Road.

The Barclays lived in a small house in Hampstead not far from Heath Street. Holmes again asked the driver to wait, and within moments a housekeeper was opening the door and ushering us into a simply furnished sitting room. Like everything else that day, the house was hot; and as in 221B, the curtains had been pulled back to expose the open windows. In this case, however, there was the shade of oak trees just beyond the walls to help lessen the heat. Within moments, Mrs Barclay joined us, and we rose to greet her.

"Would you care for some tea, Mr Holmes? For you and your young man."

"No thank you. I am here on business, and then I must return to Baker Street."

"Pray, sit down then and tell me the worst."

"It was as I feared, Mrs Barclay," he said. "The pearls originally given to you by Phillip Stanley have been replaced by these poor imitations." He handed her the box containing the newly made false necklace.

No sooner had she opened the box than a sneer formed on her lips. "These don't look anything like mine!" she exclaimed.

Holmes pointed at one end of the strand. "You will notice that Mackintosh retained the original clasp, the racing tyres."

"As if these odious pearls could fool me," she muttered. But then she brought the necklace to her bosom. "I shall save the clasp. It is all I have left to remind me of Phillip. This trash I shall discard."

"Then our job here is done," said Sherlock Holmes as he rose to his feet. "I trust that Mr Barclay will soon contact you and that some measure of calm will descend upon your household. I informed your husband that I am expecting to hear from you directly about the resolution of your marital differences." Glancing at me, he said. "Come, Billy."

Mrs Barclay escorted us to the door. Holding it open, she watched as once again we climbed into the hansom.

"To Baker Street!" Mr Holmes shouted to the driver.

VII

No sooner did we enter the outer door at 221 than the siren sound of laughter beckoned. It emanated from the kitchen, and it was there that we discovered Charlie sitting at the wooden table opposite Mrs H, who was roaring with delight. Charlie had jabbed a pair of forks into a couple of dinner rolls and, keeping his head low to the table top, was using the forks to manipulate the rolls. They appeared to be the dancing shoes of a very short body attached to Charlie's very big head. He turned his face this way and that, arched his brows, and—with an exaggerated smile, smirk, or grin— presented many the hilarious expression to accompany the mincing steps. What an entertainer! Mrs H was laughing so hard that her eyes disappeared behind the rounds of her cheeks, and even Sherlock Holmes provided an appreciative chuckle.

"Quite a show!" I cried. "It would be even funnier with musical accompaniment. Try one of Scott Joplin's rags."

Charlie nodded; but in spite of Mr Holmes's quick smile, seriousness had entered the kitchen alongside the detective, and within a minute the uproarious entertainment came to an end.

"Your report, Charlie?" Holmes asked.

Charlie confirmed that he'd personally delivered to Inspector Youghal the note about the hanged man; and while Charlie and I polished the silver tea service for Mrs Hudson, I furnished him with the details of the afternoon's activities.

Charlie worked at perfecting his performance as a Baker Street page-boy until it was time for him to leave town a few days later with the *Sherlock Holmes* touring company. I can say with great sincerity that I was sorry to see him go and not—I hasten to add—just because he'd lightened my workload.

*****

It would be two years before we laid eyes on Charlie Chaplin again, two years during which a number of major transitions occurred. First and foremost, Mr Holmes retired to a cottage in the Sussex Downs. I myself left Mrs Hudson's service to devote more time to my studies in Dulwich. As for the Barclays, they agreed to an uncontested divorce and went their separate ways.

Charlie re-entered out lives at the Duke of York's Theatre in the late fall of 1905. In point of fact, he left tickets for Mrs Hudson, Mr Holmes, Dr Watson and me to an evening performance of William Gillette's play, *Sherlock Holmes*. By then, the drama that Mr Holmes once derided had gained international acclaim. We all knew of the favourable reviews though none of us—emphatically *not* Mr Holmes—had actually seen a production. To honour Charlie, however, even the detective agreed to take advantage of the boy's largesse and journeyed up from Sussex that very day to join us for the performance. He met Dr Watson at his home in Queen Anne Street, and the two of them had their four-wheeler stop in Baker Street where I had joined Mrs H. Together we all drove to the theatre in St. Martin's Lane.

Anticipating an enjoyable evening, everyone looked pleased, everyone except Mr Holmes.

"Publicity annoys me," he muttered when, above the clatter of the carriage wheels, I questioned his dour expression.

"Oh my," sighed Dr Watson. "Here we go again. I can assure you that I've heard the same complaint regarding Holmes's appearances in my own sketches. Be forewarned, Billy, should you ever write your memoirs and attempt to include Sherlock Holmes."

Mrs H nodded in support of the doctor.

"The more people who recognise me," said Mr Holmes, "the harder the job of detecting becomes. Anonymity is key in my line of work."

"He does have a point, Doctor," Mrs H said, now in agreement with the detective.

"You too, Mrs Hudson?" said Dr Watson, "I think the man doth protest too much. They say that this chap Gillette has captured you perfectly, Holmes. They say you have much to be proud of."

"'They *say*, they *say*'," muttered the detective to no one in particular. And he hunkered down against the back cushion like a limp boxer retreating to his corner of the ring.

Soon we were walking past the delicate arches, powerful columns, golden fittings, and burnished wood of the Duke of York's Theatre on our way to the stalls. I wound up sitting on the aisle with Dr Watson to my immediate left; and once the lights dimmed and the red velvet curtain rose, I could see the good doctor nodding in expectation.

Dr Watson became even more energetic in joining the thunderous applause that greeted William Gillette once he strode onto the stage. Erect and noble, the actor smoked a golden-brown calabash; and though it was a style of pipe that I myself had never seen among those on the mantel of 221B, even Mr Holmes flashed a smile.

We all grinned approvingly at Charlie's performance as Billy the Page. Obviously, the time he'd spent learning my job had paid off handsomely. He could tug at his tunic and announce a visitor with professional ease. Just then, Dr Watson nudged me and gestured to the left in the direction of Mrs Hudson. At that very moment, she was displaying a broad smile in recognition of the very same uniform she'd given to Charlie.

For all the doctor's enthusiasm, however, I must say, that when the amiable Kenneth Rivington, the Dr Watson of the piece, came charging onto the stage, my neighbour started sputtering.

"See here," he whispered, grabbing my arm. "That fellow's nothing at all like me."

"It's merely a *charade*, sir," I reminded him.

But the doctor couldn't be placated. "These actors are a cantankerous breed. Their imaginations have run amok. They confuse fiction with reality."

Perhaps he was right—though such ambiguity doesn't bother *me*. In terms of my own writing, I don't let the issue of reality get in the way. Labels like "interesting" or "dull" mean more to me than questions of "fact" or "fiction". Take my personal situation as an example. Personally, I never considered my housekeeping chores at Baker Street as noteworthy, but here was the audience in the Duke of York's watching a boy in buttons make mundane labour seem attractive. Obviously, there is much in one's personal experiences that can entertain an audience.

Suddenly, I found myself thinking about stories that might be fashioned from events in my own life. What happened to my father after he'd run out on my mother and me in Chicago? Who was responsible for the dead body floating down the muddy river near my aunt's house in Nebraska? What was prompting Uncle Ernest to pay for my education in Dulwich? With a few pokes here and a few pokes there, I might even fashion a mystery tale in the tradition of Dr Watson or his agent, Arthur Conan Doyle.

I'd need to create my own consulting detective, of course; one couldn't expect a mere page-boy to get involved with murders on a regular basis. But at least I was beginning to espy the genesis of a plot or two. For that matter, a writer could do worse than base a narrative on the two-year-old murder in the alleyway behind 221. Ignited by a blistering, red-hot summer's day, the type with which everybody is unfortunately familiar, the tale contains a kind of universality. After all, unless you reside at the North Pole, who hasn't lived through one of those scorchers?—the sort of day that renders the bullet or the blade the simplest of solutions, the sort of day that is so hot that just about anything might happen . . . .

The Adventure of the Star-Crossed Lovers[*]

Why should the world be over-wise,
In counting all our tears and sighs?
Nay, let them only see us, while
We wear the mask.
--Paul Laurence Dunbar
"We Wear the Mask", 1896

Marriage is one of the "basic civil rights of man," fundamental to our very existence and survival . . . . [T]he freedom to marry, or not marry, a person of another race resides with the individual and cannot be infringed by the State.
--U.S. Supreme Court,
Loving v. Virginia, 1967

I

Whether one calls it the most disheartening mistake of my career or simply the most foolish, it is I who has had to live with the terrible consequences. The origins of the woeful tale actually date back to the early spring of '88; but the more immediate events, those that led to its tragic conclusion, began one bright summer's afternoon in early July of 1903. I was returning home to Queen Anne Street following an afternoon in my club and thought I might stop in at my former rooms in Baker Street to visit my friend and colleague, Mr Sherlock Holmes.

[*] With great appreciation to Samuel Williams, Jr., whose novel *Anomalous* was first to bring together two of Conan Doyle's more memorable characters, Lucy Hebron from "The Yellow Face," and Steve Dixie from "The Three Gables." (DDV)

Generally, Mrs Hudson welcomed my appearance. Today, however, with lips sealed in a straight line and arms folded across her chest, my former landlady eyed me with suspicion. Standing tall and firm in the entry hall a few feet from the outer door, she displayed an undisguised look of disapproval as I passed; and she continued to mark me even after I had mounted the stairs.

As it turned out, a client occupied my friend's sitting room. Not surprisingly, Sherlock Holmes was seated with the windows behind him. In daylight hours, the stratagem served to cast Holmes's face in silhouette, concealing his facial expressions from the person positioned opposite him. However effective in masking his reactions, such placement also served to present the back of the client to anyone entering the sitting room from the hallway, thus shielding the visitor's identity from view.

Upon arriving, therefore, I discovered my own powers of observation severely limited; all I could determine with any certitude was that Holmes appeared engaged in conversation with a young woman. I could not distinguish her facial features, yet her composed voice and gestures, not to mention her fashionable green frock and small, single-feathered hat, clearly indicated a person of substantial breeding and refined upbringing.

"Ah, Watson," said Holmes, rising to his feet, "allow me to introduce an old friend."

I had no idea to whom Holmes was referring, but I must confess to being all the more astonished when the young lady in question turned to face me and I perceived the chocolate hue of her skin. I am ashamed to admit that I froze in my tracks, mouth agape, beginning to understand the critical look in Mrs Hudson's eye. Though many a peculiar type had marched up the seventeen steps to Holmes's lair over the years, few had been female, and even fewer had been black.

"An-an old friend?" I stammered.

"Miss Lucy Hebron," Holmes announced.

"Miss Lucy Hebron?" I repeated mindlessly.

"Watson, Watson," Holmes admonished, "have you forgot our investigation in Norbury of the girl with the yellow face?"

The Yellow Face. Norbury. Suddenly, it came back to me. Fifteen years before, Holmes and I had attempted to resolve the mysterious comings and goings in that town of an Englishwoman called Effie Grant Munro. Holmes had got it wrong at first and seemed unable to put his error out of mind. Indeed, he suggested that whenever he might appear too full of himself, I should "kindly whisper Norbury" in his ear to bring him back to earth.

Fortunately, it had not taken long for Holmes to right the problem. The woman's strange behaviour, which had prompted Effie's husband to call upon my friend in the first place, had been part of a ruse to conceal the arrival of her daughter Lucy. The little girl was the product of the woman's earlier marriage to one John Hebron, an American Negro lawyer of Atlanta where Effie herself had grown up. Hebron had died from yellow fever when Lucy was very young; and Effie returned to England, leaving the little girl, who had also been struck down by the illness, to be cared for in Atlanta by a former servant.

Though Effie remarried and became Mrs Grant Munro, she soon found herself longing for her daughter. Yet fearing an angry reaction from her new husband towards the black little girl, she requested the child be sent to her in secrecy. What is more, to deter recognition, not only did Effie have her daughter cared for in a nearby cottage, but she also required the child to don a yellow mask whenever the girl approached a window.

Fortunately, the matter was happily resolved. Indeed, Holmes and I took great comfort in the tolerance that Grant Munro displayed in accepting the child into their household. I shall never forget how, after first meeting his black stepdaughter, he lifted her in his arms and kissed her. For the moment, it actually gave one hope for a future in which diverse peoples might live together in peace, an optimism I sought to recreate in the sketch I titled "The Adventure of the Yellow Face".

Obviously, the little black girl had blossomed into a beautiful young woman. She had been but a child when I first set eyes upon her; and yet I suddenly realised that during the years that followed, I had never encountered a black personage of my own social set—not to mention so charming an example. In hope of adapting my manners to a situation that was new to me, I asked, "What brings you here, my dear?" and tentatively offered my hand.

She took it up immediately. "Oh, Dr Watson," said she, "it is indeed wonderful to see you again—although, truth be told, I was too young to remember the occasion of our first meeting." She smiled in my direction, but seemed to catch herself and averted her eyes. Unless I was very much mistaken, it was not a happy circumstance that had brought her to Holmes's door.

"Before your arrival," said he, "Miss Hebron was in the process of telling me the fears she harbours for her *fiancé*. Why not lend an ear, old fellow? Your advice in matters romantic has always proved invaluable."

Compliments from Sherlock Holmes never failed to move me; yet I must also admit that, flattery aside, I was especially interested in hearing what a young lady from our past might have to say. I settled into an armchair while Holmes returned to his own seat and invited Miss Hebron to resume her story.

"As I told Mr Holmes, I am recently engaged to a fine gentleman called Josiah Fipps. He works as an accountant in the City for the banking firm of Westmoreland and Franks. We met whilst admiring the roses at Kew Gardens."

"Charming," I observed.

A smile flickered in the young woman's face though it took but a moment for a frown to replace it. "I suppose," said she, "I must also add that he is white."

In spite of the shocking nature of their mixed relationship, that last bit actually went without saying. One could not imagine a long-standing institution like Westmoreland and Franks daring to place the funds of its white clientele in the hands of a Negro.

"Mr Fipps and I are quite used to receiving hostile looks and the odd remark when we appear together in public. But one develops a thick skin in reaction to such offensive behaviour and learns to go on about his business. Which is not to say that such hostility doesn't cause great distress."

"Of course," said I, knowing full well that as a white man myself I could not possibly comprehend the depths of her pain.

"Once we announced our engagement, however, matters worsened."

Holmes brought his fingers together in their familiar steeple. "In what way did they worsen?"

"First, there was the rock thrown through the window of Josiah's flat."

"A rock, you say?" I asked.

"With a note tied round it."

Holmes leaned forward in anticipation. "Did you bring the note with you?"

I could easily envision him, lens in hand, analysing the paper, the ink, and the handwriting.

"Alas, no," replied Lucy Hebron. "It was so offensive that Jos burned it in the grate. I do, however, remember its foul language."

If ever one seeks similarities among diverse people, one need only recall the sad look in their eyes when they recount the words of insult hurled at them.

"It said, 'Stay away from niggers'"—Lucy flinched at repeating the hateful epithet—"'lest you be treated like one yourself.'"

Holmes and I exchanged looks of grave disapproval.

"What else?" he prompted.

"Jos told me of a similar letter delivered to him a week later," Lucy frowned. "It arrived at his office in Lombard Street. Sorry, Mr Holmes. He destroyed that one too—right away, in fact, so it wouldn't be seen by any of his colleagues. Jos is not naïve, gentlemen. For that matter, neither am I. We recognise the disgust with which many people regard our companionship—let alone our engagement. For that reason, Jos has refrained from announcing our upcoming nuptials at work, but neither are we shying away from the news."

"Surely," said Holmes, "for two strong individuals like Mr Fipps and yourself, there must be more that brought you here than just those two ugly notes."

"Indeed," nodded Lucy Hebron. "I still live with my mother and stepfather in the house you visited in Norbury all those years ago. One afternoon not long after the rock and letter incidents, I was leaving home to visit a friend when a closed four-wheeler that had been waiting nearby tore down the road in my direction and suddenly veered into my path. I tell you, gentlemen, at that instant, I feared for my life; but at the last moment, the driver, his face concealed behind a black scarf and wool cap, pulled the horses back to the centre of the road. It had rained earlier that day; and fortunately the only pain I suffered was the humiliation of being splashed with the mud that had collected in the roadway."

"Outrageous!" I cried.

"Could you identify any marks about the carriage?" Holmes asked

Once again, Lucy nodded. "I recognised the name of Chadwick's on its door. It's the local stables in Norbury. Anyone in the world might have hired it, and so I let the matter drop." Her voice dropped as well, her report apparently finished. She now sat staring at the two of us biting her lower lip.

"And yet, Miss Hebron," observed Sherlock Holmes, "I sense there is still more to tell. As unsettling as the events you have described must be, they occurred weeks ago. What has happened just recently that has finally brought you to my door?"

Lucy Hebron reacted to Holmes's question with silence. She had kept her hands gently folded in her lap when recounting her story; but now she raised them and, entwining her fingers, clasped them tightly together. A single sob escaped her lips.

"Take your time, my dear," said I softly and actually found myself leaning forward and placing my pale palm atop her dark hands.

The young woman threw back her shoulders as if to gain strength. "Jos was beaten by thugs," she hissed. "Sunday last when we walked through St. James's Park. We came upon three young men who, once they'd seen us, pushed me out of the way with some foul words and then set upon Jos. 'No nigger lovers here!' they screamed at him. One held Jos from behind, and the other two took turns hitting him."

The account sickened me, and I vaguely recalled a sentence from *Huckleberry Finn,* the American novel about racial intolerance—something about being "ashamed of the human race."

"This must stop, Mr Holmes!" demanded Lucy, her voice full of defiance. "That's why I have come to you. Jos doesn't know I'm here. He tells me not to worry; he says we simply have to get used to the malicious acts of ignorant people."

"Yes," Holmes intoned, "your Jos does have a point. One cannot set about correcting the foibles of everyone in the world."

Lucy arched her eyebrows. "*Foibles*, Mr Holmes?" she cried. "Is that all you can think to call these happenstances? Mere *foibles*?" Her eyes grew wide, their whiteness standing out in contrast to her dark skin. "I expected such a reaction from the *police*. That's why we never bothered to report the incident. But I did not anticipate so tepid a response from *you,* sir. My parents have always spoken of Sherlock Holmes with the greatest regard. In fact, it is why I have called upon you today."

"My apologies," Holmes said, leaning back in his chair. "Perhaps you misinterpret my meaning."

On more than one occasion, I have referred to my friend as an emotionless reasoning machine. I am afraid that his unfeeling reaction to the complaints of Lucy Hebron typified his aloofness.

"White skin, black skin," he proclaimed, waving a hand in the air, "they mean nothing to me when compared to the human brain. To express emotional concern over such distinctions is to minimise the power of thought. The most brutish of white men can stoop as low as any black, just as the minds of both races can soar. To paraphrase the Bard, 'what a piece of work is man, how meaningless his colour'. I have no patience for such distinctions when the game's afoot. It is the villainous perpetrator I seek regardless of his skin's hue. The word 'Negro' conveys nothing more to me than does the horse of that name that ran against Silver Blaze in the Wessex Cup."

Holmes did well in citing a previous case. It served to put me in mind of a corroborating comment he had made while investigating the Cunninghams of Reigate back in '87. "I make a point of never having any prejudices," he had said on that occasion, "and of following docilely along wherever facts may lead me."

However truthful Holmes's speech to Lucy Hebron, the lady's shoulders sagged at its conclusion. "Perhaps I've expected too much," she sighed. "Maybe the intolerance I have observed typifies *all* white people, and my mother simply serves as a notable exception. She and my true father had to leave Atlanta, you know, because of the ignorant and prejudicial laws there.

"Even before the yellow fever struck, they were planning to come here. I think they believed that the British people had a reputation for greater understanding—at least, compared to that of most Americans. After all, Britain ended the slave trade some thirty years before the American Civil War."

"Quite so," I was pleased to agree.

"To illustrate the point even further," Lucy went on, "after I had recuperated and finally arrived in Norbury, my mother and later my new stepfather provided me with private tutors and generally sheltered my upbringing. As a little girl, I never had reason to doubt the wisdom of their decision to live in England. And yet, with all the Negrophobia I've seen in the last few months, I'm no longer certain that the British reputation for tolerance is deserved."

It pained me to hear my race so severely denigrated, especially by such an innocent voice. "Do not disparage the British, Miss Hebron," I countered. "As you noted, we may indeed have our own shameful record of slavery, but we are a people that can rise above it. You yourself have grown up here and are testimony to that fact."

"Watson is right on that score, Miss Hebron," said Holmes. "Let me put my mind to it. Something doesn't ring true regarding these events. I shall visit you in Norbury tomorrow afternoon to explain my reasoning; and I trust that, schedule permitting, Dr Watson will join us."

"I certainly hope you *will*, Doctor," said Lucy Hebron.

Need I hear more? Naturally, I would attend the gathering. Not only was British honour at stake, but my personal reputation as well. John H. Watson made it a habit of never turning down the request of a stately young lady in distress—no matter, I had only now just discovered, the hue of her skin. Breeding, money, grooming, colour—in my mind, all are trumped by beauty.

Holmes's old friend Maupassant put it this way in his story, "The Diamond Necklace": "Women belong to no caste, no race, their grace, their beauty and their charm serving them in the place of birth and family." In fairness, however, the desire for justice had also to be included as one of the essential attributes of the young lady seated before me.

"Of course, I shall be there," said I, confident that in the name of supporting victims of prejudice, my wife would raise no objections to my venture.

A smiling Lucy Hebron rose to her feet, and Holmes and I stood as well. To Holmes, she said, "For whatever light you may shed on this matter, sir, Jos and I will be truly grateful."

"I shall see you to a carriage," said I. No need to let the charming Miss Hebron have to face the critical eye of Mrs Hudson unescorted.

It was the thought of the landlady that prompted yet another realization on my part. In spite of the tolerance shown by Mrs Hudson towards Holmes's odd behaviours—the bullets shot into the wall, the chemicals fouling the air, the bust in the window luring an assassin—one could not divorce this kind lady from the cultural assumptions of our age. However little Mrs Hudson may have intended it, her otherwise benign and stoic attitude actually provided cover for the very acts of cruelty and violence described by the latest client of Sherlock Holmes.

I boldly offered Miss Hebron my arm, and down the stairs the two of us marched, past the centurion of a landlady and out into Baker Street.

In addition to the summer's heat, the usual *mélange* of rattling carriages, shouting merchants, stinking horses, and jostling pedestrians filled the air. In my mind, the act of accompanying the young lady to the kerb amidst the chaos seemed the gentlemanly thing to do. Yet to my great surprise, it turned out to be much more than that—or so I learned as Miss Hebron broadened my understanding of social indignities.

"Thank you for coming along with me, Doctor," said she. "If a white man like yourself signals for a cab, they usually stop. When a black man or woman tries, they frequently drive right past."

I had never bothered to consider the privileges of being white. There was, I now realised, a lot more I had never considered and much more that I had always taken for granted.

*****

By the time I climbed back up the stairs, the sitting room was clouded with pipe smoke. Holding his favourite briar, Holmes sat in his armchair, knees propped under his chin.

Fixing me with his intense grey eyes, he said, "Consider, Watson—the rock, the letter, the splash of mud—they all occurred when the principals were alone. Only the beating took place when they were together. Does that not evoke an immediate conclusion?"

"Only the commonality of prejudicial behaviour," said I angrily, my thoughts still pondering those final words of Lucy Hebron.

"Of course," said Holmes with a dismissive wave of his pipe. "What I'm referring to is the strategies involved. For the rock and the letter to reach their destinations, whoever delivered them had to know the home and business addresses of Mr Fipps. And the devious carriage that almost ran down Miss Hebron—whoever rented it had been waiting for her near her home. Once more, someone knew where to find her."

"Agreed," said I, "though now that you bring it up, the attack in the park seemed unpremeditated. Unfortunately, the poor couple stumbled upon a band of prejudiced street-toughs."

"Exactly, Watson! Unless I am greatly mistaken, one must conclude that, unlike the assailants in the park, whoever sent those notes to Fipps and whoever pointed that carriage in the direction of Miss Hebron are quite familiar with the habits of both personages. It is a subject I intend to explore more fully on the morrow during our visit to Norbury."

With that cryptic pronouncement, he placed his pipe on the mantel, bade me good day, and—violin in hand—retired to his bedroom.

II

The late-morning train to Surrey deposited Holmes and me in Norbury not long past noon the following day. A few more shops than I had remembered now populated the area surrounding the railway station. One in particular, *Chadwick's Equestrian Equipment and Carriages,* caught Holmes's attention.

"A moment," said he, as we were about to set off for Pollards Hill where the Grant Munros lived. Before I could respond, he disappeared within the confines of a freshly painted red wood-barn. Not long thereafter, he emerged with a look of satisfaction. Motioning me to join him, he murmured, "As I had expected," and marched on.

Within minutes we found ourselves on the same rustic road that had led us to the little black girl and her yellow mask more than a decade earlier. Like the new shops in the village, more cottages now appeared along our route. Though numerous groves of yews and beeches and rolling pastures of green forage continued to dominate the scene, there could be little doubt that the forces of progress were beginning to overtake the pastoral countryside. It could not be more than a few years before additional roads and structures would be vying for prominence.

Soon we were passing the cottage in which little Lucy had been secreted away and then we were turning down the tree-lined lane that led to the handsome, two-storied villa of Grant Munro. (I valued it at eighty-pounds-a-year the first time I saw it.) But here too the isolation was receding. On the road above Munro's villa, a few more cottages had joined the two I remembered near the inn.

Holmes gave the entrance bell a pull; and though the door was opened by the same Scottish woman who had appeared ancient so many years before, she was immediately supplanted by the master of the house. His hair now tinged with grey, the still muscular Grant Munro ushered us into the sitting room where the principals in the drama were awaiting our appearance: his wife Effie, their daughter Lucy, and a clean-shaven, clear-eyed, straight-shouldered man whose bruised cheeks informed us that he must be Josiah Fipps, Lucy's recently victimised *fiancé*.

Upon our arrival they rose in unison, but Grant Munro quickly motioned for all to resume their seats and offered Holmes and me the two empty wing-chairs that faced the others.

I should say from the start that besides the greying hair, neither Grant Munro nor his wife had changed much since we had last seen them. Oh, there were a few more lines in their faces; but for the most part, the challenge of bringing up a child of colour in the midst of a white population seemed not have to undone them.

Grant Munro selected a long, amber-stemmed briar from a crowded wooden pipe rack. With two distinctive silver bands, the pipe appeared to be the same one to which he had been so attached upon our first meeting. He offered us tobacco, but we declined—in Holmes's case a sure indication that he wanted to move directly to the matter at hand.

"About these threatening notes," Holmes began.

"Damned haters!" Grant Munro cried out.

Effie placed a hand on his arm. "Jack, please allow Mr Holmes to continue."

Grant Munro tightened his jaw, but said nothing more.

Sherlock Holmes now repeated the inferences he had previously shared with me—that, given the fact that the threatening messages were delivered to known addresses, the writers must have been relatively familiar with either Lucy or Josiah or both.

"Nonsense!" cried Grant Munro, springing to his feet. "No one close to either one of them could have been responsible for those hateful messages. *No one!"*

A furrow darkened Effie's brow. "Jack, please," she said again. "What Mr Holmes has said makes perfect sense. Perhaps he may even have someone particular in mind."

Holmes bowed his head briefly. "Thank you, madam. Indeed, I do." He looked up at Grant Munro who had commenced the nervous pacing with which we were familiar. "Mr Munro," said Holmes, "it would be easier to proceed if you were to sit down."

Still seething, the man took his seat.

"Now, sir," said Holmes directly to Grant Munro, "I must ask you: for what reason did you hurl a rock through the window of Josiah Fipps's flat and send a threatening letter to his place of work?"

"Good God," I murmured as everyone's eyes turned to the head of the family.

"Mr Holmes!" cried his wife.

Grant Munro's face grew red; but he maintained his composure and gently set his pipe in a nearby ashtray. "I don't know what you're talking about, Mr Holmes. Certainly, you cannot believe that I, a man who accepted this wonderful girl as my own daughter all those year ago, could possibly have done anything at all to thwart her future happiness."

Lucy appeared too shocked to smile at her stepfather's compliment.

"So I too thought at first," replied Holmes. "After all, I was present the day you first met Lucy and embraced her with a fatherly kiss."

"A beautiful scene," I recalled. "I too remember it well."

"But then," Holmes continued, "I considered the matter more deeply. Take that dangerous carriage that almost ran Miss Hebron down. Why would its driver turn away at the last moment if he had truly set out to commit mayhem? If such a violent encounter had actually occurred on the wet road, if the carriage had in fact struck her, the event might well have been dismissed as an accident. Clearly, in this case there was no intent to harm. My doubts were confirmed when I described you to the proprietor of Chadwick's. He told me that although the person who had rented a four-wheeler on the day in question had swathed his lower face in a black scarf, the man's half-concealed features might indeed fit the description I offered. The stranger's money was plentiful, however, and the proprietor ignored any attempt to penetrate his mask."

As Holmes constructed his argument, Effie Grant Munro's eyes widened, and Josiah Fipps furrowed his brow. But it was poor Lucy, the victim of the aborted assault, who produced the tears. They trailed slowly down her dark cheeks.

A minute of silence ticked by. At last Effie spoke. "Have you nothing to say for yourself, Jack—you who once chastised *me* for underestimating your courage in matters of colour?"

Grant Munro, who had been looking down, now turned to Lucy and Jos. "I'm sorry," he said in a tremulous voice. "I was trying to spare the two of you the pain that always accompanies such experiments in social upheaval. I saw what your mother had gone through in seeking to protect you, Lucy—the lies, the fears, the machinations. How she secured a second house, how she kept from me her clandestine activities, how she allowed our own marriage to teeter precariously."

"Indeed," I said to Lucy, "your stepfather was quite upset when he visited Holmes and me in Baker Street all those years ago."

Grant Munro wiped at his eyes. "I was trying to save you from an ordeal you know nothing about, dear Lucy." He tried to secure Effie's hand, but she pulled it back from him.

"I've heard this tired history before, Father; and I appreciate all you had to put up with to keep our family together. But Jos and I love each other; and as far as we're concerned, nothing else need be said."

Jos gripped Lucy's hand. "It is our love," he proclaimed, "that will give us the strength to fight whatever bigotry comes our way."

"Like the attack in the park?" Grant Munro countered. "I had nothing to do with *that*; and unlike the results of *my* meagre warnings, the two of you suffered greatly."

Holmes nodded again. "I *assumed* that the assault in the park was random. Sad to say, such acts must be anticipated. If the two of you proceed in the direction you seem to have charted, I should imagine more of the same will occur."

"And yet that is precisely our intention," said the dark-skinned young lady, "to proceed—as you put it—in the direction we have already charted."

Her *fiancé* placed his arm round her shoulders.

Effie's nostrils flared as she beamed with pride at her daughter. "I should have expected nothing less," said she defiantly.

Grant Munro shook his head. "If you insist on placing yourselves at risk," said he with a note of resignation, "then I must remind you of a most significant fact."

Lucy extracted a white linen handkerchief from the cuff of her shirtwaist. Dabbing at her eyes, she asked suspiciously, "What is it?"

"A year remains before you reach your majority," said her stepfather. "Until that time, the law requires parental approval for someone of your age to wed. Grant me this one request. All I ask is that you take that time to examine your decision. If in a year from now you still wish to proceed, then you will have my blessing—my approval would no longer be needed—as well as a most generous wedding gift. Is that so great a sacrifice? I simply want what is the best for the two of you."

Lucy and Jos exchanged questioning glances followed by mutual shrugs. As best I could judge, it seemed that both of them deemed the proposition reasonable—if not desirable.

"A year seems a long time to wait," Lucy offered coldly, "but if it will make you happy, Father, I suppose we could manage."

With an accommodation in sight, Holmes took the opportunity to add, "I have no wish to interfere with anyone's personal considerations, only with the logistics of safety during the waiting time." To Lucy, he offered, "Allow me to find you protection, Miss Hebron." To her stepfather, he charged, "*You* will, of course, be asked to pay for such a service, Mr Grant Munro. But successful hops-agent that you are—not to mention the catalyst for so much consternation—producing money for such activity should not result in any major inconvenience."

"I cannot imagine that it should," he smiled. "Indeed, I relish the opportunity."

"Good!" cried Holmes with a clap of his hands. He obviously had some sort of plan in mind. "I shall communicate with you once I have arranged the matter. As for the conflicting passions aroused within your family, I trust you will resolve those issues among yourselves."

With those final words, Holmes got to his feet. I followed; and the two of us, offering the briefest of farewells, took our leave. In the railway carriage on our return to London, Holmes sat silently contemplating his next move.

*****

As I am certain the readers of my past works are aware, Sherlock Holmes, his claim of objectivity notwithstanding, displayed conflicting attitudes towards the question of race. On the one hand, confirming his view of the trivialities of racial distinctions, he could speak approvingly of Grant Munro's early acceptance of black little Lucy. On the other hand, he could just as easily hurl demeaning epithets at people of colour when he deemed such language useful. Among the more disquieting aspects of Holmes's character that I have reported, the insults he aimed at the Negro pugilist Steve Dixie just the previous May rank among the lowest.

Based on the boxer's reprehensible behaviour, Holmes could easily have limited his denunciations to the man's devoted allegiance to the criminal class. As I reported in the case I titled "The Three Gables", Holmes had voiced general suspicions regarding not only some "dirty work" Dixie had undertaken for the notorious Spencer John gang, but also a vague connection to the murder of a young man named Perkins outside the Holborn Bar. Yet instead of confining the basis of his disparagement to Dixie's criminal acts, Holmes preferred to insult the villain he called "Black Steve" with various racial stereotypes. To cite but a few of his jibes, I offer Holmes's derogatory jibes concerning Dixie's smell, woolly hair, and large lips.

Due to their antagonistic history, it was to my great surprise that when I called on Holmes the following day, I discovered the huge frame of the very villain in question ensconced at Holmes's table in the Baker Street sitting room. Dressed in a charcoal suit with grey and red pinstripes and sporting a loud yellow tie, Dixie appeared less aggressive than I had remembered. On the contrary, employing his tongue to roll a toothpick between his teeth, the one-time boxer sat listening quietly to my friend.

"She's one of yours, after all," Holmes said to him. "I should think you'd want to protect her."

"That I would, Masser Holmes. Which is why I'm payin' so much attention to you." The toothpick was now still. "It's not everyday that old Stevie gets offered a noble proposal from the likes of yourself—not with the money to back it up, at any rate. No, indeed."

"Excellent!" cried Holmes, handing the man a small piece of paper. "Here is the address in Norbury. During daylight hours you are to keep at a discreet distance from the house. You will wait for the lady in question, Miss Lucy Hebron, to emerge—either on her own or in the company of her *fiancé* or parents—and then follow her about, intervening only when you sense she might be exposed to danger. At night, you may assign one of your associates to relieve you."

Steve Dixie removed the toothpick. "Long as we're paid, Masser Holmes," said he, offering a wide grin that showed off his white teeth, "I vow that my mates and me will do right by the lady."

Holmes proceeded to draw out of the breast pocket of his coat a number of pound notes. "These should do you for a while," said he as he laid them on the table. "I'll forewarn the family of your presence. Now get to work."

With the toothpick once more nestling between his lips, Dixie picked up the bills and examined them. Then with a nod, he inserted the money, along with the Norbury address, into a light-brown, kid-leather wallet and slid the wallet somewhere inside his coat. "Gentlemen," said he, addressing us both as he rose, "it's been a pleasure doin' business with you, I'm sure."

With that, he set a tweed flat cap on his head and, tilting his chin up, thrust forward the toothpick like the bowsprit of a frigate and stalked out the door.

"Perhaps you'll make an honest man of him after all, Holmes," I offered.

"I have come to understand, old fellow," my friend responded with a quick smile, "that developing one's character is sometimes simply a matter of gaining an opportunity to prove one's worth." With a dry chuckle, he added, "Time will tell."

III

One can only strive to do one's best in this cold-hearted world. Success is never guaranteed, and yet during the next few weeks I found myself longing for good news from Norbury. With the threatening messages from Grant Munro stopped at their source and the posting of a bodyguard in the form of tough Steve Dixie, Holmes had done all that he could to insulate Lucy Hebron from the benighted society that surrounded her and her man. And yet we heard nothing from the young woman. Daring to hope that no news was good news, I found myself wondering whether Grant Munro's yearlong time-line for inter-racial harmony might actually be shortened.

The more days that passed, the more I wondered. And why not? Did a union like the one between Lucy Hebron and Josiah Fipps not offer the next logical step in helping eradicate communal prejudices? Before witnessing such a courtship involving people I actually knew, I had always deemed so idealistic a relationship as very far-off indeed, the kind of social harmony I would more readily expect to encounter in the fantasy world of my friend Mr H.G. Wells and his time machine than in the much more traditional landscape of Dr John H. Watson.

The desire to take action burned within me, and I found myself unable to wait any longer. Right or wrong, I decided, I would push the matter along on my own. There was no need to raise the issue with my wife—"Don't meddle, John," I could hear her saying—or even with Sherlock Holmes, whose disapproval would be obvious.

On the final Saturday in July, therefore, I found myself sans my old friend on the late-morning train to Norbury. Whatever the outcome, I was determined to involve myself in the personal plans of the Grant Munro family. I hoped to prod Miss Hebron into fixing a specific date for her marriage—a date, I should emphasise, to be much earlier than the one her stepfather had mandated—in short, a date not far from the present. To that end, I had sent a wire to Miss Hebron and Mr Fipps requesting a meeting that afternoon at the Munro villa.

In retrospect, I judge that it is at this point when one should raise the question I posed at the outset—foolish mistake or grievous error? For my part, I can only say that the closer I got to Norbury—

the train ride took less than an hour—the more strongly I felt possessed by the desire to make the very heavens smile upon this union. How, I wondered naively at the time, could anyone of right mind not be pleased with my effort to improve the human condition?

I sprang from the train at the station and fairly bounded down the road to Grant Munro's cottage. As expected, I espied Steve Dixie, toothpick in mouth, surveying the house from behind the trunk of a plane tree across the road.

"How goes the watch?" I enquired, tipping my bowler.

"Right as rain, Doctor," said he, offering an informal touch to the brim of his flat cap. "That is, once this Grant Munro bloke explained to the copper who kept sniffin' round just what I was doin' out here day after day."

I understood. "Not too many blacks milling about in Norbury, I should judge."

"Yeh," Dixie snorted, "none that *I've* seen anyway—besides Miss Lucy, that is. But there's so few houses out this way that there ain't too many *white* folks around to complain about me neither."

Bigotry again. Never before had I contemplated the extent of its pernicious omnipresence—never before had I felt the need. It was everywhere. Now, prompted by my little chat with Dixie, I felt my intentions even more confirmed, and I approached the house with a greater sense of urgency.

Fipps and Lucy were waiting for me. Assuring them that the black boxer would follow close behind us, I convinced them to join me in a short walk through the countryside. In the shade of the beech trees that arched the road, I hoped to convince the pair of the logic in marrying quickly. However presumptuous my suggestion, it seemed to me the appropriate action for them to take.

"Do you really think we should?" Lucy pressed me.

"Listen to the man," said Fipps before I could answer. "Dr Watson makes a valid point. Why worry about the artificial walls set up by the older generation? I love you, Lucy; and God knows we'll have lots more imposing barriers to surmount than the arbitrary timeline created by your stepfather."

Lucy smiled at her *fiancé* and clutched his hand. "Like Juliet's love for Romeo," said she, "my love for you is infinite. The more I give, the more there remains for me to give anew." Out on the open road, beneath a cathedral of arching branches thick with dark-green leaves, she dared kiss him on the cheek.

Romeo and Juliet indeed, I mused, quite enjoying the moment.

Suddenly, a wagon filled with hay came rumbling by. Its driver, an aging farmer with white side-whiskers, stared at the couple. As beautiful as had been Lucy's words, the old man, obviously repulsed by this display of affection between members of a different race, scowled and spat into the dirt. I saw Steve Dixie approach and then fall back as the wagon disappeared behind a bend in the road.

Lucy's focus would not be deterred by an act of ignorance. "We've been asked to wait," said she, "but there is also the law. How can we marry without the permission of my parents?"

Here was an opportunity for human progress, and I hoped to stimulate it as much as I could. In point of fact, I had anticipated Lucy's question and was ready with an answer. "There's Gretna Green," I offered, evoking the name of the southernmost Scottish village on the old coach road between London and Edinburgh. For years, the town had been the destination of many young English couples seeking immediate weddings. Unlike English law, the Scots required no parental approval, only two witnesses—the villagers themselves were generally eager to volunteer—and a twenty-one day residence requirement to be fulfilled by either member of the nuptial party.

"What a wonderful plan, Doctor!" cried Fipps, his speech quick with excitement. "Business is slow, and I should be able to make the journey immediately."

"Are you certain, Jos?" asked Lucy, a look of concern furrowing her smooth, dark brow.

"Westmoreland and Franks have already promised me time off," Fipps declared. "I'll travel to Gretna Green and come back for you in three weeks."

Clasping his hands in hers, the young woman closed her eyes. She must have been imagining their dream come true. Opening them again, she turned to me. "Oh, thank you, Doctor Watson. You've made me the happiest girl on the planet."

*****

The rest of the story requires but a few words of summary. What need is there to dwell on misery? For more than a month, neither Holmes nor I heard a word from the couple. One day in September, however, not long before Holmes retired to his bee keeping in the South Downs, I received a note to meet him in Baker Street. It was a solemn face he presented as he reached for the gasogene and prepared brandies for the two of us. Years before, Grant Munro had come to this very room and engaged Holmes with his own tale of woe. Today it was Holmes's turn to relate its latest permutation.

Just as I had envisioned, or so he told me, Lucy did indeed meet Jos in Gretna Green where the two were married. A blacksmith and his man served as witnesses. Once wed, the couple returned to Norbury where, thanks to Fipps's earnings, they managed to purchase a small cottage not far from the railway station. Grant Munro admitted that at first he had been outraged by the headstrong action of the lovers; but during the next few weeks Effie, appealing to the goodness in his nature, persuaded him to welcome the newlyweds into their home once more.

Would that the rest of the community had acted with the same magnanimity. As far as Scotland Yard could determine, one terrible night not three weeks after the fateful marriage, Steve Dixie's man was set upon by unknown assailants and knocked unconscious. These same vicious thugs then proceeded to set fire to the couple's house and escape into the countryside.

Fortunately, both Jos and Lucy were able to awaken, but so overwhelming was the smoke that it quickly threatened to overcome the pair. Only the young man's strength enabled him to save his bride. Though weakened by the noxious fumes, he managed to stagger away from the burning structure with Lucy in his arms and stumble to safety. It grieves me to say, however, that the smoke had done its damage. Not long after setting Lucy on safe ground, poor Jos, having inhaled too much of the thick, foul matter, expired in front of the smouldering remains of their cottage.

And still the tragedy had not fully played itself out. For Effie Grant Munro had never completely forgiven her husband's initial intimidation of the young couple. Vanquished by grief, she gathered up her distraught daughter and within the fortnight following the fire left her husband and returned with Lucy to the unfriendly but familiar confines of Atlanta.

"Playing Cupid is never easy, Watson," observed Sherlock Holmes. "I thought you would have learned by now. The role is laced with an irony one frequently overlooks. All too often, what appear to be comforting scenes of love serve to mask the hidden but circumscribing rules of logic. In this case—neither the first nor the last, you can rest assured—it was the stringent demands of society that undermined the union of two lovers—" (here Holmes paused to sip his drink and offer a sad smile) "—not to mention any attempts at correcting what ails the world. In spite of your most noble efforts, old fellow, everyone involved with this story of good intentions has been punished—Lucy, her late husband, and the Grant Munros."

I joined Holmes in sampling the brandy. It gave me time to reflect on his words. Whether purposely or not, he had omitted my name from the list of victims. Obviously, it had not been I who had fired the newlyweds' home, and yet my role in the matter had led inexorably to the tragic conclusion.

As I have already indicated, for Sherlock Holmes the name of Norbury had come to signify a mistake. Ironically, it now seemed to serve the same purpose for me. However calculating Holmes's analysis of the affair might have sounded, I have to confess that he was correct about the logic of the situation. Had I not naively attempted to right society's wrongs, a young man would still be living, a mother and daughter would still be part of a happy household, and I myself would not be shrouded in gloom.

"But wait a moment," I told myself. "Had not Holmes picked himself up after Norbury all those years ago? Had he not just a few months later successfully solved the riddle of 'The Sign of Four', the adventure in which I met my own true love? Perhaps it was my longing for Mary Morstan that awakened in me the desire to see Lucy and Jos as happy as Mary and I had been.

To be sure, colour had played no role in *our* relationship. For a love like Jos and Lucy's to be so unencumbered, the planet would no doubt have to be populated by masses of grey figures instead of individual blacks and whites. Only then would colour, which now so conveniently functions to separate us all, no longer play a role in human relationships.

"To a world free from prejudice!" I suddenly cried out, raising my glass as I did so. However distant from our present-day existence, at the very least Lucy and Jos had taken a step towards such a future.

Holmes raised his glass as well. I believe I detected a glimmer of appreciation in his steel-grey eyes.

A Case of Mistaken Identity

No amount of fire or freshness can challenge
what a man will store up in his ghostly heart.
--F. Scott Fitzgerald
The Great Gatsby

I

*W*ith a furled black brolly hooked over my arm, I stood outside my door in Queen Anne Street peering up and down the road. It was the beginning of a cool, wet June in the year 1924; and like many another evening that summer, the air felt thick and heavy beneath grey and threatening skies. To be sure, my sitting room offered more comfort; but I was awaiting the arrival of a taxi and wanted to be as punctual as possible.

Fortunately, I did not have long to wait. In a matter of minutes a dark-blue cab rolled to a stop. A wave from the rear-seat window assured me that my old friend was inside; and employing the umbrella as a walking-stick, I carefully made my way along the slippery flags to the kerb.

"Ah, my dear Watson," said Sherlock Holmes as I planted myself upon the shiny black-leather cushion beside him, "so good to see you."

Except for the silvering of his combed-back hair and thick brows, Sherlock Holmes looked as he always had—the same square jaw, the same aquiline nose, the same steely glance from those sharp, grey eyes.

"Holmes," said I, "you haven't aged a bit."

"As much as one may hope for the contrary, old fellow," said he indicating his grey hair, "one cannot cheat the calendar—let alone the occasional touch of rheumatism."

It was always a pleasure to see my former colleague and companion. And yet, though Holmes and I had not visited with each other for quite some time, I confess to having felt mystified at his quick acceptance of my dinner-invitation. Only the day before had I asked him to dine with another guest and me at the Langham, and I really did not expect him to come up to London from his cottage upon the South Downs on such short notice. Yet here he was.

Holmes must have realised what I was thinking. Perhaps he even sensed my resentment at his failure to keep me abreast of his recent adventures. For no sooner had the taxi lurched forward than he drew a small white envelope from an inner-coat pocket and slid it tantalisingly across the seat in my direction. Though the ride to nearby Portland Place would be brief, he had obviously concluded that there would be sufficient time for me to discern the significance of the envelope's contents and presumably the reason for his last-minute trip to London.

First things first, however. I noted his Sussex address scrawled across the front of the envelope and three American stamps affixed to the upper-right-hand corner bearing a postmark from New Brunswick, New Jersey. Yet what most intrigued me was the crimping at the centre of the envelope formed by the small objects within. Somehow, it all seemed distantly familiar.

Sherlock Holmes nodded at the thing. "Open it," said he.

"Open it?" I repeated, making certain that I had heard him correctly.

He nodded, and so I picked up the envelope. It took but a moment of fingering the tiny pieces within to guess the contents. Indeed, once I had lifted the flap, I was not at all surprised to discover the five small pips. Although from previous experience, I expected to see the whitish, dried seeds from an orange, these pips were brown, and I judged them to have come from an apple. Printed in red ink on the inside of the envelope's flap were the words, "Drop the case"; beneath them, the letters K.K.K.

"A copycat?" I chuckled, employing the American term. I vaguely remembered a similar message we had received in the late 80's some four decades ago. It was my initial introduction to the Ku Klux Klan, the secret American society primarily bent on terrorising Negroes—and worse. Readers may remember my account of the affair, which I titled "The Five Orange Pips".

For his part, Holmes appeared unamused, reacting to my light-hearted response with a tightening of his jaw and a narrowing of his eyes. "I received this envelope by post a few days ago," said he. "How they got my address I have no idea, but it is the reason that I agreed so quickly to join you and your friend for dinner this evening."

"He's not exactly my friend, Holmes," I protested as the taxi rolled to a stop before the many-faceted Langham. "He's a writer—an American actually. As I explained in my wire, I met him just yesterday. That's when he told me he hoped to speak with you as soon as possible about a murder in New Jersey—"

A doorman in grey livery cut me off in mid-sentence.

"Welcome to the Langham," said he, opening the door of the taxi and gesturing to the front arch of the building's three-sided stone portico.

Before I could get up, Holmes grabbed my arm and pulled me towards him. "*Two* murders, actually," he whispered close to my ear and snatched the envelope from my hand.

Two murders—Holmes was right. He may not have known the man we were about to meet, but he certainly knew about the case the man had told me about. Yet owing to both the doorman and my stick-like umbrella, I managed to exit the cab without saying a word. Holmes paid the driver, and together the two of us walked slowly through the familiar entrance hall and into the vestibule that led to the *Salle á Manger*.

Our short trek did nothing to stifle my curiosity. We passed various small tables where patrons were taking coffee, their hushed voices accompanied by some nondescript melodies offered by classical players stationed in a corner of the broad hallway. Holmes seemed to enjoy the tunes, but I would not be distracted. In spite of the music, my thoughts were haunted not only by the meaning of those pips Holmes had showed me but also by whatever connection they might have to the murders to which he had referred. For that matter, I now worried that we ourselves might be in some danger.

"Mozart's G major String Quartet," observed Holmes with a brief but self-satisfied smile. "Though the second violin is a bit off."

Under the circumstances, I admired his calm. Here he was thinking about a fiddle whilst I was worrying about our safety. At the same moment Holmes was turning his head towards the musicians, I was considering a look over my shoulder for secret assassins.

Upon entering the dining room, a large darkened hall bordered by stately marble columns on facing walls, I offered our names to the *maître d'*; and he quickly ushered us to a well-appointed table set for three. It was there that the American I had mentioned to Holmes sat awaiting our arrival. In the tall glass he was clutching, a green half-rind of lime lay submerged in a pool of melted ice—no doubt the remains of a gin rickey, a drink that he had previously described to me. When he cast his eyes upon Holmes, a look of relief seemed to bathe the American's face.

Apparently, it was left to me to appreciate the irony. Though the entire business had begun in my own house the day before, Sherlock Holmes seemed much more aware of what was going on than did I. Apple pips? The Klan? Murders in New Jersey? Of all this, I remained as ignorant as I was the previous morning when I had been working innocently at my desk and the bell at the front door clanged for attention at precisely ten o'clock.

*****

"An American gentleman to see you, Dr Watson," said my young housekeeper, Miss Ross.

I smiled at her from behind a stack of papers. The older I grow, the more I appreciate how casting one's eye on an attractive young woman each day serves as a better tonic than any diurnal medicine I can name.

"Quite a good-looking fellow, sir," she added, "if you don't mind my saying. He said to tell you he's a writer."

"A writer?" I repeated, cupping my hand behind my ear to amplify the sound. I was always surprised when my accounts of Holmes's cases attracted the literary world. But I suppose it was why—now in my early seventies—I was still hard at work compiling portfolios of those sketches of mine that had most recently been published in The Strand. *My agent, Sir Arthur Conan Doyle, had already bestowed a title upon the volume I was currently completing: "The Case-Book of Sherlock Holmes". If authors like this fellow at the door were coming to see me from as far away as the United States, there seemed little doubt that my new collection would generate strong interest.*

In all honesty, however, I should inform my readers that I really do expect "The Case-Book" to be the last. My hearing problem is but one of the physical ailments with which I must contend. Alas, I no longer move as dextrously as I once did and, as a result, spend most of my days on the ground floor of my house. Due to this lack of mobility, my sitting room looks more like a library, my grand mahogany desk at its centre, surrounded by walls of bookshelves reaching to the ceiling.

When I go out walking, I employ a stick; and Miss Ross aids me in climbing the stairs. In fact, I confess rather sheepishly that it is her physical support pressing against my body that encourages me to ascend the staircase more often than might seem necessary. In any event, since the death of my wife, I have appreciated having Miss Ross about the place. She leaves me dinner before going home.

"Sir?" said she, her voice a degree louder as she awaited my instructions regarding the visitor at the door.

"Show the man in," said I, rising from my chair.

In spite of my other infirmities, my eyesight remains sharp; and I could see that Miss Ross was quite correct about the visitor's good looks. Advancing towards me was a dapper young man probably not yet thirty. At first, I took him to be clean-shaven; but the nearer he came, the more apparent was the hint of a feeble blond moustache. I placed him at about five-foot-eight, his short legs limiting his height. The tan he bore indicated that he had not been spending his summer in London; yet his stylish suit of white linen set off by a light-blue tie suggested he seemed undeterred by our continually-dreary English skies.

Though the gentleman caller had fairly bounded into the room, I immediately sensed the contradictions. He may have greeted me with a friendly smile; but his sad, green eyes betokened vulnerability. His brushed-back blond hair, sharply chiselled nose, and thin lips presented quite a handsome portrait; yet one could detect an aura of insecurity.

Holding a straw boater in his left hand, he extended his right in my direction. "Scott Fitzgerald," said he in his flat American accent. "My friends call me Fitz."

"John Watson," said I, shaking his hand, "but then you know who I am since you've come here to see me."

"Spot on," said my guest.

Whilst Miss Ross took the man's hat, I gazed at my striking visitor. I knew the name, of course: F. Scott Fitzgerald—the author of countless short stories; inventor of *the phrase, "The Jazz Age"; composer of two successful novels*, This Side of Paradise *and* The Beautiful and Damned. *More to the point, even I, cooped up as I was here in Queen Anne Street, had heard some of the more egregious tales from New York about the man and his wife—riding atop the bonnets of taxis, bathing in pubic fountains, disrobing at parties—and always, in spite of the prohibition against alcohol in the States, the constant drinking. To be sure, much of his work had received positive reviews, yet I personally had no intention of exposing myself to his sordid descriptions of colonial sensationalism.*

In spite of my protests, however, let it not be thought that I am in the habit of shunning American writers. Faithful readers will recall that I have fraternised with such figures in the past—people like Clemens and Crane and London. Yet those encounters had taken place many years before, and all had something to do with crimes for my detective-friend to solve. With Holmes now comfortably retired, I had no idea—other than the desire to meet the biographer of Sherlock Holmes, of course—what might have pushed so infamous a figure as F. Scott Fitzgerald in my direction.

"Might I offer you some refreshments?" said I, waving in the general direction of the silver tea and coffee pots.

"Normally, I don't drink in the morning," said Fitzgerald with what sounded like a bit too much piety. "But," he added with what I regarded as equally too much enthusiasm, "I wouldn't say no to a gin rickey."

My blank expression elicited an explanation.

"An American drink, Doctor—gin, carbonated water, and half a lime."

My housekeeper moved to serve him, but I intervened. "It's all right, Miss Ross. We'll manage on our own."

"Very good, sir," said she, casting one final look at the handsome visitor as she gently closed the door on her way out.

To fulfil Fitzgerald's early-morning craving for spirits, I pointed him in the direction of the cherry-wood sideboard. Upon it stood my silver tantalus and its three bottles, one of which contained a smooth gin. For the carbonated water, he would have to rely on my ancient gasogene.

"There's ice in the bucket," I told him, "but I'm rather afraid you'll need to substitute lime juice for an actual lime. Could you pour me a glass of water while you're at it?"

I moved to the wing chair opposite the sofa whilst Fitzgerald filled our glasses. Placing the drinks on the table between us, he seated himself across from me and sampled his rickey with a satisfied smile.

"Now, Mr Fitzgerald, what brings you to London?" I asked, fully expecting some sort of homage *to my literary accomplishments.*

"It's simple really," said he. "I need to meet with Sherlock Holmes."

"Holmes!" I cried, my eyebrows shooting up in astonishment. Although I had been compiling a number of our adventures together, it had been quite a while since I had given serious thought to actually engaging with my old friend again.

Fitzgerald ran a hand through his luxuriant hair. "You see, Doctor, I'm in the middle of writing my third novel. Actually, I've been working on it for some time. I call it Among Ash Heaps and Millionaires."

I reacted not at all to the cumbersome title, and Fitzgerald immediately recognised my response as unspoken criticism.

"You know," said he with a quick laugh, "I'm not too keen on the title either. That's why I have alternatives. In fact, as of this moment, thanks to you I'm going to start calling it Trimalchio in West Egg.*"*

I continued staring blankly. "Trimalchio? West Egg?" The terms meant nothing to me.

"West Egg is my fictional name for Great Neck. It's a town on Long Island in New York. We rented a house there, and I studied the inhabitants. As for Trimalchio, he was a Roman slave who got rich through underhanded means. At least, that's what Petronius says in the Satyricon.*"*

Fitzgerald completed this announcement with a broad grin. Though he was obviously proud to show off his knowledge of the Classics, I greeted this explanation with no more emotion than I had displayed just moments before.

"It doesn't really matter," Fitzgerald said, dismissing my ignorance with a measured wave of his glass and a quick shake of his head. The point is that the fellow's a model for the main character in

my novel. It's about a rich American crook and the married woman he falls in love with." He paused to sample his rickey. "But to be honest," he said with a lick of his lips, "even though I completed a first draft, my life in New York—it's not called the den of iniquity for nothing, you know—the city had gotten the best of me. I figured that if I was ever to complete the book, I'd have to go some place where there was peace and quiet."

This observation made sense to me, and I nodded accordingly.

"We have to watch our money," Fitzgerald continued, " but thanks to what I'd earned from my magazine stories, Zelda and I—Zelda's my wife—packed up our belongings—including our little girl Scottie (she's two)—and we sailed to France in early May. It took us ten *days to get from New York to Paris!* Ten *days on a 'dry steamer', the* Minnewaska. Ten days without a drink! *Can you imagine? In fairness, I guess I've been making up for it ever since." Here he held up his glass to illustrate the point—as if I needed such a gesture to recognise an inebriant.*

"But Paris?" I said in disbelief. "Why, the cost alone—"

"Oh," he smiled, "we didn't remain there—not in Paris. You don't stay in Paris if you're trying to economise. For that matter, you don't come to London either—believe me. But we bought an inexpensive car and drove south to the Riviera. It sounds swell, but it's pretty empty in the summer. Apparently, the French consider the Riviera a place to spend the winter. As a result, we were able to rent a small house a few miles north of St. Raphaël."

"Quite beautiful, I should imagine."

Fitzgerald fairly beamed. "Our house—it's called Villa Marie*—stands on a pine-shaded hill overlooking the town of Valescure and the glorious too-blue Mediterranean. It's hot in the daytime under that flaming sun; but at night, when the liquid dark comes down, it's perfect. Mainly though, it's cheap—$79 a month—and silent—if you discount the rush of the sea. It's a place where I can work on the book and not be disturbed. Zelda spends her time on the sand with a couple of French aviators she's met."*

I drank some water while picturing the paradisiacal scene. But too much time had already elapsed without my having asked the inevitable question: "What in the world does any of this have to do with Sherlock Holmes?"

Again Fitzgerald brushed at his hair. "I need some technical help with the plot of my novel, you see. As of now, it contains at least two murders and a suicide."

"'Two murders and a suicide,' I repeated to be sure I had heard him correctly. "And how, may I ask, could a fictional work of such a nature possibly involve Sherlock Holmes?"

Fitzgerald held up his glass to me, as if to say, "Good question." Then he drank some more. "I was hoping Holmes might advise me. You see, I've re-worked much of the story. Ever since the failure of a play I wrote, I've been worrying more about Trimalchio*—the book, I mean. My original plan was to deal with the impact of the Catholic Church on the life of a little boy. I was raised Catholic. That's probably why the early effects of sin and guilt intrigue me."*

F. Scott Fitzgerald thinks too much, *I mused.*

"But lately I've been looking for a new angle. Forget about the little boy. I want to say more about the evil schemes those sins produce in adults—you know, crimes and such. It's funny. I've always liked Chesterton's Father Brown mysteries. Maybe that's why. You know, back in my youth, I wrote a murder-mystery myself. I guess I've been fascinated by curious deaths from the start, and that's what led me to writing about real-life murders."

"'Real-life *murders'? I thought your book was fiction."*

"It is," Fitzgerald nodded. "But as it so happened, Zelda and I moved from St. Paul to New York in '22—just when news of two horrific killings in New Jersey were appearing in the local newspapers.

"Mind you, I'm not in the business of writing crime stories; but to establish my Trimalchio *as a product of that era, I decided to include references to actual events—the fixing of our baseball World Series, for instance; and I offer indirect allusions to Presidential hijinks as well as scenes of people skirting our anti-drinking laws." Here, with a decided twinkle in his eyes, he held up his glass again.*

"And?"

"And for the accuracy of the historical record, I want part of the plot to be propelled by that real-life—and as yet unsolved—pair

*of hard-boiled murders in New Jersey. I've kept some newspaper clippings about them in my scrapbook."**

"I'm beginning to understand what you're after," said I—though what Holmes might have to do with a two-year-old double-murder in America, I could only guess. Affairs of a literary nature were not the sort of issue with which to bother my friend.

"You see, Doctor, I've reached a kind of impasse. I'm dissatisfied with Trimalchio*'s sixth and seventh chapters, the ones that establish the motives for the murders. I'm worried that some of it is too raw. That's why I want Sherlock Holmes to tell me more about the realities of the case—mainly, what he knows about the people involved. I want to avoid having to fall back upon the usual trashy imaginings I've based much of my other work on."*

"Look here, Mr Fitzgerald—" said I.

"Fitz," he reminded me with a winsome smile. Then quickly downing the rest of his rickey, he raised the empty glass.

"May I?" he asked.

I nodded once more in the direction of the tantalus, then resumed my argument: "Sherlock Holmes is retired. He is no longer fighting crime. And though he may have read something of this case you have in mind—"

"The Hall-Mills murders," Fitzgerald said over his shoulder while pouring more gin.

I cupped my hand behind an ear and asked him to repeat the names.

"They mean nothing to me," I murmured after he had done so. "And I would be very surprised indeed if they mean anything more to Sherlock Holmes—other than what he may have read about them in the newspapers. Besides, he and I have been out of touch."

Fitzgerald's response surprised me. "I'll *say you've been out of touch! I realise that it hasn't been reported, Doctor, but still . . . you don't seem to know that Sherlock Holmes himself went to New*

---

* Fitzgerald's interest in the aforementioned murders is substantiated by Sarah Churchwell in her 2013 study titled *Careless People: Murder, Mayhem, and the Invention of The Great Gatsby*. It must be pointed out, however, that she makes no mention of Sherlock Holmes's role in the investigation. (DDV)

Jersey back in December of '22 to investigate the very same murders we're talking about."

Holmes in America? Two years before and not a word to me? (*At least, I could not remember that he had informed me of such a trip.)*

"How is it, Mr Fitzgerald," I asked with not a little envy, "that you *have come to know of Holmes's involvement?"*

The American took another pull of his gin. "Actually, I inferred as much from the comments of Sir Basil Thomson in the New York Times.*"*

I had met Sir Basil on some occasion or another. A former head of the CID at Scotland Yard, he kept a sharp eye out for Holmes—both to learn from and to criticise. He was the type of rigorous investigator that many an objective observer of the Yard has called the embodiment of Holmes himself.

*"You see," Fitzgerald explained, "like Holmes, Thomson was also asked to evaluate the police proceedings in New Brunswick. He was in New York not long after Holmes's investigation. You can look it up. Sir Basil never offered any specific solutions to the murders, but he had plenty to say about Sherlock Holmes. He rambled on and on about how the best police work involves a team—not soloists. It is organizations that solve actual mysteries, he maintained, not solitary detectives like Sherlock Holmes. Why, he even joked that if he himself had to rely on the same methods as those employed by Holmes, then he, Sir Basil Thomson, might very well lock up the Archbishop of Canterbury by mistake."**

I had to smile. It was exactly the sort of comment one would expect from a Yarder.

"I tell you, Doctor, you could just smell the rivalry. The more Thomson devalued Holmes, the more convinced I became that Holmes must actually have investigated the affair. You just knew *it! Once I incorporated the murders into my novel, I figured a private eye like Sherlock Holmes would be just the fellow to fill me in on the details. After my contacts at the* Times *confirmed that Holmes had been to New Jersey to study the case, I knew I had to talk with him."*

---

* Thomson's comments regarding the Archbishop of Canterbury and Sherlock Holmes were made in a speech to the Royal Society of Arts and quoted in the *New York Times* of April 24, 1921. (DDV)

I drank more water.

"Max Perkins, my editor at Scribner's, contacted Conan Doyle to find out where you live. I left Zelda and Scottie at Villa Marie *so I could pop over to London for a couple of days to see you. What better way to get a hold of Sherlock Holmes than by having his noted Boswell make the connection?"*

I blushed at the compliment. Still, I had to repeat that, thanks to my questionable health, Holmes and I had not communicated since his trip to New Jersey.

"Look, Doctor," Fitzgerald said, motioning with his glass to emphasise his point, "all I ask is that you give him a call."

"He has no telephone."

"Send him a wire then, saying I'd like to see him, and arrange a visit. I'm staying at the Langham. We could meet there for dinner."

"The Langham?"

"I know, I know. I said we were trying to avoid spending too much, but you can't deny that there's always a high cost to economising. Tell Mr Holmes that to get his personal view of the case, I'd travel anywhere that would be convenient for him. I mean—it's obvious that he still gets around. Recall that it wasn't so long ago that he was in the States."

F. Scott Fitzgerald offered a persuasive argument. Obviously, Holmes did indeed "get around"—with or without my knowledge. I must admit that his failure to notify me *of his trip continued to sting. After all, was I not—as Fitzgerald had pointed out—Holmes's faithful Boswell? As such, should I not have been given an opportunity to record Holmes's investigation into these infamous murders?*

Why *not* take advantage of Fitzgerald's interest in the crimes? *Fitzgerald had said the murders were unsolved, and yet Holmes was not the sort to leave such matters up in the air. Why not use Fitzgerald's request as an excuse to hear about the murders from Holmes himself? Perhaps I might even discover an opportunity to add one final sketch to "The Case-Book".*

Truth be told, as a writer, I also felt sympathetic towards Fitzgerald's literary plight. I cannot ignore my good fortune at having actually been *to most all of the locations I have recreated in my accounts, locations like Baskerville Hall, Stoke Moran, the Copper Beeches. At the very least, it seemed to me that Fitzgerald deserved to hear the perspective of one who had studied these murders first-hand. And yet at the same time, I still found it difficult to imagine Sherlock Holmes conversing with so flamboyant a figure as F. Scott Fitzgerald about so trivial a matter as a book of fiction.*

My guest mustered a winsome, almost seductive, grin. "Give it a try, Doctor. That's all I ask. Contact Sherlock Holmes. Let me pick his brain."

In the end, the young man was quite persuasive—not to mention my own desire to see Holmes again. Besides, at the very least, I would be familiarising myself with a two-year-old mystery that—as far as I knew at the time—seemed to still want untangling. I knew nothing about this Hall-Mills murder case, but the act of examining any unsolved crime has always fired my imagination.

"All right," I told Fitzgerald. "I'll give it a go."

With an appreciative smile he held up his now-empty glass in a form of salutation.

*****

Upon seeing Holmes and me approach, the American rose to greet us.

"Mr Fitzgerald," said I by way of introduction, "may I present to you Mr Sherlock Holmes."

The American surprised me by bending at the waist in an almost formal bow. Only after he straightened up, did the young man speak. "Thanks for meeting me on such quick notice, Mr Holmes."

With a wave of his hand, my friend brushed away the appreciative words. "I've worked with writers before, Mr Fitzgerald," he offered as we settled into our seats, "though never, I confess, in so appropriate a setting."

"How so?"

"Why, this is the very room in which Oscar Wilde and Watson's agent, Conan Doyle, had their famous dinner in August of '89."

"1889?" Fitzgerald marvelled. "Why, I wasn't even born yet."

"Who was the host, Watson? Another American if I remember rightly."

"To be sure. They met with Joseph Stoddart, the managing editor of an American periodical—*Lippincott's,* I believe. Conan Doyle called the affair a 'golden evening'."

"As well he might," observed Holmes to Fitzgerald. "Prompted by that dinner party, Wilde composed *The Picture of Dorian Gray*, and Conan Doyle was able to coax a lengthy narrative out of friend Watson here. Which case was it, old fellow?"

"*The Sign of Four*."

"Quite so," said Holmes. "Who can forget the perilous chase up the Thames on the trail of Jonathan Small and the Andaman Islander with the poisonous darts?"

Who can forget indeed? I thought. But my mind focused on different memories of the case, for it was during that same investigation all those years ago that I met Miss Mary Morstan, the beautiful young woman who was destined to become my bride. Following her death, I thought I could never marry again. Fortunately, I was wrong.

Fitzgerald broke into my reverie. "As Dr Watson may have informed you, Mr Holmes, it's of a more recent case I wish to speak—the Hall-Mills murders." Suddenly, Fitzgerald snapped his fingers, and a waiter immediately approached our table. "But first we must fortify ourselves."

Holmes and I leaned back in our chairs.

"Drinks, gentlemen," commanded the writer. "It's all on me—or on my publisher. 'Get the damned book finished!' I've been told in no uncertain terms. Perkins assures me that Scribner's regards any money they advance me to that end as a good investment."

Holmes and I each ordered a sherry; Fitzgerald, another gin rickey.

"I've got to tell you, Mr Holmes," said the American after the drinks were delivered, "that I was most pleased you agreed to meet with me. You have quite the reputation for shunning interviews."

Holmes raised his long forefinger. "Don't press your luck, Mr Fitzgerald. Let it not be thought that I am here to promote your career. I have reason enough to keep these murders in the public eye."

Recalling the apple pips Holmes had just shown me, I understood his desire to get to the bottom of the matter.

"I regard neither murder nor its investigation as a subject of frivolity," Holmes explained. "Watson here can tell you how often I used to remonstrate with him for pandering to public tastes. He constantly romanticised our enquiries when he should have been presenting them as austere models for criminal study. But in New Jersey, Mr Fitzgerald, my confidential findings were dismissed so quietly that I'm hoping your novel might gain them further exposure.

"Call me 'Fitz'," said the writer, hoisting his glass with a wink of an eye.

Sherlock Holmes ignored the invitation.

"What I am truly hoping, Mr Fitzgerald," said he, "is that your book will trigger a new investigation and reveal not only what happened to the minister and the choir singer, but also some other activities of a criminal nature possibly committed by the killers."

I shook my head. "I'm afraid I'm in the dark. What minister? What choir singer? For that matter, Holmes, I had no idea that you had actually gone to America over this affair until Fitzgerald informed me of the fact. You might at least have told me of your plans. I'm a bit hurt."

"You're quite right, of course, old fellow," said Holmes. "I'm sorry about that." He sampled his sherry—no doubt to avoid the discomfort of offering further apology. "Neither one of us is getting any younger, old fellow, and Conan Doyle has told me how occupied you've been compiling your stories. Why, I had no idea if my own antiquated skills would even be helpful in the New Jersey investigations."

Fitzgerald held his glass up to Holmes as if to toast him. "You underestimate yourself, Mr Holmes."

"So what happened?" I asked, my injured pride quickly replaced by curiosity.

"I too am most interested in hearing your view of things," said Fitzgerald, "but hedonist that I am, I insist that we order our meals before you begin."

Once again, the American summoned the waiter with a snap of his fingers. I looked at Holmes who simply rolled his eyes at Fitzgerald's brashness. Still, the *table d'hôte* menu sounded appealing, and I ordered the rack of lamb; Holmes, the *coq au vin*; and Fitzgerald, the roast beef.

No sooner did the waiter depart than Fitzgerald produced from inside a jacket pocket a small notebook and gold pencil. "At the risk of stating the obvious, gentlemen," said he, "I find it vitally important to take notes about all sorts of things—especially when those things have a direct relationship to my current work."

For his part, Sherlock Holmes took a moment to study the remaining sherry in his glass, sipped a bit, and then began his narrative.

II

"From the start," said Holmes, "I followed the Hall-Mills case in the daily newspapers. It was not without its curiosities. Conan Doyle himself was mentioned by Charlotte Mills, the sixteen-year-old daughter of the murdered woman—"

"The one the papers call a 'flapper'," interrupted Fitzgerald. "She caught my interest."

"Quite so," said Holmes curtly. Never pleased at being cut off in mid-sentence, he began again. "It seems the girl had been reading *The New Revelation*, Sir Arthur's book on spiritualism, and hoped to converse with her deceased mother. The daughter wanted to ask her just who was responsible for the crimes. Needless to say, such a strategy never materialised—if you can forgive the pun."

Fitzgerald offered a polite smile.

"But to the case itself: In early December of 1922, I was invited by Mr Wilbur Mott, the New Jersey state prosecutor, to come to America. He sought my opinion of a mystery that had occurred some two months before. It seems that a pair of grisly murders had been committed just outside of New Brunswick, a quiet town situated on the banks of the Raritan River. As one can imagine, in so idyllic a setting the occurrence of such a heinous crime was rare—but then, sad to say, so were the authorities' preparations for investigating it.

"Confusion reigned from the start. In fact, it took the state about a month to discover that jurisdictional issues were severely hampering the investigation. Deciding whose case it was posed the first challenge. The bodies were found in a field in Somerset County, you see; and yet it was widely believed that the victims had been killed somewhere in the town of New Brunswick, which is in the county of Middlesex. To resolve the problem, New Jersey's Attorney General appointed a state prosecutor to oversee the enquiry."

"This fellow Mott," I observed, "the chap who contacted *you,* Holmes."

"Just so. In fact, most of what I am about to tell you I learned from him and from the ocean of papers comprising the police report that he provided.

"Do tell, Mr Holmes," said Fitzgerald, pencil poised. "We're all ears."

"The murders in question occurred on a quiet Thursday night, the 14th of September. Although the police detected bits and pieces of evidence, they found nothing conclusive. Oh, a few peripheral suspects were considered, but on 5 December a Grand Jury announced that no indictments were to be brought against anyone. It was this frustrating result that prompted Mr Mott to seek fresh eyes."

"And so he turned to *you,*" I prompted.

"Precisely—although I should add that he made it quite clear from the start that anything I might discover could never be attributed to Sherlock Holmes. 'Public funds,' Mr Mott said, 'require our public servants to do the work themselves.'"

"You'd get no credit?" Fitzgerald asked.

Holmes chuckled drily. "'Getting the credit', as you call it, Mr Fitzgerald, has never been my need. As friend Watson has documented elsewhere, I prefer to work anonymously. Even in retirement, it is the problem itself that attracts me—the more complicated, the more attractive. I've dabbled in some interesting cases since leaving Baker Street—my work during the Great War and that business with the so-called 'Lion's Mane' come to mind—but not for a long time have I involved myself in so intricate a murder investigation as the one presented to me in New Jersey.

"Suffice it to say, I readily accepted the opportunity to put my analytical skills back to work. In fact, it was with an enthusiasm that surprised even me that, after securing a neighbour to look after my bees, I employed the Cunard line to convey me across the Atlantic."

At this provocative instant, the waiter arrived with our dinners. I must report, however, that savoury though the bill of fare was, not even the fine cuisine of the Langham could distract us from Holmes's compelling narrative. My friend did pause to butter some bread—a dramatic bit of theatre, perhaps, since once he had fully lathered it, he set the slice down uneaten.

Holmes also allowed himself a moment to sample the chicken. But after a few bites and an approving nod, he resumed his tale. "I met Mr Mott as soon as I was established in my hotel in New Brunswick. A distinguished-looking jurist in his sixties with iron-grey hair, he seemed just the man to set matters straight. And indeed he wasted no time before filling me in on the general background of the case.

"'On Saturday, the 16th of September,' he told me, 'a young New Brunswick couple went out for a morning stroll. Their walk took them through the ankle-deep grass of a field just outside of town—part of an abandoned farm where lovers are wont to amble, especially at night—that is, they did before these murders took place.'"

"I've studied the area," Fitzgerald interjected. "It's just south of a park called 'Buccleuch'. I like the name. In fact, I'm using it as an ancestral patronymic for the narrator of my novel."

"Quite so," responded Holmes, clearly uninterested in the development of Fitzgerald's fiction.

"The couple's excursion," Holmes went on, "turned out to be far different from the idyllic walk the two had been expecting. It was these two, you see, who stumbled across a pair of bodies lying among a scattering of trees. In fact, the feet of the corpses were pointing towards a nearby crab-apple tree."

"I assume that's important," said I, thinking of the pips Holmes had had shown me earlier.

He held up his hand, palm outward. "In due time," said he with a quick smile.

"The dead were Reverend Edward Wheeler Hall, the rector of New Brunswick's Protestant Episcopal Church of St. John the Evangelist, and Mrs Emily Mills, a member of the church choir. Hall, husband of the wealthy Frances Noel Hall, was in his early forties; Mrs Mills, wife to James Mills, the janitor and sextant of Reverend Hall's church, in her mid-thirties. The state prosecutor admitted that the causes of death were so obvious—the reverend had been shot in the head and Mrs Mills in the face—that the authorities had accepted the morticians' reports without requiring any official examinations of the bodies. In point of fact, formal autopsies had been dispensed with. As a result, the precise extent of the wounds wasn't discovered for weeks."

"No autopsies?" the doctor in me exclaimed. "Unforgiveable."

"I said much the same, old fellow. One can only assume that upon their arrival at the murder scene, the investigators had been so overly distracted by the gruesome tableau set out before them that they forgot their usual protocol.

"You see, gentlemen, as Mr Mott described it, 'Laid out in the grass on their backs as the bodies were, Mrs Mills's head rested on one of the Reverend's outstretched arms; her hand lay on his upper leg, and his white Panama hat covered his face—with his glasses, we would soon discover, carefully mounted on his nose. Their clothing was neatly arranged on their persons, and their feet, as I have said, pointed towards the crab-apple tree. The police also found the Reverend's calling card—his name printed in Gothic lettering—placed upright against the bottom of one of his shoes; and love letters to the Reverend—written with pencil on cheap paper in the handwriting of Mrs Mills—had been scattered round the bodies.' I should add, gentlemen, that though both were married to others, it was common gossip that the two were romantically involved with each other."

"A vicar?" I gasped.

Fitzgerald smiled at my *naiveté*. "It is this illicit love affair that interests me," said he. "It's what I seek to explore in my novel—lovers who betray the people they are attached to."

Again Holmes failed to respond to the literary diversion.

"I trust the authorities came round to conducting regular autopsies," said I.

"Ah, Watson, ever the medical man. That is precisely what they did. A prosecutor from Middlesex was made responsible for the body of Mr Hall; a prosecutor from Somerset, for that of Mrs Mills. The same doctors performed both procedures."

"A pinch of consistency, at any rate," I observed

"Following the earlier problems, Mr Mott was pleased to report the new facts that emerged from the autopsies. 'We learned,' said he, 'that the .32 calibre bullet, which had entered Hall's head near his right temple, had exited at the back of his neck on the left side. Since the missile had clearly travelled downward, it can be inferred that the poor man had been shot from above."

"Perhaps he was praying," I suggested.

"Praying or otherwise," said Holmes, "he'd been on his knees and executed."

Interestingly, Fitzgerald seemed to pay little mind to the forensic details. He went right on eating as Holmes described the bloody details.

"Actually," said Holmes, "the remains of Mrs Mills proved more revealing. It turns out that she had been shot in the face not once—as had first been reported—but three times; and the scarf that had been wrapped round her neck had actually concealed the fact that her throat had been slashed from ear to ear. So deep was the cut that her head had been nearly severed."

"A veritable holocaust!" I cried. "And so many horrors missed! What sort of organisation do they run out there?"

"Quite so," Holmes murmured again.

"And who do the authorities think was responsible for this mayhem?" I asked. "They must have some ideas about the perpetrator of these atrocities."

"Yes," said Fitzgerald, pencil now at the ready, "those are the people I'm most interested in hearing your opinions of."

Holmes shook his head glumly. "Just the usual suspects, I'm afraid. As always, there were the wrong-headed possibilities—the young man who found the bodies; a vestryman who was in the area at the time. But the police reserved their hardest looks for the newly-widowed spouses."

"The initial suspects," I found myself pontificating, "whenever a husband or wife is killed."

"And yet," offered Fitzgerald as he sliced into another healthy portion of beef, "I've read that the husband, Jimmy Mills, is too dumb to have planned such a crime. In my *Trimalchio*, I say he's so dumb that he doesn't even know he's alive."

"Be careful," cautioned Holmes. "Stupidity is one of the most effective guises a guilty person can don—though I must agree that in the case of the cuckolded Mills, I believe you have read him correctly. From all the reports, such a characterization credibly excuses the man. No, from the start, the prime suspect has always been the affluent widow—Mrs Frances Noel Hall."

"The wife did it then!" I exclaimed, waving my fork, "just as I said."

Holmes placed his hand on my wrist to calm me down. "We have an alleged key witness," said he, "to thank for the identification—a Mrs Gibson, who claims to have been in the vicinity."

"The pig woman," offered Fitzgerald.

"You know of her then," said Holmes, releasing my arm.

"Oh, yes. They call her that because she raises pigs on her farm."

"Well," said Holmes, "on the night in question, she thought someone had been stealing the corn from that farm; and to have a look, she rode out to her field on a mule. She claimed that it was then that she had heard four shots and, thanks to the moonlight, seen a white-haired woman in a tan coat—a description of Mrs Hall—and three other men. She went so far as to say that someone had called out 'Henry', which happens to be the name of Mrs Hall's brother. He, along with a cousin and another brother—an eccentric the townspeople call 'Crazy Willie'—were also suspected."

Fitzgerald shook his head. "But lots of people doubted the 'pig woman's' account."

"That's correct," said Holmes. "There were too many discrepancies in her repetitions of the story. Mr Mott counted five people in one of her scenarios, six in another. She also said that the vicar had fallen when he'd been shot—yet thanks to the autopsy, as I've already pointed out, we know he was kneeling when he was killed. In short, some in authority believed her; others did not."

"What *is* the answer then?" I asked. "Whether this 'pig woman' was right or wrong, *somebody* killed those people. Who was responsible for committing such evil deeds?"

I knew I was sounding naïve once again, and Fitzgerald was quick to remind me.

"Surely, Dr Watson, a writer with your insights can detect the whiff of jealousy and revenge that hovers over a pair of marriages gone sour. In *Trimalchio*, I attribute more than one death to those same perfidious motivations."

Left to ponder Fitzgerald's fiction, we finished our meals, and the plates were removed. Both my dinner companions declined after-dinner sweets, but I could not resist the chocolate *gateau.*

III

Following the arrival of the coffee and my cake, Holmes began again. "I found myself at odds with Mr Mott. He tended to believe the Pig Woman; I didn't. I simply couldn't accept that Mrs Hall or members of her prominent family were involved. There were simply too many distracting clues suggesting otherwise. For instance, the prosecutor's conclusion ignored the role of the crab-apple tree. Why was it so important for the killer—or killers—to point the bodies in the direction of the tree? I had to see the area for myself, and I told Mr Mott so."

"'No point,' said he. 'Not only has the weather been terrible—we've just had some December snow—but large numbers of people have tramped all over the place—hundreds of gawkers. Why, one weekend in October we had over three hundred cars! The police did their best to preserve the original scene, but souvenir hunters put their fingers all over Hall's calling card and the scattered love-letters. Why, some enthusiasts have even ripped off the bark from the crab-apple tree for macabre mementos.'"

I shook my head in disbelief. *How could the police allow such confusion?* We used to think the Yarders made mistakes! Why, not even Lestrade could have bungled a crime scene so badly.

"Regardless of the prosecutor's caveats," said Holmes, "I refused to be gainsaid.

"The next day broke cold and bleak; but early that morning a black police motor-car conveyed Mr Mott and me through New Brunswick along the Easton Avenue streetcar line—beyond the shops and offices, past a few stylish houses—to the fields and farmlands at the outskirts of the town. By the time we reached Buccleuch Park where the trolley rails ended, the traffic had become very sparse indeed. Just past the columns fronting the Parker Home for the Aged, we turned left into De Russey's Lane. There remained but a short drive to the dirt road next to which the bodies had been found.

"As a precaution, a half dozen uniformed policemen stood by to keep the fields of the abandoned farm free of any wandering pedestrians. The show of force turned out to be unnecessary, however, for only a scattering of winter-thinned trees, their naked branches reaching skyward like brittle bones, interrupted the barren landscape.

"It required a single glance to confirm the contamination of the spot where the bodies had been discovered. The recent snow had saturated the area, and indiscriminate crowds had indeed stamped down the grass and marched over underbrush. Yet once Mr Mott pointed out the celebrated crab-apple tree, I knew that—manhandled as it had already been—here stood an entity that bulked large in the solution to the case."

"In what way?" Fitzgerald asked.

"Mind," said Holmes, "what I am about to tell you both I also told Prosecutor Mott. To this day he has made nothing of my findings, but I continue to believe that before long the case will be re-opened, my view will prevail, and—once for all—justice will be served."

"And precisely what *is* your view, Mr Holmes?" Fitzgerald persisted.

Sherlock Holmes placed his elbows on the white tablecloth and steepled his fingers together. It was a way he had when he wanted to draw attention to a meaningful observation. "As I have said before, the art of detection is merely 'systematised common sense'. The feet of the deceased were pointing to the crab-apple tree. Clearly, that tree was the spot where one had to begin in order to unravel this tangle.

"Even though much of the brownish-red bark had been stripped away, a close examination with my glass revealed a small cross that had been carved chest-high into the narrow trunk. Given the relative freshness of the cut, one could surmise the mark had been made at the time of the murders."

"Do you think the killings were religious in nature then?" I asked. "After all, this Mr Hall was a vicar."

"Perhaps. But there was more. You know my methods, Watson. I employed my lens to examine the ground where the bodies had been placed. In spite of the damage to the area, it was easy to note the lack of blood. In fact, with the investigating chemist having discovered only .08 of a pint of blood in the grass, it was elementary to conclude that Mrs Mills's horrific neck-wound had been administered post-mortem.

"But it was at the spot where the feet of the dead had rested that I concentrated my greatest efforts. Remember that the vicar's calling card had been found leaning against his shoes. It was in that location that I discovered what no one else had seen: mixed in with the scrambled dirt and grass, I counted five apple pips."

Apple pips again . . . .

"So what?" questioned Fitzgerald. "What's so strange about apple seeds being found near an apple tree?"

"True enough, Mr Fitzgerald," Holmes smiled, "except that these were seeds from the *Malus pumila*, the *common* apple tree, not from the *Malus coronaria*, the specific crab-apple tree near where the bodies had lain."

"Do you mean to say that you can actually tell the difference?" the writer asked.

"Oh, yes, with the aid of a magnifying lens. The seeds of the common apple tree are small, brown, flattened ovoids. Those of the crab-apple tree are smaller, redder, and more shiny."

Fitzgerald shook his head in amazement. "But what makes this so important?"

Holmes's eyes flashed as they always did when he was about to reveal a significant conclusion. "I believe that the apple seeds were transported to the scene by the killer—or killers—for distribution. This discovery, along with the cross carved into the tree, was enough for me. I told Mr Mott that I was ready to return to my hotel.

"You see, there was a witness named Frank Csister whom I wanted to question. His original testimony involved none of the major suspects, so the police had ignored it. A chauffeur by trade, he happened to be out on the road near the scene of the murders that night. I had read the account that he had furnished the authorities, and I wanted to interrogate him myself. To me, his was exactly the sort of report I wanted to hear more of. The police file informed me that Csister worked in a garage. Apparently, when he was not driving passengers about, he was repairing motor-cars."

"Lots to do with automobiles in this case, eh, Holmes?" I observed. "Chauffeurs, motor-ways, garages."

"It's America we're talking about, Dr Watson," said Fitzgerald. "My Trimalchio drives a 'circus wagon'. If the story took place in England, I'm sure I would have been writing about trains."

"Indeed," Holmes muttered and continued his narrative. "Mr Mott said he had heard all he needed to from Csister and declined to go along. So once the police deposited me at my hotel in New Brunswick, I hired a taxi for the drive to Bound Brook, the borough some ten miles to the northwest where Frank Csister worked.

IV

"I found the fellow in a small garage," said Holmes. "A ginger-haired man with inquisitive eyes and a full, red beard. He was adjusting the steering of an old Dodge touring model. He wore grease-covered overalls and a soiled flat cap.

"'Again?' he said when I told him that I wanted to ask him about the Hall-Mills murders. 'I've already talked to the cops. They don't think much of what I have to say.'

"None the less, he agreed to spend a few minutes with me and recommended coffee at the *café* next door."

"Funny," Fitzgerald interrupted, "in *Trimalchio* I put a Greek joint next to a garage."

Holmes would not be distracted. "Csister and I seated ourselves at a small wooden table with our coffees between us. 'What did you see that night, Mr Csister,' I asked, 'the night of the murders?'

"He put two cubes of sugar into his coffee and stirred. 'Like I told the cops,' he said after administering to his drink, 'a friend of mine and me was driving to Red Bank. We was on our way to the volunteer fireman's ball, you know. It was getting dark out there, but around 8.30 or so we saw a small, dust-covered car—maybe a Ford or a Dodge—parked by the side of the road. It wasn't too far from where them bodies was found. It didn't have no license plate, and only one tail-light was on.'

"'I'm sure you've seen many a car by the side of the road. What was so curious about this one?'

"'Ha!' he laughed, 'take your choice—the tire that came flying out of one of the windows just as we drove past or the three Negroes who poured out after it. They were yelling and throwing their arms around. Well, we didn't want no trouble so we speeded up and got out of there.'

"The thought of disguises immediately crossed my mind. 'Were these men truly Negroes,' I asked, 'or might they have been white men wearing black face-paint?'

"Csister shook his head. 'I tell you, Mr Holmes, me and my partner didn't hang around long enough to find out. We didn't want to get robbed or nothing—know what I mean?'

"'Anything else?'

"'Well, about two hundred feet down the road we saw another car. This one was shiny; but just like the one we saw before, the rear end was lit up by a single tail-light, and it didn't have no license. Once I heard about them murders out there, I told all this stuff to the cops here in Bound Brook. They promised they'd give my story to the dicks in Somerset County, but no one's ever come to talk to *me* about it. From what *I* hear, others seen them cars too, but the cops told me that them other folks said the cars was there way later—that I must have been wrong about the time."

"'Couldn't the cars have been out there for a few hours?' I asked Csister. 'That would explain why you and the others could see them at different times.'

"'Sure. That's why I thought my story was important.' He sipped some coffee before making his final pronouncement. 'Guess I was wrong.'

"Csister had no more to tell. I thanked him for his help, paid for the coffees, and returned with the taxi to my hotel."

Staring into our own coffees Fitzgerald and I both sat pondering the story.

It was the writer who broke the silence. "So what was it that you learned, Mr Holmes? The apple seeds, the cross in the tree, the cars by the road. What gives?"

I had a good idea of what Holmes was suggesting, so I was prepared when my friend said, "Perhaps Watson can enlighten you. The answer lies within an old case of ours, one which he has already chronicled."

"'The Five Orange Pips'," I announced for a second time that evening. "An adventure which you yourself labelled 'grotesque', Holmes."

"Yes, I did. But you must not forget that on another occasion I also said that 'there is but one step from the grotesque to the horrible'. And in this new case—two killings, a slit throat, gunshots to the face—oh, I think that step to the horrible had been taken."

I agreed. Staring some forty years into the past, I recalled more clearly the murder of John Openshaw. In spite of the warnings provided by the orange pips, those harbingers of death sent out by the Ku Klux Klan, his was a death that Holmes and I had failed to prevent. And yet, horrible as it was, his drowning near Waterloo Bridge did not seem as awful as the ghoulish deaths in New Jersey.

"The Klan?" echoed Fitzgerald after I had pronounced the peculiar words. "What in the world could a bunch of clowns running around in white sheets have to do with these murders in New Jersey? The Klan was a nineteenth-century invention—an outgrowth of our Civil War. Its basic purpose was to menace Negroes in the South."

"Quite so," Holmes agreed, "but I'm sure that as an American, you must be aware of the group's resurgence. In 1915, in your state of Georgia, a preacher named Joseph Simmons created a new version of the so-called "Invisible Empire". With inspiration from a film called *The Birth of a Nation*, the Klan, no longer content with persecuting freed slaves, began targeting any kind of behaviour they deemed immoral.

"And it continues today. When they find such sinners, they frequently administer corrective measures. What's more, they do not confine themselves to what used to be the Confederacy. One can find this newly resurrected version of the Klan active throughout your East Coast and—more to the point—New Jersey in particular."

"When Zelda and I return home," said Fitzgerald, "I suppose we should watch our backs." He flashed that ambiguous look again—half serious, half jocular—and one could not be certain if he was joking or sincerely considering the safety of his family.

"It is my contention," Holmes announced, "that the publicly known relationship between Mr Hall and Mrs Mills was exactly the kind of *outré* behaviour that would attract the Klan and which the Klan would desire to correct."*

---

* Holmes's analysis closely predicts that of civil rights lawyer William Kunstler in his 1964 account of the Hall-Mills murders titled *The Minister and the Choir Singer.* (DDV)

In spite of his suspicions, Holmes made no reference to the pips he had shown me in the taxi. It seemed clear that he had no intention of sharing that particular detail with Fitzgerald.

"But, Holmes," said I, "in our earlier investigation, the Klan sent out warnings before they killed someone. Remember that it was the arrival of the five orange pips that brought poor Openshaw to our door in the first place. You never mentioned any such warnings regarding the murders in New Jersey."

Holmes managed a chuckle. "There has been no discussion of warnings, old fellow, because the local authorities found none. Recall that the police said nothing about *any* apple pips, and they failed to regard the cross on the tree as a clue. They also chose to ignore the letters sent to Florence North, the lawyer for Charlotte Mills, the dead woman's daughter."

"The flapper," Fitzgerald reminded us with another wink.

Holmes cocked an eyebrow, but continued his explanation. "One of the letters said that in order to discover the identity of the killer, the attorney should locate the Klan members in the church of the late Reverend Hall. And when Miss North herself suggested that vigilantes might be responsible for killing her client's mother, a letter-writer warned that if the lawyer did not stop accusing groups like the Klan, then they just might have to give Miss North 'a taste of the same medicine we gave to Mrs Mills. Beware,' they warned, 'or you will see the fiery cross some night and get your due reward.'"

"My word," I murmured. Not only did Holmes's argument sound convincing, but it also rendered more ominous the threat to his own person conveyed via the apple pips.

"Motive, means, and opportunity," said Holmes, ticking off each word on his fingers. "It seems quite compelling that outside forces were the instigators of the Hall-Mills murders. I'm sure you'll agree, Mr Fitzgerald, that thanks to the proliferation of motorcars to which you have already referred, the Klan can move quite easily across state boundaries. The dirty car observed by Csister might well have picked up large quantities of soot and grime as it travelled some great distance. It would have been no trouble at all for Klansmen to have committed these outrages and then retreated to safer grounds. In such an instance, their tracks would be most difficult to follow."

Fitzgerald ran a hand through his hair. "Blaming some amorphous outfit like the K.K.K. might be all fine and good for actually solving the case," said he, his brow now furrowed, "but I'm writing a novel about thwarted love. It was precisely the *romantic* dilemma of the victims that attracted me to these murders in the first place. And now *you* want to replace the love story with a mundane morality drama played out by some prudish thugs. Regardless of what you think may really have happened, Mr Holmes, in my *Trimalchio* I hold a cuckolded lover responsible for the murders—maybe two such lovers now that I think about it."

"It's funny, Mr Fitzgerald," mused Holmes, "the prosecution in the Hall-Mills case was bent on proving exactly what you are suggesting. They couldn't blame the hapless husband, so they turned their attention to the widowed Mrs Hall."

Holmes may have felt that he had struck too harsh a tone; for when he spoke again, I detected a note of sympathy in his voice.

"If you try viewing the story through the eyes of the officials," he said to Fitzgerald, "you might see the entire affair as a case of mistaken identities. The wrong suspects accused? The wrong witnesses believed . . . ?"

"Mistaken identities," Fitzgerald mused. Suddenly, eyes flashing directly at Holmes, he cried out, "Of *course!* It's exactly the sort of wrong-headed conclusion a dim-wit like the husband in my book would jump to. *Mistaken identities*—just the thing!"

Quickly, he rose to his feet, tossed his serviette on the table, and turned to leave. "I must return to *Villa Marie* and resume my work on *Trimalchio*. You've made the resolution very clear to me, Mr Holmes."

With that, the young American threw some money on the table and bolted from the restaurant. Later we learned that he had returned to his room, collected his valise, and departed for France that very night.

"And the pips sent to you by the Klan?" I asked Holmes.

With the shake of his head, he dismissed the question. "Whoever sent that message must believe a new investigation will soon be under way. No doubt they want to prevent my involvement in it. But as I have already given my thoughts to the state prosecutor and have nothing left to say on the matter, I trust that I can safely ignore such threats. I am done with my part of the enquiry, Watson. My conclusions were never taken seriously, and thus I have vowed to

Mr Mott—before I ever received those apple pips—to remain silent if the case is re-opened."

I breathed more easily and now returned my attention to the chocolate cake before me. A few minutes later, Holmes and I extended our evening in the plush environs of the Langham with a round of port and cigars.

V

As it turned out, Sherlock Holmes had correctly predicted a second investigation into the Hall-Mills murders. The new novel by F. Scott Fitzgerald, however, was completed before the proceedings began and remained unaffected by the new legal developments. As most readers may know, Fitzgerald had changed the book's title yet again just before it was published on 10 April 1925. Formerly called *Trimalchio,* the novel ultimately appeared in public as *The Great Gatsby*.

A few days after its publication, a package arrived by post from Scribner's. Getting round even less dextrously than a few years before, I was relieved to have Miss Ross bring it to my desk in the sitting room.

Within the brown shipping paper, I discovered a gift from Fitzgerald—a first printing of *The Great Gatsby.* What is more, it was complete with the haunting dust-jacket crafted by Spanish artist Francis Cugat, a dark-blue cover featuring the disembodied face of a woman from whose sad, kohl-lined eyes—their irises containing neatly concealed reclining nudes—falls a tear. Actually, there were two copies of the book in the delivery—one intended for me, and the other to be sent to Sherlock Holmes.

A hand-written note (whose notorious grammar and spelling I have taken the liberty to correct) accompanied the books. It read:

Hotel Tiberio, Capri
March 12, 1925

Dear Dr Watson:

Along with this note, I asked Maxwell Perkins to send two copies of my latest novel to you once it was published. One is for you, and the other, if you would be good enough to pass it along, is for Mr Holmes. All in all, though I'm still not satisfied with the title,

The Great Gatsby—I still think I should have named it Trimalchio—the book looks awfully good to me. In fact, I think that the chapters I reworked in light of the help you and Mr Holmes furnished are among the best things I've ever done. Oh, I may not have recreated the specific details of the actual murders, but I do believe that I was faithful to the spirit of the dead lovers. As for Cugat's cover, I find it a delight, and Zelda agrees.

I hear that there are those in England who say that we Americans can't write this sort of thing. Believing that you and Mr Holmes are not among them, I offer you my thanks.

Like the books themselves, it was signed, *F. Scott Fitzgerald.*

*****

It might be comforting to believe—as Sherlock Holmes had hoped—that the publication of *The Great Gatsby* caused enough interest in the Hall-Mills case to account for the new trial that took place in 1926. Yet the fictional murders that appear at the end of the novel are so unlike the originals that not even the most perceptive reader could argue a connection. The truth is that Fitzgerald had written a tragic tale based on mistaken identities rather than a tawdry crime-drama dealing with a gang of vigilantes. I suspect such had been his intention from the start.

Would that I could report otherwise, but the new enquiry was initiated by no clarion call for justice. On the contrary, it was the testimony from a marital annulment case that prompted another look at the pair of gruesome murders. Catalyst for the legal action had been the complaints of an aggrieved husband, who maintained that his wife had lied to him. What connected the issue to the Hall-Mills case was the fact that the wife who was accused of lying had been a maid in the home of Mr Hall, and the lie she was accused of telling was her claim to her husband that she knew nothing of Mrs Hall's involvement in the murders.

The former maid was now admitting that four years earlier she had, in fact, heard incriminating statements from Mrs Hall during a telephone conversation. The newly offered hearsay was all the authorities needed to get them started once more.

Resurrecting the testimony of The Pig Woman, a fresh prosecutor charged Mrs Hall, along with her two brothers and a cousin, with the double murders at the crab-apple tree. On this occasion, however, an actual trial was convened. And yet, though it lasted sixteen days, the ending turned out to be no different from the earlier Grand Jury's failure to indict.

In point of fact, I learned of the *dénouement* from Holmes himself. Employing the news as motivation for a trip to London, he journeyed from the South Downs to share with me the information he had received from Wilbur Mott, the former prosecutor of the case.

"All the defendants were found not guilty," reported Holmes as we sampled the tea and biscuits provided by Miss Ross. "Ultimately," Holmes explained, "the maid retracted her condemnation of Mrs Hall."

"So there's an end to it," said I.

"Hardly," Holmes scoffed. "Mr Mott said that there are many who still believe the testimony of The Pig Woman. Even though her own mother denounced her three times in the courtroom as a "liar", people remain outraged that the suspects were acquitted. Some are urging the case be sent to the Governor for further prosecution."

I shook my head.

"Still," offered Holmes, "given my personal view of the actual perpetrators, I'm happy to say that the majority of the public seem resigned to the unsatisfying conclusion. As long as no new evidence had been disclosed, no one in the Hall family could be convicted of the murders—let alone hanged for them."

"Hanged! Surely it would never have come to that."

"No, indeed," said Holmes. "In spite of the Klan's threat to me and my own oath to be silent—I would have interrupted the legal proceedings with my personal findings in order to prevent punishment from falling on the wrong heads."

"And yet," I felt compelled to add, "the miscreants responsible for these two murders, the killers from the Ku Klux Klan, seem to have got away with the proverbial perfect crime."

"Alas, Watson, that seems to be the case. But perhaps we can take comfort in the conclusion of our previous brush with the K.K.K. You will remember that those men, having escaped the justice of an earthly court, had to face a Higher Judge much sooner than they had expected. Recall the shattered stern-post that had been seen floating in the waves, remnants of the *Lone Star* of Savannah, the ship upon which they attempted to make their escape. As the Latin proverb goes, *Res nolunt diu male administrari*."

My eyes widened in hope of encouraging the translation.

"'Things refuse to be mismanaged for long', he announced obligingly. "It is a concept cited by the American philosopher Emerson in making the case that the world is run according to compensation. What appears to go unpunished will indeed be punished in the end."

Let the philosopher have the last word. To me, the whole idea sounded like a comforting fancy to tell oneself after playing a losing hand. Glancing out the window at the lingering twilight, I bit into a chocolate biscuit and put the entire criminal business to rest. Better to spend whatever time I had left enjoying sweets in the company of my friend and colleague, Mr Sherlock Holmes.

Also from Daniel D Victor

The American Literati Series

The Final Page of Baker Street
The Baron of Brede Place
Seventeen Minutes To Baker Street
The Outrage at The Diogenes Club

"The really amazing thing about this book is the author's ability to call up the 'essence' of both the Baker Street 'digs' of Holmes and Watson as well as that of the 'mean streets' of Marlowe's Los Angeles. Although none of the action takes place in either place, Holmes and Watson share a sense of camaraderie and self-confidence in facing threats and problems that also pervades many of the later tales in the Canon. Following their conversations and banter is a return to Edwardian England and its certainties and hope for the future. This is definitely the world before The Great War."
Philip K Jones

www.mxpublishing.com

www.ingramcontent.com/pod-product-compliance
Lightning Source LLC
Chambersburg PA
CBHW030424310726
48979CB00009B/1607/J

* 9 7 8 1 7 8 7 0 5 4 6 9 1 *